Mountain Road

Mountain Road

A Milltown Novel
Book Three

Devin Sloane

Dedication

For my daughters.
The strongest women I know.

Playlist

Love – Nathan Wagner

Lullaby – The Spill Canvas

Demons – Written by Wolves

Iris – Diamante, Breaking Benjamin

A Little More of You – Ashley Chambliss

Fear – Blue October

Angel – Angels Fall

Dive – Ed Sheerhan

I'll Fight – Daughtry

Inner Demons – Julia Brennan

Changed by You – Between the Trees

What Have I Done – Dermot Kennedy

To Make You Feel My Love – Mick McAuley, Winifred Horan

As You Are – Daughtry

Simple the Best – Billianne

Favorite Color – One Less Reason

Desire – Meg Myers

HTIS – Meg Myers, Carmen Vandenberg, Luna Shadows

Mystify – Saving Abel

Duet – Penny and Sparrow, (Stephanie Briggs)

Here's My Heart – SayWeCanFly

Walk You Home – Karmina

Twist and Shout – The Beatles

Darkness in Me – Fight the Fade

Worthwhile – Nathan Wagner

Table of Contents

Chapter 1 – Perfect   1

Chapter 2 – Happy Ending   6

Chapter 3 – Are You Sure   14

Chapter 4 – Cougar   24

Chapter 5 – Thoughts and Fears   31

Chapter 6 – Full Disclosure   37

Chapter 7 - PG   43

Chapter 8 – My Boys   51

Chapter 9 – All Grown Up   56

Chapter 10 – Plans   66

Chapter 11 -Hands Down   72

Chapter 12 – Baptism by Fire   78

Chapter 13 – Ready?   86

Chapter 14 – Twenty Minutes   93

Chapter 15 - Underwear   97

Chapter 16 - Mutually Exclusive   102

Chapter 17 – Alien Sex   109

Chapter 18 - Punishment   118

Chapter 19 - Limits   126

Chapter 20 – Drivetrain   135

Chapter 21 – Butt-Smacking   142

Chapter 22 – Unhinged   151

Chapter 23 - Boundaries   159

Chapter 24 – A Study in Contrasts   166

Chapter 25 – Hope   173

Chapter 26 – Dreams   181

Chapter 27 – Personal Preservation   187

Chapter 28 - Night Terrors   198

Chapter 29 - Fuck-Me Heels   204

Chapter 30 – Saddle Up   212

Chapter 31 – Sunday Morning Duet   222

Chapter 32 – Nobody's Talking   231

Chapter 33 - White Noise   237

Chapter 34 – Intrigued   245

Chapter 35 – I Will   251

Chapter 36 – Donkey Kong   258

Chapter 37 - Cackling   266

Chapter 38 – Walk of Shame   271

Chapter 39 – Reflection   276

Chapter 40 - Checking   281

Chapter 41 – Easy   288

Chapter 42 - Knees   295

Chapter 43 - Smithereens   301

Chapter 44 - Sticky   309

Chapter 45 – Incongruity   317

Chapter 46 – Words in My Head   324

Chapter 47 – Compass   331

Chapter 48 - Heartstrings   339

Chapter 49 – Pussy Intervention   346

Chapter 50 – Thank You   352

Chapter 51 – Compensation   358

Epilogue   363

Sweet Everythings.   365

One Can Only Hope   366

Special Acknowledgements   371

About the Author   374

Also by Devin Sloane   375

Chapter 1 – Perfect

<u>October</u>

<u>Minty</u>

I walked downstairs to the living room, the house so thick with joy it physically rocked me.

The groom's parents, Jeanie and Calum, bustled back and forth with final preparations. He swatted her on the ass on her way past, and she came to a full stop, turned to him, and beamed.

He tipped his chin down, his eyes to the floor, and rested his hands loosely on his lean hips.

Her smile gentled, and she stepped into him, tipping her neck back to look up into his face. "You old softie," she teased gently.

He harrumphed, and she laughed as she cupped his wrinkled cheek in her palm.

God, how I wanted that.

The sound of women's laughter, my girls, drifted down the stairs and broke the moment. I crossed to Jeanie.

"Ah, Minty, you're back!" Jeanie exclaimed while Calum slipped away.

Handing her Calum's tie, I smiled and murmured, "I'll leave this with you."

She apologized for her husband. "He's usually very friendly. It's an emotional day."

"Woman! If I wanted Minty to know I was crying, I would have stayed there!" Calum groused amicably from the kitchen.

I laughed, and Jeanie winked at me as she flitted off to join him.

I looked to the backyard where the men had gathered to wait.

How crazy was it that they pulled together a wedding within the space of a week? A week of hilarious cloak and dagger to hide the plans from the sweet bride, Willa, my friend and one of the women I worked with.

Barrett bided his time, and when the moment was right, he swooped in and swept her right off her feet. After finding out she was pregnant, he worked his tail off to not only set up his proposal but the entire wedding. Which was taking place in approximately thirty minutes.

I carried the ties we had chosen for the men outside.

Eye candy.

Eye candy everywhere as I made my way across the lawn.

Zale looked up first and crinkled his eyes, his version of a smile. I'd met him on several occasions over the years, him being married to Willa's sister. Beside him stood Barrett who was equally stoic.

"Gentlemen," I greeted them, handing them their ties.

"Thank you, Minty," Zale expertly slid the tie under his collar and flipped the end over to tie it, while Barrett did the same.

Rhys, Bex's husband, stood a few feet away checking to ensure the flower-covered arch was secure. "He might need help, Zee," he joked, referring to Barrett. "He's only half-tamed."

He sauntered over, a grin on his too handsome face, and I handed him his tie.

"Ah, my noose. Thank you."

I smiled, then turned to Zale, seeking the comfort of his familiar face. "Please excuse me."

I felt their eyes on my back as I walked away.

I knew what they thought.

Cool.

Reserved.

Withdrawn.

Unfriendly.

I shook it off. If they knew my actual thoughts, they'd run for the hills.

"What's up, bitch! You look hot!" Junie's voice hit me, and I spun around in time to catch her as she flew at me. Her curtain of white-blond hair blew lightly around her exquisite face. She looked like a fairy princess.

She spoke like a sailor.

"Hello, beautiful." I held her out in front of me. "You're stunning, Junie," I admitted truthfully.

She curtsied and winked bawdily, looking me up and down. "I'd do you," she quipped. "You have Lenny's tie?"

If I felt eyes on me before, it was doubly apparent now with my little hooligan spouting off in front of me. I passed her the tie. "Here you go, lovely."

She ran the tie through her hands. "Nice!" she drawled slowly. "It's going to look awesome wrapped around my wrists later," she whispered.

I laughed. "You're incorrigible."

She skipped off to give Lenny, the drummer in Barrett's band and her beau, his tie.

I watched her go, a smile on my face, and caught sight of the guys watching with grins on their faces. I rolled my eyes. Zale smiled bigger, Barrett flashed his teeth, and Rhys laughed out loud. Frigging eye candy.

There was only one man left, a long, lean, blond fellow sitting on the bench to the side of the arbor, his acoustic guitar settled on his lap as he gently strummed.

Although I'd never met him, I knew he was the other lead guitarist in Barrett's band. My eyes ran over his form, and in my imagination, my hands did the same. I shook off the errant thought, although this time it brought no guilt.

Crossing to him, I held the tie out in front of me.

3

He glanced down at the tie then back up to meet my eyes.

Lucky

Cool.

Contained.

I followed her progress as she made her way across the grass to the men. Noted her discomfort, her relief as she excused herself, the tension in her frame as she walked away.

Watched her with Lenny's spitfire, Junie. Watched Junie with her. Saw how she loved her.

Made me wonder.

I caught her as she swept that cool gaze down my body, resting momentarily on my hands plucking the strings, before carrying on.

I noted the little shake she gave herself and readied myself to meet those eyes.

And dive in.

Her wide mouth tipped into a polite smile as she held out the tie, waiting for me to take it. Reluctant to end the interaction, I refrained from reaching for the tie. I glanced at it and wondered how it would look wrapped around *her* delicate wrists.

Was she the type to go for that?

Looking up, I met her eyes and something inside them flashed.

Those clear brown eyes held secrets, secrets I wanted to know.

What would it take to tame a woman like that? To gain her trust, to gain entry to the treasures locked behind that cool gaze.

I tipped my lips up at her in return, and she stepped into my space, a welcome invader.

Mistaking my hesitation, she offered, "Would you like me to tie it for you?"

Her voice was cool, slightly raspy, and I wondered what it would take to make her lose it entirely.

Gently setting my guitar to the side, I quirked my eyebrows up and smiled. Maintaining eye contact, I straightened my spine and tipped my chin back before snapping up the sides of my collar and securing the top button of my dress shirt.

Sliding closer, she looped the tie around my neck while I strove to keep my eyes from her chest, my hands from her round hips.

I watched her eyes follow the work of her hands, caught the slight pursing of her lips, heard the little hitch in her breath as she ran the tie around my neck and danced her fingers over my collarbone, the ends of the tie slipping through her delicate fingers.

"Your husband's a lucky man," I prodded.

Her eyes met mine knowingly, and my stomach clenched.

"I have no husband."

"You tied that like an expert."

Her lips curved up arrestingly. "I'm good with knots."

My mouth fell open for a brief second, long enough for her to notice, and a light, tinkling laugh escaped her pretty mouth.

Smoothing her palm over the front of my tie, she pressed lightly against my chest.

"There. Perfect."

I stared after her as she walked away.

Slipped my cell phone from my pocket.

And I wondered.

Chapter 2 – Happy Ending

<u>Christmas Day</u>

<u>Minty</u>

Decisions.

I'd made many in my forty-four years. Despite my penchant for examining every angle to assess for any possible risk factors, not all of them were good. And at the intersection of those risk assessments, sat my life.

Early Christmas morning, earlier than I usually rose, I wandered around contemplating the results of some of those decisions.

Pulling the edge of the sheers back from the wide picture window, I peeked out. The street outside was quiet, a rare occurrence. While snow had fallen overnight, the snowplow had already cleared the road in front. So many travelers on Christmas Day.

Moving into the condo was a good decision.

I dropped the curtain and headed into my kitchen. It spanned half the width of my condo, and my condo was huge, taking up the top floor of the building I owned, the building my adoptive parents left me.

When they left me.

God, I missed them.

I decorated in shades of white and whiter, and abhorred clutter. At least in the kitchen. Open, airy, and somehow, despite the starkness of the decoration, welcoming, with curved lines and gentle slopes, not a touch of metal anywhere.

Curvy chairs hugged a round tabletop set atop a sweeping center stand, that separated the kitchen from the living room.

And it was a true living room. Wide, comfortable seats, an L-shaped couch nestled into the corner, a big screen tv because I liked my entertainment, and a curvy kidney-shaped coffee table, the shelf under which was stuffed with books. My first indulgence. The places I lived within their pages where the only risk was envy.

More housing for books lined the walls, and every wall hosted a bookcase. Except in the boys' room. In that room, toys, books, and Lego lined the shelves for when my honorary nephews, the sons of my dearest friends, Amber and Ruby, visited me. Which was not as often anymore as they were getting older.

There had been some changes for those boys recently. In fact, I had just played maid of honor for Ruby when she finally married her first love, Vander. Amber and Gus, too, were finally back where they belonged: together.

The results of good decisions after a series of heartbreaking ones.

If only we made decisions with an understanding of the echo they would make in our lives. Whether they would lead to alienation or belonging.

So long as I could remember, I'd searched for somewhere to belong. Eventually, I found it in the unlikeliest of places.

Myself.

Belonging, as it turned out, came along as the bonus gift attached to the prize of self-acceptance. Who knew, in order to belong, you needed to find home in yourself first?

Ironically, the very thing that stood in the way of self-acceptance was the very thing that led me to my first sense of home and belonging to someone else.

Always a hypersensitive and anxious child, when I hit the age of five, my proclivities morphed into an array of quirks that left my parents at first bewildered, then increasingly frustrated.

They couldn't take me anywhere, alter anything in the house, or dispose of any of my things, even the baby clothes, without encountering a massive tantrum from yours truly.

By the age of eleven, after four years of their unique forms of discipline and training, a school nurse noticed the bruises and called Children's Aid. As they could no longer tolerate my behavior, my parents willingly handed me over to the state.

Immediately apprehended and placed in foster care with an older, childless couple who quickly recognized that my distress did not stem only from my life circumstances, they wasted no time in obtaining the help I so desperately needed. Within three months, they successfully advocated for me to see a psychiatrist. Several weeks after that first visit, diagnosed with anxiety and OCD, the real therapy began.

I'd like to say it was easier than the 'therapy' my parents subjected me to, but it wasn't. Effective, yes. Easy? Not at all, although it was never cruel.

I opened the glass door of the hutch, the only non-essential piece of furniture in my home. It belonged to my mother, my real mother, the one who raised me.

Only two things resided on the glass shelves inside: a China tea set, and a beat up set of art tools belonging to my father. In the long days when I first landed on their doorstep and was unable to attend school, he taught me to draw. He never once balked at the number of times I had to touch each brush before I picked it up. He never once reprimanded me for the time I wasted counting brushstrokes. And when it came time to wash my hands of paint before dinner, he stood beside me and carefully measured out small amounts of detergent into my greedy palms.

I obsessed about washing my hands, imagining the invisible germs on my skin to be as difficult to shed as the dried-on bits of paint that worked their way into the lines of my dry, cracked skin. Fearful of spreading contamination to my new family, I touched nothing and scrubbed my hands raw.

8

Science class the previous year taught me about invisible germs. If I couldn't see them on my hands, how did I know they were clean? Did I scrub in between my fingers? All of them? So many cracks and lines, hiding places for germs that could make people sick. I couldn't lose them.

Wash again.

And again.

I remember my mother leading me into the kitchen where she opened a brand-new bottle of hand lotion and added a generous amount of liquid soap. Replacing the lid, she shook it violently before passing it to me.

"There, dolly. Now you can moisturize and clean your hands at the same time."

The obsessive handwashing eased, and the practice of adding a squirt of detergent to my moisturizer continued.

My birth family refused to relinquish all their rights. This turned into a blessing because instead of Children's Aid trying to find an adoptive family for me, an almost impossible feat for a mentally ill eleven-year-old, they left me with my foster family.

On the day I turned eighteen, my foster parents took me to their lawyer where I took their name, and they added me to their will. While I did not have a new birth certificate and was never officially adopted, for all intents and purposes I was theirs, they were mine, and my new name reflected that truth.

Long before I belonged to myself, I belonged to them.

When they passed, they left me everything.

And it was a lot.

I used it to give back.

Another good decision.

I looked at my watch.

If I wanted to be on time, and I hoped I actually would be on time today, I needed to start getting ready.

Thirty minutes past the time I'd hoped to be there, I flew through the door. "Sorry I'm late!" I tossed my purse onto the table in the hall as I swept into the kitchen of the only real home I'd ever shared with anyone.

"Minty! Sweetheart!" Ezinne, the house mother, exclaimed as she swept me up in her strong arms.

I cupped my palms around her shoulder blades and held her close. I'd learned that in order for the hug to end, I had to hug her back.

It was not a huge trial.

She drew back and looked at me, her perfect teeth on display in the most beautiful smile I'd ever seen. Her skin, smooth and baby-soft with nary a wrinkle, never failed to amaze me.

"God, I'd kill for your skin, Ezzy."

"And I'd kill for your legs." She beamed at me. "Merry Christmas, sweet girl."

A decade older than me, Ezinne felt for me what I felt for Willa and Junie. Like an older sister, perhaps. A little protective, enormous admiration, and a deep, abiding affection that she never failed to communicate.

"Merry Christmas, sweet friend," I answered. "How are the girls doing today? How many are home?"

I peered into the living room to see if anyone was around.

Ezinne linked her pinky with mine as she, too, peeked into the living room. "They're all going to be here for dinner at three o'clock. Jen had Christmas dinner with her family last night and just called to say she wants to come back."

Ezinne looked at her watch. She was one of the few people I knew who still wore one. "I sent an Uber for her half an hour ago, so she'll be back any minute. Lindy will be here by three. Everyone else is here."

After my parents passed away, the house felt as hollow as my heart. It was far too big for one person, and my thoughts echoed off the walls, so I renovated and moved into the condo downtown.

A conversation with Amber after she got her first official gig as a social worker sparked the idea for what my family home became.

Kids like me who ended up in foster care, once they turned eighteen, aged out of the system. Most were left to their own devices without a single clue how to proceed.

Some of them, like Lindy and Jen, still had contact with their birth families, one of the reasons they were never eligible for adoption. They lived in a cruel sort of limbo, balancing between the foster family or families that offered them shelter for a fee, and the birth families who elected to hang on despite offering less than nothing. Oftentimes, months passed with nary a phone call nor a visit.

And I had this big, beautiful house and no one to share it with.

I kept the master bedroom closed behind a locked door. It belonged exclusively to me and was mine for when I chose to stay there.

And I stayed often.

When I needed to be close to the memories of my mom and dad.

When I needed the embrace of the walls that first gave me a sense of belonging.

When the girls needed me.

When Ezinne called me in for backup.

Grants and funding were easy to come by through contacts of my parents, other wealthy people who had more money than they knew what to do with. Running this place cost me nothing but time. And it gave these girls a fighting chance.

I had room for five girls at once. Three of the girls currently living in the house attended post-secondary school full time. They paid rent out of their government grants, that money going into an account which would be transferred into their name once they graduated and moved out. After the first couple of years, I learned a little extra motivation never hurt.

The other two girls were not ready to make any decisions for their future yet.

They were healing.

Or trying to.

The vetting process was excruciating, and I left most of it to Ezinne. Those who did not make it into the program, we endeavored to help in other ways. Many times, it was as simple as purchasing a couple of outfits suitable for job interviews. A few times we provided first and last month's rent. Very occasionally we funded short-term counseling.

I did not kid myself. These were small things and unlikely to make a huge dent, but maybe God, I prayed, would make it be enough.

In truth, there were not that many applicants. Once these kids were free of the system and handed control of their lives, they ran with it.

Often straight to hell.

The ones who ended up with us were serious and determined. They had goals. One of my girls wanted to have her own business one day. A cafe with a bookstore. I mentally reminded myself to check with Ruby to see if she could use help at Spuds. She could at least learn the business of running a restaurant from Ruby and Vander.

Ezinne jiggled my pinky with hers before releasing me. "What's new, sugar?"

We turned back into the kitchen, and I headed to the counter, pulling out a cutting board. "My friend Ruby got married."

"Ohhh," Ezinne squealed and clasped her hands beneath her chin. She was a sucker for a good love story, and I had filled her in the last time I visited. "I'm so happy they finally got their happy ending!"

A happy ending. Ezinne's smile was contagious, and I smiled back.

Wanna fuck?

I smiled serenely and turned back to my cutting board. "She deserves it. They both do. They were made for each other."

Ezinne sighed. "I love love." She looked at me sideways. "You deserve a happy ending."

You want to lick her pussy.

I took a deep breath and smiled again, irritated with the intrusion but not overly bothered. It happened so often it was mostly white noise.

"Oh, you, with your secret little smiles. What secrets do you hide behind those pretty eyes?"

I laughed but answered honestly, "You don't want to know."

She smiled knowingly and patted my cheek. "That's alright."

After far too much food, most of which I could eat, and the delicate exercise of giving gifts to those who were unused to receiving that which came with no strings, I headed out to spend the evening with Amber and Ruby. My second family. My big, fat, Greek family with whom I also belonged.

I grinned.

My boys had no problem accepting gifts and I seriously looked forward to their faces when they opened them.

Belonging did not, contrary to popular belief, eradicate loneliness. That I had in spades. The cure for loneliness rested in intimacy. Thus far I had deemed that too great a risk.

That decision echoed loudly in the silence of my condo later that night.

I wondered if there might be someone worth the risk of exposure.

I huffed out a laugh.

Or even a second date.

Chapter 3 – Are You Sure

<u>May</u>

<u>Minty</u>

Despite my best efforts at opening myself up to dating after Christmas, I put myself back on hiatus after the third first date. I told myself it was no great loss. You can't miss what you've never had, right?

The door to the office swung open and Willa breezed inside, her baby bump leading the way.

My hand wrapped around the hilt of a hunting knife, buried in her stomach, blood bathing both of us.

"Hello, beautiful," I called softly while rounding my desk to help her carry her bags.

"Minty! I can't see my damn feet. Barrett took away all my nice shoes," she laughed exasperatedly.

I looked down. Sure enough, she wore lace-up canvas running shoes with her dress.

The laces undo, Willa trips and falls onto her stomach, her face grimacing in pain.

"Did you put them on? Or did he?" I asked, amused. They were double-knotted. That was a relief. I could easily picture that big bear of a man on his knees tying her shoes.

A picture of them together flashed in my mind, his big hands wrapped around her naked thighs, his face buried between them, her head thrown back in ecstasy.

"He did," she laughed again.

She laughed a lot lately. Always blessed with a sunny disposition, now her happiness lit the whole damn sky. After freeing herself from her past, she lived her life to the fullest. Seeing that made me both proud and envious.

Mostly proud.

"Those are sizable double-knots you're sporting," I teased. "You may never get them off."

Slanting me a sideways glance and making me laugh, she assured me, "Believe me. He has no problem getting things off me."

She looked around. "Is Junie here yet?"

"Do you hear her?" I answered drily.

Willa looked quickly towards the door, then leaned towards me. "Okay, so Lenny is going to pop the question."

I raised my eyebrows. "He told you?"

"No. He told Barrett. Barrett told me. I'm telling you." She looked away from me as she busily organized her things on her desk, hung her coat on the rack, and slipped the strap of her purse over her chair. Then she took the bag I still held and began emptying the contents onto her desk.

"Who else did you tell?" I prodded knowingly, leaning my hip against her desk.

Her blue eyes blew wide. "Nobody." She paused. "And it's killing me."

"Mm-hmm," I teased. "When is this going to happen?"

"They're having everyone over for a barbecue and he's going to ask her then." She pulled a granola bar out of her bag and flopped down into her chair. "I'm so freaking hungry." She pointed at me with it. "You're invited, of course."

The city bus passed by the window.

Bus. Safe travels.

I smiled. "I thought you were offering me your granola bar."

She widened her eyes and shook her head. "Not on your life, lady."

The door opened again, and Willa spun around in her seat, a huge smile on her face. "Junie!"

Junie, her white-blond hair trailing behind her, threw her arms up in the air. "It. Is. Gorgeous outside! We should get Spuds and eat in the back. Or on your terrace, Mint." She swung her gaze around to Willa. "Why are you so happy? You get boned last night?"

Willa scoffed and waved her away with a blush.

Junie bent and stared into her eyes. "Nope. You're hiding something!" she accused. Her crystal eyes widened, and she breathed, "You found out the sex of the baby."

Willa shook her head. "No." Then tilted it to the side. "Well, we have a sealed envelope from the ultrasound tech, but we haven't opened it."

Junie narrowed her eyes suspiciously as she unloaded her bag at her own desk. "Then what is it?"

Willa's eyes flitted back and forth.

I laughed to myself as I watched her seek a believable lie.

"They're thinking about having a gender reveal party, but she hasn't been able to convince Daddy yet."

Junie's eyebrows shot up, and Willa looked like she was chewing on my lie.

She raised her eyes up to Junie's excited face. "Do you think it's a good idea?"

Junie pursed her rosebud mouth. "I want to say yes because I want to know, but I think it's more exciting to wait." Her face soured with her pronouncement eliciting another laugh out of Willa.

"Maybe you're right."

Junie turned away and Willa smiled at me. I winked in return.

Bus.

Safe travels.

The current bane of my existence was the city bus. Why my brain felt the need to point it out to me every time one passed, I could not say, but it did. Immediately afterwards I felt compelled to wish the inhabitants a safe trip. It was little enough. Like wishing someone a good morning. And I knew nothing bad would happen if I didn't do it in much the same way as wishing them safe travels did nothing to guarantee it.

Still, it persisted.

Bus. Two in a row. Safe Travels.

I resisted the urge to say it twice.

Resist the urge, not the thought.

"Mint. You have got to come to our place on Sunday. We want to get the gang together before Mama here pops."

"Sunday? I think I can make it. I'll have to check with Ezzy to make sure she doesn't need me."

I knew she didn't need me, just as I knew Junie would be suspicious if I agreed right away. I never agreed to go anywhere or do anything until I had the opportunity to assess all angles.

She continued her campaign to convince me.

"I already bought Veggie dogs and Veggie Italian sausage for you. And Lenny said he'll cook them on his hibachi so no animal juices get on them." She paused. "And you can bring a salad. I know you're choosy about what you eat, but if you bring a salad, and we have veggie dogs and sausage, that would be good, right?"

I looked into her sweetly anxious face and my heart melted. I couldn't even pretend.

"That sounds really good. I'll do that. If I have time, I'll bake cookies, too." I shifted sideways to return to my desk, and she swatted me on the ass.

"You and your cookies," she teased as she swung into her seat. "That's why you got the booty, baby!"

Bus. Safe travels.

Two days later, I flew out the back door and skipped down the stairs on my way to Junie's. I really didn't want to be late. Walking in when everyone else had already settled opened me up to scrutiny I preferred to avoid.

Is the door locked?

I halted on the bottom step, my keys in hand, then spun to scoot back up the stairs. I yanked on the doorhandle and jerked it back and forth. Put my key in and twisted it back and forth, then checked again to ensure it was secure. Most definitely locked. I hit the bottom of the stairs and headed to my car.

Are you sure you locked the door?

I smiled the thought away and slipped into my car.

Willa and Barrett were already there, their truck parked in the driveway. I wondered who else was coming. I slid in at the curb across the street behind a motorcycle, and slowly extricated myself from my car, hooking my purse over my elbow and balancing my cookie platter across my forearm before grabbing the salad bowl.

Bracing my hip against the open car door, I bumped it closed.

Do you have your keys?

I had them. I purposefully dropped them into my purse before I got out of the car.

Are you sure? What if you're ready to leave and your keys are locked in the car? You'll be trapped.

Check.

I sighed.

It wasn't worth the risk.

Lots of things weren't worth the risk.

I liked to think my OCD was in remission. The fact that I lived my life through it, around it, alongside it, and didn't allow it to take over my entire day as it used to, meant the doctors considered it to be in remission.

But remission was a long shot from eradication.

It was an insidious beast. No sooner had I conquered one symptom, subtype, or trigger, than another took its place.

Ezzy assured me if I continued to exercise trust in myself, I would continue to improve.

I had improved.

And I lived my life.

But OCD remained, hovering in the background, while its' shadow conjured a vague sense of dread, supplied a disturbing array of shocking visuals, and promoted an unhealthy dose of self-doubt.

Resting the cookie platter on the roof of the car, setting the salad bowl beside it, I opened my purse. My keys were in the pocket where I always placed them.

Are you sure those are the car keys?

I looked hard, then laughed at myself. Who else's keys would they be?

Crossing the street, I caught sight of dark, bouncy curls rounding the side of the house toward the back. Mara, Willa's sister. I followed her around back rather than trying the front door.

Willa's thirteen-year-old niece, Olivia, shuffled along nervously, sandwiched between her parents with her forefinger hooked through the back beltloop of Zale's jeans. I slowed to allow Olivia time to acclimate herself.

Being Willa's shadow, Olivia knew Junie and me well, but she'd be nervous until she saw who else was there and assessed the setup. Although she'd been to Junie's place a few times, Junie had since moved into Lenny's house and Olivia had never been.

Their little family stood just inside the gate while Olivia took in the scene.

Junie caught sight of her and bellowed at her from across the yard. "Olivia!"

Olivia startled and stepped back for a moment before her sweet face split into a grin as Junie barreled down on her.

"I'm so happy to see you!" Junie exclaimed, stopping a good arm's length in front of her to wait.

Olivia stepped into her space until they were almost nose-to-nose, or they would have been if Junie had a couple more inches on her.

"I'm taller than you," Olivia stated smugly.

"You are," Junie agreed, smiling. "Want to help me reach stuff in the kitchen?"

I looked across the yard to see Lenny hanging back. Olivia didn't know him very well yet.

Olivia nodded, still smiling. "You're very short."

"That I am, Olivia. That I am." Junie laughed and held out her hand. Olivia slid her palm against Junie's for a gentle squeeze before relieving Mara and me of our offerings.

Mara's shoulders lifted and fell with her deep breath. Zale grinned at her and smiled a hello at me before patting her backside and ambling off to chat with Lenny.

"Hello, beautiful," I greeted Mara.

Nice ass.

Did I say that out loud?

No.

Can she read my mind? What if she can read my mind?

She can't read minds. I didn't say it out loud.

Are you sure?

Don't argue with OCD. Let it go.

Mara turned, a smile on her pretty face. She held out her arms and gave me a warm hug. "It's good to see you, Minty! How have you been?"

Since we'd whisked Willa away for a girls' weekend several months earlier, we'd become friends.

"I'm good. Seems like Olivia is doing well."

Mara smiled but it didn't mask the worry behind her eyes. "Yes. She is. We're lucky that we've been able to surround her with people she trusts while she learns to trust herself."

The patio door slid open, and Barrett stepped through before turning to extend his hand to Willa.

"I'm not incapable of walking, Viking," she murmured, her brows knit.

Barrett simply stared back at her, his hand extended until she rolled her eyes and placed her palm over his.

"You can't see your feet, Curly."

"I don't need to see them to walk-"

The toe of her running shoe caught on the track of the patio door, and she pitched forward, sending my heart into my throat.

Screaming. Crying. Blood pouring from between her thighs. Barrett's face white with terror. Ambulance.

God please-

Let it go.

Barrett steadied her, his strong, white teeth a brief flash in his wild beard. "You were saying?"

"Thank you?" She looked up at him with a cheeky grin, and he grunted at her in response, making her laugh.

She scanned the backyard, her face lighting up when she caught sight of Mara and me.

I stepped forward and offered my hand. "May I take over?"

Barrett met my eyes, worry ripe behind the kaleidoscope of color. "Careful of the stairs."

"I would guard her with my life," I murmured.

He relaxed his stance and released his wife. "I believe you would, actually."

"Hi, Thor," Mara teased Barrett as she gently patted the side of her sister's bump.

Willa turned to follow me but was stopped momentarily by Barrett's hand around the back of her neck as he pressed a brief kiss to the top of her head.

I watched as she closed her eyes at the contact, her agitation momentarily soothed.

I envied her.

Not in the way that I wished her good fortune away from her. God knew she deserved that beautiful Viking, but I wondered how it would be to love like that. To be loved like that.

"I'm being a bitch," she grumbled as we walked across the grass.

"I'm sure that's not true," I soothed.

She looked at me sideways, her mouth twisted with amusement. "I assure you; I have had my moments."

I met her eyes, and we laughed.

"What's so funny?" Rebecca, or Bex as everyone but Rhys called her, folded into her chair and kicked out her feet.

"Willa's grumpy," I smiled.

"Of course, she is." Bex leaned over and patted Willa's belly. "You're what? Thirty-eight weeks?"

"That and she's got a baby Viking stuffed up her twat," Junie bounced in and perched her tiny butt on the edge of my chair.

Bex snorted out a laugh setting the rest of us off.

Mara looked around quickly. "Where's Olivia?"

"In the house with Rhys. The twins and the dogs are there, too. Rhys said he'll bring her out with him."

Bex and Rhys had two tiny chihuahuas that were well-loved by their children as well as Olivia. Bex and Rhys often brought the dogs to family events to put Olivia at ease. They made their tiny presence known a few minutes later when a jumble of laughter and high-pitched barking spilled out of the house.

Olivia gently cradled Lilliput in her arms, her bag of happiness filled with the day's necessities hanging off her elbow, as she carefully made her way down the porch steps.

Holy handsome, Rhys ambled across the grass beside Olivia, his smiling eyes resting on his wife.

Rebecca's tiny form wrapped around him, his big hands on her hips, his sexy face tight with ecstasy as he drove up into her.

I felt a shameful flutter but smiled through it.

Rhys greeted the rest of us in his deep, raspy voice, then tossed a blanket on the grass a few feet away from us, spreading it out flat for Olivia and Lilliput.

"You comfortable, Livvie?" he asked softly.

She nodded and pulled out her headphones and her iPad.

Rhys slipped a dog toy from his back pocket and tossed it down on the blanket for the dog.

"Okay, sweetness," he said to Rebecca, his big hand wrapped around her shoulder. "I'm going to go shoot the shit with Zale and Lenny."

"Charming," she teased.

He winked at her as he walked away. "I'll save my charm for when I need it."

"Mm, does that man ever need it?" Junie drawled.

Mara and Willa laughed while Bex smiled happily. "No. No, he does not."

The sound of a motorcycle sparked to life outside and I wondered if it was my curb-mate leaving.

Safe travels.

Chapter 4 – Cougar

<u>Lucky</u>

Pulling my helmet off, I ran my hands through my hair to mess it into submission before heading back inside.

I'd gotten to Lenny and Junie's hours ago and had gone inside to look for something in his garage. I don't know what compelled me to look out the back window before going back out. When I did, my eyes immediately fell on the object of my most recent imaginings. With her chin tipped back, laughter spilling from her pretty lips, her beautiful face framed by a halo of strawberry blond hair that she'd swept back in some sort of twist, I was caught.

The urge to flee wrapped around the drive to claim and froze me in place. I stood staring, the protective barrier of the window between us.

Olivia chatted away with Junie behind me while I creeped on Minty, then Olivia provided me the perfect excuse to leave when she asked if Junie had any Kraft dinner. She reminded me a bit of my cousin's kid, and I wondered if she was on the autism spectrum.

Turning, I caught the flash of anxiety on Junie's face.

"You want me to go pick some up?"

Immediately the lines in her face smoothed. "That would be great."

I knocked briskly on the counter. "I'll be back."

The truth was, I needed to escape.

I passed Rhys and his entourage returning from the park and briefly explained my mission.

"Make sure it's name brand," Rhys advised. "Olivia's got exacting standards when it comes to her mac and cheese."

These people were tight. They were a family. Made me grateful for my own.

Once on my bike, I let my thoughts wander.

Minty.

I mentally rolled her name around my tongue, thinking about the woman who had occupied rent-free status in my mind since first meeting her at Barrett's wedding months before.

She enthralled me.

No one had ever done that before.

Returning with three boxes of Kraft Dinner in hand, I parked my bike against the curb and headed up to the front door.

Junie bounced through the back slider just as I came in. I tossed the mac and cheese on the counter. "Alright, Junie?"

"It's great." Her gaze flicked down to the counter, and she huffed out a breath of relief. "Thank you."

"No problem," I muttered, returning to my station in front of the window.

Junie sidled up beside me and followed my line of sight to Minty.

"Hmm," she hummed. Nudging me with her elbow, she murmured, "She doesn't bite."

I looked down at her elven face and smirked. "More's the pity."

Junie laughed out loud, her eyes alight. "Oh, this is going to be good." She rubbed her small hands together.

"What's going to be good?" I asked suspiciously. With four sisters, I recognized that tone. Usually, it did not bode well for me.

She shook her head. "You think you know, but you don't. She," Junie nodded toward Minty in the backyard, "is probably the best person I know." She grinned. "And she's going to give you one helluva run for your money."

I watched her a moment longer. Sitting so still. Contained. In control.

So classically beautiful.

"I don't think so," I murmured, a heaviness I didn't recognize settling onto my chest. "Women like her are not for men like me."

Junie only hummed.

I tousled her hair, laughing at her scowl as I stepped out into the backyard.

I purposefully diverted my attention away from the strawberry blond beauty at the back of the garden and headed towards the men. The conversation rambled easily though I uncharacteristically struggled to participate.

Barrett, his eyes on me, tipped his head back and sucked back a long draught of beer. His gaze flitted to Minty momentarily before coming back to me with a quirk of his brow.

How he knew the things he did, I didn't fucking know, but I wished he didn't.

I shook my head once.

Minty.

Her name tasted sweet.

Something about her tugged at my heartstrings as well as my dick. Even my brain was firing on all cylinders. It was probably an illusion. I'd made her out to be more than she was. We'd barely exchanged ten words.

With everyone's attention on Lenny and his plan to propose, I snuck another look, a longer one this time. Prim and proper, her legs crossed at the ankles, surrounded by that crazy, cackling bunch, she both fit in and stood out.

I imagined she encapsulated all things good and classy and bright. Those vibrant women surrounding her, they were the good ones, and they obviously loved her.

I remembered Barrett telling me all that Minty had done to help him prepare for his and Willa's wedding, and the obvious respect he had for her. I pulled in a deep breath, relieved to have finally figured it out. It was the stories I'd heard from Junie and Barrett that created this push-pull. Then, with her being so fucking easy on the eyes, I'd built her up in my mind.

That didn't explain the immediate attraction at the wedding, but everyone gets sentimental at weddings. Even, apparently, certified single dudes like myself.

Several minutes later, after forcibly pulling my attention from her yet again, Barrett met my eyes and grinned.

I came crashing back to earth. "Too rich for my blood, Bear," I warned.

His eyebrows shot up in surprise while he quickly appraised me. He looked out over the yard, his eyes softening as they found his wife.

"Some women are just too good. Yet here we are."

Minty

Happy couples surrounded me. Like twin rings soldered together and linked to the next set of twin rings, forming a human necklace. Willa and Junie and their crew on one side, Amber and Ruby and their crew on the other, the children catching and spreading the light like diamond pendants.

I was the clasp holding the necklace together.

Functional, but discreet.

No link to call my own.

No diamonds.

I mentally chastised myself.

I loved Amber and Ruby's boys, Jace and Alex, as though they were my own. And I had George now as well.

Amber and Ruby were as good as sisters. Better, even.

Their Yiayia reminded me of my late parents, and she treated me like one of her own.

Ruby's husband, Vander, had slowly worked his way into my heart, and I'd always loved Gus, even before he married Amber.

Between Ezinne, the people in this yard, and my big, fat, Greek family, love filled every nook and cranny of my life.

At times I thought about whether I would have liked to have had a child but knew that kids were not the best idea for me.

Definitely not full time.

Especially not with my issues.

I smiled away the last of the shadowy thoughts and returned my attention to Junie who was talking animatedly.

"I came off the pill, but we want to make sure all the hormones are out of my system before we start trying for a baby bump. So, I got fitted for a diaphragm." Her eyes went wide, and she drew an imaginary circle in the vicinity of her nether regions. "Let me tell you, there is much more space up in there than you think! I mean, a diaphragm is not that small and digging that fucker out the first time required both me and the doctor. I've never had so many fingers inside me at the same time."

Bex wrapped her arms around her waist and howled while Willa did the same, albeit in considerably more discomfort. Mara's hands muffled her snorts, and Olivia drew on, her earphones keeping her oblivious to the conversation going on around her.

"By the time I left the doctor's office, I thought I had it all figured out. I was feeling all sexy mother earth, like a fertility goddess on the prowl. Lenny was due home, so I put on a bit of sexy and waited for him on the bed." She guffawed then pulled herself together. "He comes in, catches sight of me on the bed and goes all caveman. He yanks me by my ankles, pulls me down to the bottom of the bed, whips my legs open and the fucker flew out of my coochie and hit him on the chin."

Mara barked out a laugh, shot out of her seat, and ran for the house, her thighs squeezed shut.

"She's going to pee," Bex laughed. "She always pees when she laughs."

Willa groaned as she shook with laughter, clutching her stomach.

Junie excelled at making people laugh. She had no qualms about sharing and no filter. Her transparency and honesty were refreshing and reassuring.

The roar of the motorcycle coming down the street drew Junie's attention. Perhaps my curb-mate was back.

Junie cocked her head to the side. "Oh, good!" She jumped up from her spot. "Lucky's back with the KD."

Another flutter, this one higher up and unburdened by guilt, set my heart racing. Keeping one eye on the back porch, I noticed the exact moment when Lucky, all lean and long, stepped out the screen door, prowled across the porch, and dropped lazily down the steps.

With his gaze fixed on the men, mine was free to roam. In all fairness, he was the only bit of man candy strictly permitted.

His hair had grown out a bit since the wedding, much more befitting the image of the rock god I'd made him out to be in my mind. Tall, over six feet for sure, he had the body of a runner. Long, lean, graceful. He walked like a big cat, all prowl and predator which stirred my womb.

In contrast, the two deep dimples that creased his cheeks when he laughed made him boyishly cute. Perhaps he was even younger than I thought. Careful now not to give myself away, because the man had to be four or five years younger than me, I drank him in.

I had enjoyed the bit of flirting we indulged in at the wedding. I knew, had I allowed it, we might have taken it further. But then, how awkward would gatherings like this be?

Maybe I'd look at a dating site for older people, I mused. I wouldn't mind finding a man who was a bit older. A widower maybe. A man whose children were grown. A companion. Someone to travel with. He might even be retired. What would sex be like with a man the likes of which I pictured in my head?

Hmm.

Well.

Sex wasn't everything.

I looked at Barrett, Zale, Rhys, and Lenny.

Then my eyes drifted over to Lucky, and I admitted to myself that, for me, it was important.

Lucky remembered me.

I caught glimpses of him checking me out. Finally, I caught his eye and sent him a wink. I nearly laughed out loud at his reaction. He probably thinks I'm a cougar.

Lenny's proposal went off without a hitch. Afterwards, Junie was uncharacteristically quiet, spending many long moments staring at the ring on her finger, her face soft. Finally, Lenny scooped her up and put her on his lap where she settled in until she found her feet again.

Well, her voice at least.

Although Lucky's glances became emboldened, he did not approach me. And other than a few pleasantries exchanged over the course of dinner, we did not speak.

We sent Willa home to rest and helped Junie clear up the kitchen.

When I returned to the backyard to gather my things, Lucky was gone.

Chapter 5 – Thoughts and Fears

Lucky

Throwing my leg over my bike, I settled myself to wait.

It didn't take long before the front door opened and Minty stepped outside, immediately followed by Junie, a huge grin spreading across her pixie face when she spotted me sitting at the curb.

"Fuck." I laughed. I should have known there'd be an audience.

Minty looked over her shoulder, her raised eyebrows giving away her surprise.

As the afternoon hours slipped past, the craving to know her overcame all but one ounce of the self-preservation I had left. Slipping away to wait outside, I thought I was being discreet.

Not for my sake. For hers.

There was no help for it now.

Both women watched my progress as I swung off my bike and headed up to the door, relieving Junie's arms of the weight of Minty's dishes.

"I'll carry these to your car," I murmured.

Junie opened her mouth to speak, her eyes dancing, but I cut her off with a laugh. "Go inside, Junebug."

Junie giggled and waggled her fingers at Minty. "Have a good night," she sang, closing the door.

Minty assessed me quickly, a hint of uncertainty flickering over her face before she composed herself and murmured, "Thank you."

Our brief trek to her car was made in silence. She opened the door, and I slid her dishes across to the passenger side.

Crossing her arms over her chest, she met my eyes and coolly announced. "I don't play games."

"What makes you think I do?"

"You didn't say more than three words to me all day and now you're waiting by my car?" She answered softly.

I nodded. "I can see how that might look." I turned to lean against the side of her car. "Here's the thing. I'm reasonably certain you're too good for me." Her eyebrows flew up, but I continued. "My sense of self-preservation insists that I keep my distance, but watching you all afternoon..." I petered off, unsure how to finish. Finally, I turned and faced her head-on. "There's something about you that pulls at me, and I want to get to know you."

The sound of feminine laughter spilled from around the side of the house as Mara and Bex burst around, bumping into each other as they walked, Bex's arms waving as she talked. Rhys and Zale brought up the rear with the kids and the dogs.

Mara caught sight of us first, stopped walking, and grabbed Bex's arm. "Bex!" She pointed right at us. "Look!"

Bex's head swung around, and she clapped her hands.

Zale snaked an arm around his wife's waist and pulled her around to face him. I watched as she melted against him.

I wanted that.

What the fuck? Since when?

Rhys wrapped his hand around the back of Bex's nape and laughed at her antics.

"For fuck's sake," I huffed, looking at Minty. "This was perhaps not my best plan. I thought by slipping away I could ask you out discreetly, but no such luck."

Something flashed behind Minty's eyes, and she smiled.

I stared harder at her than I should, but I wanted to know what was behind that smile. What it was that flashed in her eyes and pinkened her cheeks when she looked at me.

I needed to know.

Minty

I wonder what it would be like to have sex on his bike?

Our audience had grown, and I, for one, did not know my lines.

He tipped his chin down and scuffed the toe of his boot against the road.

Words failed me.

Thoughts failed me. It had been a long time since I'd felt this awkward in any kind of social situation.

I counted each finger starting with my pinky. *1-2-3-4-5*.

Now back, starting with my thumb. *1-2-3-4-5*.

Each finger gets a 1, each finger gets a 5 so in the end they weigh the same.

Again.

1-2-3-4-5-1-2-3-4-5-1-2-3-4-5-1-2-3-

He cleared his throat, then tipped his chin up to look at me, a wry smile on his sweet face. "I think, perhaps, I misjudged."

4-5.

Finding my voice, I met his eyes. "No. No, you did not. I, um, I'm usually not this tongue-tied."

"I'm hoping that's a good thing. Would you like to go out for a coffee?" he asked, looking at me hopefully.

"I would." I cleared my throat. "I would like that very much."

He grinned, both dimples winking at me. "Are you going to let me pick you up and take you on my bike?"

Straddling his lap on his bike, my head thrown back, his hands gripping my waist, his mouth latched onto my nipple while I ride him hard, all the boyish softness wiped from his face...

Can he hear your thoughts?

Can he read your mind?

Did you say that out loud?

He stepped closer. "I need to know what goes on behind those eyes."

"Be careful what you wish for," I warned ruefully.

"I'll take my chances," he muttered. "You going to let me take you on my bike?"

Oh, yes.

"Are you a safe driver?"

He grinned and touched the tip of his forefinger to my cheek. "The safest. I even have an extra helmet for you."

An irrational surge of jealousy shot through me, and my eyebrow quirked in irritation.

The finger touch turned into a feather light stroke that ended with a firm finger underneath my chin, tipping my face up to his.

"It's my sister's helmet. She won't mind you borrowing it. If she hadn't left it at my place, I wouldn't be able to offer you a ride."

I swallowed and nodded, suddenly exhausted from the day and the hours of continuous mental warfare. My reserves were dangerously low.

I smiled to soften my rejection of his offer. "I'm not ready to trust you with my life on that bike, but I'll meet you for coffee."

We exchanged phone numbers, and I watched him ride off from the safety of my vehicle before slowly pulling away from the curb and heading home.

Once home, I shed my clothes, tossing them on top of the heap I started a few days ago. Clothes. My second indulgence. And this room, my bedroom, was where they congregated and multiplied. The one room in my home that was never pristine.

In the ensuite bath, I dug through my basket of cosmetics, found my makeup remover and cotton pads and wiped my face clean.

I dumped a scoop of lavender scented Epsom salts into the tub and filled it to the brim with hot water. Next, I connected my portable speaker, lit my scented candles, and grabbed my Kindle.

I allowed the scented water to welcome me into its warm embrace.

Tomorrow I'd tidy my bedroom.

Tomorrow I'd sort through my thoughts and fears about Lucky.

Oh, frig.

Tomorrow I'd have to face Willa and Junie. I laughed to myself. If anybody could get me out of my head, it was those two.

Hopefully, Willa would stay at home and get some rest.

I shook my head. There was no way. She'd be in if only to grill me.

At three a.m. my cell phone rang.

Junie's name on the display set my heart to racing.

I snapped it up.

"Hell-"

"It's a girl," a half-sobbing Junie laughed into the phone. "Barrett just called. They have a little girl."

"A little girl," I breathed, my breath stuck in my throat. "How is Willa? Did she come through okay?"

"She's fine. Barrett said she was a rock star," Junie hiccoughed.

My smile spread clear across my face. "Of course, he did. Are we allowed to visit her tomorrow?"

"Just try to keep me away. I dare you!" Junie threatened.

After a few more minutes in which Junie relayed the time of birth, 2:04, the baby's weight, 8 lbs, 11 oz, the baby's length, 20 inches, then lamented the fact that she forgot to ask the baby's name, Lenny coaxed her back to bed.

While I burrowed back down into mine, I did not sleep.

A little girl.

A precious baby girl.

A Viking, his queen, and their princess.
Lucky little bean.

Chapter 6 – Full Disclosure

<u>Lucky</u>

So, it was official.

For the first time ever, I wanted to hide my man-whore status.

Never, in all my life, did I care what a woman thought or felt about my dating habits.

Until now.

That spark of jealousy in Minty's eyes when I mentioned the extra helmet warmed my heart and shriveled my balls.

Because I cared what Minty thought. A lot. And I didn't want any obstacles to stand in the way of getting to know her.

I gave my head a shake at the intensity of my feelings. We hadn't even had one date. It didn't matter. I could reason to myself all I wanted but having watched Barrett and Lenny fall like two great trees the previous summer, I knew it was possible. I had started to believe myself immune to that type of experience.

Now I feared? Hoped? Thrilled? That I wasn't.

Because I wouldn't mind having what Barrett and Lenny had. Hell, Rhys and Zale had it pretty damn good, too.

I wondered if Minty wanted that, too.

The light turned green, and I rolled through the intersection, flicking on my indicator to turn into the hospital parking lot.

I grinned at the thought of Barrett being a girl dad, then twisted my mouth in compassionate solidarity.

Zale and Rhys walked out of the hospital with their wives just as I was heading in.

Mara's face lit with excitement when she saw me. "Hey! Are you going to see the baby?"

I smiled at her obvious joy. "You've seen her?"

Zale snorted. "She hasn't left since Willa called her to go with them last night."

It was only then that I noticed she was wearing the same outfit as yesterday.

"Minty's up there now," she informed me, her gaze narrowing in on my face expectantly.

My heart skipped a beat and my eyebrows shot up before I had a chance to school my reaction.

Mara looked pointedly at Bex, who assessed me curiously, her clear blue eyes searching my face.

Zale and Rhys met my eyes over their heads and smiled in commiseration.

Rhys laughed and cupped his wife around the back of her neck. "C'mon, sweetness. Give the man some space."

Zale held up his fist for a bump, his smile wry. "Good luck, bud."

With an extra bounce in my step, I hit the stairs instead of the elevator, and bounded up to the second floor.

Finding Willa's room, I peeked in to find Minty sitting in a chair enraptured by the tiny pink bundle nestled in her arms. Barrett stood sentry, a modern-day Viking, between his girls and the door.

I rapped softly on the doorframe to announce my presence, and two pairs of eyes swung in my direction. One alert, that alertness softening only marginally when he took me in, the other anxious, and belonging to the object of my fascination.

"Hey, come on in," Barrett called quietly. "Wash your hands over there and then come see my girls."

I heard a scoff from the direction of the bed and caught the flash of amusement in Barrett's eyes.

"They're not coming to see me, Viking."

He swung around to face his wife and muttered. "They are definitely coming to check on you, too."

I dried my hands and threw my arm over Barrett's shoulders. "And you, too, big guy. Congrats."

"Thanks." Not much for words, his face expressed his pride and joy. And more than a hint of wonder. He'd waited a long time for Willa.

It occurred to me that, like me, Barrett didn't fall in love too readily, but once he fell, he went down like a mighty oak. I wondered if I had it in me to fall that hard.

I went to the bed first and leaned down to kiss Willa's cheek. "How are you doing? I hear you pushed out a Viking-sized baby."

Willa laughed. "No kidding. I was there. The doctor said it was a good thing I went a couple of weeks early."

I handed her the bear I bought for the baby then crossed to where Minty sat cuddling her.

"Hello, beautiful."

Minty continued to smile down at the baby.

I tapped Minty's cheek lightly with the tip of my finger, and she looked up at me in question.

"Hello, beautiful," I said again, smiling into her eyes.

Her tinkling laugh spilled out, and I grinned back at her. "So, who do we have here?"

I leaned over and peered at the tiny, perfect face with its rosebud lips pursed in a tiny frown.

"She's frowning," Minty cooed.

"Ah, so she has her father's disposition."

Willa barked out a laugh and Barrett chuckled. "Let's hope she's exactly like her perfect mother."

Minty

"This is Rena," I said softly. "It means joy or melody."

"Well." Lucky swallowed hard, his jaw tightening as he took in Rena's perfect face. "That is entirely fitting."

"It is." I heard the smile in my voice.

Without asking, Barrett had transferred the tiny, perfect bundle into my arms the moment I finished drying my hands. A thousand shockingly violent images flashed behind my eyes, and I covered her fragile head with my palm protectively as I carefully maneuvered myself into the only available chair.

I breathed deeply, the sweet smell of her little head filling my lungs while I waited for the shock of the images to dispel so I could enjoy her.

By the time Lucky knocked the door, I was just beginning to settle in. I didn't want to give her up.

His presence served as an excellent distraction to my disturbing thoughts. In the quiet of the hospital room, I found I liked the sound of his voice. Knowing he played guitar in Barrett's band, Drivetrain, I wondered if he also sang. Did he play any other instruments? I wondered if I'd gone with Willa and Junie last summer if we would have hit it off.

Music opened doors inside me like nothing else could. It allowed me to feel, to cry, to dream, to breathe.

It stimulated my brain in ways that left me relaxed and offered me a reprieve.

Lucky reached out a long, lean finger and touched Rena's tiny ear.

"It seems a shame to touch this perfect skin with these calloused fingers," he murmured.

You can touch mine.

I felt my face flush. No man had affected me like this in years. I searched my memory for the last one who elicited this type of reaction. Just as I suspected, there was only one.

"I won't ask to hold her today," he said to Willa. "She looks too comfortable nestled up against Minty. I'll wait and come visit you at home in a couple of weeks."

The clock on the wall showed that it was nearing six o'clock and there had been visitors for the past few hours. It was time to go.

I stood and nestled Rena back inside the cradle of her mother's loving arms. Saying our goodbyes, Lucky followed me out of Willa and Barrett's room.

Lucky rested his fingers lightly at the small of my back. "Have you eaten yet?"

"No. Not yet."

"Would you like to grab some dinner with me?"

I blew out a quick breath. Spontaneous changes in plan were not my strong suit.

I looked up to find his eyes on me. Waiting. Assessing.

"I'm kind of a fussy eater," I admitted. "Would it be okay with you if I picked the restaurant?"

He shrugged. "Works for me. It's not vegan, is it?" he joked.

I smiled guiltily, and he slapped a hand over his heart. "You're killing me," he groused, laughing. "Alright. Let this be a testament to my interest in you that I'm willing to visit the dark side."

"You're that interested, hm?" I teased, beginning to feel my feet under me.

"I am," he readily admitted with a smile.

"Well, if we get to know each other better and we decide to go out and eat again, I'll take you to Spuds. My best friend owns it, and you can get all the meat you want."

"Will I also get grilled by your friend?"

I groaned. "You did not just make a punny."

He laughed. "I did." He nodded and pressed his lips together tightly in mock apology. "However, I also play electric guitar in a rock band which I hope is enough to balance out my dorky side." He held up a finger as if he just remembered something. "And I have abs."

I laughed out loud. "Certainly, a good set of abs covers a multitude of sins." I glanced up at his smiling face, his dimples a mere tease. "I do not have abs. I feel it's only fair to let you know considering we are revealing our innermost secrets."

He smiled bigger, his dimples deeper. "I'm definitely down with that. I prefer my women soft."

"Hm. And how many women do you have?"

"One at a time," he answered quickly.

I laughed again. "You answered rather quickly. Did you practice?"

He huffed out a laugh in response.

"I sense there's a story there," I prodded.

Meeting my eyes, he replied, "I've given enough away for a first date, and we haven't even made it to our cars. How about we hold off on discussing stats until at least our third date."

"Sure." I shrugged. "But in the interest of full disclosure, I do not share. Ever."

"After which point?" he asked, his head cocked to the side curiously.

"Before my clothes come off," I answered wryly.

He laughed and threw his arm around my shoulders, squeezing me to his side. "Fair enough."

Only a couple of inches shorter than Barret, he towered over me, his body deliciously hard against mine.

A zing of awareness skittered along my spine swelling my breasts.

I drew in a deep steadying breath.

"Yeah," he said, his voice a bit wobbly. "I feel it, too."

Chapter 7 - PG

Minty

He followed me to Bliss Kitchen, my only 100% trigger-free restaurant aside from Spuds.

Sitting across from me at a table for two by the window, I perused the menu looking for something for him to eat. Coming here was a mistake. I should have chosen somewhere different. Something he would like.

"What are you ordering?" he asked.

I looked up.

His friendly grey eyes rested on my face.

"I'm sorry. I should have thought this through better."

His eyebrows rose. "What are you sorry for?"

"For bringing you here. Is there anything here for you to eat?"

"Loads," he assured me. "I already know what I'm going to order. What are you getting?"

"I'm going to go with the burrito bowl."

He smiled. "We have similar tastes. I'm getting the loaded burrito fries. See? We're all good."

He closed his menu and asked, "Do you ever eat meat?"

"I do," I answered carefully.

How much to disclose? Usually, I didn't get past the first or second date with a man so there was no need to reveal such personal information.

Lucky was different, he would show up in my life sporadically one way or another. It wasn't that I felt ashamed of having OCD, I just didn't like to give it center stage in my life. Bringing it front and center on a first date seemed to be doing just that.

His husky voice interrupted my musings. "Is this a difficult question for you?"

I pursed my lips then smiled. "It shouldn't be. I don't much like discussing my food preferences. I do eat meat occasionally," I answered slowly. "But I can get turned off of it really easily."

"Ah," he nodded. "It's mostly psychological."

"Yes," I nodded, then waited to see if he would push it further.

"My sister is like that," he said easily, tipping his chin up to smile at the server.

"Hi, folks. What can I get for you?"

Lucky chatted with her then ordered for both of us, confirming with me that he got mine correct, then asked what I wanted to drink.

This date already rated far and above any in recent memory. The last man I went out with ordered his meal first, criticized my choice, then had the audacity to put his big fingers on my plate to steal my fries. The very same food item he criticized for its trans fats.

"You have a sister?"

"I have four sisters," he corrected.

"Oh my!" I laughed. "Tell me you're not the middle child."

"I am," he chuckled. "But I share that space with my older brother."

"So, you had a built-in partner-in-crime."

He laughed outright. "I did. He's more crime oriented than me. It was his schemes that got us into trouble. My skills lay in the area of charming our way out of it. He's better looking and smart as a whip. I'm much more charming and charismatic."

I laughed out loud. "And humble," I added. "Mustn't forget humble."

44

"I'm the humblest," he agreed.

Easy to talk to, easy on the eyes, he didn't push, he didn't prod, and he listened as well as spoke.

"What was it like growing up in a large family?"

He shrugged. "It's hard to answer that question. It's what I knew, what I know. It's normal for me. There were a lot of personalities in our house, which made it difficult at times. Holidays were a blast. My mom was chronically tired, but she was happy. And she worked hard to ensure we were as well."

"Was?" I asked gently.

He nodded. "Was. She passed away many years ago. My youngest sister was only twenty. My dad was older than her and followed five years later." The faraway look in his eyes revealed his trek into the past. "Those five years were brutal for him." His attention came back to me. "Her death came as a shock. Car accident."

"I'm sorry, Lucky."

"Me too. She was a good woman. Always smiling."

Like you.

"And your dad?"

"Good man," he replied immediately. "Loved his wife, loved his kids, and didn't shy away from showing it, although as a kid I could have done without the PDA. They set the bar high."

"Is that why you're not married with six kids of your own?"

He slapped a hand over his chest in mock alarm. "You're going to give me a heart attack! No six kids for me. Too busy. And with the state of the economy, I just don't think it's feasible to have that many children and be able to give them everything I'd like to give them."

He wanted kids. Not six, perhaps, but it was clear he planned on having some.

I couldn't give him kids.

First off, I was too old. If I got pregnant tonight, I'd be forty-five when the baby was born. Which wasn't terrible. My foster parents would have

45

been forty-five when I was born. However, my meds, which had taken years to get right, did not mix well with pregnancy and I could not function without them.

So, while Lucky was indeed charming and I could admit he made my lady parts sing, this would not amount to more than friendship or perhaps a temporary fling.

"I feel like most of the conversation is going on inside your head," he mused.

I tilted my head to the side. "How old are you?"

He smiled deeper, his dimples winking at me. "No stats until the third date."

"Okay," I grinned. "Tell me more about your siblings."

Two of his sisters were happily married, one was divorced, and one had not yet met 'the one'. His brother was a confirmed bachelor. He had seven nieces and nephews all equally adored.

I told him I was an only child, which was not strictly true, and that my parents passed when I was in my early twenties.

"And why aren't you married with six kids?" he asked, giving me a taste of my own words.

"I think, like you, my parents' relationship set the bar high. Not only because of the way they treated each other, but for how they treated me, how they taught me to treat other people." I thought some more. "Just look around at the relationships around us. Would you want to settle for less than what Willa and Barrett have now that you know it's possible? I see how happy Lenny and Junie are, and I see the same thing in my two best friends and their husbands. I've never felt like that about someone else." I needed to qualify that in the name of honesty. "At least, I've never felt like that about someone who felt the same for me."

"I'm thinking he must have been a fool," Lucky murmured, his eyes soft on my face.

What if you're too much for anybody?

I smiled, knowing the chances of him turning tail and running would increase astronomically once I let him in.

If I let him in.

I gave myself a mental shake and reminded myself that we would only ever be friends. "We shall see. How about you?"

He leaned back in his chair and ran his hand through his hair. "I can honestly tell you I've never felt that way about anyone before. Marriage requires work and self-sacrifice if it's to be done right. Your partner's happiness must be as important as your own if not more so. Every decision you make affects them. You essentially live your life for them as well as with them, and so far, I've never felt driven to that level of commitment."

At least we were on the same page. I liked him. A lot. We would have a bit of fun and then we'd go our separate ways. And hopefully he'd find someone he wanted to build his life around who could give him a couple of kids.

Lucky

The vegan place wasn't nearly as bad as I thought it would be. Minty even managed to finagle a promise from me that I'd go back in exchange for her assurance that our next dinner would be at Spuds where I could load up on souvlaki.

And that was happening tomorrow for lunch.

"Okay, miscreants," I yelled over the cacophony of too many musical instruments in the wrong hands. "Back to your seats."

I wrote out the homework due for next week on the board and promised I'd update the student website. A promise I made daily and broke almost as often. We had a deal. If I forgot to update the website, and they forgot to do their homework, they got a day's grace.

It was rare they did not get their day's grace.

Working at an inner-city high school had its challenges.

Unlike the suburbs, many of these students did not have internet at home, never mind access to the laptops and desktops that their suburban counterparts upgraded every couple of years.

They did however have cell phones, guns, drugs, knives, and some already had a rap sheet. Oh, yeah. And fake IDs. Which I found out when a group of them showed up at one of Drivetrain's shows.

I saw them file in, dressed tough, looking hopeful. I told Barrett between songs. He welcomed them and warned them their continued presence depended on their beverage choices.

I laughed out loud when they looked at me, mouths hanging open. I made the universal sign for 'I'm watching you', then ordered a shit load of apps for them to eat while they watched the show.

When they left it was with fists in the air screaming, 'Mr. Triggs'.

The ACEs scores some of these kids carried curdled my stomach. The fact there was little I could do made it worse.

Food scarcity, a political term that meant half my students didn't bring a lunch and most likely had cookies for breakfast, did not fuel their brains to learn.

Last Christmas, the board sent around student feedback forms asking students what would help them succeed. It was anonymous. Forms were filled out and popped into my mailbox throughout the week.

The first day of Christmas vacation, I sat in my kitchen and read through the responses. Fifty of my one hundred and twenty students filled out the forms. These were the students that still had hope. Based on the handwriting, most of them were female. Forty-five forms included underwear on the wish list.

It was fucking Christmas.

Underwear was on the list of things they felt they needed for success.

After reading the last form, I placed it gently on the table on top of the others and stared out my window.

I was a thirty-eight-year-old man and my female students needed underwear.

What the fuck was I supposed to do with that?

My students filed out, but I remained at my desk thinking about my first date with Minty. Conversation flowed easily between us despite my belief that more than half of it took place in her head.

After meeting her at Barrett's wedding, I purposefully decided not to pursue her. She seemed like a nice woman, a good girl, and giving her my regular spiel didn't seem right. Especially considering the connection through our mutual friends.

In the months between that first meeting and the barbecue at Lenny's, my interest did not wane. I struggled all afternoon, much to Barrett's amusement, to convince myself my earlier decision to leave her be was the correct one.

At the hospital I could wait no longer. I wasn't sorry. If anything, she intrigued me more.

Classy, gracious, soft-spoken, and funny, she was not my usual type. I worried a little about how we would be between the sheets, but I wanted to find out. I huffed out a laugh. The fact that she wanted to be exclusive before her clothes came off was different. The fact that I was considering it a testament to my growing fascination with her.

I was even willing to brave a vegan restaurant which turned out much better than I expected. After we ate, I walked her to her car.

"That was delicious," I admitted.

"Yeah?" She looked up at me hopefully. "I'm glad."

My eyes dropped to her pretty mouth. "Hm. I want to kiss you but not with burrito breath."

She studied me for a moment then surprised me by stepping into my space, her breasts brushing against my abdomen.

I tipped my chin down, staring into her upturned face.

Her hand gently cupped the back of my neck. "You forget I have burrito breath, too." She tilted her head back and offered me her mouth, a tiny smile teasing her lips. "Let's see what you got."

Holy fuck. The challenge in her eyes jerked my dick just as surely as if she stuck her hand down my pants.

I palmed her lower back and pulled her firmly against me, arching her back.

The gratifying sound of her sharp inhale combined with the surprised quirk of her brows made me smile.

"I'll keep it PG this time," I promised then pressed my lips gently against her laughing mouth.

At the first brush of our lips, she stilled, and her eyes flew open.

A zing of awareness like nothing I'd ever felt before lit me up inside, and my arm locked around her tight. My other hand cupped the back of her head while my lips moved over hers, softly at first as her breathy sigh escaped into my mouth and her eyelids fluttered shut.

So sweet.

I needed to go deeper.

I pulled back half an inch to find her right with me, eyes half-closed, mouth soft and willing. Watching the heat build in her eyes, I moved my hand up to grip her sleek ponytail and gently pulled her head back and to the side before going in again, slanting my mouth across hers, and begging entrance with my tongue.

She tipped her chin up further and opened her mouth under mine.

My fingers tightened and I held her still while I explored, licking inside her mouth, stroking her tongue, and nibbling gently on her bottom lip before covering her mouth the way I wanted to cover her body.

Her hand tightened around the back of my neck, and she pressed her full breasts into my chest.

I ground my hips into her stomach, letting her feel what she was doing to me, the little noise she made in her throat urging me to strip her pants down her legs and sink to my knees.

She slid her hand to my chest and gently pushed me back a couple of inches.

Not ready to release her, I simply stared down into her face, her ponytail trapped in my fist, my fingers flexing against her back.

Her eyes dropped to my mouth. "Mm-hmm," she hummed.

"Fuck me," I whispered.

A tiny smirk lifted the corner of those lips to which I may have already become addicted. "Not tonight, darling."

I wondered when she'd give me a different answer. I hoped it would be soon.

Chapter 8 – My Boys

<u>Minty</u>

My parking spot at the back of the lot offered me an excellent view of the mess of students spilling from the front door of the high school. George's school. The same one Jace and Alex would attend in September. So far, every time I'd come to pick him up, he'd come out alone.

George, Vander's son from his first marriage, had resided full-time with Ruby and Vander since Christmas. His situation broke my heart, but thankfully, he was beginning to come around.

Just not at school.

There was nothing inherently negative about his experience at school, there just wasn't anything all that positive.

I looked around at the students coming out. The split between those who had, and those who had not, hit roughly 60/40, that 40 being those who could not afford private school and were forced to make do with what the neighborhood offered.

The 60.

Good Lord.

George's curly head finally made an appearance, and I exhaled the breath I didn't know I'd been holding.

My eyes widened. A pert little blond bounced along beside him, hugging her books to her chest, her face tipped up toward him.

He slanted a glance in her direction and gave her a short nod.

She veered off away from him toward the buses. She looked back once.

He did not.

At the edge of the lot, he stopped and scanned the cars, a look of amused determination on his young face. He looked like his dad, exactly like Vander did when he was amused. The look he usually aimed at Ruby.

I smiled. This was our game. I hit the start button on the timer.

His eyes skipped past me then flew back and he pointed, a victorious smile on his face. 9.7 seconds. His best time yet.

He loped to the car and swung into the front passenger seat.

Is it okay that he's alone with you?

"How did I do?"

I showed him the stopwatch. "Best time yet."

His eyebrows flew up and he whipped out his cell phone to document the evidence. "Hold it up to your face, Minnie," he murmured and took the picture. "They'll never beat this time," he crowed.

"It's unlikely," I agreed.

You want to kiss him.

Carefully pulling out of the lot, I continued our routine. "Three good things."

He pulled in a deep breath. "Three?" he asked as he always did.

"Three," I confirmed.

"I passed my history test."

"Good! What did you get?"

He slanted me a sneaky glance. "I passed and I don't have a note to be signed."

I chuckled. "Fair enough. Next?"

"The cafeteria had the giant chocolate chip cookies today."

"Mm-hmm." We turned onto the main road.

Twisted metal and screams, a bloody gash on George's head, his eyes vacant.

The sun sparkled off the windshield. George cranked his window down and stuck his hand out the window to feel the rush of the wind on his palm. We passed the turn-off to Spuds and my place, and then pulled off the main road towards the elementary school.

"I don't have any homework for the weekend. My one teacher, he's different. Gives homework every day but says we don't have to meet the due date if he forgets to update the website." He looked at me, his head cocked to the side. "He literally never remembers. Then, on the day when it's due, he gives us the entire class time to complete it. If anyone has it done ahead of time, he opens up the recording room."

"Recording room?"

"Yeah. It's music class."

"You like music class?"

"I don't know. I like this teacher. I don't care too much for my instrument."

"What are you playing?"

He sighed. "What almost everyone is playing. The recorder."

"There are no other musical instruments?"

"No. The teacher brings in his own to let us try them. He's even leant them out a few times. There's a drum set, but someone has already claimed that. A couple of ukuleles. Two guitars. One set of bongos. There's not much."

"What would you want to play, honey?"

He shook his head. "No, Minnie. Anyone who walks in there with a new instrument..." He petered off. "There are so many kids that have nothing. To walk in there with a brand-new instrument when most don't have that option, most people don't take it too well."

"I understand." I paused. "But would you want something to play at home?"

"Maybe," he murmured. "Maybe guitar. Maybe bongos. Ukulele looks fun."

"Acoustic or electric?"

He laughed, the sound joyous with disbelief. "Electric, of course." He turned to look out the window and his voice softened. "My dad will buy me anything I want, Minnie. You don't have to worry about that."

"I know, honey. You should ask him." I pulled into the school parking lot and allowed George to pick our hiding spot.

He was right. Jace and Alex did not beat his time, which meant he got to choose where we went to eat.

As usual, and much to Jace and Alex's temporary chagrin, he chose Spuds.

The place he was most comfortable.

I started the car and took a steadying breath. Elementary school dismissal was the absolute worst time of day to drive.

The crosswalks closest to the school were not bad because the elementary schools utilized crossing guards which helped to verify the messages my eyes sent to my brain. But as we drove further out, there was less need of crossing guards, and I lost my security blanket.

I pulled to a stop at a stop sign where a few kids waited to cross. They set out, a small hive of pre-teens, bumbling across the street.

The boys jabbered away to each other about their day, teasing George about the girl who texted him.

Go.

I could almost feel my foot stomping onto the accelerator, the boy in front of my car crumpling.

I swallowed hard and pressed my foot to the brake harder.

Oh, God. What if I lose control?

Relax.

Smile it away. It's just OCD.

Joke. Make a joke.

He's only worth two points. Not worth the jail time.

Breathe.

Smile.

"Minty?"

I looked carefully to ensure the way was clear before moving through the intersection.

"Yes, Alex?" He was up to something. I could always tell by the sound of his voice in combination with the silence from the other two. My heart smiled.

"We were thinking, if you think it's a good idea, that we could take the day off school on Friday, you know, take a mental health day?"

I laughed. "Sounds good to me. I'll talk to the parentals and see if I can get them onboard. What is it you would like to do on this mental health day?"

The rest of the drive was taken up with planning, effectively stealing my attention from the insidious beast that danced with doubt and fed off my fear.

I parked around back, and the boys tumbled out of the car.

Walking behind them, my heart throbbed with a mix of joy and pain.

I wrapped my palm around my throat to soothe myself. Perhaps it was just as well I did not have my own children. I'm not sure if my anxiety could handle the constant worry, the unpredictability, the upheaval of emotions. I smiled. At least I had my boys. I wouldn't trade them for anything, and the ability to offer them understanding, especially George, made my history worthwhile.

Chapter 9 – All Grown Up

<u>Lucky</u>

"I can't," she shook her head, her sweet laughter ringing around me. "The boys made me take them yesterday, and Junie and I had it for lunch twice this week. I cannot look at another potato."

"But you promised me souvlaki!" I protested.

After agreeing to meet me inside Spuds for a late lunch on Saturday, she texted and asked me to meet her in the parking lot behind her building instead. I'd never been to Spuds, but the smells drifting through the back door had me salivating.

I held my hand over my chest. "You're crushing me," I moaned.

"How about I let you take me out in your car?" she suggested, her head tilted slightly to the side, her eyes alert on my face.

I perked up, and she smiled.

"Yeah? You trust me enough to get into my car?" I twinkled at her.

"Your car, yes. You've received stellar character references from our mutual Viking friend." She teased before a cloud passed through her eyes. "Although reports from our mutual lady friends are mixed."

"Mixed?" I drew back, shocked.

"Mm-hmm. They love you. They also warned me that you have a busy dating life."

I studied her face.

She did not look pleased.

My heart raced.

Fuck.

I stepped closer and was gratified to see her eyes widen.

With a touch to her delicate chin, I reminded her. "No stats until the third date. No clothes come off until we're exclusive."

She swallowed hard, and her voice when she answered was husky. "Okay."

Opening the passenger side door and tucking her inside gave me a feeling of satisfaction I didn't recognize. Getting in beside her, taking her with me, there was something elemental about it.

She spoke easily about the little men in her life. It was a shame she wasn't a mother; she would have been a good one.

That thought led to another, one I wasn't willing to entertain yet, so I shut it down.

Twenty minutes of following her directions later, I pulled into the parking lot across from Baranga's on the Beach.

Minty waved her hand towards the restaurant with a flourish. "Souvlaki."

"Ah, a woman who understands my needs," I joked.

I rested my palm lightly at the small of her back as we walked into the restaurant. She stiffened at the first touch before leaning back ever so slightly against the lightness of my touch.

The barest hint of roses brushed her cheeks. Perhaps Minty was not quite so cool and collected as she seemed. That blush did things to me, and I looked away before my face gave away my thoughts.

Seated on the patio, we had an excellent view of the beach. Tall plants and vivid flowers nestled into corners and lined the half wall where we sat. Greek music piped through the speakers. Between that, the sunshine, the smell of the food, the sound of the waves, and the fragrance of the flowers, I could almost imagine myself in Greece.

We ordered our meals and settled in.

She ordered Greek salad with a side of fries.

"I thought you couldn't look at another potato?"

"You'll see," she exclaimed. "These are not ordinary potatoes, and if you're good, I'll share."

"Oh, I'll be good," I laughingly replied. "I promise. At least until I get your French fries. And no, that's not a euphemism for something else," I added drily.

Small talk always bored me. I tried, but my mind buzzed with questions, things I wanted to know about her.

"Have you ever been married? Any children?" I blurted out.

A wall came down over her eyes, and she withdrew slightly. "No. You?"

"Never married, but I do have a child. A little girl. She's two and her name is Brayleigh."

"That's lovely!" she smiled with her hands clasped in front of her face. "You'll be able to talk babies with Barrett!"

I chuckled. "Definitely. It's not quite the same thing. Sharing custody gives you so much more free time. Although, for those first six months we did live together. Those were difficult months, and I didn't want to bail on her."

"Do you and your ex have a good relationship?"

I looked at her seriously. "She's not my ex, we never dated, but she is my best friend." I watched as she withdrew even more and realized she probably thought she was stepping into the middle of a love triangle. "We've been best friends since we were in grade school. Grade four maybe?" I shrugged. "We slept together once. It was hilarious. She got pregnant."

She leaned forward in her seat. "Why was it hilarious?"

"We went out one night and got to talking, too much drinking, and decided we should see if we had any chemistry." I stopped and looked at Minty, a wry smile on my face. "We don't, by the way."

She tilted her head to the side. "Tell me the story?"

"Alright. The next morning, we woke up at the same time, both of us with hangovers. I didn't even remember what we did at first. Seeing her beside me was no big deal, it wasn't like it was the first time we'd slept in the same bed, we'd just never had sex." I shrugged. "Never wanted to."

I shook my head in disbelief even now at the thought before continuing.

"We're just squinting at each other, kind of complaining about dry mouth, she's saying something charming about considering drinking her own piss then she looks at me with this look of horror on her face."

"I start panicking and whisper, 'What is it?'"

"Minty, my eyes are bugging out because I'm thinking there's a spider on me, the light from the window is hitting me in not a good way, there are hammers in my head, and my stomach is staging a rebellion."

Minty's smile grew as she listened to my story, feeding the hope that me having a child was not going to be the end of what looked like a really fucking good beginning.

I couldn't help laughing at the next part.

"So, she says to me all quiet, 'you put your willy in me.' As soon as she said it, it all comes flying back to me and it's like the biggest WTF moment in my entire life, because seriously, what the fuck were we thinking?"

"So, I just looked at her and said, 'I did.' Then she puts her hand over her eyes and says it again, but louder, and she's laughing. 'You put your willy in me!' And I'm stunned. Literally stunned stupid."

Minty covered her mouth with her hand to hold in her laughter but she could do nothing about the tears in her eyes. I took a breath in relief and continued with my story.

"Then she looks incredulous and says, 'You *came* inside me!' Now, I'm panicking. I say, 'You said you're on the pill!'"

"She yells, 'I am! But you *actually came* inside me! Like, you enjoyed it!'

I hold my hands out and yell back at her, 'It's warm and wet, what do you expect?'

She covers her ears and starts saying, 'Ew!'"

I looked at Minty with my eyebrows raised. "Ew? Can you believe that?"

Minty shakes her head. Her face is flushed, her eyes are crinkled, and she jerks her chin up for me to continue.

I loved seeing her like this, a glimpse of the real woman, her laughter freeing her.

"Now we're both laughing and screaming and holding our heads and it's all just really funny. Then I think about it, feeling sure she orgasmed. So, I ask her, 'Wait a minute. Are you a faker?'"

"'What?' she looks at me all confused. 'A faker! Are you a faker? Because I'm pretty sure you came, too!'"

"She gives me this high-and-mighty look and says, 'I was thinking about my book boyfriend!'"

Minty slapped both hands over her face and curled into a c-shape across from me. Her shoulders shook with laughter that didn't sound nearly as ladylike and genteel as it usually did.

When she finally looked up at me, I grinned at her.

"We laughed it off, mutually agreed to never speak about it again never mind do it again. Two weeks later she shows up with a positive pregnancy test, scared out of her mind." I shrugged. "She talked. I listened. We have a baby."

"Do you regret it?" Her eyes and voice were soft.

"No." I shook my head definitively. "She's the best thing that's ever happened to me."

"Your friend or your baby?"

"My baby, but Hope ranks pretty high as well."

"Do you see Hope a lot?"

I understood how this might be a problem for some women. I hoped Minty wasn't one of them. "I do. We have dinner at least once a week, usually when we exchange Brayleigh, and if there's a kid event we want to bring her to, we both try to go."

"That's nice, actually."

"It is. Our relationship didn't change that much."

"Why did you move out after six months?"

60

"I never really moved in. I just stayed there at night to help with the nighttime feeds so Hope could get some sleep."

"You never gave the relationship a go?"

"We have a relationship. Sex has no place in it. Never did. It was a fluke that turned into a gift."

Minty

"That's the most serious romantic relationship I've ever had, and it lasted about fifteen minutes." He flashed his dimples and his eyes flashed with humor. "Glad I got that out of the way. I won't even ask you about your dating life until the third date."

"Oh, really?" I teased. "You didn't actually tell me about your dating life. You just told me about how you came to be a father."

His face grew serious. "I've never worried much about what anybody thought about my dating habits until you. Junie and Bex were right but they're also way wrong. It's true that I don't date. I hook up. More often than I'd like to admit to you. But I have no interest in anyone else and will not be hooking up with anyone while we explore what this might be between us."

Floored by his sudden bout of blunt honesty, I decided to return in kind. Bringing it out into the open brought relief because we could simply let it end here if it was too much for him.

"I had one serious relationship. About a year into it, a mental health issue I've battled my entire life flared up. I hadn't disclosed it to him up until that point because I believed I had it under control. But my parents had just passed away, and the stress of losing them triggered a relapse."

I smiled softly and folded my hands gently in my lap, taking care not to clench my fists or squeeze while I waited for him to respond. Our food arrived before he had a chance.

Baranga's served their French fries dusted with oregano, drizzled with olive oil, and sprinkled with feta cheese, diced tomatoes, and black olives. His eyes flickered between my meal and his own souvlaki on a pita.

"I'm a little bit jealous," he admitted.

"Help yourself." I set the French fries between us, hoping he forgot what we were talking about.

No such luck.

"So." Lucky raised one eyebrow, his eyes compassionate. "He left?"

I nodded, maintaining my smile. "He did."

"I'm sorry." Lucky fiddled with his napkin then looked up at me. "Do you want to tell me what it is? Or would you prefer to wait?"

Seagulls squawked. Waves rolled in. Kids laughed and played. People walked the pathway with their dogs. And I sat across from a funny, sweet, interesting, sexy, unfortunately younger man who I very much wanted to taste.

It was a perfect day.

A butterfly flitted gently on the breeze and came to rest on a flowering plant beside our table.

"I can tell you, I'm not ashamed of it. I have OCD."

Its delicate wings beat back and forth lazily.

I popped a French fry in my mouth.

You're eating a butterfly.

I stared down at the plate of French fries and focused on the flavors in my mouth, willing my brain to release the mental imagery.

I bit down on the French fry and started chewing.

You're crushing it between your teeth. A picture of the black body embedded in the grooves of my molars invaded my brain.

The bitter pungent taste of oregano registered on my tongue.

That's the taste of the butterfly, its body crushed, its body fluids spilling over your tongue, its tiny legs trapped between your teeth.

"Obsessive Compulsive Disorder."

Lucky's voice came from far away as I attempted to focus on the conversation instead of struggling with what was in my mouth.

"Yes."

My stomach churned. I wondered if I could swallow without chewing. I took a sip of my water, my eyes scanning the surface for bugs.

That water is contaminated. Feces. Insects. Germs.

Focus. Focus. Find something to look at and swallow.

"I don't know too much about it, but I've had students over the years with the diagnoses so I'm not entirely ignorant of it. From what I've seen, it can be a real ballbuster."

I looked up at his face, his sensitive, compassionate face that somehow comforted me and thought about fucking him to distract myself long enough that I could swallow the offensive French fry.

I laughed. "Yes, indeed. That's a rather apt description." Time to move on to another subject or I'd never get another bite in. "Are you a teacher?"

He leaned forward and his eyes lit up. "Yes. I'm a high school teacher. I teach music."

"Your eyes just lit up. You enjoy your job."

"I do. Most of the time. At my school there's a lot of poverty. Even the school itself doesn't get enough funding, especially not the music department."

"My nephew takes music. He was telling me that there aren't enough instruments, not much variety. I offered to buy him a guitar, but he said coming in with a brand-new instrument would get him the wrong kind of attention."

Lucky nodded thoughtfully. "He's right. I'm working on something for my classroom. I'm going to talk to Barrett about doing a fundraiser night with Drivetrain."

I took a deep breath. Relaxed. Started eating my salad.

Is the lettuce properly washed?

"Drivetrain is your band, correct?"

"Yes," he said, again with the light-up smile. "We're having our first show of the season soon."

"What would you buy with the funds?" I was curious, for my own purposes as well.

"Ukuleles, guitars, portable keyboards, maybe some bongos. Shit, I'd even throw in a few xylophones." He laughed. "The problem is some of the kids want to take the instruments home. But there's no way I can hope to buy enough instruments for all my students to be able to have exclusive use of them." He looked uncomfortable as he admitted, "And it's not unheard of for an instrument to be lost and a few days later turn up in a pawn shop."

"So, a class set that remains in the classroom would be better. What would you need for a class set?"

"In a perfect world? A classroom set would include a drum set or two, five guitars, five or six ukuleles, three or four bongos, three portable keyboards, one full-size, and a couple of xylophones. I have roughly half of that. There's no way my school could afford decent wind instruments. That's a dream for a utopian world."

"Are most of the high schools in Milltown operating under the same lack of resources?"

"No. The schools in wealthier neighborhoods have more because parents and kids can participate in fundraisers and raffles and such. Schools in impoverished areas don't have that option, those families are just trying to swing lunch for their kids."

"What school do you work at- actually, how old are you, Lucky?" Perhaps it was time to inject a small dose of reality.

He leaned his elbows on the table and looked at me steadily, his grey eyes heating even as I watched. "I'm all grown up, Minty."

Despite the lightning bolt of desire his answer sent straight to my clit, I pushed further. "Are you going to ask me how old I am?"

He sat back and took a swig of his beer, placing it back on the table before answering. "Third date."

At least he was aware there was an age gap. Perhaps it didn't matter for his purposes. If we were just having a good time, and he wasn't looking for 'the one', someone to start a family with, age was just a number.

I ate a few more fries and Lucky plowed through the rest. Our server packed up my leftover salad to go.

On the way to the car, Lucky interlaced his long fingers with mine, his thumb gently caressing the outside of mine. He released my hand in the car but picked it up again as he walked me up the stairs to my door. There, he turned to face me.

I looked at him. Considering.

My body was ready. My heart still neatly detached. It wouldn't be a terrible way to wile away the rest of the afternoon. Perhaps I could ditch my rules for dating and dip my toes into Lucky's pool of hook-ups.

The thought left a bitter taste in my mouth. I didn't want to be one of his many hook-ups.

He stepped into my space and cupped my jaw between his palms, his calloused fingertips caressing the tender skin under my ears as he studied me.

Conflicting thoughts and feelings flickered across his face so rapidly I couldn't even attempt to read him.

Finally, he seemed to come to a decision and huffed out a short laugh. "The only thing I want more than to be invited in is a third date."

My chest inflated with my deep inhale and my hands came up to wrap around his wrists. It had been so long since I'd been wanted, so long since I'd wanted someone like this.

His eyes darkened. "Will you go out with me again?"

"I'd like that," I replied softly.

Smiling, his lips met mine with the softest of touches before kissing me firmly on the forehead and heading to his car.

I watched him.

At his car door, he looked back, and smiled.

Chapter 10 – Plans

<u>Minty</u>

Junie dropped her pen on her desk and spun round in her chair with a dramatic flourish. "Done! Let's close up and go to Willa's."

I tilted my head to the side, wondering if it was too soon to be landing on her. "It's barely been a week. Don't you think it's too soon to drop in?"

"Nope." Junie's lips popped on the word as she tidied her desk space. "Barrett went back to work today. Let's call her and see if she wants company. Doesn't hurt to check in."

Forty-five minutes later, after a quick trip to the grocery store and a pitstop at Tim Horton's, Willa met us at the door with her finger over her lips telling us to be quiet.

Junie passed her a coffee from Tim Horton's.

"I swear to God, Junie, if there's no caffeine in here, I won't be held responsible for my actions."

Junie held up her hands. "Caffeinated. Promise."

Willa closed her eyes and took her first sip while still standing in the open doorway.

"Okay, beautiful," I soothed. "If you let us in, we might even be able to wrangle you a shower and make you some lunch."

"Sorry," she mumbled, before backing up and taking another sip. "Oh, Lord, this is so good."

Junie looked at me smugly. "Told you."

I got busy in the kitchen, and Junie hovered over the sleeping baby in between tidying up all the baby paraphernalia. By the time Willa came back freshly scrubbed and slightly more awake, I had lunch on the table and two casseroles in the oven.

"Oh my gosh, Minty! You're so fast!" Willa exclaimed.

"She's a machine," Junie concurred, nodding.

"Pfft," I waved them away. "Lunch was take-out, and the casseroles take ten minutes to throw together. The oven does the work."

"Thank you, Minty," Willa murmured, her face soft, the dark circles under her eyes emphasizing the midnight blue of her eyes.

Before we finished lunch, Rena woke, fussing for her mama's breast. Willa moved to a large comfy chair and drew a nursing pillow onto her lap beneath the baby.

Watching her tuck her sweet baby in close, noting the way Rena's tiny body curled in around Willa's torso, weighed heavy on me. Rena's tiny hands grasped fitfully at Willa's breast, and she mewled in her haste to feed. It sent a prickling awareness to my own breasts.

Watching them turns you on.

No.

Your breasts are tingling.

It's not sexual.

Are you sure?

I smiled gently and took a slow breath in. Reminded myself not to argue with OCD. There was no winning that way.

In any case, there were similarities. But with a man those tingles signified a desire to be touched. Instead, I yearned to give. As if seeing Willa nurse her child reminded my brain of what my body, too, was built to do.

The heaviness built. The sudden sharp yearning for a child of my own surprised me even as it cut me in the deepest parts of my soul. For the first time in ages, I wondered if I'd made a mistake in cutting off this part of myself.

I shook away my wayward thoughts.

The unvarnished truth was that I could not cope without my medications, and my medications were not safe for a developing baby. Some people could switch between meds and mitigate the risks during pregnancy. I was not one of those people.

"Um," Willa cleared her throat. "I know it's early days, but I don't think I'm coming back to work at the office."

Junie's head whipped up. "Okay..." Her eyes skittered over Willa's face. "Are you sure? It's not just hormones?"

Willa nodded. "It's not just hormones. I have my art, the shelter, and the store. Doing all of it will be impossible with Rena. I can't give up the shelter and I don't want to give up my art. My favorite part of the business was the fact that you two were there."

Her eyes filled with tears. She laughed and sniffed before pointing at her face. "This is hormones!"

"You can't get rid of me so easily." Junie bent over her and kissed her cheek then asked gently, "Do you want to sell the business?"

Willa shook her head. "I want you to think about it. If you want to slowly buy me out or if you want to sell."

"Do you mind if I put some feelers out?" Junie asked.

"Not at all." Willa turned to me. "Minty..."

I held up my palm. "Don't worry about me. I can find another tenant. You two do what's best for the both of you."

"What about your job?" Willa's pretty face creased with concern.

"Oh, don't worry about that," I dismissed her concerns. "I have the women's shelter and my art. I only work with you two because I love you so much." I turned to Junie. "I'm still in to help you if you want to go on your own, even if you're not renting the space." I contemplated Willa. "We might be able to team up with the art component. Perhaps next year we can look at doing the craft circuit together." I smiled. "You won't lose me, and I'm definitely not losing you."

"How hard will it be to get another tenant?" Junie worried.

"Not hard," I assured her.

Willa swept her finger beneath her eyes. "Barrett wants to eventually have a place downtown. I know he'd be interested in that space."

That surprised me. "He wants to leave the shelter?"

"It's not that he wants to leave the shelter so much that he dreams of custom-designing a clinic with more space for his Viking-sized body." Willa snorted. "And he also wants to set up a program to help lower income families care for their pets."

I raised my eyebrows. I loved that idea. If I gave him the same rental agreement I offered Willa and Junie, it would go a long way toward cutting his costs. Those cost cuts could be passed along to his clients.

Junie interrupted my musings with a sly look in my direction.

"Enough shoptalk. I've been exceptionally good." She looked pointedly at Willa, getting her nod of agreement. "I haven't asked her a single thing about Lucky."

Both girls turned to look at me expectantly, and I laughed.

"There's not much to tell," I protested.

"Did you bang?" Junie asked baldly.

I looked at her with all the affection I held for her in my heart. "A lady doesn't tell, Junie."

Junie, uncowed, studied me. "I can't tell if she did or she didn't," she said to Willa.

"She didn't," Willa answered. "Lucky told Barrett he's taking it slow."

My mouth fell open, and I shut it just as quickly. "Lucky talked to Barrett about me?"

"Yup." Willa winced as she detached Rena from her breast and switched sides. "Barrett asked him about it when they were setting up on Saturday. He was kind of pissed that we told you about his busy dating life and told Barrett you're different and he's taking it slow."

I schooled my features but my mind spun.

Flattered and fearful in equal measure. I didn't love the idea of Lucky putting so much thought and planning into us. Because there wasn't going to be an us. Not seriously. I needed to take back control of the direction of this relationship or one of us would get hurt.

Yet, I could not help myself from digging for more information.

"Have you met Hope?"

"Who's Hope?" Junie asked.

"His best friend and the mother of his child," I answered drily.

Willa's head popped up. "Lucky has a child?"

"You didn't know that?" Junie asked.

"No! Why didn't I know that?" Willa exclaimed.

Junie shrugged. "It's not like he spends every weekend with us. He's got a big family, too, and they're close." She turned to me. "I've only seen the baby once and I've never met the mother. I should have mentioned it to you. I'm sorry, I didn't even think about it."

"No worries," I replied easily. But I was worried.

The way he told the story of Brayleigh's conception assured me that he and Hope were only meant to be friends. But the more I got to know Lucky, the more I wondered about a woman who would not want to make a family with him. Especially one he considered to be his best friend. One who'd already given birth to his child.

I wondered if perhaps there was unfinished business between them.

Something Junie said niggled at the back of my mind.

"Setting up? Setting up for what?" I asked.

"Drivetrain. They played Saturday night. First gig of the season."

Junie's fiancé, Lenny, played the drums for Drivetrain. Lucky played lead guitar, Barrett covered guitar and vocals, and they lost their bass player after she made a play for Barrett last summer.

Realization dawned. Maybe that was why we had an afternoon date. I had assumed he already had a sure thing lined up for Saturday night.

My eyebrows went up and I stared into space. It was still possible. If he played Saturday night, it's more than likely he had the opportunity to hook up with someone afterwards. He said he wouldn't while we explored what might be between us, but I wondered if that exploration period started before or after our clothes came off.

And if I'd decided this was going to be a sweet, sexy, romp, why did it matter?

Perhaps pursuing this thing with Lucky was a mistake but I was long overdue a bit of fun. Not everything had to be planned to the nth degree.

On Friday we had plans to go out for coffee. If I still felt this way, I'd lay out my plan for him then.

Chapter 11 –Hands Down

Lucky

For the first time in my life, I found myself on the receiving end of the 'I'm only in this for the fun' talk.

It was far from enjoyable.

As much as I wanted to get her into bed, and in that respect, this felt like a win, I figured it was going to take me the entire summer to get her to trust me enough to loosen up.

And I desperately wanted her to loosen up.

Getting her to that point held all kinds of promise but based on her proposed timeline I guessed we would just be at the point where things were getting good when she would be planning her exit.

My mind spun with possibilities, or in Minty's case, impossibilities.

Insecurities I never knew I had reared their ugly, misshapen heads. I'd grapple with those later, after dealing with the mystifying woman in front of me.

I sat back in my seat and studied her eyes. So much went on behind them, all the things to which I was not yet privy but hoped to access.

I never pegged her as the type of woman who would want a casual arrangement. The way Willa and Junie warned me to be good to her certainly hadn't given me that impression.

She was protecting herself. At least, I hoped that's what it was. Either that or she really wasn't interested in anything deeper with me, and my over-inflated ego would not accept that.

"What do you find so funny?" she murmured, a small smile curving her pretty mouth.

I smiled wryly. "So, what I'm hearing is that you'd like to date and maybe fuck me for the summer and call it quits before Labour Day?"

Her back went ramrod straight. She blinked once, slowly, then raised her eyes to mine and answered me coolly. "If you strip it back to the bare bones, I suppose that's exactly what I'm saying." Whatever she saw in my face had her softening marginally. She sighed. "I like you, Lucky. I like you a lot. But the truth remains that you are thirty-eight and I am forty-four. I can't give you what you want long-term."

I mentally cursed myself for admitting I wouldn't mind another child.

"And what if I decide it's you I want long-term?"

Who the hell was speaking? It wasn't until the words left my mouth that I consciously realized I'd been considering anything long-term. I dried my sweaty palms on my jeans and shook my head. Looked like things were about to get interesting.

She raised her hands then let them flop down on her lap. "See, that's just it. Eventually you'll resent me, and you'll always wonder about the family you might have had. Lucky, you could go find someone like Willa and make a family. Someone like Hope," she added pointedly. "I'm kind of past that."

She deflated right in front of me. Her lips tipped up at one side. "Perhaps this was a mistake." She twisted in her seat to gather her things.

"Hold up there, pretty lady. I accept your generous offer so long as we're exclusive. Beginning right now."

She looked at me with suspicion, and I grinned at her. "You drive a hard bargain, but I think if I can manage my intense need to commit, we'll have fun. And we could both use a bit of fun."

Her lips twitched while she fought, and lost, the urge to smile. "You're sure you can manage? You're not going to ask me my ring size?" She wiggled her ring finger and raised one eyebrow.

"I'll do my best," I promised.

I looked around. As nice as it was, I couldn't wait to get out of this coffee shop. "Want to get out of here?"

Her eyes widened. "Now?"

Indicating her empty coffee cup, I asked. "You're done, right?"

"Oh!" She stood and gathered her purse. "So, that's that? Negotiations complete we head to your place?"

My mouth fell open in shock. I barked out a laugh and quickly pulled her into my chest, wrapping my arms around her back.

She stood stiffly in my embrace. More than ever now I knew this was not her usual modus operandi.

I dipped my head to her ear and spoke softly, though I could hear the laughter in my voice. "Give me credit for a little bit more finesse. Allow me to seduce you into my bed. Get you to the point where you really want to be there, hm?"

She relaxed in my arms. Her hands came up to my waist and she leaned back to look at me, a wry smile twisting her mouth to the side.

"I guess you can tell I haven't done this in a while?"

I bent my neck and kissed the tip of her nose. "It's just like riding a bull."

"A bull? Don't you mean a bike?" she replied huskily.

I tilted my head back and forth as though thinking it through before continuing. "If it's a bike, it's definitely a Harley."

Understanding dawned and her tinkly laugh broke free. "You're setting my expectations pretty high. I hope I'm not going to be disappointed."

"You won't be," I promised before releasing her.

I linked my fingers through hers and led her out of the coffee shop.

Minty

Holy fuck, I'd been dating the wrong men.

Lucky had me pinned against my door, his pelvis locked against mine, my thighs spread, my toes just barely touching the ground.

74

My hands clung to his waist as he cupped my jaw between his palms and slowly and methodically devoured my mouth with single-minded attention. His tongue toyed with mine, then he gently sucked my bottom lip into his mouth, releasing it only to nibble at the corners of my mouth.

He reduced me to a wanton, panting mess.

I tipped my chin back further, surrendering my mouth, offering my throat.

He dropped one hand to wrap around my ribs, his thumb barely brushing the underside of my breast.

I gasped at the contact, breaking the kiss, my breasts swelling with anticipation.

He stared into my eyes as his thumb skated across my cheek, dragged across my lower lip, and ran along the line of my jaw to the other side of my throat. With his thumb on one side of my jaw, and his forefinger on the other, he palmed my throat and pushed firmly on my jaw, forcing my chin up.

My low groan broke the silence of the night as his mouth hovered over mine and his thumb grazed the underswell of my breast.

"Lucky," I whispered.

He didn't smile as he went back in, his mouth firm, his cock hard against my stomach.

I rolled my pelvis against him, my body pleading even as my brain attempted to take back the reins.

Would it be so bad to let him in?

We were adults. Consenting adults. One of us at least was an uber-consenting adult.

"One more minute," he muttered, rocking against me. "One more minute and then I'm leaving you here. This was not what I had in mind when I said finesse."

Disappointment mixed with relief. But if there was still an ounce of relief, it was time to stop.

After another sweet, mind-fucking kiss, he pulled back and dragged his palm down the center of my chest, separating our bodies inch by inch.

"Minty," he murmured, his face tipped down to look at me. He wrapped both hands around my ribcage, settling me firmly on my feet. "Can I see you Sunday?" He dragged his knuckles down the side of my face. "I'd ask to see you tomorrow but I'm not free."

I studied his light grey eyes. They looked like molten silver in the dark. It was wrong to want to know what he was doing tomorrow. I'd never been the suspicious type. Never been the jealous type. For some reason, I suffered from twinges of both. "You're busy tomorrow?"

"With the guys," he said. "I'll be with Barrett and Lenny. Just rehearsing with the new bass player. No women. Gigs are sporadic until July and then it's every Saturday."

I huffed out a laugh, embarrassed to realize I'd been assessing him for truth as he spoke. It would have been better if Willa and Junie hadn't informed me of his dating or non-dating habits. But then, what kind of girlfriends would they be if they didn't?

His lips tipped up in a half-smile. "That information did a number on you." With a sigh, he dipped his knees and stared into my eyes. "I promise I will not lie to you or go behind your back. I wouldn't do that to anybody, but especially not to you. And not just because Barrett would kick my ass."

Placing both palms on his chest, I eased him back. "I'm sorry. I believe you. I would like to see you Sunday. I have an exhibit at the craft fair until four, but I can see you after that."

Serious Lucky transformed into boy-next-door Lucky with a single flash of his dimples. "Come to my place. Five o'clock. Will that work?"

When I nodded, he kissed the tip of my nose and headed to his car. He turned and looked back for a moment before opening the door and sliding behind the wheel.

I slipped inside and leaned against my door from the inside, thinking about our date.

After the coffee shop, we'd driven down to the Bay and walked along the pier. When the waning sunlight was no longer a match for the breeze coming off the water, he took me for dinner.

I'd never talked and laughed with a man the way I'd talked and laughed with Lucky.

Eating at a new place proved to be difficult as usual, and it did not go unnoticed. When Lucky pulled out the dessert menu, he discovered my passion for chocolate. I admitted that while I struggled with eating, I somehow never had an issue when it came to dessert. In fact, when my OCD flared up, I often lived on nibbles of cookies and chocolate.

Especially chocolate.

When our server came to our table, he ordered me the most decadent chocolate dessert on the menu.

"What about you? Are you not having dessert?" I asked.

"Considering I ate my entire meal and half of yours, I think I'm good. To be honest, I'm not much for sweets, but I fully plan to taste the remnants off your tongue before I say goodnight," he grinned lasciviously, making me laugh yet again.

The fact that he had not lied, made it all the better.

Hands down, the best date I'd ever had.

Chapter 12 – Baptism by Fire

<u>Lucky</u>

Hope was late. She'd gone shopping for the morning with her girlfriends, dropping Brayleigh off on her way.

After taking Brayleigh to the park and out for lunch, I put her down for a late nap while I tidied up in preparation for Minty coming over.

I planned to take Minty out on my bike. Earlier I texted her to think about it, asked her to wear jeans and flat boots or shoes if she was feeling adventurous.

Everything was going according to plan until Hope called to tell me she was running late. Normally, it wouldn't bother me in the least, and guilt that it bothered me now weighed heavily. Not once in the past two years had I ever not wanted to be with my daughter. We spent enough time apart that I treasured any extra time I got.

If Hope knew I had a date, she would have been on time, but I was loathe to inform her. Hope was well aware of my habits. She knew there were women, she did not care, and I had no reason to hide anything from her.

But I wanted to hide Minty.

Which piled more uncomfortable feelings on top of the guilt. I'd unpack that later.

A few minutes after five, Minty pulled into my driveway.

I watched as she swung her long legs out of the car and looked around. Gratified to see she wore flat ankle boots and slim-fitting jeans, I returned my attention to her face and wondered what she thought as she took in my home.

My house was small, old, and situated on a quiet side street lined with equally small, old homes. Eight years earlier, when the housing market dipped, I bought it and poured every extra penny into renovating. Far from the only one to have that idea, the neighborhood now teemed with young professionals and families who spent their free time and extra funds updating and refinishing their homes.

Lawns were well-cared for, huge trees lined the street, and flowers spilled off porches and into the gardens below.

I bought it strictly for its investment potential, but having Brayleigh turned it into a home.

Minty smiled as she looked around.

I pulled open the front door before she reached it and watched her walk up the path. At the bottom step, she stopped and waved her hand to indicate the last of my tulips. "I never took you for a gardener!"

I let the door close behind me and grinned. "I'm not. That's my sister's handiwork."

Minty's eyebrows rose as she walked up the steps towards me. "She does your gardening for you? You're lucky."

"I am Lucky. I didn't come by my moniker by accident," I quipped. I drew her in to my gentle embrace, pleased to find her face tipped up to mine. "Don't worry. She plants but she makes me weed."

She leaned in, her breasts pressing lightly against my chest, as I looked down into her face.

"So, what is Lucky short for?"

"Lucas."

"Mm. I like that name. It means 'light'."

"You can use it, but I probably won't answer," I warned with a smile.

Five years of being called Lucas the Mucous in grade school, back when I was short and scrawny, inoculated me against my name for life.

In grade five, the same year we moved, I picked a winning lottery ticket for my parents and earned my new name. I wasn't about to give it up. Not even for Minty.

I stared down into her pretty face, my view unimpeded by her mass of hair. Swept back from her face and coiled into a knot at the nape of her neck, it pinpointed the exact spot I longed to press my kiss.

She looked beautiful, as always, but her smile belied the wariness in her eyes, reminding me of the need to tread lightly.

"You know I'd never hurt you in any way."

Surprise widened her eyes. "I know." She took a breath and the tension in her shoulders released. "I do know that. I'm not worried about that."

"What are you worried about?" My eyes skittered over her face.

"Our age difference, how attracted I am to you, the fact that you have a child, that we are temporary."

All the things she'd already said to me. All her reasons for not wanting to dive in with me. All the reasons she put an expiration date on us.

"I can't do anything about the first and wouldn't even if I could. I'm delighted with the second. She's not too scary although she is bossy, and we'll take it one day at a time," I replied.

Minty's emotions flashed through her eyes though her lovely face remained politely composed.

I wondered at the need for that control.

I dipped to kiss the tip of her perfect nose, noting the flare of pleasure in her eyes, before leading her inside.

"Hope is running late but she'll be here soon to pick up Brayleigh," I explained. Minty didn't respond. "She was supposed to be here by three. I thought that would give her plenty of time. We've always been flexible with pick up times. Next time I'll let her know when we have plans so she won't be late." I continued, nervously filling the silence. "I'm sorry."

"Brayleigh is here?"

I nodded, my breath held. "She's napping."

"Okay," she replied easily. "Want to give me the tour while we wait?"

Relief momentarily weakened my limbs, startling me with the depth of my investment in her already. I was not enamored with this feeling of trepidation. I pushed it to the side, focusing instead on the pleasures of watching Minty take in my home.

"You did some of the work yourself?" she asked.

"I didn't do the electrical or the plumbing. Barrett's brother is a contractor and he helped me in his spare time, gave me all the grunt work to do while he worked his magic on the rest. Actually, what am I saying? You know Rhys. He did the tough stuff."

"It's beautiful." She took in the kitchen, its bright, white cabinetry, raw-edged countertops, and patterned ceramic floors. Her concentrated gaze seeming to replace her physical touch as she strangely kept her hands to herself. "What parts did you do?"

"I tore everything down and helped hang the cabinetry. Rhys did the back splash. I did the flooring; I did all the flooring," I added as we walked out into the living room and its warm wood floors.

I tried to see it through Minty's eyes. The wide baseboards, wood floors, new windows, and reclaimed brick fireplace were all beautiful but could not hide the lack of a woman's touch.

I rubbed my hand over my shaggy hair. "I'm not much of a decorator."

She spun towards me and reached out to touch my arm, the first time she'd touched anything. "It's beautiful, Lucky. Truly. I'm not one for clutter and I love the clean lines of your place. Its... soothing."

"Da-da-da-da-da!"

"She's up!" I grinned and held out my hand. "Come on up. You can see the upstairs while I get the baby."

Minty

Wow.

This was not what I expected when I pulled into his driveway. Certainly nothing I prepared for. I swallowed my trepidation as I trailed him up the narrow staircase to meet his child.

He bounded up ahead of me, his long legs eating up the stairs. Low-riding jeans ending in frayed hems brushed the tops of his bare feet, and he wore a simple t-shirt that skimmed his lean physique and high-lighted the ropey muscles of his arms.

He didn't dress to impress and that's what impressed me. Most of the men I'd dated over the past decade were so bent on peacocking that they barely tried to get to know me at all.

Plus, there was something about men in jeans and bare feet.

I huffed out a breath. Maybe if some of those other men had worn jeans and showed a little arm porn, I might have been more interested. I almost felt sorry for them because I suddenly found myself in the unenviable position of wanting to impress somebody. A toddler somebody at that.

"Da-da-da-da-da!" Rang out even louder as we approached Brayleigh's bedroom.

Maybe if this meeting went well, I'd be buoyed to meet his baby-mama. I smirked. What the hell was I getting myself into? After this, riding with him on his motorcycle would be anticlimactic.

He looked back to make sure I still trailed him and jerked his head with a grin for me to follow. When he opened the door, Brayleigh squealed in delight, her tiny mouth wide open, eyes sparkling, little fingers grasping the air.

That look told me everything I needed to know about what kind of dad he was.

"Da! Pick up!" she demanded, her little feet stomping into the mattress.

Lucky laughed as he swept her from her crib and wrapped his muscled arms around her cozy baby body. "Hello, Tweetie!"

Immediately, she curled her tiny body into his chest and flung her chubby arms around his neck. "Hi, Da," she murmured. The tips of her little fingers turned white where she pressed them into the back of his neck, and my ovaries exploded.

She cuddled in for a moment more then shot up straight, her entire body wiggling to get down.

Lucky set her down on the floor and she stepped behind his leg, wrapping her arm around his thigh as she peaked around to look up at me.

Blond, gravity-defying curls stood straight up on top of her head while round, cornflower-blue eyes studied me quietly. Those eyes along with her supremely rounded cheeks made it clear how she came by her nickname.

"Hello, Brayleigh," I greeted her softly.

She hid her face in her dad's leg.

Lucky laughed. "She's not usually shy!"

I spotted the corner of her room where she kept her toys and settled myself on the floor. Out of the corner of my eye I watched her taking me in.

"Lucky, these are nice toys," I commented softly. "I like your toys, Brayleigh."

She took a tentative step forward, her hand still grasping Lucky's leg. Lucky untucked her arm and sat down on the floor, placing her between his thighs, the toys somewhat between us.

"Them toys mine," she told me with big eyes.

"Your toys," I agreed.

She crawled forward and chose a stuffed bear. "Mine bear," she declared, then got to her feet and dumped it into my lap.

"This is a handsome bear," I told her, picking it up to admire it.

Lucky drew his legs up and rested his elbows on his bent knees, his clasped hands dangling between them. His brows knit as he watched us. Perhaps he didn't want me to play with her?

I caught his eye, and he gave me a warm smile.

He wouldn't smile at you if he knew the thoughts in your head.

I smiled away the false warning in time to receive a stuffed bunny. "Mine bun-bun."

"Lovely bun-bun," I replied, and so on until my lap was covered in stuffies.

Brayleigh began to knock them away, and once she'd cleared a space she swung her leg over mine, the momentum knocking her on her diapered bum on my lap. She picked up my necklace. "You sparky," she said, her eyes shining brightly.

I laughed. "Yes, I've been told that before," I agreed.

She dropped it back on my chest and patted it roughly. "That nice. That mine?" She cocked her head comically to the side.

Lucky jumped to his feet, laughing. "Come on, magpie. Not every sparkly thing is for you." He scooped her up and winked at me. "Some sparkly things are for daddy."

I laughed as he reached a hand down to pull me to my feet. He yanked me into his side briefly, sweeping his hand down my spine to the top of my ass before releasing me, all kinds of shiny sparks leaping between us.

I startled when I heard a female voice holler from the main floor. "Where's my favorite girl?"

Lucky offered me a wry smile. "Baptism by fire."

I laughed and made sure he took the stairs first. I did not want to be the first face Hope saw.

He loped down the narrow staircase, Brayleigh wiggling excitedly in his arms.

My hands, his back, one push, screaming, tumbling, lying broken at the bottom of the stairs.

The violence of the image forced me back a step before I was able to accept it and follow Lucky down the stairs where I came face-to-face with the most beautiful woman I'd ever laid eyes on in my life.

Eyes the exact shade as her daughter's, smooth peaches and cream complexion, long honey-blond hair, she was tall and slender but somehow blessed with bust and butt.

"Hi, Tweetie-bird!" Hope nuzzled her nose into Brayleigh's neck while Brayleigh nestled in Lucky's arms. They were a picture. A family. Young and beautiful and together.

Three blond heads bent together, their soft laughter linking them as surely as the child tucked between them.

Brayleigh laughed and threw herself into her mother's arms and it was at that point that Hope looked up and caught sight of me.

"Oh!" Her eyes skittered back and forth between Lucky and me, her questions loud in the silence.

Lucky cleared his throat. "Hope, this is Minty. Minty, this is Hope. Minty and I have plans this afternoon."

She slanted a sly look at Lucky before extending her free hand out to shake mine. "Hello, Minty. It's a pleasure to meet you."

Her smile, wide and genuine, pulled me in. It was no hardship to return her smile.

"Lovely to meet you as well," I replied.

"So." She stepped closer, her head tilting to the side reminiscent of her daughter as she studied me. "It's not often I get to meet Lucky's-"

You want to fuck her.

My mouth twisted with distaste for a split second before I schooled my features and dismissed the thought with a smile. A smile that said, 'Yes, yes. I see you, I hear you, on you go.'

Lucky cupped Hope around the back of the neck and cut her off with a laugh. "Thank you, Hope. You were just leaving, Hope? What's that? You can't stay for dinner? That's too bad. Maybe next time?"

She huffed out a breath. "Okay, okay. Fine," she muttered. She peeked up at me and quirked a perfect brow. "Maybe I'll see you again sometime?"

"I look forward to it," I smiled politely and watched as she drew back.

Brayleigh's bright eyes looked at me from over her mother's shoulder. "Bye, sparky!"

Lucky stared out the front door after them with his hands on his hips for what seemed like a million years before turning back to me, a small, uncertain smile on his lips.

"Are you completely freaked out?"

Chapter 13 – Ready?

<u>Minty</u>

"Not completely," I answered honestly.

He walked toward me and dipped to separate my linked fingers, intertwining them with his instead. "What part freaks you out?"

"You're a family," I asserted, watching for his reaction.

"We try," he countered, then sighed and leveled with me. "I get that she's beautiful. I'm not blind, but I'm not into her. She doesn't do it for me, and I don't do it for her. She's my oldest and dearest friend." He nodded as if acquiescing. "And she's the mother of my child which makes things all kinds of weird. And I know you'd think with the fact that we love each other, because we do love each other, that we'd want to make a go of it, but it's not true."

"Have you ever thought about it?"

"It came up when we first told everyone she was pregnant. My youngest sister pressured us something awful. Hope and I talked about it. She didn't want to settle for less than everything and I didn't want to settle period. Not once in all this time have either of us been tempted to sleep together again." He dipped his knees to bring himself down to my height, his grey eyes earnest as they searched mine. "Worst date ever?"

I could not help my smile and squeezed his fingers. "Let's just say you're lucky yesterday was the best date ever."

His brows quirked and he smiled a slow, sweet smile. "Well, alright then. I'll take it." He stood up straight. "You want to go for a ride and get something to eat?"

"Not too far, okay? Just in case I'm not a fan."

"Fair enough."

Fifteen minutes later, most of which was spent squeezing my head into that damn helmet, he eased us down the driveway. With his feet braced on the ground, he twisted in his seat and wordlessly beckoned me closer.

I wiggled closer and nervously fisted his shirt in my hands.

Sitting forward on his bike, straddling the seat, my hands on the handles as he drove into me from behind, one hand wrapped around my ponytail, the other at my waist.

A delicious heat sparked to life in my belly at the picture in my mind, but I drew back slightly, needing physical space where in my mind there was none.

He turned off the ignition, momentarily silencing the rumbling beast beneath me.

"I need you to get close and hang on tight. Mold your body to mine," he instructed.

"This is just a play to get my thighs wrapped around you," I accused him with a nervous laugh.

"It's fucking genius," he replied, then grasped me behind my knees and hauled me closer, every inch of the inside of my thighs aligned along the outside of his, my breasts plastered against his back. Unfurling my fists from his shirt, he pulled my hands around his flat stomach.

I itched to explore the ridges beneath my fingertips. My fingertips twitched and flexed into his abdomen.

He patted my hands firmly. "Keep them there. No exploring," he directed, then laughed. "You won't hear that from me again." He twisted his neck to peer at me over his shoulder and his deep, raspy voice was quiet. "Alright?"

Alright? Good Lord. I wasn't sure. Plastered against him, I was both too close and not nearly close enough. Thank goodness we both had these round alien heads attached to hide my face.

I nodded briskly. "Mm-hm."

He chuckled as he patted the outside of my thigh, leaned forward, and brought the beast to life.

My senses exploded. Spread open around him, the motor rumbling beneath me, his body close, muscles clenching and bunching as he maneuvered us down the driveway and out onto the street, his attention focused forward, adrenalin pumping through my veins from the threat of the bike, maybe also the threat of the man, and suddenly I was caught in the vortex of fight or flight or cleave, and I desperately wanted to cleave unto him.

He patted my hands. "Here we go."

The thrum of power, a burst of speed, my heart pounding in my breast, my brain devoid of everything but the man between my thighs and the thrill of our dual flight through space.

The world whirled past, delivering a mix of disappointment and relief each time we rolled to a stop.

"You doing okay?" he shouted over the sound of the engine. "Want to keep going?"

"Yes, definitely," I hollered back and felt his chuckle coming from his gut. I squeezed him tight, excitement quivering in my chest.

He dropped his hand to my thigh and gave me a squeeze before flicking on his indicator.

A few quick turns brought us to the edge of the city and the long, uninterrupted expanse of rural roads that ran between Milltown and the nearby village of Bridgewater. We picked up speed and my heart settled into a steady rhythm. My head emptied and my body aligned itself to his as he steered us over hills and around soft curves, the countryside fading to a blur. I closed my eyes and filled my lungs with air.

The whip of the breeze gentled as he rolled us to a stop at the side of the road and brought the beast to rest. Buffered by open fields on either side, the air ripe with the sweet sounds of the earth, we found ourselves a world away in only fifteen minutes.

He pulled off his helmet and ran his hand over his shaggy hair while I fiddled with the strap of mine.

Twisting around, he reached for my hands. "I'll help you," he murmured, carefully and expertly removing my tight helmet.

I smoothed my hands over my hair and turned my face up to the sun, not yet ready to speak.

"You liked it," he confirmed, watching me over his shoulder.

I met his eyes, feeling both sleepy and alive. I didn't even put my feet down onto the ground, relying on him to keep us upright. Was this what it was to feel calm? Was this happiness? Freedom?

"I loved it," I confessed. "Surprisingly."

"Why surprisingly?"

"I like to be in control. More than that, I hate feeling out of control."

My comment was ripe for innuendo, but he didn't bite, instead taking my words at face value, his mouth tilting upwards with genuine happiness.

"We'll ride for another ten minutes then head back?" he asked.

"That sounds perfect," I sighed.

Without the extreme anxiety and trepidation of the first leg of our trip, my attention drifted, reveling in the sensations of time and space, muscle and man, proximity and pursuit.

Lucky

A different brand of tension marked the ride back home. It wasn't often I took a woman out on my bike other than one of my sisters, and even that was rare.

Having her behind me on the bike, not just close but wrapped around me, not only responding to my movements but moving with me, sharpened my desire to feel her move with me as I gave her pleasure and brought her release.

Seeing her open and vulnerable, her face tipped up to the sun, sated and relaxed, lit a craving inside me to elicit that expression again and again. On my bike, in my bed, every fucking day of her life.

When Barrett told us about Willa, I was pleased for him though I didn't understand it. I laughed when Lenny fell so fucking hard for Junie, having no idea of the mix of pleasure and pain one woman could render.

A heady mixture, the potent opposition between pleasure and pain driving me homeward. I wanted to take her out on the town and tie her to my bed. Kiss the tip of her nose and tongue-fuck her mouth. Run my fingers through her hair and wrap her ponytail around my fist. Draw on her back until she fell asleep and slap her ass until she couldn't breathe. Suck on her clit, drive her to her knees, fill her with my cum, spill myself on her breasts, take everything she had to give and pay her back tenfold, one hundredfold, a thousand-fucking-fold.

I wanted to see behind those eyes, know her secrets, seek her truth.

I rolled up the driveway and her hands dropped from my stomach to rest on my thighs, her fingers flexing as she shuddered against my back.

I took the keys out of the ignition and covered her hands with mine.

"You ready?" I asked, my voice gritty with need.

"Yes."

Her voice was breathy. She understood the question, answered it, and I wouldn't risk a different answer by asking again. Tension buzzed loudly between us as I ushered her into the house, making the lack of conversation unnoticeable.

With my hand at the small of her back, I guided her to the stairs.

She stopped and offered me a cool little smile over her shoulder. "I take it this means we're not going out to eat?"

"Oh, I'm eating," I assured her darkly, giving her a little push. "And I'll take you out to eat later."

She turned and headed up the stairs, her round hips swaying in front of me.

I ran my hand over the curve of her hip. There were so many ways I wanted to take her. Facing her first. I grasped her hips and gently squeezed. Pulling her hips up and driving into her from behind.

"Or we can order in," I mumbled. I wondered how much she'd let me do tonight.

Her light, tinkling laugh filtered back to me, and I grinned. She was an enigma, a gift. Layers upon layers and I planned to remove every single one.

She stepped inside my bedroom for the first time and turned to face me.

Seeing her in my most intimate space set off a craving to get her under me as soon as possible. I stalked towards her, forgetting my plan to go slow, but checked myself when I encountered her palm pressed firmly against my chest.

Meeting her eyes, witnessing that flash of insecurity, stopped me in my tracks. I rocked back onto my heels and steadied myself.

I took a deep breath and nodded. "You're in charge," I assured her. "Only as far or as much as you want."

"Condoms," she asserted.

"Of course," I agreed.

She trailed her palm over my pectorals and tweaked my nipple through my t-shirt.

My cock jerked and my eyes locked onto hers.

"No one else?"

I captured her wrist, brought it to my mouth, and dragged my teeth over it. "No one else."

Her eyelids fluttered to half-mast.

I pulled her arm further around my neck until the front of her body pressed firmly against mine, then brought my hands up to the tie she still wore in her hair and released it, allowing the silken curtain to hang heavy down her back. Tunneling my fingers into the area where it had been secured, I massaged her scalp, gratified when her head dropped back into my hands.

She would be pliant.

She moved with me on my bike.

She fell into my hands.

My blood heated.

She'd be submissive.

That was my last coherent thought.

Chapter 14 — Twenty Minutes

Minty

The divine pressure of his calloused fingers on my scalp had me arching my back, pressing closer, giving over to him and the pleasure promised by his hands.

He mumbled something under his breath that I didn't catch. He gave me no time to ask before fisting my hair, tugging my head back, and dropping his soft mouth to mine.

So soft, his lips gentle where his hands were rough and demanding. The contrast sent shivers down my spine simultaneously urging me to both squeeze my thighs together and spread them wide.

Releasing my hair but not my mouth, his hands got busy at the button of my jeans and within minutes I stood completely naked before him.

He stared down at me for a pregnant moment before grabbing his t-shirt at the back, yanking it forward over his head, and pulling me against his chest. His hand ran firmly down my spine, jerking to a stop at the top of my ass and veering off to cup my cheek as he backed me up to the bed and lay me down, crawling over me, his jean-clad legs caging me beneath him.

I moaned at the sight and rolled my pelvis.

"Baby," he murmured. "You're so beautiful. I knew you'd be like this."

Cupping an ample breast in each hand, he murmured over me as he tongued and tugged and soothed my nipples. "You hide your sweetness. I love that it's just for me."

I tunneled my fingers into his hair. Thick and coarse, exactly how I imagined, I held him to my breast, silently demanding more.

He willingly gave but only for a moment before trailing his lips down my abdomen, his hands grasping my hips. The dip of his tongue into my belly button sent a lightning bolt of awareness to my clit and caused my hips to buck off the bed.

Sliding off onto the floor on his knees, he lifted my hips and yanked me down to the edge of the mattress before flattening his palms on the inside of my thighs and spreading me wide.

"Oh!" An involuntary exclamation escaped at the sureness of his handling. The unwelcome thought that he'd done a lot of this and probably in this very bed intruded on my psyche, but his tongue lapping through my slit to circle my clit circumvented my brain.

"Oh!" Delicious shock, I couldn't even remember the last time. "Lucky..."

"Right here, baby."

With his hands beneath me, he lifted my hips, pulling my pussy flush to his mouth. His words vibrated against my body. "Legs around my head. Do it now." He paused and added almost as an afterthought. "Please."

I readily complied and he groaned as he dipped his face into my folds, nuzzling my clit, tonguing my lips, spearing my center.

A brief quiver fluttered, and he moved his hand to push down on my abdomen above my mons and went back in, sucking, nibbling, swirling, spearing, before taking my clit into his mouth and gently, oh so gently, sucking it, calling my attention away from the two fingers that sought my opening, entered, and curled.

I arched up, crying out, and he flattened his tongue against my clit, pulsing with me, stroking, drawing it out, coaxing the crest of the next wave, until I lay back limp and sated on the bed.

"Lucky," I whispered.

He came off the floor and lay beside me, pulling me up the bed. "Are you okay to taste yourself, baby?"

His mouth, slick with me, hovered inches from my mouth.

I groaned as I cupped the back of his neck and parted my lips under his.

No longer soft, his mouth fused to mine, his tongue demanding entrance. His body shook above me, and he groaned deep in his throat.

"Gotta fuck you now, okay, baby?"

"Yes," I nodded.

"Sweetest word in the English language," he muttered.

Jackknifing off the bed, his jeans and boxers hit the floor. Thirty seconds later he lay on his back while I straddled his hips and lowered my body onto his, the relief of being filled sending waves of satisfaction and bliss through my system.

He cupped my breasts and tweaked my nipples as I rode him, his eyes lazily stroking the lines of my body.

Needing more but lacking the strength to go as hard as I wanted it, I leaned forward and flattened my breasts to his chest.

His arms came around me tightly and he thrust upward, the pleasure arching my neck back and away from him.

"Please, Lucky," I rasped. Kissing him lightly, I tugged on his shoulder and rolled to my back, pulling him with me.

He reared up over me, his broad shoulders shadowing me, his stomach muscles contracting as he pumped into me, deep and slow. No sign of the-boy-next-door dimples as he watched me.

Oh, the bliss, the sweetness, the ache! To be filled, to be wanted, to be taken, used, handled. To give. And receive.

My brain reached for that space where reality faded, and rapture reigned. My senses alight, my walls began to pulse. I dug my heel into the back of his thigh and pressed my fingers into the muscle of his ass, every atom of my mind and body focused on the burn between us. My inhibitions fled, blissed out freedom beckoned.

"Fuck that pussy, baby," I gasped.

He jerked back in surprise for half a second. "Fuck me," he breathed.

95

"No, darling," I responded, lost in sensation, momentarily freed from my mental prison. "Fuck *me*."

A low rumble sounded from his chest and his big hand gripped the back of my neck tightly as he crushed his mouth over mine, no gentleness left. His hips hammered deeply inside me while he ground against my clit again and again.

He groaned low, his muscles shaking, face tight with need, restraint, and desire, sending me over.

I cried out as I detonated, arching back hard and breaking free of his grip on my neck.

His back bowed and his mouth clamped down on my collarbone as he groaned out his own release.

Filling my lungs, my head lolled as my body melted into the mattress. I ran my hands firmly over his back, kneading the muscles along either side of his spine as his breath slowly evened out and the tension left his body.

Lazily, he pushed himself up onto his elbows and peered down at me, a mix of curiosity and amusement on his boyishly handsome face. "You've, uh, got quite a mouth on you."

I stared back at him boldly. Old enough to know what I wanted in bed, knowing he could handle it, I had no intention of holding back. "Is that a problem?"

He grinned, his eyebrows raised in surprised delight. "Fuck, no. Give me twenty minutes and we'll go again!"

I laughed out loud, more relieved than I wanted to admit.

His grin softened to a smile, and he cupped my cheek. "With you I'm never going to be bored, am I?"

You might be, I answered silently.

The age difference concerned me because I couldn't give him the family he wanted.

My issues concerned me because they slowed me down.

Would I be able to keep up with him?

Should I even try?

Chapter 15 – Underwear

<u>Lucky</u>

Minty blew my mind.

I mean, I wasn't sure I had a single, functioning brain cell left.

Not an ideal state of affairs when you're supposed to be passing on your wisdom to future generations.

I turned my mind back to the issue that had plagued me since the Christmas break.

I met, once again, with the principal about the underwear problem. He was slowly working on it, but how fucking hard was it to put together a feminine hygiene kit? We passed out condoms like beaded necklaces at Mardi gras but shied away from underwear?

I frowned as I drummed my fingers on my desk in my empty classroom.

I took a deep breath. The indignity of it broke my heart.

"Mr. Triggs?"

My head swung around. "Yes, Sasha? What can I do for you?"

Sasha had just turned eighteen, this year being her victory lap, and hopefully the one in which she graduated.

"Can I sit down?"

"Of course." My heart rate picked up. This was one of three things. She wanted to take an instrument home, somebody was hurting her, or she was...

"I'm pregnant," she blurted out. "I think I'm pregnant."

I nodded and held her gaze. "Okay. Thank you for telling me. Is the father involved?"

Her face twisted. "Yeah, with my sister."

My spine snapped straight, and her startled eyes flew to mine. I forced myself to shift back in my chair. "Sash, was it forced?"

"Not exactly... It's complicated." Tension coiled around her body. She was about to bolt.

"Sasha, I'm really glad you told me. You did the right thing. I would like to know if you have taken a pregnancy test yet."

"No. But, I'm late. I'm never late."

I stood up and extended my arm. "C'mon kiddo. Let's go to guidance and see about getting you a test."

With her arms crossed she tucked herself against my side. I lay my hand on her shoulder, wishing I could give this child a hug. Her chest heaved once and then she seemed to pull herself together.

"It'll be okay," I whispered.

"Will you stay with me while I take the test?"

"I'll be right outside."

Minty

"Underwear, Minty. Can you believe that? Fucking underwear. And while the powers that be fuck around trying to find the politically correct way to hand out fucking underwear, they're tossing condoms like candy."

"It's horrendous, darling." I stroked his hair back from his forehead.

We were supposed to go out to see a movie tonight, but he showed up at my door positively wrecked so I invited him in instead. Now I curled up sideways on my couch, leaning against him while he slouched back, his head resting on the back.

"I may be able to help." I scratched his scalp lightly, brushing his hair back from his tired face.

Dull, grey eyes swung in my direction. "How? Everything has to be approved by the principal and the board. It's a fucking ridiculous process. If a girl requests a pair of underwear in grade nine, she might get them in time for graduation," he bit out bitterly.

"I run a shelter. A small one. My best friend, Amber, is a social worker. The woman who runs the shelter with me, she's also a social worker. We've got connections out the wazoo. Let me put my feelers out. See if there's an organization already approved and in place. Then we just need to drum up some funding. It won't take long."

"I feel bad for wanting instruments now," he admitted.

"Lucky, education is important. It's vital. It shouldn't be a toss-up between underwear and educational equipment. Underwear should be a given."

He nodded.

"This girl, the one who thought she was pregnant, is she safe?"

His laugh was hollow. "Physically, I think so. She's just surrounded by assholes."

He threw his forearm over his eyes. "She's agreed to talk to the social worker at school. Hopefully they'll get to the bottom of it." His Adam's apple bobbed a few times in his throat. A tear rolled into his hairline.

Carefully, I set my glass of wine down on the coffee table and slipped his beer from his hand. Swinging my leg over his lap, I nestled down, my head on his chest. Both his arms came around me tightly, my entire body rising with his deep, shuddering breath before settling in comfortably.

His grip loosened bit by bit until he slumped into sleep.

I kissed his cheek, whispered, "I'll be right back," although he did not answer. I covered him with a blanket and retreated to my kitchen table with my laptop, the plan already taking shape in my mind.

Ezinne and Amber knew each other well. Amber went out to the house once a month and ran sessions for the ladies on various topics, all aimed toward empowerment. Within ten minutes I'd sent them both an email detailing the problem. Amber held a master's degree in social work, her area of study, community resources. Ezinne had worked in this community for her entire career, and I swore she knew everyone and everything. My specialty was funding. We could do this.

I opened up the search engine and started compiling a wish list of musical instruments.

Lucky stirred on the couch, and I realized with a start that more than two hours had passed. In that time, both Ezinne and Amber had gotten back to me with a total of five possibilities, organizations that were already approved and working with the school board. We only needed one to take us in as a special guest and allow us to distribute care packages.

"Hey," I called quietly before standing up and walking toward him. "Um," I stopped and clasped my hands together in front of me, suddenly unsure. "I think we've got a way in. I just need a few days to secure funding."

He stilled, his head cocked to the side. "What?"

I twisted my hands together then forced them to relax and linked them together loosely in front of me. "Um.."

He shook his head. "I heard you. Come here." He grasped my hips and pulled me down to straddle his lap, his face pressed against my breasts. "Thank you," he breathed. "Even if it doesn't happen, thank you."

"It's going to happen." I massaged his scalp firmly. "We're just going to piggyback in on someone else. We will essentially be donating to one of the pre-approved organizations and helping them to distribute. Amber is going to contact them tomorrow; she knows most of the people involved. I'll work on funding. Ezinne will wrangle the girls to put together the care packages."

He didn't speak, but his hands began to roam up and down my back.

"Are you hungry?" he asked gruffly. "Or can you wait?"

"I can wait," I assured him.

Digging his fingers into the cheeks of my ass, he stood from the couch.

I wrapped my arms around his neck as he boosted me further up, nuzzling my temple with his nose. Turning, he stalked down the hall to my bedroom.

I remembered the mess, in stark contrast to the rest of my condo. "Um, I should warn you-"

He stopped short and drew his chin back to look at me, a small smile on his face. "That a bomb went off in here?"

I laughed, feeling my face heat. "Yeah, something like that."

His dimples flashed and he tossed me onto my bed before crawling in after me. "At least I won't be worrying about making a mess."

Chapter 16 – Mutually Exclusive

Lucky

Friday evening, while I waited for Minty to finish getting ready, I ran my finger lightly over the keys of her piano.

It was old. Well-loved. Perfectly in tune. And matched nothing else in her condo except maybe the dark wood of the China cabinet.

Minty came from down the hallway from her bedroom, twisting her hair into a knot and securing it.

"I noticed this the other day before you dragged me off into your bedroom to ravish me," I teased. "Do you play?"

"My recollection is that you grabbed my big butt and literally hauled my ass down the hall and threw me on the bed!" Minty laughed, her eyes sparkling.

Her eyes amazed me. At times cool, bordering on unfriendly, I could no longer believe I ever found her calm and controlled. It was an illusion, barely skin deep. She was all heart. All kindness. All passion.

"You don't have a big ass," I protested, then spun her around so I could take a look. "It's perfect."

"Yeah," she teased, looking over her shoulder. "Perfectly round."

"Mm-hmm," I agreed, my hand following the path forged by my eyes.

"Want to hear me play?" She stepped away from me and slid onto the bench seat, tipping her chin up to take me.

"I would love to hear."

She smiled and lightly ran her fingers over the keys. I didn't recognize the piece she played, but no matter, it quickly became my favorite. Her eyes closed as her fingers danced, her chin dipping when the music crested, she swayed and moved, brow tightening, lips pursing then parting to take a deep breath, her face tilting upwards, the music filling her, taking her away to a place I wanted to go.

When she finished, she sat back and looked up at me again, her eyes calm.

"What was that?"

"It's called 'The Darkness in Me' by Fight the Fade. It's a favorite of mine."

"You play beautifully."

"It calms me. I love music. All kinds."

"Did you ever play professionally?"

"Oh, no. I wasn't good enough for that." She laughed. "I used to be in a band though." She quirked a brow, waiting for my reaction.

"Really?" I cocked my head to the side, picturing folk music, tambourines, and flowy skirts.

"Evanescence was my jam back then." She paused. "Still is, actually."

My eyebrows went up. "You played keyboard?"

"No, darling." Her voice dropped and she winked. "I sang."

This woman was full of surprises. "Please," I begged. "Tell me you have pictures."

She brightened. "I do! I'll get them if you want to see?"

She opened the photo album up on the kitchen table. I pulled out the chair beside her and slowly turned the pages. "How old are you here?"

"Twenty-two," she said, her voice strained.

"Was this before your parents passed?"

"Yes."

"Before your relapse?"

"Yes."

One-word answers. The scraps and pieces of stories she revealed began to piece together.

"And what happened to the band?"

She cleared her throat. "Remember I told you there was one once who couldn't handle my OCD? It was our band. I walked away. Not that I had much choice, at first. I wasn't functioning. But even later, once I had a hold on it again, I couldn't be in the band with him while he moved on."

I pointed to a photo of Minty leaning against one of the band members. "Is this him?"

"Yes." Her voice was soft, almost nostalgic. "You know, I miss the band more than I miss him at this point. And I don't really miss the band. Sometimes staying causes more hurt. But there were some good times."

"Has he ever been in contact since?"

"Sporadically over the years. He married, had a couple of kids, divorced, remarried, had a couple more." She grinned at me. "All in all, I think I dodged a bullet."

I laughed. "Looks that way."

She turned a page, and I zeroed in on her outfit. "Did you dress like that all the time?"

I looked at her sitting demurely beside me, her ankles crossed and tucked to the side. Her floral sundress nearly hitting the floor, blond hair upswept, silvery-blue pearls at her ears and a single teardrop pearl dangling from a silver chain at her throat. "I can't imagine you dressing any other way than you do."

She shrugged and smiled. "Well, I certainly didn't dress like that." She pointed to the picture. "That was my on-stage persona and was a ton of fun." She tapped her finger on the man beside her in the picture. "I think he loved her, not me."

"He was a fool," I said softly.

She laughed softly and shook her head. "You don't know how bad it was, how bad it can be."

"I wouldn't leave you, Minty. If I told you I loved you, I would never leave you."

She dipped her chin for a moment before looking back at me, her smile sad. "You're going to make some woman incredibly happy someday."

Her words cut me, and I had to take a moment to draw my breath.

Minty

Was that reminder for him or for me?

The idea of him being with someone else now or ever was beginning to grate on me.

"Well, lucky for you, I'm all yours right now." He broke the silence. "And I really need to elicit a promise that you'll dig up your on-stage persona and wear it to one of my shows."

I laughed though it sounded forced. "Maybe I'll do that."

"Would you ever get onstage with me?"

"I won't lie and say I don't miss it; I do. But that me I keep under wraps for your eyes only?" I tapped his chin and teased. "Everybody will see her up there."

"It just might be worth it," he retorted, making me laugh.

It had been a long time since I'd looked at those pictures and not felt the humiliating sting of rejection. Up until now, I don't think I'd ever seen those pictures and felt happiness, or at least a bittersweet nostalgia, rather than heartbreak and loss.

He closed the album. "I have a show tomorrow. You want to come? I can make sure a table is set aside for you. You can see if Junie's going."

"I can't tomorrow." I wished I could. I wondered if he would regret our agreement to be exclusive. "Are you still okay with our agreement?"

"What agreement?"

I huffed out a sigh. "To be exclusive. I imagine these are the nights when you'd date?"

He laughed. "Are you jealous?" I felt my face close up and his smile faded. He touched his finger to my cheek. "First of all, I didn't date. Second of all, I'm only interested in you."

"But these would be the nights," I pushed.

"Yes." He sighed and his lips tightened. "I don't blame your girls for giving you the heads-up they did, but they really poisoned your opinion of me. I never found anyone I wanted to date. Never met anyone I wanted around Brayleigh. I'm not going to screw up what we have."

He spoke like we had something bigger than what we did. His words stole mine and I stood silently before him. Dipping his head to meet my eyes, he implored, "I'm not going to hurt you, baby. I'm just not." He stood and held out his hand. "We're going to miss the movie if we don't leave. You can tell me what big plans you have that you're leaving me lonely on a Saturday night on our way."

Summer nights smell better than any other fragrance on the planet. Better than Christmas, better than freshly fallen snow, better than chocolate, yes, better than chocolate.

I inhaled happily as Lucky pulled out of the lot to take us to the movies.

"It's Bookstagram night with Amber and Ruby, but speaking of Amber, I actually have things to tell you! Amber has two solid leads. Both are willing to help us out and they have already contacted the board. We've made it clear that we're starting with your high school, and I need to fill in some paperwork. What school is it?"

Lucky told me the school and my mouth dropped open. "How many high schools are in Milltown?"

"Twenty? Twenty-five? More than twenty between the Catholic system and public system for sure."

"Do you have a student named George Vitalis?"

"Yes," he answered, surprised. "How do you know George?"

"George is Ruby's stepson. He's my honorary nephew. I pick him up several times a week!" I stopped, realizing. "Oh my gosh! It's your music class we've been talking about getting instruments for!"

"Well, yeah, it's my class I've been thinking of doing the fundraiser for..."

"Yes, oh my gosh, this is so funny!" I clasped my hands under my chin. "The girl. The girl you were upset about the other day. She takes music?"

"Yes," he looked at me oddly.

"What instrument does she play?"

"Usually, the recorder like everybody else but she wants a guitar."

"Okay, okay, hear me out." I splayed my hands out in front of me. I expected a fight, but I wasn't sure why. "I make a donation every year to something that means something to me. My nephew, George, was telling me about his awesome music teacher and the lack of instruments. I'd already decided to donate instruments to your school before I even met you! Remember that night I quizzed you on what would be good for a class set? That's why!"

Lucky's jaw tightened and he flicked on the indicator.

"Lucky? What's wrong?"

He slanted a look at me sideways. "Not going to make it to the movies tonight, baby."

"What? Why? Are you mad?" I reached out and lay a hand on his arm.

"Don't touch me right now, Minty, or we won't even make it home."

I stared at him, the truth slowly dawning on me. "Are you turned on?"

He gripped the steering wheel.

I dropped my voice. "Does all my talk of musical instruments do something to you?"

He looked at me meanly, but his mouth tipped up on one side.

I gathered my dress up inch-by-inch, sliding the fabric along my thigh. "Guitars, and," I gasped theatrically, "Ukuleles..."

He chuckled and I grinned at him even as his gaze dropped to my lap where my fingers danced along the inside of my thigh. His Adam's apple bobbed.

With one leg completely bared, I went to work on the other side. "Drums to beat, violins to stroke...eyes on the road, darling..." I pulled my underwear off and let it fall to the floor before tossing it into his lap. "We haven't even begun to talk about wind instruments..."

He pulled into the parking lot we'd left not fifteen minutes before and turned toward me, frowning. "I can't even get out of the car without embarrassing myself."

I laughed as I swung my legs out of the car. "I guess I'll meet you upstairs." I closed the door and walked around the car to his side, backing away from his open window. "Should I wait?" I pretended to think. "Maybe I'll get started without you..." I turned and headed for the stairs leading up to my door, gathering the hem of my dress up higher with every step.

I heard the car door close with a slam. Looking back over my shoulder, I saw him prowling after me like a large, golden cat. A big cat with a bit of a hitch in his step.

I ducked my chin and laughed at his predicament before racing my way up the rest of the stairs.

Breathless, I jammed my key in the lock right before he slammed into my back. "I don't know whether to spank you or fuck you," he growled.

I tossed him a teasing look over my shoulder. His flushed face sent waves of tingling anticipation to my womb. "Are they mutually exclusive?"

With his hand over mine, he stared at me hard as he turned the key in the lock.

We made it as far as the kitchen table.

Chapter 17 – Alien Sex

Minty

"I'm seeing a man," I blurted out.

Two sets of wide, curious eyes swung around to rest on my face.

Tonight was girls' night, otherwise known as Bookstagram night. We used to have it at Amber's condo, but since she and Gus reconciled, we switched to my place.

This past month, Amber, Ruby, and I dipped our proverbial toes into the realm of alien romance, and I felt all kinds of things, not all of them comfortable, as we worked through our review for @aphroditesharem.

"I did not think I would like this," I admitted. "This is so far from my usual genre, but I liked it. A lot."

"When you boil it all down, muscles, a big dick, the knowhow to wield it, and total devotion is all women want," Amber commented drily.

"To wield it?" Ruby guffawed, and I snorted.

"Orgasms," Amber clarified with a laugh. "We want orgasms."

"From someone who loves us with a love bordering on worship."

"And wants you and no one else."

"Okay...so I think we can safely say alien romance sums up the universal female wish list. A mate or partner who wants you and only you, no other woman will suffice."

"Yes, that, certainly," Amber agreed. "And it should also be noted that those feelings of devotion and protection go both ways."

"Trials are weathered together," Ruby added.

"I love it that they are equals. The alien mates revere and respect their women."

"How's this: *The foray into the category of alien romance marks a significant departure from Aphrodite's usual fare of contemporary romance with the occasional side dish of dark and dirty romance or BDSM. Curiosity led me to pick up the first book, and curiosity met surprise as I quickly found myself completely invested in the characters and the world they inhabited. While half of me wondered at the pull of these non-men, the other half dove in and fell in love right along with their human female counterparts. By the time I put the 8th book down, I figured it out. Alien romance, at least this series of alien romance, nails down exactly what women want: a strong mate who wants them and only them, orgasms and plenty of them, devotion bordering on worship, the opportunity to reciprocate, and someone who respects their needs, wants and opinions. That last point seems to be a truly alien concept in today's world, which makes it understandable that female readers might look for escape in a different one.*"

"What do you think?" I asked.

"It's true," Amber laughed. "Especially that last point. You've had a phenomenally long run of bad luck with men."

Which is when I blurted out the fact that I was seeing someone.

Amber topped up Ruby's wine then curled herself into the couch. "Since when? Who is it?"

"You remember I told you about Willa and Bex from work? Willa is married to Barrett and Junie is engaged to Lenny who is the drummer in their band. Lucky is the lead guitarist."

"He's in a band?" Ruby's eyes lit up. "That's so freaking sexy."

"He is. He really is and he's very sweet. Anyway, I met him at Willa's wedding but neither of us pursued it. Then we met up again at Lenny's and he asked me out."

"This is fantastic!" Amber exclaimed. "Do we get to meet him?"

"Well, see, this is what I've been thinking about. I wouldn't mind introducing you but we kind of have an expiration date."

Ruby drew her chin into her chest, her eyebrows scrunched. "An expiration date? What do you mean you have an expiration date?"

Amber eyed me steadily. "I think the question is *why* do you have an expiration date?"

I chewed the inside of my cheek. "Because he's younger than me and I can't give him a family. Because he has had a rather busy dating life from what I've been told, and I don't think he's ready for forever. Because..." I trailed off, sure I had more reasons but unable at that moment to recall a single one.

Amber leaned over me, passing me a dessert plate with her Yiayia's cookies on it.

I swing my head forward and bash my forehead into her nose, blood streams down her face, she cries out, covering her face with her hands. Blood pours through the cracks between her fingers.

"Thank you, beautiful," I murmured, taking the goodies. Amber knew my weakness was cookies and never failed to bring some when Yiayia baked.

I bit into one and hummed my appreciation. "She's never going to give me the recipe, is she?"

Ruby lit up. "She invited you over to bake with her. She doesn't actually have the recipes written down and she can't write in English anyways."

"Oh, I'd love that!" My mind began to whirr. "You think she'd come to the shelter and bake with the ladies?"

Amber cut in, "Absolutely. I'll go, too. The girls know me. It'll be fun. But we're getting off topic. Tell us more about your man."

I suddenly remembered the other point. "He has a child, a two-year-old girl, with his current best friend."

"What?" Two sets of surprised eyes rested on my face.

"I know, I know. See? And she's beautiful. Stunningly beautiful. And she's his age. They share custody, have dinner together at least once a week, do activities with their little girl...it's not just me, right? That's a red flag, isn't it?"

"You think you're walking into some crazy love triangle?" Amber rolled her lips between her teeth. "Have you met her?"

"Yes! And that was even more bizarre! Lucky introduced me, made it clear she was interrupting our date, and kicked her out! She laughed!"

Ruby relaxed back into the couch and shrugged. "Maybe they really are just friends."

"Or maybe they're not and he's just not ready to settle down," I mused.

"That would make him the biggest kind of asshole, though. Don't you think?" Amber asked.

"Yes. And he's not. I don't think."

"What's he doing tonight?" Ruby asked.

"His band is playing at a bar downtown. He asked me to come, but I told him I had Bookstagram with you guys."

"Let's go," Amber sat up straight. "We're done talking about alien sex, I haven't been out on the town in ages, he already invited you, let's go!"

Ruby held up her hands. "Wait. Where is it exactly?" Ruby, like myself, liked to have all the details before she committed to something. None of us were very spur of the moment, this was even out of character for Amber. I suspected her protective instincts were aroused.

After several more minutes of discussion, they raided my closet and we set off for the bar. It was late, but we'd at least catch some of the show.

A gurgle of excitement welled up in my tummy as I pictured the flash of his dimples when he saw me.

We got there just after the start of the second set. Most people were on their feet near the stage or seated at the few scattered high-top tables nearby. A small table near the back opened up and we snapped it up.

"Good Lord!" Ruby breathed. "What is that?"

I followed the line of her sight and laughed. "*That* is Barrett. You know Willa. That's her husband. The fellow on the drums is Lenny, Junie's fiancé. I haven't met the bass player yet, but his name is Bax. Lucky is the blond on lead guitar."

Ruby's eyes lit up and she chortled. "I cannot wait to talk to Willa and Junie on Monday!"

"How do you keep your panties on?" Amber laughed, eyeing Lucky on stage.

"I didn't," I winked.

Ruby looked betrayed. "You couldn't have told us that part at home?"

Laughter, music, camaraderie: the sustenance of the gods. Barrett's voice dripped sex, and I laughed to myself as I remembered how hard Willa worked to steer clear of him.

I'd never seen Drivetrain play. If I had, I would never have agreed to any kind of arrangement with Lucky.

In this environment, the difference between us became all too clear. Younger, more energetic, no hang-ups, and the women, the women hanging around half-dressed at the foot of the stage made it abundantly clear he had no lack of options for female companionship.

Wearing ripped jeans and a tight tee, his hair a mess, he looked the part of the quintessential rockstar, and I just knew his students must love him. Happiness radiated off him. He loved the stage, his joy in playing almost palpable.

All kinds of turned on watching his fingers fly across the fretboard, knowing how they played across my skin, made me happy I hadn't seen this side of him before. Because I would have missed out on getting to know a genuinely good guy. And I would have missed out on a night of spectacular sex. With the promise of more to come.

Barrett closed the show, passed his instrument to Lenny, and bounded off the stage sparing nary a glance at the beauties buzzing around waiting.

I watched Lucky, smiling and laughing with Lenny and the other fellow. I couldn't help but smile.

Standing, I slung the strap of my purse over my shoulder, suddenly bursting to let him know I'd seen him play. "Alright, girls. I'll introduce you."

Lucky jumped down off the stage into the midst of the groupies. Jealousy sharpened her claws, but he only nodded and smiled as he dismissed them.

I breathed out a sigh of relief. So silly. You have no reason not to trust him.

He looked my way and his eyes lit up, sending the butterflies in my stomach into flight even as I wondered how he found me so quickly. Smiling widely, his deep dimples fully on display, he opened his arms.

Two laughing women, gazing up at him with open adoration, moved in and wrapped their arms around his waist, while one lay a proprietary hand on his chest.

Amber sucked in a breath and Ruby made a noise as if she'd been punched. My stomach dropped to the floor along with my eyes while my heart thumped wildly in my chest. Humiliation stained my cheeks, and I blinked back the sting of bitter disappointment.

I looked up in time to see him turn his head and press a laughing kiss onto the temple of one of the women even as he squeezed the other close to his side. He walked out of the bar with both of them.

My girls moved in close, Ruby practically vibrating with fury. Amber laced her fingers tightly through mine. By unspoken decree, we hung back, not wanting to meet up with Lucky in the parking lot.

I remembered our first kiss up against my car. That was not something I wanted to witness.

Two women.

Two.

If I'd had doubts about my ability to keep up with him before, they were now doubled.

"Aliens for the win, I guess," I broke the silence.

Not a single tear fell until I reached the solace of my bed.

And then they flowed.

Lucky

I checked the time again. She should have been here already. I wondered if the craft fair ran late. Maybe she forgot? Or was too tired to get together?

With both of us busy last night, we made plans to meet late this afternoon at my place. I texted to confirm as soon as I woke up, but she didn't answer. She didn't strike me as the type of woman to blow me off without an explanation and I began to worry.

I pulled out my phone and shot off another text.

Lucky: You were supposed to be here half an hour ago. Are you okay?

I had to pick up Brayleigh in a few hours. Shaving half an hour off my time with Minty did not sit well. I'd planned a repeat of our last date, culminating with her curled up beside me on my couch watching a movie after putting Brayleigh to bed.

Minty: I didn't realize we were still on.

My mouth twisted to the side. What the hell?

Lucky: Why wouldn't we be? Want me to come there?

Minty: I don't think that's a good idea.

Had something changed between Friday night and this morning? She saw her friends last night. Did they somehow convince her I was a bad bet? Why would they? They didn't even know me.

Lucky: Are you having second thoughts?

Minty: Aren't you?

Lucky: No! Not at all! I've thought of nothing save being with you today.

Minty: Even last night?

Lucky: Of course. Minty, what's this about?

Out of patience and buzzing with apprehension, I zinged off another text without waiting for her reply.

Lucky: I'm coming to your place.

Minty: No! I'll meet you for coffee.

She named a place, and I headed out. When I got there, I ordered myself a coffee and realized I didn't even know what she liked to drink. I looked at the display case. They had chocolate cookies.

"I'll take six of those to go."

Fifteen minutes later, just as I began to lose hope, the door opened.

She looked beautiful as always, but instead of the smile I hoped for, she wore the blank, composed mask I mistakenly believed was a thing of the past.

I stood to pull out her chair. "I didn't know what you wanted to drink but I got you cookies." I pushed the little box of cookies toward her, but she barely spared it a glance. "What can I get you?"

"Nothing. I won't be staying."

Her words jolted me, like a chain hooked to my spine, wrenching my guts backwards.

I eased into the chair across from her. "What happened?"

Sitting with her hands clasped in her lap, she met my eyes coolly. Regally.

Red rimmed her eyes. "Have you been crying?" I asked, suddenly alarmed.

She waved my concern away. "That is neither here nor there. I saw you. Last night."

I brightened and smiled through my confusion. "You came?"

She did not look at all happy. "I did."

"Why didn't you stay? I don't understand. I would have loved to have seen you." Wracking my brain, I could think of no reason for her to be upset. I scanned her face, watched as her eyes flashed with anger, and red splotches painted her cheeks.

"Really? I mean," she waved a graceful hand, "I imagine if you're used to two at a time, three would hardly be a crowd." She gathered her purse into her lap and icily dismissed me. "This is a waste of time. I'm leaving."

In that moment, all became clear, and fire glazed my vision. I stood abruptly, my chair legs screeching across the floor, the sudden noise staying her departure.

I leaned over, looked past the mask of composure on her face, and stared into her eyes. They were blank, her protective walls pulled high and wide.

"No, baby." I shook my head. "I'm leaving." Her eyes flickered with doubt in the face of my anger.

Thank, God.

I took my time scooping my helmet off the chair and gathering my wallet and keys off the table. Letting her stew a moment longer though it killed me, I dipped down to meet her wide eyes. "Those two women? My sisters. I would have been happy to introduce you had you made your presence known."

Her mouth gaped open, and the color drained from her face. "Your sisters?" she squeaked.

"Yeah, baby. My sisters." Anger over the warnings Junie and Willa delivered mixed with remorse for the lifestyle I'd indulged in, the lifestyle I'd worried would turn her away from me right from the beginning. "Despite what your friends have told you? I'm not a cheating asshole."

"Lucky..." she whispered.

"I'm going." I noted her flinch with both satisfaction and relief. I knocked sharply on the table. "And I'll be back tomorrow. You've got twenty-four fucking hours to get your head on straight or I'll straighten it for you. You feel me?"

Her mouth opened and closed a couple of times, but the door to the coffee shop slammed behind me before she was able to string two words together.

Chapter 18 - Punishment

Minty

I stared at the small box of cookies on the kitchen table in front of me, knowing I'd screwed up colossally.

1-2-3-4-5-1-2-3-4-5-1-2-3-4-5-1-2-3-4-5

I tapped out the numbers, equal weight on each finger, two full rotations make it even. Sets of two, always.

As soon as I got back from the coffee shop, I phoned Amber and Ruby and filled them in. Ruby summarized the situation perfectly. "Shitfuckdamn. We screwed up."

Amber offered to come over, but I needed to think things through on my own.

"I'm going to offer you a piece of advice a wise woman once offered me. Let that shit go. Whatever he did before you has no bearing on what you two have now."

"It was so much easier to say than it is to do," I admitted.

"Yes," Amber replied immediately, and bestowed one further piece of advice before hanging up. "But the baggage of the past makes the present so much more painful than it needs to be. There is joy to be had, but we can't grasp it if our hands are full of fear."

I carried the box of cookies to my window seat and curled up on the padded bench. The late afternoon sun cast long shadows, and if I listened carefully, I could hear the sounds from the street below.

1-2-3-4-5-1-2-3-4-5-1-2-3-4-5-1-2-3-4-5

You didn't even give him a chance. You didn't just jump, you leaped to the wrong conclusion, then treated him like shit.

Insulted him.

1-2-3-4-5-1-2-3-4-5-1-2-3-4-5-1-2-3-4-5

I could have been with Lucky right now.

Bus.

Safe travels.

I slept fitfully and it was a relief when the sun finally rose. Instead of going straight to work, I texted Junie to tell her I'd be late and went to my childhood home.

And Ezinne.

Just pulling into the driveway provided a hint of the peace I sought.

I sat in my car and remembered paints and brushes, a guiding hand over mine, sweeping color across a canvas. "You're a marvel, my girl. Math and art and music. A miracle," he used to say.

Dish soap mixed with hand cream. "Here you go, dolly. This will do both."

Baking cookies. "Try this, dolly." Mom putting her hands over mine, twisting the glass to release the perfect circle of dough underneath.

Weeks of homeschooling when going to school overwhelmed me. Mom did most of it, but Dad handled the math. "You've a fine mind, my girl. A fine mind."

Encouraging smiles, gentle touches, firm guidance, loving eyes. Gentle hands.

Half of me wished I could simply sneak past Ezinne and hole up in my room, what used to be my parents' room, and cocoon myself in memories. See if their closet still held any of their smell. I kept the bottles of perfume and aftershave on a box on the shelf.

Today was a day I would open it.

I looked up and could not help but laugh.

Ezinne's elbows filled the doorway where she stood with her legs braced, her hands on her hips, head cocked with that beautiful smile on her face.

By the time I reached her, her smile had faded.

"You're having a tough time."

"Yes." There was no point in denying it. Ezinne knew and understood me better than anyone and she had stood by me all these years.

"You want to talk, or do you just want to be here?"

I looked out across the wide front yard. Situated on the edge of town, the property stretched long and wide, offering space and privacy. Misery, in my case, did not love company, and there was nothing I wanted more than to hide but I knew that wasn't what I needed.

I sighed. "If you have time, I'd love to chat."

"Hmm." She leaned over and looked in my eyes, a smile in hers. "Yes, you really look like you'd love to chat."

Huffing out a laugh, I leaned against her as she pulled me into her side and welcomed me into my own house.

Her round breast pressed against the side of my arm as she squeezed me.

You like that.

I closed my eyes. I was too tired for this today.

You want to fuck her.

I dropped my eyes to the floor and mentally replied, *'Okay. I hear you. Thank you for your input.'*

We stopped by the kitchen to get drinks and cookies to bring out to the porch. Twenty minutes later, having told Ezinne the whole of Lucky's and my very short story from start to finish, I waited for her to speak.

"What is the scariest part of being with him?"

I didn't answer, but Ezinne possessed unearthly amounts of patience and never felt compelled to fill the silence. Instead, she permitted me space and time to know my own mind.

"There are two things," I began slowly. "The first is that I fall for him and I'm not enough, or perhaps I am too much."

She hummed her acceptance of my statement.

"The second is the little one, Brayleigh. She's going to turn my recovery on its' head," I whispered.

I heard the lie in my words even before Ezinne spoke.

"It's not recovery if you're still avoiding. And, Minty, you are still avoiding."

"It's not as bad anymore," I protested weakly.

"Do you have those boys over for sleepovers by themselves? Or do they always have to come in pairs?"

She was referring to Jace and Alex, and now George. I never had them on their own. The visuals were too much to handle. They frightened me more than any other thing. "In pairs."

"Why?"

The shame of it all was inescapable. Admitting to this type of OCD crushed my spirit. Confessing my self-doubt felt tantamount to an admission of guilt. "Just in case it's not OCD. Just in case I am the monster it says I am, and I lose control. They are safer with me if they are not alone."

"You know in your heart it's OCD."

"I do. But my brain won't let it go without exposure and response prevention and it feels like too great a risk."

Ezinne drummed her fingers on her desk. "You know, when you are cerebral, as you and I are, it's counterintuitive to ignore our brains in lieu of listening to our hearts. There are cases when our hearts know better."

A tear rolled down my cheek.

I didn't bother to wipe it away.

It was loss.

And it demanded a witness.

Silence rested easy between us for several minutes.

"Okay." I broke the silence and smiled at her wryly. "I'll work on it."

"That's good, Minty. You're filled to the brim with love. It would be a shame to deny yourself the joy of a good man and the love of a child if that's what you want."

After eating breakfast with Ezinne and the girls, I headed into work where I found Junie cooing over Rena while Willa sorted through the mess at her desk.

"What happened?" Willa asked. "You look like you've had less sleep than I have."

"It's Lucky," I said and watched as the brows of both ladies contracted into frowns. 'No, no. He didn't do anything wrong. I did."

I relayed the events, skipping over the finer details, but finishing with the coffee shop. "He was so angry. Insulted. He said I had twenty-four hours to get my head on straight or he'd do it for me."

Junie looked at Willa, wrinkled her nose, and nodded. "That's kind of hot."

Willa laughed in agreement, then turned to me. "I'm sorry, Minty. I think we set him up for this. We shouldn't have undermined him." She rubbed her hands up and down her thighs. "We felt like we needed to give you a heads up." She looked back at Junie again. "Now I feel like we owe you both an apology."

I stood up with a sigh. "No. It's me that owes him an apology." I reached my hands out toward Junie. "Give me that baby. You've hogged her for long enough."

I open my arms wide and drop the baby on the floor.

I nestled Rena against my breast and cuddled her close.

You like that.

Yes. Yes, I do, I answered defiantly.

I kissed her downy head and closed my eyes to the outside world while I waited for the beast to retract its' claws.

"Sweet little bean," I murmured as I breathed in her sweet baby scent. "Such a lucky little bean."

I held her close and after a little while it was just me and her and no malicious whispers from the monster inside.

"So, I was thinking to resume art lessons at the house next month."

"Already?" I asked, surprised.

"Yes. I'm getting bored at home, but I'm not ready to bring Rena to the shelter. At the house Ezinne can hold her while I run the art lesson. Even the girls would probably be happy to hold her."

"That's excellent! They will love that."

That news helped my mood, and by the time we closed up the store for the day, I felt ready to approach Lucky. Should I text him? Call him? Wait for him to call me?

No.

I accused him of doing something he promised he'd never do. I needed to take ownership of my mistakes.

I walked out the back and headed up the stairs to the back door of my condo, my attention focused on my cell phone as I tapped out a text.

On the top stair, I encountered two large feet.

I gasped and went to step back which would have sent me catapulting down the stairs, but Lucky's hand shot out and grasped my waist, pulling me in quickly.

"Sorry!" he exclaimed, his eyes wide. "I should have let you know I was sitting here."

I splayed my palm over my chest. "Holy fuck!" I took a deep breath. "It's okay. I'm okay."

Fall backwards. Let yourself go. Allow the steel and concrete to break your bones, shatter your skull, end your pain.

Those thoughts didn't even warrant the acknowledgement of a smile. Huh. Perhaps the other thoughts could be neutralized just as easily. Easily. Right.

I offered him a small smile. "Would you like to come in?"

He moved aside and swept his arm out, indicating for me to step forward and unlock the door.

As soon as I closed the door, I spoke. "I'm sorry. It was insulting and rude and immature. I should have approached you. I should not have jumped to conclusions."

"You're right. At the very least, you should have contacted me and demanded an explanation."

"Yes," I agreed. There was nothing else for it. I was wrong.

"I'm not going to lie. That hurt, Minty." He dragged a hand through his hair. "Look. I've never cared about my dating history until you. I worried from the beginning it was going to be a problem. But I have never ever cheated on a woman. I have four sisters. I have a daughter. My best friend is a woman!" His eyes widened. "I could never do that."

"I'm sorry, Lucky," I breathed. "You didn't deserve that."

He braced his hands on his hips and looked at me from beneath his brow, then sighed before stepping toward me with his arms open to draw me in.

"Minty," he murmured, one hand at the small of my back, the other gently cupping the back of my head. Gentle fingers tangled in my hair and pulled, raising my face to his.

"I will not hurt you," he promised, his stormy grey eyes catching mine. "Can we carry on like we planned? Continue seeing each other?"

I tried to nod but he didn't release my hair. The moment I relaxed back into his hand, the line of his mouth softened, and his eyelids closed to half-mast.

"Yes, Lucky. I'd like that."

My eyes fell to his mouth, my lips parting of their own accord.

He tightened his hold on my hair, bringing my eyes up to his. His mouth quirked up on one side, almost regretful, and he murmured, "For your punishment, I'm not going to fuck you."

Taken aback, I went to pull away, but he held me closer and smiled, this one reaching his eyes. "But because that will also punish me, and we've already agreed I didn't do anything wrong, maybe you'll agree to let me take you out on Wednesday. I can't wait until Friday to see you again. Besides, I already bought us tickets to a show I think you'll like."

He flashed his dimples.

I laughed.

Then, dropping his smile, he dipped his knees and searched my eyes. "We good?"

"Yes," I immediately answered. "We're good."

"Good."

The breath left his chest, he dropped a kiss onto the tip of my nose and, true to his word, we did nothing more than cuddle up on the couch and watch a movie.

It wasn't much of a punishment.

Chapter 19 – Limits

<u>Lucky</u>

What the actual fuck?

I pulled the tickets out of my pocket, wondering if somehow we'd been admitted to the wrong gallery.

The Goddess at Play – A Celebration.

Those same words hung from the ceiling at the center of the exhibition. And there was no better word for what I saw.

At the entrance to the exhibit, the hostess explained that the walk-through of the exhibition took approximately two hours, allowing seven minutes at each of twelve stations, the remainder of the time spent perusing the open gallery. She requested that we neither rush nor delay, so as not to intrude upon the attendees either in front or behind us but pay heed to the soft bell that indicated when it was time to move on.

Narrow pathways swelled into intimate pockets, called stations, which again narrowed into a pathway until we happened upon the next. I imagined if we could see the layout from above, it would look like the unfurling of a rose.

The music, a heavy, lustful beat, seemed almost out of place.

At first.

The first pocket, or station, featured flowers. They reminded me of something, but I couldn't quite put my finger on it. Following the flowers, we were treated to increasingly erotic depictions of women, first alone, then in pairs, then in larger groups, sometimes with men, sometimes without. As the number of characters in the paintings increased, the amount of clothing decreased.

We now stood in the next pocket, henceforth known as the 'what the actual fuck' station.

I cleared my throat. "Um, Minty. I had no idea," I whispered.

Her tinkling laugh broke out and she squeezed my biceps. "I know," she admitted. "I thought it was a strange choice and wondered if you knew what we were getting into. Watching you," she laughed softly, "has been incredibly entertaining!"

I huffed out a breath in relief. "Thank, God," I exclaimed, splaying my hand over my chest. "I thought it had something to do with mythology, or female empowerment and creativity. I pictured celestial paintings, maybe a trident if things got racy! I'm almost afraid to go to the next station."

We worked our way through, and I began to appreciate the beauty and spirit of this celebration of female sexuality. Knowing the end approached, I relaxed, watched Minty as she took it all in.

I was still looking at her when the hallway opened up into the last station and saw the surprise on her face.

It should have served as a warning.

It didn't.

The large, open space featured a live art installation of BDSM featuring women in both Dom and sub roles in various stages of undress, freeze-framed for several moments as they worked through a series of poses.

Like a live action flip book in slow motion.

Scattered vignettes included several props. Women and men were cuffed to spanking benches, wooden frames or crosses. One woman hung suspended from the ceiling, ropes cleverly placed to conceal nothing.

Some of it looked frankly painful.

Minty

The final station, set up in a large room, staged and furnished to look like the playroom of a sex club, stipulated no time constraint.

Which was good because Lucky was about to have a coronary.

At the sight of the nipple clamps, his face paled.

The gentleman sub cuffed to a cross, his nether regions encased in a cage, elicited a pained curse.

Fortunately, that was as racy as it got.

I hooked my hand through Lucky's elbow and gently tugged him forward. "Come, darling. Let's go."

Once outside, Lucky lifted my hand from his arm and laced my fingers through his. "Let's walk for a bit. I need some air."

Working to quell my smile, I strolled along beside him. Located across the street from the lake, taking a walk along the pier was almost a given after visiting the art gallery.

"I, uh, I really want to apologize." He cleared his throat.

I cut him off. "It's quite alright, darling. It's not a big deal. It was interesting."

"Really?" He twisted his neck to look down at me.

I shrugged. "Sure. I've read lots of romance books featuring BDSM. It was interesting to see a visual representation."

"And what did you think of it?"

We crossed the road and took the path along the lakeshore.

I wrinkled my nose. "It's much sexier in print than in reality."

"What about it appeals to you?"

"The open communication and attention. Couples talk about their sexual limits, what they do and don't want to do. Sometimes they allow each other to push to expand those limits. The focused attention on your partner, I'm not sure anything can beat that."

"So...not the whips and chains and cages."

"Not those things, no," I confirmed with a laugh.

He covered his chest with his hand. "Thank, God. I don't think I could give you that. I'm not sure I can even perform tonight. Did you see that one man?"

I grinned up at him. "I did. You sure you don't want to try it?"

He shook his head adamantly. "I'm sure." He paused. "But I wouldn't mind seeing you in some of those outfits."

"Oh, yeah?" I teased. "Which one?"

Dimples flashing, he pulled me to a stop at the side of the path and looped his arms around my back. "Any of them. Except for those pinchy nipple things. I would never want to do that to your pretty nipples."

"That's good. My pretty nipples are not fans of extraneous pain."

"Extraneous? A little pain is okay?"

"They are more than happy with your teeth, darling."

I felt him growing firm against my stomach and smiled up into his handsome face. "Looks like you'll be able to perform tonight after all."

Later that night, Lucky told me he'd been tested and cleared. We decided to forego the use of condoms.

There was no chance of pregnancy. I explained to him how I'd had my tubes tied over a decade before due to my dependance on my medication and the fact it did not mix well with pregnancy. We were slowly getting to know each other, inside and outside of the bedroom.

We still had a way to go. Lucky held a false impression of me. I knew this with a certainty because on Friday he took me to see Shakespeare.

I hated Shakespeare.

"Do you like theatre, Lucky?" We stood in the lobby waiting for the doors of the theatre to open.

He slanted a sideways look in my direction. "I'm not a huge fan, but I wanted to do something special." Huffing out a laugh, he continued, "Especially after the art gallery debacle."

I squeezed his arm to my chest. "It all worked out in the end. All your parts are still in working order. No lasting trauma," I teased.

No man had ever worked so hard to please me. I needed to tell him exactly how to do that before I found myself at an opera. Not sure I could sit through that.

The first scene took place behind a backlit screen. While the language was distinctly Shakespearean, it appeared as though the actors wore leotards and large masks.

Before scene two began, the lights dimmed and not a sound was heard while the screen rose revealing a frozen tableau.

In the silence, Lucky's pained whisper easily reached me. "How is this happening?"

Shakespeare.

But naked.

Full frontal nudity, both sexes.

"It's Shakespeare," he whispered again in disbelief.

My shoulders began to shake.

The sudden visual of Lucky and me fucking on stage made me laugh harder.

The woman behind me cleared her throat, making her irritation known.

You want to lick her pussy.

I momentarily grimaced in distaste but swept the thought away.

Lucky shrank down in his seat which at his height was not an easy feat.

We waited until intermission, and then got the hell out of dodge.

"Minty," he began. "I'm sorry." He scrubbed his hand through his hair.

I looked down at the ground while we walked to the car. "Lucky, I think you have the wrong idea about me..."

He cut me off. "No. Honestly. This was a mistake." He held his hands out as if to stay my words. "Another one. I know how it looks, but I just wanted to do something nice for you. Something cultured. Classy. As you are."

He gave me the perfect opening and I wasn't about to waste it. "Lucky, I like music. I like going to the movies. Coffee shops are my soul food, and bookstores are my catnip. I love art, and don't mind going to the occasional art gallery or museum, but I prefer to practice rather than view. I don't mind theatre, but I like modern. And funny. I like to read. Bake cookies. Listen to music. One day I'd love to travel. I'm not really a classy kind of girl. It's not hard to please me. Especially not for you. You please me just by being you."

His jaw hardened as I spoke. When I finished, he just stared at me. "You're too fucking good for me. I knew it then; I know it better now."

He led me to the car and headed straight to his place. The tension between us ratcheted up with every mile.

Inside, he pushed me none too gently up the stairs to his bedroom where he immediately spun me around to face him.

With his forehead pressed to mine, he made short work of my blouse and the zipper of my skirt, shimmying it down over my hips.

He groaned at the sight of my midnight lace bra and panties.

"You like it, Lucky? I bought them for you," I murmured, ready to unleash a little more of me.

With one calloused finger, he traced the edge of my bra, following the swell of my breast. "I like it," he answered huskily.

"Would you like it better off?" I pushed. "Would you like to lick my pretty nipples, darling?"

Narrowed eyes darted to mine before returning to my chest.

I trailed my own fingers after his, then cupped my breasts in my hands and offered them to him.

He bit down over the lace of my bra, the sting of his teeth a wondrous precursor to the warm wet sweep of his tongue. With both hands, he pulled the straps down my arms until my breasts bounced free of the cups.

"You would bind me with my bra?" I trailed my fingers down my abdomen, noting with supreme feminine satisfaction his flushed face, how he stilled while his eyes followed my hand, unblinking.

I dipped my fingers down the front of my tiny panties.

Heard him swallow.

His minty breath fanned out over my face as I dipped lower and swept my fingers through my slit. I lifted them within an inch of his mouth, then snatched them away as soon as he opened, and painted my nipples instead.

His hands grasped my ribs, his fingers digging in as he bent me backwards to latch onto my breast. With teeth and tongue and lips he tasted me.

Quickly hazing over, and wanting to push him further, I whispered, "Do you want to fuck me with your fingers, darling?"

He dropped to his knees, tore my panties down to my thighs, and pressed his face at their juncture.

I grasped onto his shoulders, my mouth falling open at the first sweep of his tongue.

With his thumbs, he spread my lips, exposing the little bundle of nerves that cried out for attention.

"Spread your legs," he ordered, his tone hard.

I opened my thighs as far as I could with my panties still half on.

He curled a finger inside me, then two, the sound of my arousal loud in the quiet of the room.

"It's obscene," I whispered. "How wet I am for you..."

Bounding to his feet, he pulled the straps of my bra down. "Take your arms out," he demanded.

The harshness of his voice sent a shiver down my spine.

Spinning me to face the bed, he pushed me forward until both my hands and knees met the mattress.

Over his rasping breath, I heard his belt hit the floor followed by the sound of his zipper.

"So dirty, isn't it, darling? Me naked and you fully dressed..."

"Minty," he warned. He knelt on the bed behind me. The cool fabric of his pants slid along my thighs.

"You want me to soak your pants. You want my sweetness on your pants the same way you want to watch your cum leak out and drip down my thighs..."

Hauling my hips up further, he growled, "We need to talk about fucking limits."

He notched himself at my entrance and drove inside.

I gasped at the intrusion, his urgency stealing my breath, and he plowed into me again.

"Hold on," I gasped, my body recoiling from the pain. "I need to adjust."

His thighs shook against the back of mine as his fingertips dug into the soft flesh of my hips. Leaning over me, he dragged his tongue along my spine and pressed a kiss to the nape of my neck.

Rocking against him, I urged my body to give way to allow him deeper.

"Ah," I breathed out in relief, feeling my body soften, then whispered throatily. "Go ahead, baby. Feed me that cock."

"Fuuuckkk..." Palm between my shoulder blades, he pushed my chest down to the mattress and groaned. "Finger to your clit, my baby."

Circling my clit, I clung to the edge as he filled me deeply, rolling his hips.

My thighs quivered.

His hands shook.

"Fucking come, Minty." He pressed his thumb against my ass and my pussy convulsed around him.

"Thank, fuck." He drove into me twice more, his dick swelling beautifully within my walls, pulsing his release deep inside me.

Stilling, his hands gentle, he trailed kisses down my boneless spine as he pulled out. One hand remained splayed against my back holding me down as he stood behind me, watching. His orgasm leaking from my body elicited a satisfied rumble from his chest. With one finger, he scooped his cum and pushed it back inside me.

A claiming.

His palms caressed the curve of my ass then gently cupped my hips. He turned my body, urging me onto my side before curling up to face me, his knees butting mine.

"You okay?" he asked gruffly.

"I'm good, baby." I smiled into his eyes.

He cupped my cheek, and my smile turned into a grin.

His eyes snapped up to mine, a bemused look on his face. "What's so funny?"

I shrugged, my laugh escaping. "Fucking limits?"

He snorted and pinched my chin, his eyes alight, dimples on display. "Thou shalt not makest a mockery of thy lover."

Chapter 20 - Drivetrain

<u>Minty</u>

Junie picked me up shortly after eight on Saturday to go watch Lucky and Lenny play. Wanting a redo of the previous week, I invited Amber and Ruby, and they met us there.

Ruby found a willing dance partner in Junie while Amber and I sat at the table Lucky reserved for us, knees bouncing to the music.

As soon as we settled in, he found me and flashed his dimples.

Amber chuckled. "Dimples: the devil's mark."

She would know. Her husband Gus was blessed with a deep dimple on one side, and he knew how to use it.

I loved music. The louder the better. Listening to live music pushed it to a wholly different level. It was the difference between watching a game on tv or cheering in the stands. Waves of energy bouncing off the people around me intensified the sensuality. The music rolled over me and through me, taking me out of my mind and into my body.

Lucky's hands, Barrett's voice, Lenny's beat, Lucky's freaking hands.

Those calloused fingers.

As if it were happening again, I felt them sweep the inside of my thigh, scooping himself up and pushing it back inside me.

I'd never let a man come inside me before.

I involuntarily shuddered at the remembrance of the erotic intimacy.

It scared me, especially knowing the obstacles between us and any kind of forever. But I'd watched Amber struggle with her own abandonment trauma, and years of therapy enabled me to identify it in myself. I refused to let it interfere.

Barrett announced the break. Lucky said something to him while Lenny sidled up alongside and clapped him on the back, then all three stepped down from the stage.

Barrett nodded a brief thanks and the seas parted for his massive frame.

Lenny smiled, his eyes scanning above their heads looking for his tiny fiancée.

Lucky jumped down, eyes on me, and the women closed around him. He smiled and nodded, his dimples flashing, then shook his head a couple of times before extricating himself from their grasp.

Sharp prickles of jealousy wounded my pride, and I sharply berated myself.

My claim on him was temporary.

Like a beloved library book.

Or a kindle unlimited book boyfriend, mine to enjoy for a little while before we both moved on.

It made me sadder than I wanted to admit.

I watched as Lucky loped across the bar, making his way to me, and my heart smiled.

"Hello, ladies," Barrett dropped down in one of the chairs before turning to Amber and extending his hand. "I'm Barrett. I'm married to Minty's friend, Willa."

Amber shook his hand. "Amber. I think you helped my husband, Gus, move a few things from my condo back to our house a few months back."

Barrett's teeth flashed in his beard. "Gus? You're married to Gus? Love that guy. We work out together at BOXXX sometimes."

"Yes, that's right," Amber agreed. "You must know Vander, too, then?"

Barrett laughed. "Everybody knows Vander."

Ruby stuck her hand out toward Barrett with a grin. "I'm Ruby, Vander's better half."

"Ah, yes. I've heard good things."

At that point, Lucky barreled down on me, scooping me out of my chair and depositing me on his lap with his arms tight around my waist. "I'm all sweaty and now you're all dirty," he murmured in my ear.

I sat stiffly in his arms, feeling all kinds of unworthy and unmatched. Looking briefly at the beauties who watched him walk away, I caught their questioning looks. I didn't blame them. I questioned, too.

He ran his palm firmly down my back, easing me against his chest, even as he turned to Amber. "I'm Lucky."

Looking pointedly at my ass on his lap, she asserted, "You certainly are."

"Don't worry," he replied, staring her straight in the eye. "I'm aware."

"Uhh," I stuttered, giving Amber the stink eye before drawing his attention away. "This is Ruby."

"Good to meet you, Lucky. I've heard mostly good things," she chirped.

Lucky looked momentarily taken aback until Barrett chuckled, telling him, "That's Vander's wife."

Lucky laughed, and Ruby scowled. "Do you guys gossip about us at BOXXX?"

BOXXX was a private gym Gus and Vander attended with some of the other husbands. I wondered if Lucky went there, his next statement answered that question and I marveled at the intersections in all our lives.

Lucky waved away her concerns. "No, but anybody who can stand up to Vander has got to be a bit of a ballbuster. Like Junie, here," he teased.

"My balls are in perfectly good hands," Lenny protested.

"Yes, and if you want them to stay that way you'll mind your step," Junie quipped, earning a delighted look from Ruby.

Our server greeted all the guys by name, dropping waters and a few beers on the table.

"Where's Bax?"

"He's hanging out in the back. That guy makes me look sociable," Barrett grumbled.

By the end of the break, Lucky succeeded in completely charming Amber and Ruby, convincing them to bring Gus and Vander out to a show before the end of the summer.

Patting me on the ass to get me off his lap, he stood, cupped my face in his hands, and kissed the tip of my nose. "Lenny's going with Junie after this, and you're coming with me. We can stay at your place if you want. I packed an overnight bag. Or we can drop by your place to pick up your stuff and you can stay at mine. But I want to wake up with you tomorrow morning."

My mouth fell open.

He laughed as he pressed a finger beneath my chin and gently closed it. "You'll be okay."

I watched him as he headed back to the stage but turned away before he walked through the beehive.

"Things are good?" Amber asked as soon as he left the table.

"Very. For now, at least."

A sleepover? We've never had a sleepover.

Her sharp eyes pinned me. "Why just for now?"

"I'm not sure," I admitted. *Is a sleepover moving too far into non-expiration date territory?* "I've never let a man get as close to me as he has. And we have an expiration date. I'm just not sure I'm going to escape unscathed."

"An expiration date you insisted on," she reminded me.

"For good reason," I retorted.

I can let him come inside me with no condom but can't wake up with him in the morning? How does that make sense?

"You sure about that? Remember what we decided? Rows to hoe, mountains to climb, and all that? Unmaking decisions that no longer served us?"

After a particularly sauced Bookstagram night, back when Ruby and Amber were working through their issues with their men, we all admitted we had made decisions meant to protect which in reality were only hurting us.

"It's a big mountain, Amber. The age difference, my OCD, his child..." I petered off.

I was only starting to get comfortable having him in my home. Why does that seem like a greater intimacy than having him bare inside me?

"I want to understand your hesitations. I'm trying to understand, but I feel like I'm missing pieces of the puzzle."

So do I.

Barrett welcomed everybody back from the break.

You want to fuck him.

For fuck's sake. I waved it away, disgusted with myself.

The music kicked off, thankfully stalling any further conversation, washing over me and taking me out of my mind.

A couple of hours later, I flopped back on my bed, breathless. "I am never missing another show," I declared.

Lucky laughed and reached over and squeezed my breast. "We're all pretty ramped up after playing. It's one of the perks of having a boyfriend in a band."

"Oh, yeah?" I smirked. "So, you're my boyfriend?"

"Well, what else would you call me? Hot man-candy?"

"That might work. How about boy-toy?"

His eyes bugged out. "Boy toy? Uh, no. Mighty man meat, maybe, but not boy toy."

"Man meat," I scoffed. "How about life-size vibrator?"

He splayed his hand over his chest. "I'm feeling objectified! I could get on board with purveyor of pleasure or commander of orgasms. I'll be your COO or your POP."

"Pop? How about I just call you 'daddy'?"

"Well, I don't know," he pretended to ponder as he rolled into me and tucked me beneath him. "Are you going to be a good girl?"

"Well, I don't know," I mimicked. "Do you want a good girl?"

He tucked his face into my neck and ran his tongue along the line of my throat. "Not in this room."

Lucky

I can't believe I ever believed her face to be impassive when it was anything but.

Tonight alone, the barrage of emotions included jealousy, insecurity, shame, embarrassment, joy, and now pleasure.

Deeply flushed with it.

Her hair spread out over her pillow.

Mouth soft and gasping, gasping my fucking name.

She could call me whatever the hell she wanted so long as I was the only one between her thighs.

I drove inside her slowly, drawing it out, waiting for the telltale sounds that told me she was close.

Temporary wasn't going to be enough.

"Lucky," she gasped, running her hands down to my ass and digging in. "Please, baby."

"Please what?"

"Go hard."

"Are you going to be a good girl?"

"Most of the time," she mewled.

I maintained my steady pace, sweat beading my brow.

I recalled her face when I stepped off the stage. I'd slept with a few of those women. I knew what we offered to each other. Minty had nothing to worry about. And suddenly I wanted to offer her everything.

"And when I want you to be bad?"

"I'll do that, too. Oh, God! Please, Lucky!"

"And if I want you to be bad only with me?" I pushed.

"Sure," she nodded, her neck arching.

"I'm going to hold you to that," I promised. I reached under her leg, pulling it up to rest in the crook of my elbow to get the angle I sought, and picked up my pace.

"Yes," she hissed, her palms flexing into my chest.

I watched her come undone, then emptied my seed inside her. The knowledge that we'd never make a child together caused a momentary pang of loss, but it was a loss that paled in comparison to losing her.

Holding my weight up on my elbows, I stared down into her sated face.

"Mr. Incredible," I declared.

"I was thinking Captain Cock," she murmured back.

I dropped my laughing mouth down onto hers, murmuring against her smiling lips. "I'll take it. Captain for short."

"Done."

Chapter 21 – Butt-Smacking

<u>Lucky</u>

Early Sunday morning, the bed shifted as Minty eased out. I snaked out an arm and hauled her back in.

"Oh no," she said with mock horror. "You're not one of those types that sleep in till all hours wasting the day away?"

"Nope, but I'm also not somebody who has had the privilege of waking up beside you and I don't want to rush through it."

She relaxed back and turned into my arms. Throwing one leg over mine, she nuzzled into my chest.

"You smell so good," she murmured.

"Definitely a point in my favor," I agreed, and felt the soft vibrations of her chuckle.

"I had fun last night. I'd kind of forgotten about watching you play the first time because of my misunderstanding, but last night I was much more relaxed. I love the music. You have fun up there?"

"I do." I cupped my hand around her shoulder and leaned in to rest my temple on the top of her head. "I love playing guitar all the time, at home, for Brayleigh, for my family when we have get-togethers, for Willa and Barrett at their wedding, I love it all. But being on stage, with my friends, you feed off each other's energy and the energy of the crowd. Was it not like that for you?"

"Not like that. Not like I felt last night. It's indescribable. Maybe because we didn't have the friendship you guys have. I wonder what it must be like for the huge rockstars."

"I imagine it's a huge adrenalin rush. But the thing is, the adrenalin drop is real, and I can understand how their lives spin so out of control."

"Did you ever want that?"

I shrugged. "Sure. I also wanted to be a professional baseball player, a secret agent, and Batman. It was never something truly within my reach. What I have now is fun, it's healthy, and it doesn't take over my whole life. I don't want more." Except for you, Minty, I added silently. "What about you? What are your dreams? Are they different from what they were when you were a kid?"

Her stillness told me I hit a nerve, but I wasn't going to let her off the hook. Finally, she sighed and melted back into me.

"I guess you could say I was a late bloomer in the dreams department. Around five or six years old, I developed some weird quirks. Instead of coming up with dreams of the future, I counted, balanced, and argued against the nightmares conjured by my brain."

Her voice was soft but almost monotone. As if she'd either told the story a thousand times before or recited it by rote, but more likely, knowing how close she held her cards, the rawness of the wound still burned. Bringing it into the light took work. I remained silent in the face of this unexpected gift and waited for her to continue.

"My birthparents dealt with them and me in an unhealthy way. The nurse at school noticed the bruises."

My body jerked involuntarily, and I drew her closer, pressing my lips into her hair. I hated that for her. My mind flitted to some of my students. I knew her. I'd met her thousands of times.

"Children's Aid apprehended me and placed me in a foster home. At age eleven, they considered me too old for adoption, and my birth family didn't want to completely give up their parental rights."

"Jesus Christ."

She rubbed her hand over my chest in a soothing circle. Comforting me. For fuck's sake.

"It was the best thing that ever could have happened. I stayed with them until I aged out of the system at age eighteen. On my birthday they took me to their lawyer and added me to their will as their sole beneficiary." She sniffed and her voice shook. "They offered me their last name, and I took it. They officially made me their own at the very first opportunity."

"Did they love you the way you deserved?"

"Oh, yes." She wiped beneath her eyes. "They got me the help I needed, beginning with a diagnosis. My mom homeschooled me until I was able to go back to school. My dad taught me to paint. I loved them. I love them still."

"I'm so sorry for your loss, baby," I murmured. "I'm glad you had them."

"Me too." Her breath released with a shudder. "So, I spent most of my time either combatting OCD or working through therapy to neutralize it as well as come to terms with the rejection from my birth family. Dreams, for a long time, were a luxury I could not afford."

"When did things begin to get better?"

"The day I moved in with them, but progress came slowly. They put me through university. I have a degree in engineering."

I squeezed her tight. "Smarty-pants."

She shrugged again. "Yes, but so stressful. I lasted two years working in that industry before I could no longer hack it. My parents passing in combination with the job stress pushed me overboard. Stress is not good for OCD."

"I can imagine," I replied. I couldn't, not really. But I wanted to.

"I got back into art and music. Taught piano and singing for a little while. Eventually I started working with Willa and Junie. My parents left me with full financial freedom so I could afford to, well, dream."

Minty

Talking about my parents eased the ache of missing them. Explaining what they gave to me, expressing how much it meant to me, filled a tiny bit of the hole they left when they died.

"What's it like?"

"What? OCD?"

"Yeah. What does it sound like in your head?"

I looked inwards. "It's difficult to isolate it from my regular thoughts."

How to explain something that was simply part of my normal. If I asked him to explain how his brain was different from mine, he wouldn't be able to do it. Did we even see colors the same way? Hear music the same way? Maybe my green was closer to his yellow. I barely knew what it was like to not have OCD. Then, I brightened with the perfect example.

"You know in the summer, at night, when you're in bed and you think the whole house is quiet and suddenly the air conditioning shuts off?"

I tilted my head back to look at him.

"Yes." His grey eyes scanned my face, listening intently.

"It's like that. I notice the quiet. I notice when it's not there."

He tilted his head, looking almost relieved. "So, it's just background. White noise."

I winced. "Most of it."

His eyes tightened on my face. "What parts aren't?"

My heart galloped once.

Hard.

I forced myself to relax and smiled.

"That's a story for another time."

After breakfast, we parted ways, him to meet Hope to take Brayleigh, and me to the craft fair.

"Will you, uh, be spending time with Hope?"

His gaze sharpened on my face. "Probably for a little while. Minty..."

I waved him away. "Well, say 'hi' for me and I'll maybe see you later, okay?"

For me to be jealous of Hope made no sense. If anyone was the interloper here, it was me.

"Sure," he responded easily. "I'll say hi for you. After all, I need to tell her my new status as your hot man-candy, right?"

I huffed out a laugh. "Captain. Captain Cock."

He grinned. "If I tell her that, she'll puke. She might even punch me." His face twisted with disgust. "Or she could tell me about her own sexual exploits, and I just can't."

"It bothers you?"

"Yes! In the same way it would bother me if my sister, any of them, told me any of that stuff."

"You're sure it's not jealousy? I don't want to be in the way of something good for you." My stomach clenched.

"Minty," he warned. "You know how I would feel if you told me something about one of your sexual exploits?" His mouth twisted into a snarl. "Enraged." Grasping me firmly by my shoulders, he pulled me around to face him. "I can't talk about this. Suffice it to say that my feelings for you are nowhere near sisterly." He turned his face away. "Fuck. Tell me you're a virgin," he laughed, pained.

"Now, now, Captain," I teased. "You know I'm not. I can still feel you from last night."

"That's your own fault," he retorted. "Lucky, fuck me harder. Please, Lucky. I need your massive cock, Lucky," he teased in a falsetto voice, earning himself a smack and my laughter.

One hand curved around my hip to press against the small of my back while his other wrapped around the front of my throat, his index finger and thumb pushing the hinge of my jaw, tipping my face up.

His eyes crinkled with laughter. "I'll see you at my place around five. We'll cook and watch a movie and play with Brayleigh. If your pussy has recovered from my ginormous love rocket by then, I'll do my best to put you out of commission until at least Wednesday."

His words, by turns warming my heart and tickling my funny bone, stayed with me throughout the long, hot day. I couldn't wait to get back to him.

By the time I walked off the lot where the craft fair was held, I'd sold another fourteen commissions. At this rate, I wasn't going to make it through the season.

I supposed it wouldn't be a bad thing. I could take a couple of weekends off, give my table to Bex and Willa if they wanted it for the day. Even if they didn't, it didn't mean I had to do it.

That's wasteful.

So, better that I make myself stressed and exhausted?

You're wasting. Someone else would have loved to have that table. You're taking someone else's spot. That's inconsiderate.

Taking a deep breath, I smiled and packed all my paraphernalia into the back of my car and headed to Lucky's.

I heard Brayleigh long before I saw her.

Every few seconds, she screamed, a godawful blood-curdling sound that frayed my nerves, accompanied by raucous laughter. What the hell was going on?

I knocked on the door, fully knowing there was no way Lucky would hear it, then let myself in.

I rounded the kitchen to find Hope and Lucky collapsed on the couch, turned toward each other, their eyes flitting back and forth between the tv and their daughter.

"Press play, press play," Lucky wheezed. "One more time."

You are a homewrecker. This is a sin.

"You ready, Tweetie?" Hope's voice was throaty with laughter.

The tv screen sprang to life, a black and white YouTube video of Twist and Shout by the Beatles sounding over the speakers. Brayleigh began to dance. After about twenty seconds, she screamed along with the vocals, and Lucky and Hope clung to each other, their two perfect blond heads pressed together, laughing.

I stood frozen at the entrance, halfway between the kitchen and the living room. Unable to move forward, unwilling to go back.

"Okay, enough," Hope finally said. "She's going to hurt her voice." She stood. "I'm going to boogie before your girlfriend gets here," she teased with a shimmy of her hips in Lucky's face.

He smacked her ass, laughing. "Get your fat arse out of my face."

"Don't say 'fat arse', you want Brayleigh to grow up with a complex?"

"Never. Get your skinny arse out of my face. Better?"

"Better." She leaned down to kiss his cheek. It was on her way back up that she caught sight of my face, and hers fell.

Lucky looked up at her. "What? What is it?" He turned. As soon as he saw me his entire face lit up. "Baby! You have to see this!" He turned to Hope holding up one finger. "One more time? One more time so Minty can see."

I cleared my throat. "I've seen quite enough."

Hope had not moved throughout the entire exchange. She opened her mouth to speak, and I pinned her with my gaze. "Do not."

Her mouth snapped shut.

Lucky spun round and took me in fully for the first time. "What's wrong?" He took two steps toward me, but I held up my hand.

My voice dripped with ice. "If you have to ask, there are not enough letters in the English language to spell it out for you."

I spun on my heel, ready to leave, when I heard a jubilant cry, "Sparky!"

I jerked to a stop, unable and unwilling to ignore the little one. I drew in a deep breath before turning to greet her. "Hello, dolly." Startled by the endearment that slipped from my lips, I retreated a step.

Brayleigh held up a stuffed penguin. "Mine Pinwin."

"Yes, darling," I murmured. "That's yours."

"Mine Sparky," she pointed to my necklace.

"No," Lucky interjected harshly. "That's Daddy's."

I looked up to find Hope twisting her hands together and Lucky glaring at me furiously.

"Now, now, Daddy. You can't have every sparkly thing you set your eye on," I said softly.

My furious gaze swung to Hope, and I softened. It wasn't her fault. In truth, I had encroached on her territory. "I wish you all the best."

I backed up quickly and spun toward the door. I had my hand on the knob when Lucky's hand smacked flat against the door and he pressed his long, hard body behind mine.

"Step back," I demanded quietly.

He dropped his lips to my ear. "Minty, please. You misinterpreted."

"Did I?"

"Yes." His body vibrated with his nod.

His chest against *my* shoulders, his abdomen against *my* back, his strong arms caging *me* against the door, his sweet voice in *my* ear, but this man wasn't mine. Not even temporarily. Yet I couldn't help myself from leaning back against him.

"Let's see, then," I replied smoothly. "Were you sitting with your arms around each other on the couch laughing?"

"Yes, but-"

"Did she stand up and shake her ass in your face?" I continued politely but firmly.

"Yes," he gritted out. "But it didn't mean-"

"Did you or did you not slap your hand on the aforementioned ass?"

His jaw clicked with the force of his grinding teeth. He leaned into me harder. "Please..."

"You don't want to answer that one?" I questioned lightly. My shoulders drooped and I rested my forehead against the door, losing the ability to lock down my disappointment. "Please step back." I sounded defeated.

"Okay. I'll step back. For now," he answered resignedly. His hands slid down the door while he bent and pressed his lips to the nape of my neck for a pregnant moment.

God help me, I soaked it in, closing my eyes to imprint it in my memory.

He moved away, taking his warmth with him.

I opened the door and walked briskly to my car.

He stood on the porch, his hands on his hips, watching me.

I raised my hand in goodbye. We would never be friends, but we could be civil. We would have to be.

Chapter 22 – Unhinged

<u>Lucky</u>

"She's psychotic. Fucking unhinged," I fumed.

"Hmm," Hope hummed.

"Come on," I griped. "I've told her in no uncertain terms there's nothing between us."

"Except for that." Hope pointed to Brayleigh. "And the fact that we love each other. That we enjoy spending time together." She sighed and looked out the back window. "Honestly? I don't know how anyone could put up with it."

"What are you talking about?" My whole life I'd been surrounded by women and my understanding of them was still less than rudimentary.

Hope turned her cornflower blue eyes on me, more serious than I'd ever seen her. "Do you know how many men I've gone through because they can't accept our friendship?" She laughed but it wasn't a happy sound.

"You have?" This surprised me. I knew she dated; I just didn't think she'd found anyone worth pursuing long-term. Which was true if they couldn't get past her having a male friend. Who fucked her. Got her pregnant. And still hung out with her on a weekly basis. "Fuck."

I sat down on the couch and dropped my head into my hands.

"Da-da?"

I looked up and smiled. "Hey, Tweetie-bird. Come give Dad a hug."

I helped her climb up into my lap where she stood and dug her little fingers into the back of my neck. "Mine Da-da?"

"Yes, Tweetie. Yours."

"Do you want to go after her?" Hope asked, twisting her hands together.

"No. Not right now. I need to think things through." My stomach dropping to the floor told me like nothing else that I teetered on the edge of a mistake, but I could see no way forward at this point.

Brayleigh settled in and pointed at the tv, asking for her favorite show. I flicked it on, and she curled against me.

"I'm going to go into the kitchen and make us something to eat," Hope said softly. "And then I think we should talk."

By the time Hope called me to bring Brayleigh in to eat, I was chomping at the bit to get to Minty.

"I can see you want to go. I get it. But I need you to put the brakes on for just a few minutes." She held her hands out to placate me. "If we ever hope to find love, we need to put up some boundaries in our relationship."

"I treat you like I'm your brother," I sighed.

"Yes. You do. And that's been fine up until this point. But now I think you must treat me like an attractive woman with whom you have a child and an amicable relationship." She inhaled deeply. "You are my best friend. You may as well be gay. I may as well be gay for all the romantic feelings between us, but that's not what the world sees. And that's not what Minty sees. How would Minty feel if you slapped my ass in front of her friends?"

I pictured them, Barrett, Lenny, Junie, Willa, Mara, Bex... frig, Amber would castrate me. "I see what you mean."

"Lucky," Hope whispered. "She'd be humiliated. She was humiliated. And if I was dating someone? Well, let me put it to you like this. If Lenny or Barrett patted Minty on the ass? Would you be okay with that?"

I saw red. "No fucking way."

"So, who's unhinged? I don't think it's Minty."

A single tear slid down her cheek.

I scooped it with my thumb. "Why the tear?"

"Because this is the end of our friendship as we've known it. Because Lucky, even though we don't have sex, even though we don't live together, in every other way that matters we are partners. You can only have one partner. And you've just found yours."

I fed the baby and ate what I could, my mind lost in Hope's words. She was right. But change was hard.

So was loss.

Hope broke the silence. "I'm going to stay here until you get back, and then I'm going to go home. Or, if you want, I can take Brayleigh home with me."

"No, please don't do that. Can you stay for a couple of hours? I need to see if she'll talk to me, but I don't want to disrupt Brayleigh's routine."

Minty

I blasted my music and lay back on my bed. The nice thing about living above the stores is that after hours there was nobody to complain about the noise.

1-2-3-4-5-1-2-3-4-5-1-2-3-4-5-1-2-3-4-5

There was just nobody there at all.

1-2-3-4-5-1-2-3-4-5-1-2-3-4-5-1-2-3-4-5

I turned it up another couple of notches, but it still wasn't enough.

I pulled my headphones out of the drawer beside my bed and settled them over my ears to block out the world. It hurt more than it should for the short time we were together. I let him in too quickly, much deeper than I should have.

I turned up the music, allowing it to counterbalance the chaos, to buffer the whirling tornado of emotions inside me that threatened to sweep my feet from under me.

The tangle of blankets on my bed, that he'd held me in just that morning, wrapped around my legs.

I ripped the headphones off my head. Grabbing my pillow and a blanket, I went out to the living room and curled up on the window seat.

This was my life. Alone behind the glass, looking out on the rest of the world.

Even so, I was fortunate. I'd been loved. There were good people and unfathomable love in my life. Financially free, I could pursue my art or nothing at all. My time was my own. Truly, I was blessed.

It was foolish of me to give so much of myself so soon. Obviously, Lucky and Hope had something special, even if he could not yet see it. Hopefully, he would.

Because if you have that kind of love, you should hang onto it. Some people never find it. That is the cold, hard truth.

My breath released with a sob.

I had much to be grateful for, but just for tonight, I would allow myself to cry for what I yearned for.

With my legs pulled up tight, I wrapped my arms around my shins and rested my forehead on my bent knees.

I drifted off only to be awakened by knocking at my door.

Jumping to my feet, I ran to the alarm panel. Had I set it? I checked. It was armed.

Are you sure?

I looked again. I looked hard. Armed. A-R-M-E-D. Armed. Disoriented from sleep and logy from crying, my brain struggled to make sense of the world around me.

Are you sure?

I took a deep breath.

Don't check.

The risk is too great.

The pounding at the door began again.

I checked the panel.

Armed.

I looked out the window.

Bus.

Safe travels.

Pounding at the door.

I crossed to the door and slid down to the floor, my back pressed against it, lending my weight to keep it closed.

"Minty?" A man's voice yelled through the door.

My heart jumped to my throat, and I screamed.

"Minty! Are you okay? Open the goddamn door!"

I covered my pounding heart with the palm of my hand and pushed myself to my feet. My hand shook. I turned the knob and pulled open the door.

Immediately, the screech of the alarm went off. I stumbled backwards and slapped my hands over my ears. "Oh, God!"

Crossing to the alarm panel, I punched in the code. Got it wrong. My whole body shook.

Lucky aligned his body behind me, his arm wrapped around my waist, his mouth at my ear. "What's the code, baby? I'll put it in."

I gave it to him, watched him punch it in, and sagged back against his chest as silence reigned once more.

He turned me to the side, then bent and scooped me up in his arms.

I pushed against his chest. "I'm okay."

"You will be," he replied, carrying me down to my bedroom.

He lay me on my bed where I stared up warily at his drawn face. Sighing, he dropped down to sit on the side of the bed.

I sighed, my breath catching. "It's okay, Lucky."

"What's okay?" he asked gruffly.

The sting of tears threatened. "You and Hope. You have something special. It's good if you recognize that."

Pulling in a deep breath, he slanted a sideways look at me then shook his head.

"You exasperate me," he huffed. "You're right. We do have something special. We always have, and Brayleigh didn't change that. Or alter it."

I swallowed my tears. What the hell did he want from me? He could save the long explanation; I didn't need it.

"Hope and I talked. Rather, Hope talked, and I listened. She told me that no matter who she has dated, none of them could get past her and I being friends." He picked up the edge of the sheet and covered me with it. "I told her I thought it was ridiculous. She asked me how I'd feel if Barrett or Lenny smacked you on the ass." He met my eyes. "I saw red." His mouth quirked up on one side. "I couldn't see it as a problem because I truly have no romantic feelings toward that girl."

"Would you smack your sister on the ass?" I challenged quietly.

"Yes." He nodded emphatically. "I would. I have. I do. And they do the same. We're a butt-smacking kind of family," he joked softly.

"She's not your sister," I whispered.

His mouth tightened. "I get that. She gets that. Hope and I are going to make some changes. There's never been anyone else's feelings to consider before you. But to me, Hope is just like my sister. Can you get that?"

I nodded slowly, painfully aware of the abyss that awaited me if I ventured deeper.

He released his breath. "Okay. That's good. Do you get that I do not see you in remotely the same way?"

I looked down. Agreeing to this seemed to be stepping back into the ring I'd just been knocked out of.

"Minty?" he prodded.

I nodded.

He leaned forward and pressed his forehead to mine. "No more butt smacking. I'll treat her the way I'd want Barrett and Lenny to treat you. But baby...she is my best friend. I don't want to lose her. I will if it means the trade-off is keeping you, but I'm begging you not to ask it of me."

The tears I'd successfully held back up until that point, released with a sob.

Bending over me, he pulled me into his arms and lay down beside me. "I'm sorry, baby. I'm so sorry. I would never hurt you. Never."

He rocked me against him while I cried, his head bent over mine, his arms tight.

How did I fall so far so fast? And how would I ever climb back out? "Oh my gosh," I moaned. "I'll pull it together. I'm sorry."

"You have nothing to be sorry about. But, Minty, I've never done this relationship thing before. I don't want to be worrying that you're going to walk away every time I fuck up."

I nodded. "I know. I get it. It's not fair. I'm sorry."

He scoffed. "Enough with the sorrys. We're okay." He paused. "We are okay, aren't we?"

I nodded against his chest. "Yes. We're okay." I drew in a shuddering breath. "I'll apologize to Hope."

"You don't owe Hope an apology. She knows that. She pointed it out. Don't be surprised if she apologizes to you."

"Not really looking forward to seeing her to be honest." He went still. "I'd never give you that ultimatum, Lucky. Don't worry about that. I just need a bit of space between her and me right now."

"No problem." He eased me back down onto the bed, and I turned to reach for a tissue.

"I'll be right back." He went into my bathroom and rifled around in my makeup basket, returning with two makeup remover pads.

My laugh sounded watery. "What are you doing?"

He sat down, pulling the pads away from my reaching hand. "You do not want to see this." He drew a circle in the air around my face.

My mouth gaped open at his audacity.

He nodded, his eyes twinkling. "Now be a good girl and close your eyes so I can relieve you of the raccoon mask."

I laughed again. It sounded better that time.

Gently, he swabbed the pad around my eyes. "There. I think it's safe for you to go and finish up. Then you need to come and lock your door because I have to get back to Brayleigh so Hope can go home."

I took a shaky breath and swung my legs off the bed. Looking at myself in the mirror, I admitted he was right to get a jump on things. Red, blotchy, and swollen. How much worse it must have been with mascara running down my face.

I quickly finished the job he started and slapped on my night cream before following him to the door.

"Minty." He dragged the back of his knuckles down the side of my face. "I want you to come and meet my family. We're having a barbecue for Canada Day in a couple of weeks. I already told my sisters you might be coming. They're very excited to meet you. They'll probably be obnoxious." He stopped talking and stared down at me. With his thumb he smoothed a line over my eyebrow and whispered, "Come. You're the first girl I've brought home since prom."

I laughed and turned my cheek into his palm.

"You think I'm joking," he chuckled. "Will you come?"

I cleared my throat. "Yes. I'll come. Um, will Hope be there?"

His brow furrowed. "She usually comes. I can ask her not to."

I shook my head. "It doesn't matter. I'll come."

His eyes searching mine once more, he leaned in and brushed a gentle kiss on my trembling lips. He opened his mouth as if to say something, then seemed to change his mind and straightened up.

"Lock the door, baby."

"Goodnight, Captain."

He laughed as he made his way back down the stairs.

I went to bed and cuddled under the blankets we'd left in a tangle from our lovemaking the night before and dared to dream.

Chapter 23 – Boundaries

<u>Minty</u>

Monday morning, it all came together. The Board, the sponsors, and the funding. The initiative was to provide underwear. Anything else that came in the care package was a bonus, and there were a lot of bonuses.

Apparently, wealthy women found the indignity of not having underwear utterly appalling.

Which was good for us.

The only other time I'd seen something like this come together so quickly was related to a food scarcity program. And it was to that star we hitched our wagon.

With only two weeks left of school, I'd entertained more than a few doubts.

"You look," Junie cocked her head to the side, her sky-blue eyes flitting over my face with concern, "puffy."

I turned to offer her a reassuring smile. "Lucky and I had a misunderstanding. It's settled now."

Her gaze sharpened. "Is everything okay? Listen, Minty. I don't want you settling for less than you deserve." She shook her head, white-blond hair flying. "I know we warned you about him, and maybe we should have, maybe we shouldn't have, but don't take any shit, okay?"

I took a breath. "Junie, it's possible that the reason we had a misunderstanding is partially because I keep waiting for him to fuck up."

Her eyes widened at my use of the expletive. In general, I had to be pretty upset before I resorted to curse words.

"Thus far, he and I have had two fights, both of them due to me thinking he was being a dog, and both times I was wrong. It was an insult to him."

Junie opened her mouth to continue but I forestalled her with a raised hand.

"He has assured me that he will not hurt me, that he will be honest with me, and that we are exclusive. Now, saying all that, do you have any reason to believe he would lie?"

"No." She shook her head immediately. "He's a good guy."

My shoulders dropped and I rolled the tension from my neck. "Then let us assume going forward that he will be a good guy and not jerk me around."

'Yes, ma'am," Junie smiled softly. She spun around to her desk, then turned back. "I'm happy, you know. Happier for him, maybe," she winked, "but I'm happy for you, too. I'm sorry if my warnings contributed to your fights. It won't happen again."

"Thank you, beautiful."

I picked up my cell and tapped out a message to Lucky.

Several minutes later he responded with celebration emojis. In the next line he wrote, *You're the best. I cannot believe this is happening. You've made me so happy.* The third line contained more emojis.

"Junie, what does a tongue, a cat, water droplets, an eggplant, and a waterfall mean?"

Junie barked out a laugh. "It means he's going to lick your pussy until you come then fuck you so hard you explode."

"Oh!" I laughed. "I shouldn't have asked."

Junie lifted her coffee cup in a toast. "I'm glad you did." Turning back to her desk, she teased, "Somebody's in for a good night!"

The musical instruments were next on my list, but unfortunately, those would have to wait until next year.

Unless they were donated.

I sat up straight in my chair. Rich people loved to dabble in different hobbies. They picked things up and discarded them just as quickly. Relaxing back, I sent a brief email to Amber, then several more to the committee ladies who enjoyed dabbling in local charities in addition to their larger commitments.

These instruments would not be for the school, they'd go directly to the students. I could store them in the basement of the house. Have them refurbished, tuned, and ready to go.

There were bound to be a lot of flutes. Maybe those could go to the school.

My spine shot straight up. A wish list. Online. Students could fill them out, indicating where their interests lie. Cameras! Cameras were another luxury item often out of reach for many families.

I'd have to go through the parent committee. The committee would set up the program, but the donations could come from anywhere.

The girls at the house who were currently floating, this could be their project. I sat back in my chair. I wonder if they, too, could benefit from a program like this.

"Are you done?" Junie asked drily.

Startled, I swung my gaze to her amused face. "Pardon me?"

"You're thinking so loud it's hurting my ears." She laughed. "What's going on?"

I smiled widely, and Junie's face broke into a grin.

"Two pet projects I had for fundraising for George's school just came through!"

I went on to explain the issues, watched her face fall the same way mine did when I heard about the underwear, then told her about the measures we had come up with to fill in part of the gap.

"They are small things. Regretfully, embarrassingly small, but perhaps it is the little things that make a difference." I paused, knowing it was nowhere near enough. "A small difference."

"That's it," Junie declared. "I totally fucking want to be you when I grow up."

I laughed even as I studied her. "If I were you, beautiful, I'd never want to be anyone else."

Lucky

Usually, we met up on Wednesday for our midweek date night, but the drive to see her rode me hard.

I couldn't get her face out of my head. At my house when she shut down, then cut me down before she walked away, and worse, at her place, mottled and swollen from crying.

After this morning's text, the craving grew only worse.

Lucky: Come over tonight. I've got Brayleigh so I can't come to you.

Minty: You sure? Yesterday brought a lot of drama. Maybe we should take a few days?

Lucky: It's because of all the drama yesterday that I want to see you today.

Minty: I'm okay, Lucky. Truly.

Lucky: I'm not. Come over.

Minty: (happy face.)

Lucky: (tongue, cat, water droplets, eggplant, waterfall.)

There was a lengthy pause.

Minty: Oh my gosh, Lucky. I asked Junie what that meant!

Lucky: (hiding behind hands.)

Minty: (laughing face) See you at six.

Knowing I'd see her after work settled my nerves about the weekend, and the news about underwear-gate lifted my spirits.

Sasha dropped a card off on my desk on her way out the door. A Hallmark. $6.99. That's a lot of money for a kid like her.

"Fuck."

I nearly cried when I opened it.

By the time Minty arrived, I'd picked up Brayleigh from daycare, taken her to the park, dropped by the grocery store to pick up vegan sausage as well as pasta, three different types of sauce, and sour dough bread. I threw in cherry tomatoes, cucumber, bocconcini cheese and olives hoping that would satisfy her fixation on salad.

Cookies. I forgot cookies. I looked at Brayleigh, unsure if she could handle one more stop and determined she could not.

It irritated me that I didn't have cookies.

In all my years, I'd never felt so driven to provide for a woman. Even when Hope had the baby, staying with her simply struck me as the correct thing to do. I would have done it even if I wasn't Brayleigh's father.

But this drive to provide for Minty, to feed her, care for her, make her smile, please her, this came as a surprise.

I slapped my hand on the steering wheel. "Brayleigh? Uber eats. Uber eats is the solution and Bliss kitchen is the Holy Grail of desserts for Minty."

"Hi, Da," Brayleigh replied.

I smiled at her in the rearview mirror. "Hi, Tweetie. Daddy got you popsicles. You want a popsicle when we get home?"

A popsicle guaranteed twenty solid minutes in the highchair. Twenty minutes to chop vegetables, boil pasta, and fry sausage.

"Popsit, Da. Mine popsit."

"Yes, Tweetie-bird. Your popsicle."

Twenty minutes later, Minty knocked on the door while Brayleigh reclined shirtless in her highchair, her face and chest stained pink.

I rushed to open it and drew her immediately into my arms. Only then, with her head tucked under my chin, did the anxiety ease.

"Hello, sweetheart," I murmured.

Her hands came around my back, her fingers flexing on either side of my spine. She sighed, melted against me. "Hello, Captain."

I huffed out a laugh then pulled back, cupping my hands around her face. "It's good to see you. Did you have a good day?"

Her smile lit up the room. "I had a great day!"

"Before you tell me everything, order us dessert from Bliss Kitchen." I handed her my cell with the app open.

"I can get dessert, Lucky. You've already gotten dinner," she protested.

"Minty, I feel this overwhelming, caveman-like urge to feed you. So, if you don't want to be thrown over my shoulder and dragged off and fucked, make the order."

She held my gaze, a tiny smirk on her wide mouth. "With an ultimatum like that, you're making it really quite difficult to place the order."

"Alright. Tell you what. I'll caveman you after Brayleigh goes to sleep, if you make the order."

She bent her golden head to my phone, muttering, "Now, we're talking."

Over dinner, which we finished cooking together, Minty voiced her concerns.

"Lucky, I would never ask you to give up your friendship with Hope. Anyone can see your relationship is special."

I stilled, cognizant of the fact that her insecurities around other women, and Hope in particular, were at the root of each of our blow-ups. "I'm listening, baby."

"But I do have my own boundaries around the way I expect to be treated, and those are non-negotiable."

I crossed my arms on the table and held her eyes. "Hit me with it."

She swallowed, looked down at the table, and gave a little nod as if to encourage herself. "I expect that your hands do not land on any other woman unless it's a handshake, a quick hug, or your sister."

I nodded. "Agreed."

"If you and Hope are in the habit of kissing each other on the cheek, I can accept that. I don't like it, but I can accept it."

I cleared my throat. "We're not. She only kissed me last time because I told her about you and how I feel about you. She was happy for me."

Minty's cool gaze searched my face. "And how do you feel about me?"

I jerked my chin up. "Finish telling me your boundaries and then I'll tell you mine."

"Um," she hesitated. "Don't be so nicey-nice to the women at the bars. Barrett plows right through, so does Lenny. I don't want to be sitting there with Barrett and Lenny, Junie and eventually Willa, while you smile and wink and nod and flash your dimples at your fan club."

"Done. Anything else?"

She eased back in her chair. "No. I think that's it."

I sat forward. "Alright, here's mine. No expiration date. We take it one day at a time and see how far we can go."

"Uhh…"

I rubbed the heel of my palm against my chest. Cleared my throat. "It's, um, non-negotiable."

"Non-negotiable?" she whispered.

"Yeah, baby. I'm getting in too deep. If you're going to cut me loose, you gotta do it now."

Brayleigh leaned across the table of her highchair and lay her grubby little hand on Minty's bracelet. "Sparky. Mine sparky?"

Minty moved her arm closer so Brayleigh could play with the shiny beads. "No, dolly," Minty murmured, aiming a half smile in my direction. "I'm Daddy's sparkly."

Chapter 24 – A Study in Contrasts

<u>Minty</u>

Once Brayleigh fell asleep, I fully expected Lucky to toss me over his shoulder and charge into the bedroom.

Instead, he linked his long, calloused fingers through mine and led me upstairs. Closing the bedroom door, he stood before me and lifted my hand to his lips, kissing the tip of each finger.

1-2-3-4-5-1-2-3-4-5

Each finger on my other hand received the same treatment.

I counted it off, twice, just the same. Same for both hands, the same weight of numbers, 6, on each finger. 1 and 5, 2 and 4, 3 and 3, 4 and 2, 5 and 1, and repeat.

He turned my hand over in his and pressed his lips to the inside of my wrist, then slowly made his way up my arm until his lips met the strap of my sundress.

Slipping it off my shoulder, he kissed the naked skin beneath.

I turned my face toward him, closed my eyes and inhaled, breathing in the smell of his shampoo, his aftershave, the warm fragrance of his skin.

Encircling my waist, he ran his hands up my spine before dragging them back down again, the zipper pinched between his talented fingers. Piece by piece, my clothing and his hit the floor.

Laying me out on the bed, he immediately covered me with his long, lean, hard, body. Braced on his elbows, he stared down into my face, his thumbs gently caressing my cheekbones, the tips of his fingers grazing my temples, his mouth soft, eyes serious.

His eyes spoke volumes.

"Lucky," I whispered.

I'd heard the old saying, 'It's the quiet ones you gotta watch', but my Lord, when the mouthy ones, the jokesters, the charismatic entertainers, the ones who command the center of attention, when those ones go quiet, it's like the whole world comes to a standstill.

"Baby." He touched the tip of his nose to mine. "This is no longer casual. You get that, right?"

"Yes."

He spread my thighs with his, notched himself at my entrance and slowly entered me, pushing deep.

The exquisite pleasure of being filled. His hips rolling. His sweet mouth dropping gentle kisses on mine, his fingers gently tangling in my hair.

I cupped one hand around his ribs and lay the other over his heart. My eyelids slowly closed, cutting off one sense to heighten the others.

The tremor in his limbs, the soft touch of his lips, the gentle fan of his breath.

The heat of his skin, the steel of his body, the rasp of his voice.

His breath fluttered against my eyelashes in the half second before his kisses fell on my closed eyes.

"Keeping you," he muttered.

"Okay, darling," I breathed, fear of the fall tightening my grip on him.

His heart beat steady against my palm as he pressed his forehead to mine, the painstaking sweetness of his claiming a balm to my soul.

I lifted my mouth to his, tipped my hips to take him deeper, and undulated against him.

Tugging my leg up over his hip, he continued his steady assault, rocking slowly and deeply inside me, pushing me up, up, up, then watching as I floated over the edge, surrendering to the wonder of it all.

Fusing his mouth to mine, his thumbs sweeping away my tears of release, he quickened his pace, his entire body releasing inside me, a great sigh of relief.

"Minty."

My name the only word on his lips as he rolled me onto my side, curled himself around my back, and pressed his mouth to the nape of my neck.

Lucky

We spent most of the week together, and I couldn't believe how far we'd come in just a few short days.

On Friday I took her out to see the movie we missed previously, and all day Saturday we hung out around the house. I completed my yardwork while Minty worked on an art commission. When I finished, I pulled out my guitar while Minty continued.

At times she paused and watched my hands as I played.

I could see her canvas from where I sat and I watched her hand fly across the empty space, slowly filling it with life.

Tonight, we did not have a show or a rehearsal. It was the last free weekend before the summer schedule picked up.

I was not one bit sorry to have that time with her.

She stretched, her back popping as she twisted out the knots, and moved to lie beside me on the double lounge chair.

"You okay if I read for a while? Or is there something you want to do?" she asked.

"You couldn't get me out of this seat with a crowbar," I assured her.

Satisfied, she settled in and opened her kindle.

I glanced down. Was she reading about alien sex? I contained my laughter. One hundred percent I planned to get an alien costume and chase her around the house with my dick hanging out.

Over the past few weeks, I'd laughed more than I could ever remember laughing. And I generally laughed a lot. I was a happy guy.

But Minty? She catapulted my happiness to a higher level.

I tucked her close to my side and stretched my legs out to rest my bare feet beside hers.

A cool breeze provided a welcome relief to the heat of the sun, and I drifted off to sleep, perfectly content.

"Lucky," Minty called softly, shaking me awake. "Darling, you need to go pick up the baby."

I rubbed my hand over my face, then nuzzled into her neck. "Thanks for waking me." I lifted my chin to catch her smiling at me. "Why don't you come with me? Break the ice."

Her smile faded. Uncertainty clouded her eyes.

"Not this time." She smiled apologetically, then closed her eyes for a quick moment, her brows knitting. "I'll get over it. I promise. While you're gone, I'll make dinner. This way we'll have time to take the baby to the park."

I managed a smile, but I worried about the sudden separation of the important people in my life. "You drive a hard bargain," I teased, hoping to alleviate the sudden weight in the atmosphere.

Pushing myself up, I dropped a kiss on her nose, and headed off.

When Hope opened her front door, she looked for Minty in the car. Noting her absence, she gave me a knowing look, her sadness apparent.

"We'll work it out. Give her some time."

She nodded and offered a smile that did not reach her eyes. In that moment, I wanted nothing more than to give her a hug, comfort her, and I knew she was entirely correct in her assessment of us as partners.

I sighed. "We'll work it out. She knows how much I love you and has no desire to interfere with our relationship. I don't know if I should even be telling you this." I scrubbed my hand through my hair. "The issue is she's not entirely convinced there's nothing romantic left over between us."

"Left over? There's never been anything romantic between us."

169

"The baby we share begs to differ." I waved away her protests. "I know, I know. But look at it from her point of view."

"Yes, yes," she replied impatiently. "I was the one who told you that."

A tear rolled down her face. "I cannot lose you."

"You won't." I reached for her hand and squeezed it. "You won't."

She squeezed back, then let go and brushed her tear away. "It'll be okay. I need for it to be okay. Brayleigh needs for it to be okay. And I'd like to think that I'll find someone someday who is going to be okay with our family dynamic."

I secured Brayleigh into her car seat and drove away, painfully aware of the strain in our friendship and the fact that I'd spent no time at all with Hope before leaving with Brayleigh. I hoped to God these were just growing pains, that we'd morph into something stronger, something that allowed us to expand our little family rather than dissolve it.

Minty searched my eyes when I came back in. Looking behind my careful smile, her face fell marginally. "I promise, darling. I'll pull it together."

I leaned my forehead against hers. "I need for you to do that. I want to expand my family, not abandon it."

Her body jerked at my words, but her eyes remained thoughtful.

We went to the park, ate the dinner Minty made, then I gave Brayleigh a bath while Minty tidied up the kitchen.

The domesticity of it all appealed to me. I laughed to myself. I was turning into a regular suburban dad. I raised my eyebrows. Who knows? I might even be husband material.

A few hours later, sprawled on my back in my bed, I admitted to myself I could definitely be husband material if it meant I had Minty in my bed every night.

She stretched out on top of me with her hands folded over my chest, her chin resting on top. Her eyes were closed, the only sound her soft hums of pleasure as I trailed my fingers lightly over her back.

Did she feel tied down by Brayleigh's routine? I wondered how she felt about Drivetrain's summer schedule.

"Is it a pain, having Drivetrain monopolize every Saturday night in the summer?"

"No, not at all. I'm not missing out on anything. I love music, especially when it's you up there playing." She sighed. "I just hate the women. They're so, so...*fertile*."

I laughed. I couldn't help it and eventually she joined in.

Though we'd dropped our temporary status, it didn't seem to alter her reservations about Hope or her insecurity about other women. Was it just our age difference? If I was older, would she still suffer pangs of insecurity?

As far as I could tell, the issue was her belief that I wanted more children. Part of me did, but that part only wanted one with her. No one else.

Never before had I felt that yearning to possess, that craving to belong to someone else, to answer to someone else.

While I definitely felt possessive of her, I wasn't jealous. I'd also never seen unattached men vying for her attention. I imagined if some man tried to move in on her, my response might be less than sedate.

Truthfully, I loved and hated her jealousy in equal measure.

I loved the possessive nature of it, hated the insecure edge with which it cut her.

I ran my hands up and down her back, pressing her lush breasts flat to my chest.

"I'm going to have your name tattooed on my cock...'Minty'... huge letters. Will that satisfy you?"

She looked at me from beneath hooded eyes that held more than a hint of amusement. "It'll look like you're advertising for freshness, trying to compel the ladies to suck you off."

My cock twitched, and by the expression on her face, she felt it. The fucking words that came out of her pretty mouth.

She was a study in contrasts.

Light and dark.

Dignified and dirty.

Perfectly composed and un-fucking-hinged.

"Hmm. You may have a point. Is Minty your full name?"

"No." Her smile spread, sending light up into her eyes. "It's Erimenthea."

My eyes widened as I wrapped her up and rolled her onto her back. "Fuck, that's a lot of letters."

Laughter bubbled up and spilled over. Thirty seconds later, when I entered her, she was still laughing.

Fuck, life was good.

Chapter 25 - Hope

Minty

Usually, I looked forward to Sunday mornings.

But leaving the warmth of Lucky's embrace chafed. It wasn't so often that we spent the entire night together that I took the cuddly mornings for granted.

I finished showering and slipped back into Lucky's bedroom, dropping a kiss on his sleepy face.

Looking down at him, I shook my head. In sleep, he looked even younger.

"What am I doing?" I whispered.

"Getting railed by Captain Cock every night," he murmured.

I barked out a laugh.

"Da-da-da-da-da! I up!"

He groaned, throwing his forearm across his eyes. Mornings were not his favorite time of day. "There's nothing like the sound of that voice first thing in the morning."

"Can I go get her? Bring her to you?" I held my breath.

He lifted his forearm and peeked at me. "You don't have to ask to pick her up, Minty. You can touch her, play with her. I'll share."

You want to touch her.

Bile rose in my throat. I swallowed. Smiled. "I'll just bring her in here to you and then I've got to run. Okay?"

"You ever going to tell me what's behind those smiles?" His stormy blue eyes narrowed on my face.

"There's nothing really to tell. It's OCD. The smile is me kind of dismissing it."

Are you sure it's OCD?

I took a deep breath, smiled again, tried to make it look more natural as I aimed it at him.

"I don't have to get her," I began backpedaling.

"Nope!" His hand shot up in a stop sign. "You already offered. No takebacks!"

"I up now!" The sound of her sturdy legs bouncing up and down on the mattress made him laugh.

"She's getting impatient," he sang.

Chuckling, I walked out to the hall. Gently pushed her door open.

She caught sight of me and full-out screamed.

"Sparky!"

With renewed vigor, she pounded her little feet into the mattress and wagged her head back and forth like a miniature head-banger, her hair a tuft of golden smoke on top of her head.

Lucky enjoyed his A/C which meant Brayleigh slept in footy pajamas year-round. Last night's boasted scattered bunnies on a fuzzy pink background. She looked like a stuffed toy.

"Hi, dolly," I murmured as I offered to pick her up. "Would you like to come to me?"

She reached out for me with no hesitation.

She's vulnerable. She can't protect herself.

Picking her up she curled her little body around mine the exact same way I'd seen her do with Lucky. I wrapped my arms around her warm little body, one hand supporting her tiny back, the other supporting her diapered bottom.

174

Your hand is on her private.

I inhaled deeply and waited for the beast to retract its' claws, refusing to give in and move my hand from her hip. I focused on the sweetness of the tiny body in my arms. Wished for just a moment that she was mine. Yearned for half a breath that it had been my belly that had swelled with Lucky's seed.

OCD eased its' grip.

My body relaxed.

I tipped my head to the side, resting my temple against her soft baby cheek.

"Good morning, dolly. You want to go see Daddy?"

"Yeah, Da."

I walked out to the hall.

She reached for the bauble I wore around my neck, pulling it away from my skin as she leaned back to get a better look. "Mine sparky?"

"Daddy's Sparky," Lucky corrected, and I harrumphed out another laugh.

That man made me laugh every damn day. My face was beginning to hurt.

"Mine sparky," she whispered, putting her face right in mine.

"Okay, dolly. Your sparky," I whispered back with a smile before releasing her into Lucky's arms.

Hours into my day, I could still feel the weight and the shape of her in my arms. I could still smell her, feel the warmth of her head tucked under my chin, the imprint of her tiny fingers pressing into the back of my neck.

After lunch, I sat back to watch the crowd. It had been a slow day, which was good. The number of commissions I'd already racked up were beginning to stress me out.

Stress and I never mixed well.

"Hi."

I swung my gaze around to the source of the hesitant greeting, a ready smile on my face.

"Hi! Hope, um, hi," I stuttered.

Tall and gorgeous, her cornflower blue eyes wide and wary, long blond hair blowing lightly in the breeze, she could have been a fashion model.

Maybe she was, I mentally shrugged. I had no idea what she did, who she was. The stranglehold of jealousy tightened around my throat.

She indicated the empty chair to my right, half behind my table. "May I sit down with you for a bit?" She held up a cardboard Tim Horton's drink carrier. "I brought you a cold drink and a cookie. Um, Lucky said cookies are your weakness..." She trailed off.

Nervous. She was nervous. And I had made her that way.

Shame heated my cheeks.

I swallowed.

"Please," I invited, waving to the chair.

"Yeah?" she checked.

"Yes," I said firmly. Nodded. "Please sit."

She released a breath and eased around the edge of the table, perching on the edge of the chair. "I, um, brought iced lemonade and iced cappuccino. I wasn't sure which you preferred. I like both. I'll take either. You pick first because I bought them for you. Well one of them. I mean, you can have both if you want," she rushed to add.

"Hope, thank you for bringing me a cold drink. I appreciate it. But it's the cookie that will really make or break this visit," I teased gently.

She sat back in the chair, a rueful smile on her face.

"You got me." She handed me the bag. "I got one of every flavor. I wasn't taking any chances."

I peeked in the bag, buying myself time.

Why is she here?

Is this where she tells me she has feelings for him?

Is this when she asks me to back off?

You're the interloper. You intruded on their family. You're practically a homewrecker. It's immoral.

176

"You really did buy every kind." I closed the bag and sighed. Looking into the distance, I asked, "Should I be nervous about whatever it is you came here to say?"

"I don't think so?" she trailed off.

I met her eyes. "Are you going to ask me to walk away?" I didn't add that I would because I was no longer sure I could.

Her eyes widened comically, and she waved her hands back and forth even as she sat forward. "No! No, no, no, I want you to come closer," she stressed. "To me, I mean. Well, to Lucky, but to me as well." She paused. "I'm not saying this well." She smoothed her palms down her jeans. "I prepared something. Can I just read it to you?"

I'd never seen a more nervous woman in my life. Was this how she was normally? Was it the situation? Did I make her feel like this?

"Please relax. I don't bite."

She laughed, "For Lucky's sake, I hope you do." She clapped a hand over her eyes. "Oh, God! I'm sorry!" She deflated right in front of me, her face drained of animation. "Look. I have the same sense of humor as a teenage boy. I'm a tomboy. Always have been. I never had girlfriends as a kid because I wasn't interested in the same things they were. By the time I hit my teens, I had all this to contend with," she circled her finger in the air indicating her face and her body, "and the girls wouldn't let me in. The boys changed as well, and not for the better. The ones that stuck around soon left when they got girlfriends." She took a breath. "Except Lucky."

"Hmm," I hummed and opened my mouth to speak, but she continued.

"He never asked me for anything more than friendship. He also never dumped me."

"He's a good man," I murmured.

She looked at me earnestly and replied fervently. "He *is*. And there are things I want you to know. He has never had a serious girlfriend. Not ever. Since Brayleigh was born, I don't even think he's dated. I mean, he's hooked up. A lot." She stared at me, eyes wide with horror.

I barked out a laugh. What is it with everyone telling me about him hooking up?

"Oh, God. I take that back. Okay. Stay on topic." She braced her hands in front of her as if to hold off my speech. "I know it's weird, him and me having a child and being best friends." She closed her eyes for a moment and shook her head in smiling disbelief then met my eyes. "I'm fucking thankful I remember very little about that night. He is just as thankful. He and I have never been remotely romantically involved. It was a one-off. It was alcohol and affection and probably a good bit of loneliness. On my side. Not his."

My Lord, she babbled worse than Willa and Ruby put together.

She dropped her face into her hands. When she looked back up at me, she was miserable.

"I can't lose him," she whispered. Tears came to her eyes. "I just can't."

I reached for her hand and held it between both of mine while I stared at the ground. Wondered if she was being one hundred per cent honest.

You're in the way. This is not where you belong.

"I believe it best if we speak honestly, woman to woman. It will simplify the situation and clarify each of our paths moving forward."

She gripped my hand tightly and felt her whole body move as she nodded.

I tipped my chin up. "I'm only going to say this once. You'll never get this offer from me after today. Think carefully before you answer as it is quite possible that our collective peace and happiness hinges on your reply."

Her gaze caught mine and she didn't turn away even as she swiped her tears away with her other hand.

I stared into her beautiful eyes and my heart squeezed. "Do you want me to step aside and give you guys a chance to be a family?"

She froze for a moment, then flew into movement, sitting forward in her chair, her other hand clasping around both of mine.

"No. I want you to accept me as part of Lucky's life. I need you to set the precedent that what we have is normal, give me hope that someday someone might want me enough to accept Lucky's place in my life. I'd like to have a place in your life if you're with him. I don't want him romantically. I just love him so much. He's more family than friend." Her mouth twisted. "But I don't, like, want to be a couple with him. I don't want to be family in that way." She waved her hand again. "I get that he's attractive. I understand why you'd want to fuck him, but to me he's just my friend. My best friend. The one person who has never ever walked away."

She took a deep breath at the same time as I did but recovered from hers faster and yanked my hands, jerking me slightly forward in my seat.

"I can't think about having sex with Lucky without gagging. It was practically incestuous. But. He is my oldest and closest friend. I don't want to lose him. I'm trying to impress upon you the fact that I am not a threat. I will never be a threat. In fact. If you love Lucky, I love you. I'll be your biggest fucking ally."

She sat back and huffed out a breath. "There. That's what I really wanted to say."

"Okay."

"Okay? That's it?"

I smiled wryly, amusement and possibly the first faint embers of affection lighting my gaze. "I think you've said enough for both of us and possibly everyone else who's here today, no?"

She barked out a laugh. "Good. Phew!" She reached for the bag of cookies. "Now that that's settled, I'm having the peanut butter cookie." She pulled it out of the bag and bit into it, rapture on her exquisite face. "Frig, that's good."

"There better be chocolate chunk in there," I grumbled. "I was looking forward to that one."

She held it up. "Noted. I'll get doubles next time. Hey! These are really cool! I want to buy one of Brayleigh for my parents. Is that okay? You can take the picture. I trust you."

"I'm really behind," I warned. "When would you need it for?"

"Christmas?" she shrugged.

"That I can do."

She finished chewing then indicated the cookie bag. "I'll let you have the next pick."

"Fair enough," I laughed, reaching in.

"Lucky's right. Your laugh is like music. You're so refined and he's so like me." Her right eyebrow raised as she assessed me. "Your chemistry must be off the fucking charts."

I held up a hand. "We are not going there."

"Yeah," she said, sitting back again. "Now *that* would be weird."

Chapter 26 – Dreams

<u>Minty</u>

Lucky was busy the following week with it being the end of school.

I caught up with him after school one day when I picked up George, and I saw him briefly when I volunteered to help distribute the care packages, but other than that, we didn't see one another.

Saturday, I took Jace, Alex, and George, to the movies and the bike park, then ate dinner with my big, fat, Greek family.

Yiayia was in fine form as usual, divvying out extra potatoes, advice, and threats indiscriminately. Shortly after dinner, Yiayia went to lie down, and the boys headed to the games room, leaving the five of us sitting around the kitchen table.

It was comfortable. Familiar. Part of me wanted to stay there where it was safe.

It was only a small part.

"Lucky is playing tonight," I announced. "I'm going with Willa and Junie to watch."

"Have we met Lucky?" Vander asked Gus. "We know Barrett from BOXXX, but I don't think we've met Lucky."

Gus shrugged. "He's the tall, blond that hangs out with Barrett sometimes. We could ask Barrett about him the next time we see him."

"Uh," I huffed. "Thanks, daddy, but I think I've got this," I reprimanded them both.

"Daddy. Kinky," Vander teased. "Do you call him 'daddy'?"

"No, actually," I began softly. Both Amber and Ruby perked up. They recognized the tone of my voice.

Gus went on alert, his eyes wary.

Vander grinned at me, unaware.

I met his eyes, and his grin faltered.

Ruby chortled, her eyes alight with expectation.

"I call him Captain Cock," I replied softly, taking in Vander's stunned expression with a deep sense of satisfaction.

Amber laughed, leaning into Gus as he wiped a big hand over his face, groaning.

Vander began to laugh and looked at Ruby affectionately. "I thought you were trouble."

I stood to go, wrapped in their happiness. For the first time, I was not the slightest bit envious

"Minty," Gus called out.

I turned, my eyebrows raised.

"Call any of us if you need anything."

I softened. I knew that. The knowledge warmed my heart. "Thank you, Angus. I know that."

A few hours later, I arrived at the bar and a different type of happy energy filled me. Being the holiday weekend, the place was packed and the atmosphere super-charged.

Willa, Junie, and I settled at our table and ordered a round of drinks, virgin for Willa who was nursing.

"Ten minutes to spare!" Junie crowed. "Lenny said we'd never make it on time." She turned to me. "How are things with Lucky?"

"Good." I cleared my throat. "We're, uh, no longer casual."

Junie grinned. "He was so gone on you the day we had the barbecue."

"How do you figure?" I asked. She hadn't mentioned this before.

"He was staring at you out the window. Said you were too good for him," Junie informed me, her voice suspiciously soft.

"Well, I'm not," I replied briskly. "He's a good man. An incredible father. You know he's a teacher? My George is one of his students and he's told me such good things about him. Oh. I met his best friend. Hope. Brayleigh's mother. She can't say enough good things about him."

"How'd that go?" Willa asked.

I smiled ruefully. "A little rough at first but I think we are good now."

"Don't take any of her shit," Junie advised. She and Lenny had to work through their own issues with Lenny's ex-wife.

"I think it'll be okay. There might be some growing pains," I conceded. "But I don't feel like I'm moving in on her territory or taking him away from her."

Barrett stepped up to welcome everybody to the show. Then smiling, he indicated Lucky, and continued, "This cocky son-of-a-bitch wants to kick off the show with a dedication to the hottest woman alive. He says if I say her name, she may kill him. So, I won't. Okay, Minty?"

Oh. My. God.

Straightening my spine, I resisted the urge to hide, though I sent him devil eyes just the same.

I don't think he saw because his happy chuckle carried over the mic. "Just officially taking myself off the market, Bear. Want my lady to know where I'm at."

A chorus of boos sounded from the foot of the stage. When he paid them no mind, they turned their curious glances to seek me out in the crowd.

"This song will do it." Barrett rumbled as the opening notes of the song sounded.

I listened to the lyrics, a little shocked at first not knowing the song, then it got to the chorus, and I understood.

"Oh. My. God." I laughed, hard, reaching for both Willa and Junie at the same time. We fell together, our joy in being together mirrored by the energy of the men onstage. "He makes me laugh until my face hurts."

I remembered what Lucky told me about being up there. I also remembered the affect it had on him and what I'd be getting treated to at the end of the night.

I looked over at Willa. "Barrett's on fire," I commented.

"Yes, well, Rena is six weeks old, Willa went lingerie shopping, and he's getting back in the saddle tonight," Junie teased.

"I'm going to feed that baby so fast when we get home," Willa added, her eyes on her man.

At the break, Lucky broke through the crowd with ease and wrapped me up in his sweaty embrace.

I smiled into his face so close to mine. "You're disgustingly sweaty."

He smiled back. "You love it." He waited for my confirmation, pressed his lips to mine, and smiled bigger. "Did you like the song I dedicated to you?"

I snorted. "To me? Or to your fan club?"

His eyes opened comically wide. "I wasn't declaring my affections to them, I was declaring my affections to you!"

"Sounded like you were commiserating with them."

"No. Not commiserating. Just miserating." He grinned again, delighted with himself. His happy vibe never failed to pick me up.

"Affections?" I raised my eyebrows.

"Yeah," his face softened. "Like. Lust." He paused. "All those 'L' words."

"All of them?"

"Getting there," he admitted, eyes narrowed on mine. "Am I alone in that?"

"No." I looked away for a moment to give myself space, then turned back and bravely met his eyes. "You're not alone."

Things were moving fast. Maybe too fast. Was I just caught up in the excitement? The romance of it all? Should I pull back a bit and regroup?

Would be kind of difficult to pull back when I planned to head home with him tonight then go with him to his sister's house for dinner tomorrow.

What was the risk? How big was the risk?

You're going to hurt him. You need to be responsible with his feelings. You shouldn't be getting so involved unless you're sure. It's not just him you have to consider, it's Brayleigh, too.

"Hey," his raspy voice interrupted my thoughts. "Stop thinking." He tugged the hem of my dress then nuzzled into my neck. "I like this. You're all sexy librarian, looking like somebody's mother, or the nice women at the bank, and only I know what lies beneath it all."

He went rigid for a moment and drew back to look me in the face. "Only I know, right? No, that's ridiculous." His eyebrows scrunched together. "How many people know?" He held up a hand. "Don't answer that!"

I laughed lightly, lay my hand alongside his face. "Not as many as you'd think. If you're asking the number of men who actually know me the way you do, it's the number of fingers on one hand." I reconsidered, then added with a smirk, "If you were a sloth."

He inhaled deeply. "I'm a hypocrite."

"No. You're not judging, are you?"

"Not judging. I'm jealous?" Half pained, half confused, his mouth twisted around the word.

The break ended and as he made his way back to the stage, the curious eyes of the women stayed with me rather than follow him.

Most of them were younger than me. Any one of them would gladly take my place. Every one of them surely wondered what I had that they did not.

I wondered that myself.

Lucky

She had me losing my fucking mind. Dragging her teeth so fucking lightly up my cock, then licking every-fucking-where else on my body except the one place that literally wept for her touch while I lay there and tried not to come from the wisp of her breath as she passed over my balls.

Fucking finally, she straddled my hips and welcomed me into her tight, wet, heat.

I grasped her round hips, arched my neck back and away from the sight of her riding me slow, her thighs straining as she raised herself up then slowly engulfed me in her heat, gasping and grinding into me each time I bottomed out.

"Baby, baby, baby," I gasped, struggling not to come.

"Say my name," she demanded, breathless. "I need to know you know who you're fucking."

As if.

As if there could ever be anybody else.

Ever.

I rolled her onto her back and drove into her hard, stayed deep, and rocked against her.

"To me?" I grunted. "To me, it's baby, sweetheart, beautiful."

I entered her with short, shallow thrusts and watched her neck arch back. My tongue traced the sweet curve of her throat.

"I'll further elaborate to add my baby, my sweetheart, my beautiful lady, my soul, my heart, my happiness, my fucking eyes, Minty." I strained to hold back but couldn't. "You're everything that's good in my life. You want to be sure I know who I'm fucking? It's you. Even in my fucking dreams."

My back bowed as I came deep inside her. Clamping down onto her collarbone with my mouth, she fluttered around me, plastering her cheek to my temple, her breath releasing with a series of husky 'ohs'.

I cleaned her up.

Turned her limp body onto the side.

Curled myself around her back and pressed my lips to the nape of her neck, breathing her name.

This.

This was happiness.

Chapter 27 – Personal Preservation

Minty

Lucky drummed his thumbs on the steering wheel as he drove, tapping out the rhythm to Saving Abel's *Mystify*.

The summer sun was performing its level best to ensure it was too hot to even marginally cover up. I looked down at my sundress. A dainty floral with narrow straps, it fell straight to my ankles. I felt exposed. When did I start dressing to hide my sexuality?

1-2-3-4-5-1-2-3-4-5

1-2-3-4-5-1-2-3-4-5

1-2-3-4-5-1-2-3-4-5

The counting both soothed and irritated.

I wanted to stop but I itched to make it even.

1-2-3-4-5-1-2-3-4-5

I took a deep breath.

It started with Jace. He was maybe Brayleigh's age. Ruby needed help and I took him for the day. I wasn't sure why. The details were difficult to remember.

I looked down at my lap.

But I remembered the feeling of horror, shame, and revulsion.

Where Alex played with Amber's hair, twirling it around his baby fingers, especially when he was drifting off to sleep, Jace stuffed his little fist into Ruby's cleavage.

We used to laugh.

Say he was going to be a boob man.

It was innocent. Sweet. A leftover habit from his nursing days.

And then, that day when I had him alone, he did it to me.

You like that.

What?

The blood drained from my face so rapidly it was dizzying. It could not have been the first time he'd done it. He did it to everybody. Yiayia, Amber, Ruby, and me as well.

But something about that day struck me differently.

I removed his fist.

He put it back.

I changed my shirt for something with a high neck.

Did you enjoy that? Are you sure? Did you molest that baby?

That memory still had the power to make me shudder.

"Cold, baby? Want me to turn down the A/C?"

"No, darling. I think we should take advantage of it while we can. It's brutally hot out there."

"Not as hot as it is in here, baby." He ran his forefinger under my strap. "You look beautiful. Your skin, Minty, your skin...if I was a man of words, I would write a sonnet to your skin."

"How about you compose a song instead?" I teased. "It's lovely and cool in here."

I rested my head back and closed my eyes to block out the street and the buses and the safe travels. I splayed my fingers wide and rested them on my thighs to avoid touching any of them and inadvertently adding weight to make them uneven.

I don't think I ever took Jace or Alex alone after that. If I ever did, it was a rare case.

My eyes stung.

When the boys were five, I started picking them up from school occasionally. Every time, I felt the urge to crash the car. I knew it was OCD. I knew it. But in combination with the other thoughts of harm and especially those of sexual harm, I began to question if I should be around them.

At my next appointment, I told Ezinne that I was worried I might be a danger to them because of my OCD. God bless her, she didn't make me explain my symptoms. She lay it out on the table, literally and metaphorically, explaining the different subtypes of OCD and the fluidity with which the disorder switched out one subtype for another, often causing the person to deal with several sets of symptoms at a time.

As long as I could remember, I always battled on multiple fronts.

Exposure. Desensitization. Response prevention.

What seemed at first to be an unbearable risk, treatment reduced to a niggling doubt, an annoyance. White noise.

Even the pedophilia OCD, I pushed past, getting to the point where the only accommodation I required was not spending one on one time with either of the boys for any amount of time.

Logically, I knew I was not a pedophile.

But OCD capitalized on my greatest fears. Perhaps it was more accurate to say it focused on those things that would be most abhorrent.

What if you lose control?

What if you're wrong?

What if this is how all pedophiles start out?

Logically, I knew it was OCD.

But the pain of those doubts made any time I spent with those boys unbearable. And I was selfish. I wanted my time with those boys.

But also...

What if I was wrong?

It was possible, wasn't it? Was it? I never felt one hundred per cent sure, therefore I never took the risk.

"Baby? You're too quiet. What's going on in that head of yours?"

"Give me a minute darling? I'm working through some OCD stuff. I'm okay," I murmured, not wanting to lose my train of thought.

It had been more than a decade. I could trust myself.

I huffed out a laugh. In all the years OCD had offered options and suggestions for hurting people, physically or sexually, not once had I ever acted on any of those thoughts. Though at times I felt the physical sensation as if I was about to do it, I never had. I never wanted to.

I was safe. I was a safe person.

But the thoughts alone had the power to shatter me.

I didn't make accommodations to keep the boys safe from me, I made accommodations to keep myself safe from the thoughts.

Perhaps it was time to overcome that as well.

I opened my eyes, relaxed my fingers, and placed my hand on Lucky's hard thigh. "Okay, darling. Give me the run-through of all the names one more time."

By the time we arrived, I'd made him go through them twice and felt reasonably confident I wouldn't make a complete fool of myself.

"Is your family quiet or boisterous?" I'd never thought to ask that question. "Is this likely to resemble a barbecue with Willa and Junie and everybody?"

Lucky smiled ruefully. "It's definitely on the boisterous side."

"Well, that's good. Makes for easier conversation," I breathed a sigh of relief.

"True!" Lucky perked up. "You'll be lucky to get a word in edgewise."

Foodwise, I was prepared. One of Lucky's sisters was vegan, and he'd already told me my preferences aligned fairly closely with hers, which quelled that anxiety at least.

"Is Hope coming?" I asked.

He chuckled. "Ten minutes of her craziness and she had you converted."

I smiled. "Well, she did bring me cookies."

"She is. And of course, she's bringing Brayleigh, and we'll take Brayleigh home with us afterwards."

"Excellent." I sat a little taller in my seat, knowing there were at least two other people there I knew, even if one was a toddler. "How old is your oldest sister?"

"Forty-three."

"Are they going to think it's weird that you're dating me? I'm older that you're oldest sister. Do you know that?"

He sent me a look of such exasperation, I laughed out loud.

"I'm not even going to answer that question," he growled as he pulled the car to a stop at the curb.

I swung my legs out of the car, then spoke over my shoulder, my voice pitched low. "Don't growl. It makes me wet and you're not in any position to do anything about it."

"Oh, so it's going to be like that, is it? Tease and run? Alright, baby. Game on." He grinned at me, wagging his eyebrows.

I gave him a slow once over, beginning at his feet, pausing at his groin, licking my lips at his shoulders, and finishing with fuck-me-eyes.

His eyes lit with interest, his entire body swaying in my direction.

I smirked. "Amateur."

He laughed, caught me around the waist and plastered my body to his. "Don't push me," he warned. "I'll haul your ass into the nearest bathroom and have my way with you."

"Hi, Uncle Lucky!"

I froze and tried to pull away, but Lucky wrapped me up tighter and turned us towards the owner of the voice.

"It's mine," he shouted. "You can't have it!"

A boy about Jace and Alex's age laughed while his counterpart, a girl slightly younger, insisted, "We just want to look at her!"

"She's not a zoo animal," Lucky protested. "She's sparkly and she smells good and she's so pretty!"

191

I finally succeeded in pulling my face out of his neck to find not just the children, but an older teen looking on as well.

"Hello," I tried for normalcy.

Lucky nodded towards the two tweens. "These hooligans are Ben and Abby. They belong to Darcy, my second oldest sister. And that gorgeous woman, wearing a skirt that is entirely too short, is my niece Rosa, Daniela's youngest."

Lucky finally released me when I extended my hand to Rosa, Rosa of the rolling eyes. Ah, good. I'd remember her name.

"Nice to meet you, Minty," she offered her hand along with a sweet smile. Lucky had not exaggerated. She was beautiful with caramel skin, dirty blond hair and light eyes.

"Hello, Ben. Hello, Abby."

"Hello. It's nice to meet you," they said, but made it clear that it was Lucky who held their interest. "Did you bring your guitar?"

"Of course. Ben, you can get it and put it in the house. Abby, you open the doors and make sure he doesn't scuff the guitar. Or Aunt Daniela's walls!" he added as an afterthought.

Rosa rolled her eyes. "Mustn't scuff the walls."

"Oh, please," Lucky mock complained. "Spare me the teenaged angst. What are they making you do? Have a part time job? Come home before one o'clock in the morning? Study?"

Rosa's face fell, and Lucky stood up straight. "What is it, Rosa?"

"Nothing. It's okay. But maybe you can talk to them later? They want me to go to school for business and I want to go for music!"

"Ah, yes. I'll talk to your mom and dad." He linked his fingers through mine and stepped forward to throw an arm around Rosa. "Put it on the back burner for now. Let's have a good day together?"

"Yeah, Lucky. Okay."

"Lucky? Not 'Uncle' Lucky? I've been demoted?"

And so it went with each member of the family.

Lucky and his siblings all had the same signature blond hair. stormy grey eyes, and larger than life personalities.

Daniela, the oldest at forty-three and today's hostess, had three kids with her husband Carlos. The oldest, Rafael, was twenty-six. They got started very early, then took a six-year break before having Isabella and then Rosa. Their father's Mexican heritage combined with Daniela's blond hair and grey eyes made them a stunning couple and gave each of their children luminescent caramel skin. Only Rosa had light eyes.

Darcy, mother to Ben and Abby, the driveway greeting committee, appeared harried and overworked. Lucky whispered that after her divorce her husband had pulled a slow-mo vanishing act, leaving her to parent alone.

Several picnic tables created a semi-circle, each covered with a tablecloth and laden with beverages, napkins, paper plates, condiments, and coolers. Music blared from a speaker tucked up on the back patio, and lawn chairs dappled the grass. It was not a large backyard.

The number of people, the tables, the tweens, the toddlers, and the toddler pop-up shelters stuffed with toys, made the space even cozier.

Lucky's brother, Raiden, handed Lucky a drink and clapped him on the back. "Well, I haven't met one of your girlfriends since prom night. Introduce me?"

Just as handsome as Lucky, but somehow harsher, Raiden had lost the boy-next-door look somewhere along the way. If he ever had it.

A picture of myself as the filling in their man sandwich flashed in my brain. You want to fuck him. You want to fuck both of them.

I smiled it away and extended my hand. "Hello, it's nice to meet you."

My voice sounded cool, distant.

Oh, no. He would think me unfriendly.

The vision flashed again, same picture. This time it stayed.

Can he read your mind? What if he can read your mind and thinks you want that? What if Lucky thinks you want it? He'd be so hurt.

I focused on the man in front of me and forced a more natural smile. "So, Lucky tells me you were the instigator of all the trouble you two got into as kids."

His bushy blond eyebrows rose as he thought about it. "I am going to have to agree, however, his life would have been boring without me. I rescued him from having to play dolls with Tracy."

"Somebody say my name?"

Gorgeous and curvy, with a wide smile, Tracy came up beside me and hugged both Lucky and me. "I've got a deal on toddlers today. Any two for the afternoon. Pick any two!"

Lucky laughed and pointed out two little girls picking the heads off the flowers in the beds.

Tracy followed his gaze and clapped a hand to her face and excused herself. "Sloane! Paige! No picking Auntie Dani's flowers!"

Lucky whispered, "They make Brayleigh look angelic."

"I heard that, Lucky," Tracy called.

"You could not possibly have heard me," he protested.

"Maybe not, but I know what you said!" she replied.

"I'm reconsidering! I'd like a paternity test," a man shouted from across the yard.

Tracy lifted her head and laughed. "We need a border collie. I'm telling you..."

Lucky tipped his beer in the man's direction. "That's Sean, Tracy's husband."

I watched him approach his wife and kiss her mouth before bending to scoop up his daughters. He pretended to run away from Tracy who turned into a monster eliciting squeals of delight from the captured fairies.

"Is Ava here yet?" A hint of a frown marred Lucky's brow as he looked around the yard. I'd never seen him worried.

"She's inside. Waiting for Hope," Raiden said meaningfully.

I froze. "Ava is your youngest sister, correct?"

194

"That would be her," Raiden answered, a twinkle in his eye. "She can be stubborn, but once you get to know her, she'll never let you down."

Darcy approached me shortly afterwards, introducing herself before turning to Lucky. "I'm stealing Minty. We're finding shade and pretending to be women of leisure. Please bring us drinks," she instructed her brothers.

Lucky and Raiden immediately turned to each other to rock-paper-scissors it out.

"Aw, thank fuck. I didn't think I could last another minute in that heat." Darcy settled herself and sat back on her chair. "Is it okay that I stole you away?"

"Absolutely." I settled myself and looked around. It seemed slightly less harried from the edges.

"It's boisterous, but it's good. Mostly." Darcy smiled.

Lucky brought us drinks while we chatted, and I found I quite liked Darcy. There was absolutely no pretension in her. Not once did I worry about what she thought because it was unlikely she possessed any type of filter.

Just as I began to relax, the back door swung open and an absolutely stunning blond, curvier even than Tracy, stepped outside.

"Ava!" Darcy yelled. "Come over!"

Ava raised her chin and coolly took me in.

"Hmm," I hummed.

"Oh, don't worry about Ava. She's a little slow to warm up to new people but she's sweet as honey."

Lucky intercepted her on her way across the grass and gave her a big hug before leaning back and talking to her seriously.

She scowled.

Darcy laughed. "Big brother is mighty protective of you."

"I can usually hold my own," I answered with a smile.

Ava held her hand out and introduced herself. Far from unfriendly, she simply struck me as wary. I felt her assessing gaze, but there was no malice in it.

After a few minutes the back door cracked open again and I could not help but smile as Brayleigh's voice preceded her.

By this time, Lucky was seated with Sean and Raiden, Sean and Tracy's little girls rounded up between their chairs, while Dani and Tracy ran around preparing things.

"I think I'll go offer to help." I wanted to avoid Hope. What if the come to Jesus' moment we shared at the craft fair didn't hold up?

Darcy laughed and even Ava smiled.

"We're on clean-up crew. By that time, Dani will have wound down and will no longer care. That's when we take over."

I watched Hope scan the yard and her face brightened immeasurably when she caught sight of Lucky.

My stomach tightened.

Heading straight for him, Hope dumped Brayleigh in his lap and gave him a noogie before heading over to us, dragging an extra chair behind her.

She squeezed her chair in between me and Tracy, forcing Tracy to shift over.

She pulled several Tim Horton's paper bags out of her enormous handbag. "Contraband cookies."

Ava laughed, then explained to me. "We're not allowed to bring food to Dani's house when she hosts. She likes to keep things healthy."

"Here, Minty. It's peanut butter. I owe you one." She dropped her hand between our chairs and passed me the cookie. "Be stealthy. If any of the short people come over, don't share. Especially toddlers. They have no sense of personal preservation."

Several hours later, a freshly bathed Brayleigh asleep in her crib, Lucky and I hit the shower as well. His touch was tender, almost unsexual, as he asked how the day went for me, that worried crease reappearing on his forehead.

I reassured him as best I could.

But it was afterwards, spent and limp in his bed, his face tucked against the back of my neck, that I really thought it through.

The conversation with Hope at the fair, her adamant assertion that there was nothing romantic between them.

The anxiety on Lucky's face as he put distance between himself and his best friend, who also happened to be the mother of his child.

I thought about the accusations I leveled at him when I saw him with his sisters at his show. The groupies that turned out to be Darcy and Ava.

He had never given me a single reason to doubt.

I was my own worst enemy and the solitary obstacle blocking the path to happiness.

I made a decision.

A good one.

No more jealousy.

When the thoughts came, and I knew that they would, I would smile them away the same way I did with every other fucked up thing my brain threw at me.

Chapter 28 - Night Terrors

<u>Lucky</u>

If someone had told me a six weeks ago that I'd be aiming to ask Minty to move in with me, I would have laughed.

Hard.

Side-splitting, snorting, hacking-up-a-lung kind of laughing.

I can't pinpoint the day I fell in love with her with any kind of certainty, but if I had to bet, it would have been at Barrett's wedding when she knotted that tie around my neck.

Brayleigh loved her.

Hope loved her.

Raiden and my sisters were fully on board, even Ava, not that it would matter if they weren't.

But it helped.

Would moving in with me strike her as too great a risk or would it finally eradicate her doubts?

Why could she not see me?

I cuddled Brayleigh against my chest as her tears, finally, shuddered to a stop and her body grew limp and heavy in my arms.

Fucking night terrors. The unholy screams. Just thinking about it sent a shiver down my spine.

The first night it happened I found myself in her room ready to fight before my eyes were fully open despite the fact that Hope had warned me. I didn't even remember her warning at first.

Brayleigh stood in her crib, staring into space and screaming. I scanned the room for intruders, scooped her into my arms, checked the window, checked inside her crib for whatever giant insect had bitten her.

I felt like I'd somehow been transported into that scene in The Lady and The Tramp where I couldn't find the rat.

Nothing was out of place or out of sorts and still she screamed. She didn't acknowledge me, just looked past me, though she clung to my shirt. It stopped as suddenly as it started, the only evidence the sniffles and hitches in her breath.

The next morning, she woke as happy as a lark while I'd aged a decade. The doctor assured me night terrors were not uncommon and usually passed on their own.

I rubbed a hand down the side of my face.

They couldn't pass soon enough. The explosion of adrenalin at the first sound of her screams, no matter how many times it happened, was unavoidable.

And exhausting.

I snickered to myself, remembering when Hope admitted she near pissed herself the first time Brayleigh woke up screaming. It wasn't funny, but Hope could make anything into a joke.

I didn't know Hope had planned to confront Minty but based on our earlier conversation, I should have.

"She thinks I'm a dog. That I'm going to lose interest and move on. That she's temporary," I admitted.

At first, she laughed, and teased, "You are a dog."

I hung my head. "I'm really not. I'm honest and straightforward." I spread my hands wide in supplication. "Was I supposed to pretend interest where there was none? Lead a woman on for a few months until she caught feelings? Become a monk? Those were my options."

Hope's big blue eyes scanned my face. "You've really never felt a spark of interest other than sex?"

"I really haven't," I replied, exasperated. "When I turned thirty, I wanted it. I tried. Remember Judy?"

"I do." She nodded, her full lips pressed tightly together. "I always wondered why that didn't work out. She seemed perfect for you."

"On paper, she was. But there was no drive to be with her. I barely thought about her other than to remind myself when we had plans. Nothing like what Dani and Tracy have with Carlos and Sean, nothing close to how my parents loved each other, and seeing Barrett and Lenny fall? What I had with Judy doesn't even register on that scale. It was..." I searched for the word, spitting it out like a bad taste. "Clinical."

"So, what happened?" Hope asked, picking at a loose thread in one of the many holes in her jeans.

"I broke it off. She was upset, maybe angry more than upset. Honestly, I don't believe I meant more to her than a few ticked boxes. She wanted a child and a family, accused me of wasting her time. And she was right."

Hope gaped. "Oh, fuck off! How else do you figure out if someone's for you if it's not by spending time with them? How long were you with her?"

"Four months?" I tried to recall.

"Pshaw, that's nothing. Four months," she scoffed. "She wanted a proposal and guarantee of forever after four months?"

"I'd move Minty in with me tomorrow," I admitted. Fearful of what I might find in Hope's eyes, I avoided her gaze. What was I afraid of?

That she secretly hoped for something more between us?

That she wouldn't accept Minty?

That she, the one who knew me best, might reduce me to what everyone else sees?

Her slender fingers wrapping around my knee propelled me to look at her. Determination shone from her face.

"Don't let your past get in the way. Be honest with her. Don't let her go." She studied my face for a moment before whispering, "Lucky, you're my best friend and it's not because you're good-looking or play guitar in a band. It's not even the fact that you smile and laugh and make the air brighter in any space you occupy. You are steadfast, loyal, honest, and *kind*. You're so kind, Lucky."

"So, I'm a good catch?" I smiled wryly at her.

She withdrew her hand but not her attention. "You are. If anyone deserves the love of a good woman, it's you. I want you to have a woman who appreciates you like I do, but puts you first before anyone else, and also wants to jump your bones."

I laughed, because that's who I am, but I wondered if Minty would ever see past the good-time guy to the man who wanted to love her.

Because I could admit it to myself at least. I wanted to love her.

I wondered if she would ever see what Hope saw in me.

I transferred Brayleigh back into her crib and prayed she'd sleep until morning.

Minty

Junie spent less and less time at the office. We still met there every morning, but by early afternoon, she was ready to call it a day.

With Willa gone, the atmosphere in the office had shifted. Junie's interest in the entire business had waned, and I found myself with less and less to do. Usually, a change in routine like that would stress me out but with Lucky in my life, free time was play time. As if she could read my mind, Junie tossed her pen on her desk and twisted sideways to face me.

"You know, I just don't have the heart to go after the bigger clients without Willa." She drummed her fingers on her desk.

"You don't have to hang onto this office space, Junie," I reminded her. "I can rent it to someone else tomorrow."

Junie's eyebrows arched up in surprise. "Oh, I'm not worried about that. Not at all. Willa wants to keep it until the end of the year at least, and I think they are trying to work out whether Barrett can swing the move. Would you be open to renting it to Barrett?"

"Of course," I replied. "I meant what I said. In fact, I should make it clear that the rent will not change. That may help them decide."

"She doesn't expect that," Junie confided gently. "Neither does he."

I waved her off. "I'm happy to do it. I'm still making money and I don't honestly need that much. Besides, I'd be helping her and that pleases me. And you, sweets. You don't need to pay rent here for me to keep up with your administration tasks. You'll be saving money, too. Which might give you room to seek out only those niche clients you want to take on."

Junie relaxed back in her seat and grinned. "In that case, how about we meet here Tuesday, Wednesday, and Thursday mornings only. Anything else that needs doing we can do from home." She made a point to look at the time. "Which means we're done for the day!"

As soon as I told him, Lucky wanted me to stay with him on my days off. We had only spent the night together a few times so this was novel territory for us. Our relationship was so fresh that everything was new territory. He offered to come to my place on the nights he didn't have Brayleigh if I preferred, but something about that didn't sit well with me.

While I loved what Lucky and I were building, I still craved my familiar, undisturbed space.

It was a matter of needing a space to regroup rather than space away from him. I had not considered that angle when I decided to jump back into the love game. With a child in the mix, it would be even harder, ha, it would be impossible to keep tight control over my environment.

I didn't need everything to be just so, but there were some things that were almost non-negotiable. I needed to see clear surfaces. Especially in the kitchen. Particularly around food preparation. One of the thoughts I struggled with was insects in my food. Clear counters were important.

Tightness in my jaw alerted me to the fact my teeth were grinding. I relaxed my jaw and my brow. These were small things. A relationship with Lucky did not mean I had to give up clear counters.

Although, compromises would have to be made. By both of us.

If things continued with us, would he want me to move in with him? Did I want that?

I'd worked so hard to create a comfortable space.

I pushed the thought away. It was too soon. Too soon to even think about it.

My brain threw up obstacles left and right, but my heart had charted its course back in October when I first met him. I feared I was too far gone to pull back now.

It was too soon for declarations of love, and I couldn't think about what it might mean for me if he didn't feel the same. It's one thing to dedicate a song tongue-in-cheek and quite another to declare yourself. I pushed the thoughts aside.

Even good decisions brought consequences, and these musings were mine.

I embraced them.

Junie and I closed the office, and I went to Spuds to have lunch with Ruby and Vander.

Then I packed a bag and headed over to Lucky's place for the weekend.

Chapter 29 - Fuck-Me Heels

<u>Minty</u>

I lay back on the lounge chair in Lucky's backyard, a sparkling water in my hand.

The sound of Lucky's fingers lazily plucking the strings of his guitar mixed with the breeze, the birds, and the sound of children laughing two yards over.

I filled my lungs with warm, fragrant, summer air.

"I could get used to this," I murmured.

He smiled, his eyes warm. "I want you to get used to this."

His words sent a giddy warmth spiraling through my stomach.

I tipped my head back and closed my eyes. I could only take so much of his tender attention. Like a sudden bright light coming on in the dark, I struggled to acclimatize myself to his open adoration.

When I walked into Lucky's house Thursday afternoon, Brayleigh greeted me with a smile and her 'Pinwin'.

Lucky stood behind her in bare feet and ripped jeans with his hands tucked loosely into his back pockets and his deep dimples on display.

I laughed. "You look delicious."

He plucked his hands out of his pockets and raised his eyebrows as he headed toward me, stepping around Brayleigh's small form and cupping his hands around my face. He tipped his chin down and smiled.

"Good enough to eat?" His eyes widened. "Shit! I did not just ask you for a blow job!"

I huffed out a small laugh and answered, "Definitely good enough to eat." I offered my mouth for a kiss.

He moved in but was interrupted by a tinny, high-pitched voice from the vicinity of his thighs.

"I has bow job, too?"

Lucky's face fell. "Fuck me," he breathed.

I snorted as I slapped my hand over his mouth. "For Pete's sake, Captain, stop talking!"

"That Daddy, not Captain."

I smiled into Lucky's twinkling eyes. "Your daddy, my captain."

Several hours later, Lucky crawled over me in his bed, caging me in with his thighs around mine, his elbows braced on either side of my head.

"Hi," he whispered happily. "I like having you in my bed."

"Mm," I hummed throatily. "I like being in your bed."

I dragged my hands down the length of his back, kneading the muscles along his spine, lining his ribs. I quirked my eyebrows at him. "Let's talk about blow jobs."

"Minty, I didn't mean anything by that." Wary apology shone from his eyes.

I wondered why. While we hadn't gotten around to that, I'd given him no indication that I was opposed. Perhaps he still held onto the version of me he believed in when we first met.

Running my hands down to the front of his hips, I closed in around his shaft and gave him a gentle rub through his shorts. "This is not a sexy kind of conversation," I admitted. "But it's a necessary one."

"Okay. I'm listening." He held himself over me, his thumbs stroking the hair at my temples.

I kept hold of him, then edged my fingers under his waistband, wanting the assurance of my hand wrapped around him, for both of us.

"You know I have OCD and that OCD is defined as intrusive thoughts. But that definition doesn't really do justice to how disturbing those thoughts can be. A lot of my intrusive thoughts involve things being in my mouth that have no business being in my mouth." I pressed my lips together and turned my head to the side, taking a long, calming breath to clear my thoughts.

"Minty, you don't have to do it. I don't care."

"Please, Lucky. Please listen hard. This stuff is difficult for me to talk about but it's important to me that you understand. And I really only want to say this once." Whenever I told someone about OCD, I usually recited the basic, textbook definition. It removed the emotion. The more I explained, the closer I got to how it really was for me, the stronger the trigger.

His whole body relaxed as he switched gears into listening mode. How I could ever have thought this man was shallow, I'll never understand.

"Go ahead, baby."

"It's really got more to do with food than anything else, but occasionally it might bleed over into other areas. Remember when we went to Baranga's on the Beach, and I couldn't eat my Greek fries?"

He nodded slowly, his eyes steady.

"My brain told me I was eating bugs, specifically butterflies."

His eyebrows shot up.

"I know I'm not," I rushed to reassure him. "But the images are so vibrant, the idea so persistent, it's difficult for me to get past it. Oftentimes, with food, I simply can't. Saying this, there are times I am incredibly orally sensitive. So, if I ever stop or pull away, even from a kiss, it's not a rejection of you, or your beautiful body, any part of it, it's my OCD symptoms screwing with me."

Understanding dawned on his face. "That's why you're a sometimes vegan."

"Yes," I replied with relief. "That's my super safe food."

He shrugged. "I get it. No problem." He shifted his knees between my thighs and moved down my half naked body. "Lucky for you, I have no such oral sensitivity." His head shot up. "Shit, that was really insensitive."

I opened my mouth to reassure him that I wasn't offended, but he was already up, thumbs hooked into the sides of my panties, grinning wickedly. "I'll just have to make it up to you."

His talented tongue alongside the tender touch of his calloused fingers made short work of my answering laughter, effectively short-circuiting my brain of any thought other than the pleasure wrought by the man between my legs.

The next night, I planned to return the favor, but he wasn't having it.

"Lucky, I want to," I protested when he stopped me.

"I know," he said, closing his eyes for a moment as if pained. "But I felt that, what you said, the horror of it, and I need to get my head around it, trust that you're not going to do something you don't want to do." He opened his eyes. "We have time, we'll get there." He grinned. "I'm highly motivated."

It struck me, in that moment, how well he had listened, how easily he had grasped the horror of it all. It flooded me with gratitude, floated a minuscule vessel of hope that he might be able to handle it.

Handle me.

Saturday morning, Hope blew in the door on with coffee and donuts from Tim Horton's. After regaling us with tales from her work week, she scooped up Brayleigh and her penguin to take her home until Lucky picked her up again on Thursday.

Saturday afternoon, Lucky did yardwork while I read and worked on my commissions. Saturday night he played at a bar in downtown Milltown, and I watched with Junie, then reaped the benefits of his adrenalin.

Sunday we all landed at Barrett and Willa's where I hogged Rena for most of the afternoon, which brought us to Monday. Lazing on loungers, the sound of the neighborhood kids playing, Lucky lazily strumming on his guitar, me reading.

I could definitely get used to this.

Monday night I headed home. For the first time since I moved in almost two decades before, I wasn't looking forward to the solitude.

Thankfully, it was short-lived. Alex, Jace, and George, landed on my doorstep about ten minutes after I got home.

"Minnie!" Alex shouted when I opened the door.

"Boys!"

I opened my arms, and they piled in. Jace and Alex immediately wrapped their arms around me. George sidled up beside me and gave me a gentle squeeze once the others released me.

"We want to stay with you tonight," Alex began.

"My mom's going to text you," Jace added.

"It's okay if you're busy," George interjected.

"We just thought we'd stay here tonight and then already be here tomorrow to go to the movies!" Alex finished off.

"It's a solid plan," I assured them. "Are we ordering in or going out to eat?"

"We should go out," Alex said, indicating George. "Seeing as how Spuds is closed, he can't pick it."

George punched him lightly on the arm.

My cell lit up with messages from both Ruby and Amber. I took a few minutes to assure them both I was onboard with the change in plans, and then took my boys out for dinner.

Tuesday morning, they played video games while I went downstairs to the office with Junie. Tuesday afternoon we made homemade pizza then went to the movies before I dropped them home.

Wednesday was supposed to be a quiet day, but Willa showed up at the office with Rena just before lunch.

We ate at Spuds, where Junie determined that I needed an injection of sex into my wardrobe just as Ruby swung through the connecting door to the back. She overheard and chortled in agreement. The door closed behind her momentarily before admitting Vander to the front.

"What are you laughing at?" Junie appraised Ruby in her jeans and t-shirt. "You could use an injection of sex as well."

"What the fuck?"

"In her wardrobe, Vander." I clarified, chuckling as his confusion cleared.

"Ah," he said, giving his wife the once over before grabbing her. "You're perfect. Don't listen to them. Unless they're going lingerie shopping. In which case, I insist."

"Definitely hitting the lingerie store," I answered.

Vander threw up his hand in the universal stop sign. "Nope! I do not need to know about you and the Captain." He released his wife. "Go, Ruby. And take your friends and their foul mouths with you."

"Don't worry, Vander," I replied soothingly. "I'm not going to say a word, but isn't it ironic that we all know about you?"

He took off his glasses and rubbed a rough hand over his face then sighed and winked at Ruby. "Well, you better buy something nice so I can give you something to talk about."

Willa nursed Rena and then we piled into the huge SUV that Barrett bought for her the week after they got married. She grumbled about missing her tiny compact car and her independence up until the day she put Rena in it for the first time on the way home from the hospital. And then she got it. Told me she wanted to trade up for a Hummer.

Ruby texted Amber from the car, and she met us at the food court of the mall, joining us at our table.

"I'm here to ensure this one," Amber indicated Junie who she'd met several times over the years, "doesn't have you dressing like a rockstar, and this one," she indicated Ruby, "doesn't have you dressing like a teenage boy. Willa's going to keep us all in line."

"I have a list," Willa assured her.

"When did you have time to make a list?" I asked.

"When Junie called me last week to tell me you needed a wardrobe overhaul."

I turned to Junie who shrugged. "It's true. You're dating a man who looks like Lucky and plays lead guitar in a band. You can't go see him play looking like a wealthy PTA Mom. Okay," she allowed. "A wealthy PTA MILF." She assessed Amber. "You could use a bit of a sex injection yourself."

Amber laughed. "I get plenty of sex, thank you very much!"

"In your wardrobe," I clarified.

Willa looked her over as she fussed over Rena, setting the shade of the car seat low so strangers wouldn't stick their fingers in to touch her cheek. She was such a pretty baby I could see how they would struggle to resist, but ew.

Amber smiled like a fat cat. "I could use some new lingerie."

"How about some shoes?" Junie quipped. "Some fuck-me heels?"

We all knew about Amber's penchant for flip-flops and slippers.

"You find me a pair of sexy heels to wear with lingerie to bed, and I'll buy them," she promised.

Junie nodded with a smile. "Challenge accepted."

Following Willa's list, we passed by all my usual stores, and I thought about how accurately Junie had summarized my look. I didn't used to dress like that. At some point, clothes became my armor rather than a spotlight to highlight my best features. I hid behind my beautiful, but modest, clothing. The clothes were on display, they did not display me. Or even reflect me.

By nature, I was not a modest, conservative kind of girl.

Somewhere along the way, I decided hiding my sex appeal was safer.

I thought back. I think it was when Angus came on the scene. The images OCD threw at me about that man, especially in the beginning, made me want to curl into a ball and put a bag over my head. I worried incessantly that he could read my thoughts by looking at me. That Amber would know. After a while they eased off. To say that was a relief was a massive understatement.

I considered for a moment and realized I still got them but could dismiss them easily. I loved him. I felt no guilt about that. Gus's heart was made of gold. His heart made me safer than any amount of clothing I could put on. If I allowed OCD to scare me away from him, I'd lose Amber and I could not entertain that.

Eventually, I became desensitized to those pictures.

Eventually, I trusted that they were fear based, not lust based. I'd never act on them. I didn't want to act on them. Those images were unwanted and caused me all kinds of distress. Sexual OCD was like having your brain sexually assaulted. But. There was the added assurance that Gus would never see me like that which enabled me to relax around him. He was one of only a handful of people I'd allowed close to me.

So, it wasn't Angus, but somewhere along the way, I decided I was a threat. Maybe even a contaminant? That I needed to find a way to make sure I didn't lose control and one way to do that was to camouflage myself, fade into the background.

Maybe it was when the boys started sleeping over.

Yes. That bit of truth clicked. It was the boys. How could I feel so relaxed around Gus but not around the boys?

They were vulnerable.

If I lost control and did something inadvertently, they'd be hurt. I knew I'd never hurt them, but, oh, God! *What if?*

"What are you thinking so hard about?" Junie elbowed me lightly.

I looked up to find everyone's eyes on me. I smiled. "Fuck-me heels."

Chapter 30 – Saddle Up

Minty

Thursday, I packed a bag with my new look and set off to rock Lucky's world.

I'd made a mistake in telling him about my oral OCD issues. I'd meant to be honest and transparent, but somehow, I communicated a distaste for oral sex. It wasn't his fault. Or mine. Who could understand the fuckery of the OCD brain except someone who had it?

I did not have a distaste for oral sex.

At all.

With the right man.

And he was definitely the right man.

Lucky instructed me to walk right in when I arrived. I closed the door gently and Brayleigh toddled out of the living room to meet me in the hallway.

"Hi, Sparky!" She squealed with her arms up.

I set my bags down and held my hands out to her. "Hi, dolly," I murmured as she pressed her fingers into the back of my neck. I'd seen her do it so often to Lucky, and also Hope, that I could picture the chubby, little, white-tipped sausages clearly.

She drew back and lifted my necklace up to her face.

"This mine sparky?"

I smiled.

"Daddy's," Lucky growled from the other room.

"You think Daddy would look nice in Minnie's sparkles? Hm?"

"Not daddy's," she whisper-shouted. "Mine sparky!"

At the mall with the girls, I ran into Claire's Accessories. At the back of the store was a toddler section complete with furry purses, hair extensions, tiaras, and enough glitter to choke a unicorn.

The woman who worked there, Amanda, had a diva of her own. She had no trouble outfitting me with the best and brightest, emphasis on brightest, for my little dolly.

"Minnie brought you your own sparkles. You want to see?"

She squiggled in my arms, grabbing onto my breast for leverage as she struggled to be put down faster than I could bend.

I grabbed her wrist and yanked her off.

Ouch.

You liked that.

My nipple was definitely harder than it was a second ago. Just the one. The one that she squeezed. That's normal. If I was turned on, both would be hard.

Lucky came down the hall.

What if he can read your mind?

He can't.

But if he could, what would he think?

Nothing. Because there's nothing to think.

Are you sure?

Don't argue with OCD.

I smiled. Thank you for your input.

"There you go again." Lucky offered me a half-smile as he covered the distance between us. "You having conversations all in your head again? You want to let me in on this one?"

Absolutely fucking not.

I smiled. "I went shopping. Bought presents for Dolly." I lowered my voice. "Bought a treat for you, too."

His face lit up. "You bought me a present?"

"Mm," I pondered. Seemed Lucky liked presents. I loved to buy presents. I foresaw more shopping in my future. Happiness filled my chest. "More like an experience."

His smile broadened. "I like the sound of that."

What kinds of things would Lucky like? I'd only ever heard him talk about things he wanted for his students, his classroom. Not once had I ever heard him talk about something he wanted for himself.

Brayleigh and I sat on the floor of the family room. I tucked my long sundress around my legs, ensuring there were no revealing gaps, and passed her the gift bag.

Lucky sat directly across from me on the couch, his legs spread, his elbows resting on his knees, hands loose between his thighs.

I so badly wanted to crawl up between his legs, push him back against the couch, and undo the zipper of his jeans.

His chuckle interrupted my chain of thought. "I think I know what you're thinking this time."

I held his gaze until the heat flared in his eyes. I winked at him and promised, "I'll show you later."

"Please, God, let her go to bed easily tonight," he muttered.

In typical toddler fashion, Brayleigh pulled each item out of the bag and tossed it to the side before going in for the next. Only after she'd emptied everything out onto the floor did she go back and examine each item.

"Mine sparky?"

"Yours," I agreed.

"Mine sparky," she whispered to herself over and again as she rifled through hair ties, bracelets, purses, hair extensions and finally the tiara which she picked up. Her face twisted into a grimace as she tried to rip the tag off.

"Here, let Minnie help you." I reached for it, but she drew her arm back, her eyes going wide with a warning glare at the same time as her mouth drew down into a heavy frown. "Oh, my!" I laughed, looking at Lucky. "She looks like she's going to slug me!"

"She does! Dad's going to get the scissors, Brayleigh, so we can cut off the tags. What do you say to Minty?"

She threw her hands up and laughed. "Mine sparky!"

Princessed to the max, Brayleigh spent the rest of the afternoon squealing her three favorite words, 'look at me'. She said it to Hope when she dropped by after Lucky called and invited her. She said it to Lucky's sisters, Ava and Darcy who met us at the park. She said it to Tracy and Dani via Facetime.

And she said it to Lucky and me over and again as she danced and spun and ate and stared at herself in the mirror. She said it in the house, in the backyard, at the park, at the kitchen table, in the tub, and finally, in her bed.

By the time she fell asleep, I could honestly say I hated the sound of her voice. And yet, I could not wait to see if she was just as enamored with her sparkles tomorrow.

Lucky lay back in his bed. It was a rare occurrence that he looked tired.

He turned his head and offered a half smile. "You didn't happen to bring a ball gag for her for tomorrow?" Then he covered his face and groaned. "I forgot to tell you something. You're going to hate me."

"Well now, that sounds ominous. Perhaps you'd better just spit it out," I teased. Half of me braced for I didn't know what, the other half didn't believe for one second it could be bad.

"Brayleigh's been having night terrors." He watched my face as I took in the news.

"Indeed."

He raised his eyebrows. "You know what those are?"

215

"Yes. Alex, that's Amber and Angus's son, had them. I slept at their house a few nights a week when he went through that phase. It was truly horrible." I sighed. "I have to tell you something, too."

"What is it?" He looked concerned.

"I cannot stand the sound of Dolly's voice," I whispered.

His eyes widened momentarily and then he laughed and grabbed me.

"I'm serious," I continued. "If I hear her say 'look at me' one more time, I'm going to poke my own eyes out with a screwdriver, just so I don't have to comply."

Rolling on top of me, his hips pressed me into the mattress. "You're never going to buy her sparkles again."

"On the contrary, I'm going to the Disney store to buy her princess dresses. There will be a plethora of sparkles."

"She'll never shut up," he teased.

"I know." I smiled at the thought. "And now you're telling me that she's going to be screaming, at the top of her little lungs, in the middle of the night?"

"Yeah," he admitted with a small frown. "It's really bad. The first night it happened, I was in her room ready to fight somebody before I'd fully opened my eyes. Hope warned me." He paused and shuddered.

I finished his sentence. "But there is no warning that can prepare you for that level of terror in their voices. Poor Hope."

He chuckled. "She said she near pissed herself the first time it happened."

"She's incredibly funny. I can see why you guys are best friends." I smiled into his eyes.

"Mm," he agreed, brushing the backs of his fingers against my cheek. "Are you going to be okay with it?"

"Yes, darling. This is not my first rodeo."

He grinned. "You going to saddle up?"

"Actually, I thought I'd practice my roping skills. Well, my knot-tying skills."

216

Sparks ignited behind his eyes. "Now this sounds interesting. I'm all for supporting skills development. How can I help?"

I slid out from under him and retrieved the silk scarves I'd packed in my bag and brought them over to the bed.

"You seem to be under the misguided impression that I don't want your cock in my mouth."

He groaned and threw his forearm over his eyes. "Damn, Minty. Your mouth kills me."

"Well, darling, let's see what you think of my mouth in about twenty minutes."

He swallowed and peeked at me from under his arm. "You're not going to do anything you don't want to?"

"Lucky," I looked at him seriously. "I want to." I slid a scarf through my fingers. "Just to prove it to you that you're not pushing for this, I'll tie your wrists to your headboard. You okay with that?"

His eyebrows went up. "I've, uh, never done that before."

"Really?" I flicked open the button of his jeans and drew the fly down before easing his jeans and his boxers off. "In all your adventures you've never been tied up?"

"One-night stands don't tend to get too adventurous," he admitted, his voice hoarse.

I trailed my fingers up the insides of his thighs, around to the outside of his hips, then up over his ribs under his shirt.

He ab-crunched and reached back to yank his shirt off over his head. He dropped it on the floor, wrapped his arms around my back and pulled me on top of him. His wary eyes bore into mine.

I rolled my pelvis against his erection.

His brain may not have been fully on board, but his body was ready to go.

"How about I just thread the scarf through the headboard, and you just hang onto the ends?" I murmured.

"How about I not be a pussy and you go ahead and tie me to the headboard?" he answered. "Take off your clothes."

"I think I'm going to tie you up first so you can't touch," I whispered along the line of his jaw.

I secured his wrists to the headboard, stripped at the side of the bed where he could see me, then climbed up on the bed and threw my leg over his hips. My tongue traced the contours of his beautiful mouth, and I ground against his cock.

His hips bucked up against me.

I lay my palm against his chest. "You're going to stay as still as you possibly can until you can't help it, then you're going to fuck my mouth like your life depends on it."

Lucky's face flushed, and his arms yanked against the restraints. "Fuck. I want you on your back," he rasped.

I laughed lightly. "Now, now, patience is a virtue, you know..."

With tongue, and lips, and teeth, I licked and nibbled and kissed my way across his chest and down his abdomen as he lay rigid beneath me.

I trailed my tongue up the underside of his penis, from base to glorious tip.

He inhaled deeply, the muscles of his ass clenching, but did not move.

At the tip, I opened my mouth wide and took him to the back of my throat.

His breath released with a grunt, and his hips bucked.

"Fuck! Sorry!"

Ignoring him, I opened my throat and pressed forward until my nose hit his groin and swallowed.

"Minty, Minty, Minty..." He trembled beneath me.

I lavished him with attention, leaving no place unlicked, unkissed, unloved.

His heels pressed into the mattress, he grasped the scarves in his fists, and still he did not move.

I released him with a gentle pop, and he grunted.

Moving up, I flicked his nipples with my tongue on my way to his mouth. I kissed him gently then positioned myself over his hips.

He looked up at me, his eyes hazy.

"The rules are the same. Do not move. And Lucky," I warned, "Do not come."

"I won't, I won't. Fuck, I hope I don't," he babbled.

Reaching down, I stroked through my wet and brought my finger to his mouth as I slowly sank down, sheathing him deeply inside me.

He sucked my finger into his mouth as his eyes rolled back in his head.

I rode him slowly, taking him as deep as I could, rolling my hips, letting him fill all my empty places. My head fell back. I was going to give in before he did.

I forced myself off him, dragged my mouth along the side of his cock, then kissed him.

"Baby, sweetheart, my beautiful, dirty girl, I can taste you..."

"Yes, and now I'm going to taste you."

Moving back down to kneel in a ball between his spread thighs, I licked and teased without mercy, pulling sounds from his throat and his chest I'd not yet heard as he struggled to hold back. His hips punched up once, twice, before he locked it down.

He gasped. "I don't want to come in your mouth. Are you wet? Tell me you're wet."

"Soaked," I replied throatily. "My thighs are slippery from having your cock in my mouth."

He groaned. "Climb up here. Give me that pussy. I want to come inside you. Fuck, Minty, hurry."

I moved to straddle his lap.

"No, wait. Up here. Get on my face," he demanded.

We'd never done that position. I froze. "With your hands tied down?"

He lifted his head to look at me, his eyes smoking. "Yes," he hissed.

"Are you sure?"

"Never been so sure of anything in my entire life." He thrust his hips up, bumping my ass and shifting me forward. "Up."

A few careful adjustments later, I hovered over his face.

He turned his head to the side and licked the wet off my thigh. His breath came in harsh pants. "Get down here," he growled.

I spread my knees and he latched onto my clit causing me to cry out. Oh, the pleasure! I ground down against his face.

What if he doesn't really want this?

He does.

He's tied down.

"You want me to release your hands, darling?" I panted.

"No. Fuck, no," he answered before driving his tongue inside me.

What if he's only doing this because you want it?

"I need you to talk to me, Lucky," I panted.

"Give me that pussy, baby." He licked and fucked me with his tongue. "Make yourself feel good."

I ground down and he groaned. "That's it, sweetheart. Come on my face."

Oh god! His tongue, his lips, his teeth, his scruff.

His hips punched the air. "Fucking drown me in it."

I cried out, womb clenching, pussy fluttering, back bowing, my man groaning beneath me.

"Untie me," he growled. "Fucking untie me."

I reached up and frantically pulled the end of the scarf to release him.

He slid out from beneath me then flipped me onto my stomach, pulled up my hips, thrust inside, and flattened me to the bed, his lips pressed to the nape of my neck as he found his release.

After several long minutes, when I was beginning to wonder if I was going to suffocate under his weight, he shifted to the side, bringing me with him.

"So," he cleared his throat. "Safe to say, I'm a fan of your knot-tying skills."

I laughed weakly, my body limp and sated.

He pressed a gentle kiss to the nape of my neck.

A godawful scream, the sound reminiscent of a horror movie, shattered the sweetness that rested between us.

We flew off the bed, a tangle of naked limbs and heart—pumping adrenalin.

He recovered from the shock first and laughed. "At least she let us finish!"

Chapter 31 – Sunday Morning Duet

Lucky

The weekend unfolded like a wash, rinse, repeat of the previous one, and I wondered when I could convince Minty to make the routine daily. And permanent.

Monday morning, she lay curled against me.

I wished I could shift to better see her beautiful face, but I didn't want to disturb her sleep. In sleep, her limbs took on a different type of stillness than she possessed while awake. Awake, she controlled her movements. Asleep seemed to be the only time her awareness slipped.

My dick saluted, reminding me of the other time she sometimes relinquished control.

To think I'd worried about chemistry. I thought back to the day of the barbecue when Junie teased me about Minty giving me a run for my money. She knew what I was getting into. I pictured her rubbing her little mitts together and her glee on the front porch when she saw me waiting for Minty that same day and couldn't help the small chuckle that escaped.

Minty stretched out languidly beside me, pressing her breasts against my side and throwing her thigh over mine. She lay her palm over my heart and dropped a kiss on my chest before nestling back into my shoulder.

"Good morning," she murmured.

That was another thing I hadn't expected. Other than the first time we woke together when she was loathe to abandon her strict routine, mornings signaled a time for gentle caresses, fleeting kisses, murmured plans, and a slow revving of engines for the day's race.

"I learned a song for you." My heart pounded in my chest.

She bent her neck back to look at me, giving me her beautiful face.

I loved seeing her without make-up. Soft mouth, the lightest sprinkling of freckles on her pale skin, golden lashes, and clear brown gaze unaltered by the effects of eyeshadow.

"A song? You learned a song for me?" She sat up, pulling the sheet to her breasts, and twisted back to look at me. "Are you going to play it for me?"

"I kind of thought you could learn it too, maybe sing it with me. If you wanted to. It's a duet."

"Play it for me. Please," she murmured.

I grabbed my pajama pants off the foot of the bed and tossed her my t-shirt.

While I liked to be naked with her, and I loved keeping her naked, the song exposed me enough. I needed my pants. And if she didn't feel the same way, she'd want my shirt.

I plucked the opening notes of Penny and Sparrow's *Duet*, then began to sing the words my heart demanded I say.

Other than a few glances, I kept my eyes on the strings.

When I finished, our room was utterly silent.

Our room. When did I start thinking about this bedroom as ours?

When I finally manned up enough to look at her, to ask her what she thought, the naked yearning on her face shocked me back into silence.

She sat smack dab in the center of the bed, her arms wrapped around her drawn-up knees.

My heart leapt to my throat.

She cleared her throat. "Do you mean it?"

I nodded firmly, my eyes steely and determined.

She unfolded her legs, stood straight up on the bed, and took the first step toward me.

I quickly set my guitar to the side, and the next moment she landed on my lap, her shins digging into my thighs.

She cupped her hands around my jaw, and I filled my palms with her ass.

"Are you sure?" Her eyes skittered back and forth as she searched mine. "Can you handle it? Can you handle me? Are you sure?"

Now that I knew where her head was at, I relaxed back into my seat and pulled her closer, forcing her legs to drop to the sides. "I'm sure."

"Sure, sure?" A mix of hope and disbelief widened her eyes and knit her brows.

"Positive."

I held her gaze. Unwavering.

"Do you..." Her mouth clamped shut.

"Ask, baby," I coaxed.

"Do you...um..." She cleared her throat. "How do you feel about me?"

"I feel like I want you to move in with me. I feel like I want you to be Brayleigh's other mother. I feel like I want to be able to find your face in the crowd when I play a gig, wake up with you every morning and go to sleep beside you every night. I want to be the one to hold you when you're down, soothe you when you fear, and fuck the insecurities out of you whenever they raise their ugly little heads. I breathe easier when you're near and I laugh harder. You make me stronger, and I want to be the one who does the same for you. I want you. And Minty, I've never in my life said these words to any woman in a romantic sense, I love you."

"Are you sure?" she whispered.

I gathered her up in my arms and held her against my chest. "I'm sure. It's easy. For me, it's as simple and necessary and complex as breathing. You're in my soul."

"Lucky," she began.

"You don't have to say it back, sweetheart. I'll wait on you," I promised.

"Captain," she melted in my arms, "I love you, too. I just, I never, I mean, I hoped, but never expected you to feel the same."

"Whyever not? My God, I'm so damn thankful no one scooped you up before I got my chance."

"I just never, I mean, when I decided to find someone, I pictured a man of retirement age-"

"Retirement?" The very idea was ludicrous. "You? You'd give the man a coronary!"

She laughed, the sound like Christmas, and wrapped her arms around my neck.

She pressed her forehead to mine and tilted her chin up so the tips of our noses touched. "I love you, Lucky."

"Good. So. When are you moving in?"

Minty

Alex, Jace, and George lay on the couches looking at their cell phones. They seemed off kilter somehow.

"Boys. Are we going out or ordering in?"

George shrugged.

Alex tucked his head further into his neck.

Jace's shoulders drooped, and his chin dimpled.

I edged onto the couch between Jace and Alex, across from George who lounged on the chair. Which of the three of them would be most likely to talk. Normally, that would be Alex, but he was turtling so hard I feared for his vertebrae. I lay my hand gently on Jace's knee.

"Jace? What happened?"

He met my eyes for a painfully, pregnant moment, then dropped his face into his hands. At that, George stood up abruptly and stalked down to the bedroom, slamming the door.

Alarm bells rang loudly. Turning to Alex, I leveled him with a look that brooked no arguments. "Alex, tell me what is going on immediately."

Alex curled into himself, wrapping his arms around his stomach. "George's mom called him on his cell. She cried and stuff. Said he abandoned her just like his dad. Told him he was just like Uncle Vander. And not like it was a good thing."

"Huh." I sat back on the couch for half a second before sitting forward and grasping him lightly under his jaw. "Thank you for telling me. Does Thia Ruby know?"

Alex shrugged.

"Jace?" I turned to him.

He shook his head miserably. "George doesn't want them to know. Said Thio Vander will be even more mad, and he'll never get to see his mom or his sisters again."

"Okay." I exhaled long and slow, surprised I didn't breathe fire. "I can see how he might think that but it's not true." I sat back and opened my arms.

Both boys leaned in, their heads on my chest, arms crossing over each other's around my waist. The fact they hugged me like that betrayed the depth of their angst.

I ruffled my fingers through their hair. Alex's fair and floppy like Angus's. Jace's curly and unruly like Vander's. And George's.

"I'm going to tell you a secret. You mustn't tell George, but you knowing the truth will be helpful for him in the long run."

They nodded against my chest.

"Fact number one. George's mom is not a good woman, and she hates your uncle Vander. That's between the two of them, and that's where it should stay, but she cares more about hurting Vander than she does about sparing George."

They nodded again. Jace sniffed. Alex reached for the end of my ponytail and twisted it around his fingers. His forearm stretched over my breast.

His arm is on your breast. Are you enjoying that? Are you molesting him? Are you sure?

I shrugged off the thought. I'd deal with the fallout later. Right now, my boy needed me.

"Fact number two. And this one is even more important than fact number one. Nothing that woman will do will stop George from wanting her to love him."

Jace slumped further against me, and Alex twirled my hair faster between his fingers.

"What we need to express to George is that he has our love. That he is loveable. And one day he will realize that she is the way she is, and it's not because of anything lacking in him."

I took a deep breath attempting to ease the familiar ache around my heart and cool the fire in my gut. "The other thing we must do is protect him from her bullying. This means we can't keep this secret."

"He's going to be mad at us," Jace whispered.

"Maybe," I nodded. "But underneath that he'll be relieved that he doesn't have to carry this by himself."

A noise from the hallway alerted me to George's presence.

Jace and Alex lurched up ramrod straight, their anxious eyes shooting to George.

George stood with his hands pushed deep in the pockets of his shorts, his face drawn and pale. "You can tell Ruby, Minnie." He looked at the boys. "I'm not mad. Not at you."

"Alright!" I stood up. "I'll tell Ruby and your dad later if that's okay, unless you'd rather I just did it now?"

"Later," he replied, some of the tension dropping from his shoulders.

"Okay." I clapped my hands sharply. "Get ready. We're going go-carting."

"Are you going to race?" Alex asked tentatively, the beginnings of a smile spreading across his freckled face.

"Damn right. If Ruby can beat Vander, I can definitely beat you three."

"You're going to wear a helmet?" Jace asked skeptically, studying me as he moved closer to George.

"I am."

"I can't picture Minnie in a helmet," George mused, smiling faintly at Jace as they found their shoes.

"I'll have you know my boyfriend rides a motorcycle and when he takes me for a ride I wear a helmet."

George's eyebrows shot up. "Mr. Triggs rides a motorcycle?"

"Indeed." I grabbed my purse and keys.

"And you go on it with him?" Alex asked as he pulled his shoes on, still skeptical.

"I do," I confirmed, opening the door, my small posse surrounding me.

"Are you going to get your own motorcycle?" Jace asked.

I laughed. "I am not."

Much later, after I beat them around the track, after I took them down to the beach for fish and chips and ice cream, after we watched Jurassic Park and I screamed, much to their delight, at all the obligatory parts, after they went to bed and I called Ruby and cried, especially when she put Vander on the extension and I heard the pain and disbelief in his voice, after all that, I slid into my bed and I wished for Lucky's arms around me.

And I thanked God he had a child with a woman who loved him.

A soft knock sounded at my door.

"Come in," I called softly, pushing myself up against the headboard and ensuring the sheet was tucked around my body. I wore pajamas, thick ones, but the lack of a bra made me feel exposed.

I fully expected to see Jace. There was no place in his tender heart that could fathom such an astronomical betrayal, but it was George who peeked his head around the door jam.

"Minnie, can I come in?"

"Of course," I replied. "What do you need?"

"Can I talk to you?"

"Yes. Of course." I moved to swing my legs out of the bed. "Do you want to go in the kitchen?"

"No." He turned and gently closed the door. "I don't want them to hear me if they get up."

"No problem." I moved over to the far side of the bed and patted the side closest to him.

He ducked his head and walked over, slowly easing himself down on the edge of the bed.

Alarms screamed in my head. Nothing about this situation felt safe. Should I call Vander to come and get him?

"Why doesn't she love me?"

All my attention swung back to the broken boy in front of me.

"Oh, honey. If she doesn't love you, she's not capable of loving anybody."

His back bowed, his shoulders curled in, and his face screwed up until a sob ripped from his throat.

I launched myself across the bed and gathered him up in my arms.

He grasped onto the back of my shirt and fisted the material tightly in his hands while his body shook with the force of his repressed sobs.

"Okay, my darling." I rocked him. "Okay, my honey." If she was in front of me in that instant, I believe I would have killed her. I knew the years ahead of him would be difficult. His ability to trust dampened, relationships strained. Especially with women. "You've got every right to cry. She hurt you. You didn't deserve it, darling. Do you hear me? You never deserved it."

After several minutes, he broke away from me. Lifting the edge of his shirt, he exposed his baby six pack and wiped his face. "Can I stay with you for a bit?"

"Yes, of course."

I crossed to my reading chair, grabbed the fleece blanket from the back, and threw it over him before getting back into bed.

He lay down. "Can I ask you something?"

"You can ask me anything. If I can't answer you, I'll tell you."

"Your mom and dad..."

"Ah, yes. What would you like to know? I'm an open book."

"How..."

229

I waited, but there were no more words forthcoming. "How did I cope?"

"Yes," he choked out.

I turned on my side to face him and reached for his hand and held it tightly. "Fortunately, I met some people who fell in love with me." I paused, wondering how much to tell him. "It never filled the hole left by my parents, but it taught me that I was loveable. The failure to love me belonged to them, not me."

"Am I loveable?" His little Adam's apple bobbed in his throat.

"What do you think?" I whispered.

He nodded, then hiccoughed. "I am."

"Indeed," I whispered. "We all love you. So much. Your dad, Ruby, Amber, Gus, Jace, Alex, Yiayia, and me. Your stepdad loves you. Your sisters love you. We can't all be wrong."

"I'm just going to stay here for a little while then I'll go to bed, okay?"

"That's fine, my darling."

I did my best to stay awake.

I failed.

When I woke up a few hours later, George's fleece blanket was tucked around me, and George was gone.

Chapter 32 – Nobody's Talking

<u>Minty</u>

Vander knocked on my door first thing in the morning so he and George could go pick up coffee and donuts for all of us. Vander told him he wouldn't keep him from his sisters but couldn't allow his mom to be abusive. He assured him of his love and asked him if he wanted to hang out with him for the day or stay with me and the boys.

George decided to stay. Last night's crises called for an all-day affair: the mall, dinner, and the movies. But first, Spuds for lunch. And an excuse for George to touch base with his dad one more time.

"She beat us, Mom!" Jace nodded emphatically, brandishing a potato wedge to make his point as he regaled them with the tale of my prowess on the racetrack the night before. "She was awesome!"

"I think it's from riding the motorbike," Alex commented.

"She doesn't drive the bike, Mr. Triggs does," George added.

"Yes." Alex held up a finger. "But now she has a need for speed."

We all laughed, George hardest of all, while Ruby narrowed her eyes at me.

"I challenge you to a race! You and me. We'll see who the real champion is."

"Certainly," I agreed. "Did you ask the boys if I had to cheat to win?"

"Low blow!" she protested. "Vander, tell her I won fair and square."

"Sorry, Ruby-mine. No can do."

Their joviality was forced but had the desired effect on the boys.

"I'll still race you, Ruby. Maybe we can ask Amber, too."

Ruby laughed. "She'd be ruthless."

"Indeed." I grinned at her. It's those quiet ones you have to watch.

By the time I dropped the boys off home, George had regained his equilibrium, but I had not.

I had broken one of my cardinal rules. Not just one. Three.

First, I was alone behind a closed door with one of the boys.

Second, I was not dressed appropriately in their presence because I was not wearing a bra under my pajamas.

And third, I fell asleep while alone in my fucking bed with him. It was paramount that I remain vigilant. Falling asleep meant letting down my guard. What if I lost control? I fucking knew I would never touch any of them, but I could not tolerate the distress wrought by those thoughts. That's what the rules guarded against.

Did you touch him while you slept?

No.

Are you sure? Maybe you rubbed up on him thinking he was Lucky?

I did tend to do that in bed with Lucky, backing up until my booty nestled into the cradle of his groin. Did I do that with George? The thought horrified me.

All day long I'd searched George's face and manner for hints or clues that I might have down something untoward. There were none that I could discern. He smiled at me and seemed much more relaxed. But what kind of barometer did he have? His mother was a fucking monster.

If anything happened, he wouldn't tell anyone. He was ready to let his mother run roughshod over him. He was too vulnerable. Oh, God! How did I let this happen?

I should have taken him out to the kitchen.

Lucky called and picked up on my mood immediately. I confided in him about what happened with George's mom but couldn't bring myself to tell him about the OCD thoughts.

"Some people should not have children," I murmured into the phone.

"Yes, I agree," he replied firmly. "But the world would be a far bleaker place without you in it. I can easily say the same thing about George. He's a great kid."

"True. We'll just have to love him harder."

"That's it, baby."

"You understand about the broken kids."

"My classes are full of them." He sighed. "There's only so much you can do. George is surrounded by good people. I have to believe he'll be okay."

Grateful that he wasn't pushing me about moving in, I remembered something else I was thankful for.

"It's because she hates Vander so much, and she's a freaking monster, that she's hurting George. I'll tell you, after seeing George's face...after hearing Vander's voice, I'm so grateful that Hope loves you."

"Aw, baby. Your heart is so pure, do you know that?"

"Lucky..."

"Tell me, baby. What's wrong?"

"I'm having an OCD flare-up. It's not serious, but I need to regroup. I'll still be there on Thursday. I'm just letting you know I'm currently at a low point."

"Is there anything I can do?"

"I don't think so. If I think of something, I'll ask."

Wednesday morning, as soon as Junie left, I headed out to the house to see Ezinne.

She met me at the door, filling the frame with her smile as usual. "Well don't you look like a used dishrag."

"Ha," I barked out a laugh, grateful for her straightforward manner that left me no room to misinterpret. "I feel like a used dishrag."

I stopped at the door, almost too tired to step over the threshold.

Ezinne held out her hands for mine and tugged me inside. "Let's go to my office first, then you can talk to the girls. They all have news they'll want to share with you. Your friends have been here. Mara and Bex? Those two are a hoot together! Anyway, the girls all have things to share with you and I think you might even get a little gift."

"I don't deserve them," I muttered.

"The very fact you value them tells me you do."

Ezinne took her regular seat, and I took mine. Her office sat off the kitchen. A hundred years ago, it probably served as the cook's bedroom. It was always cozier, but since Ezinne took over and filled it with vibrant color and life-giving plants, it was a haven.

The silence stretched comfortably between us, clearing space for me to think, beckoning me to share, inviting me to trust.

"Do you think I'm a danger to anyone?"

"Under the right circumstances, anyone could be a danger. Why should you be any different?"

"Do you think my OCD makes me a danger?"

"Are OCD thoughts dangerous?"

"Only to the person thinking them," I grumbled.

The simple act of walking through these doors allowed me to lower my guard. Well, that and the fact that Ezinne had been my sounding board for years.

"Are your OCD thoughts things you want to do?"

"No."

"Do they cause you distress?"

"Yes."

"What makes you think they might make you dangerous?"

"If I lose control. If I somehow capitulate to its demands. Even accidentally."

"Lay it out for me."

I looked at her steadily, my anger rising.

For once, she broke the silence. "You know, when you first brought this up, I lay it out for you. I explained about harm OCD and pedophilia OCD as well as the others, and I didn't ask you to specify what was going on. I knew by the distress on your face it had to be one of the big, bad, ones." She paused and frowned. "I wonder now if that was a mistake. Hiding it is not serving you."

"How does saying it out loud help?"

She shrugged. "Doesn't it?"

I maintained my silence.

"Let me ask you this. Of all the other types of OCD you've had, all the symptoms you've overcome, how many of those did you bring out into the light?"

I sighed. "All of them."

"You want me to tell you that you're a safe person. You want me to tell you that you're trustworthy." She shrugged. "You are safe. You are trustworthy. It doesn't matter that I believe it. You gotta believe it."

Ezinne caught me up on some of the happenings around the house, and I visited with the girls before I left. They gifted me with a delicate linked bracelet they made with Bex. I put it on immediately, noting how the tiny gemstones caught the light, while they caught me up on the rest of their news. One had decided to start working part-time with Ruby and Vander, and a couple others jumped at the chance to attend to craft fair with me on Sunday.

It was the last one. By the end of July, I typically had so many commissions that it did not make sense to continue into August. This year I had more than usual. I would have thought with Willa and Junie pulling back I'd have more time to work, but I had less. The drive to be with Lucky and Brayleigh ate up all the extra time.

I headed home with full intentions of working on my portrait commissions. Halfway there, it occurred to me that I could not be the only OCD sufferer with obsessions related to sex, harm, aggression, or pedophilia. Surely, somewhere in the world wide web, someone had shared how their thoughts looked and sounded.

If I could compare my thoughts to theirs, if I could prove to myself that those disturbing thoughts I had were indeed OCD and not some deviant desire that I needed to repress, I could dismiss those thoughts in the same way I dismissed the other types of OCD thoughts. They would no longer interfere.

What does your OCD sound like?

Who is the voice of your OCD?

What does OCD look like for you?

How do you know it's OCD?

Is your OCD an accusatory voice?

Is OCD your voice or someone else's?

Is your OCD you arguing with yourself, or does it talk to you as if it's someone else?

After six hours of searching, my bleary eyes could take no more and I headed to bed.

I found nothing to reassure myself.

I wasn't the only one who wasn't talking.

Chapter 33 – White Noise

<u>Lucky</u>

"We're upstairs! Come on up!"

Minty's light step sounded on the stairs followed by her tap on the door.

"Come in, baby. Brayleigh is in the tub."

"I'll just wait downstairs?"

"Come talk to me while she plays. This will take a while."

Minty stepped tentatively around the doorframe. Her eyes bounced around the bathroom, then snapped back to Brayleigh and she laughed, the tension easing out of her frame.

Brayleigh grinned. "Hi, Sparky!"

"Hi, Dolly," Minty replied softly, linking her fingers together in front.

I wondered what had wound her up and determined to ask her about it later.

I stood up and patted the closed lid of the toilet as I pulled Brayleigh's stepstool over to sit on. "Here. You sit here."

"Oh, I get the throne, do I?" she teased.

"Well, you're the queen, it's only fitting." I dropped a kiss on her soft mouth then dropped down onto the stool.

"What happened?" she asked with a nod toward Brayleigh.

"I thought it would be a good idea to feed her early so we could take her to the park and maybe get ice cream." I scrubbed a hand over my hair and laughed. "It was an amateur mistake. I turned my back to do the dishes and clean the pots and," I waved a hand at the spaghetti monster in the tub, "that happened."

Minty looked at Brayleigh, affectionate amusement in her eyes. "She looks happy enough."

I snorted. "Yes. She loves pasta, she says."

"Loves to wear it, maybe," Minty murmured with a soft smile. "She's so soft and squishy, Lucky."

I heard a note of yearning in her voice. "You want to bathe her?" I offered, but even as the words left my mouth, I saw her draw back.

"No, no. I'll just keep you company."

I looked her over for the first time. "What are you wearing? Stand up!"

She complied and gave a little spin. Fitted shorts, tight cami, sheer blouse. Her tiny ribcage, large bust, and shapely ass all on display.

"Good Lord, woman! I thought we were going to keep that under wraps for my eyes only!"

Her face fell. "You don't like it." She smoothed her palms down the front of her shorts. "I went shopping with the girls. They said I dressed like a PTA MILF and encouraged me to dress more my style. A little less covered."

I tugged her hand and kissed the back of it. "I do like it. I love it. I'm just not used to seeing so much of your skin, your *shape*! I'm not complaining. I'll have to start carrying a baseball bat to beat off the competition."

She didn't give me the smile I expected.

I stood and cupped her cheek. "Minty. You look beautiful. You're a beautiful woman and you should not be afraid to celebrate that."

She took a breath. "It's not too much?"

I shook my head decisively. "Not even a little bit. It's sexy as hell only because you're sexy as hell. You look beautiful." I shook my head again. "I'd planned to stay home but I need to take you out and show you off. Let me get Tweetie out of the tub and we'll go out. Sound good?"

Her shoulders relaxed and she gave me a genuine smile.

I jerked my chin toward the door. "Get out of here. She's going to splash up a storm and I don't want her ruining your outfit. I'll meet you downstairs."

Within the hour, we sat surrounded by Minty's family as Brayleigh enchanted her Yiayia and her sisters. I knew they weren't blood-related, but they were sisters just the same.

Around her family, Minty relaxed her usual control, although it snapped back into place when the boys barreled into her.

"Whoa," I involuntarily exclaimed even as I wondered at the change in her demeanor. Why did she feel the need for that control around the boys?

"Yeah," Gus replied apologetically. "They still plow into her like they're two years old. We've tried to correct them, but Minty reprimands us."

His blue eyes twinkled as he tipped his beer into his smiling mouth. Gus, I could relate to. Vander was just as open and friendly but possessed an underlying intensity, perhaps a darkness, I didn't recognize.

"They love her." I said as I turned my attention back to Minty and the boys. My heart broke at the mix of joy and yearning on her face. "She would have made a wonderful mother."

"They do," Vander agreed. "And she would."

His eyes strayed to Brayleigh before sliding back to me, his challenge clear.

I smiled easily, unaffected. "Brayleigh would be blessed to have her." I took a swig of my beer and laughed. "She's not much of a wingman. Keeps trying to steal her for herself."

Gus lifted his beer. "I'll be your wingman."

Vander assessed me. I looked steadily back at him, wondering at the source of his mistrust. Finally, he sighed. "You got me, too."

"Well, don't be too enthusiastic," I grinned.

"She's special," he retorted.

"I know," I clapped back, some of my good humor dissipating. "I appreciate your care for her. Don't make yourself an obstacle."

The corner of Vander's mouth tipped up in a half smile, then he leaned forward and tapped the neck of his bottle against mine. "Cheers."

I didn't need them to have my back.

But it couldn't hurt.

Minty

Waking up curled up against Lucky's heat quickly became my favorite thing, and it wasn't because he kept his house unfathomably cool at night. It didn't matter, he was better than any electric blanket.

Just as I rolled into him, watching the smile grow on his face as I slipped my fingers over his abdomen, Brayleigh announced her intentions for the day.

"Da? Da! Park, Da?"

He groaned and tucked me underneath him. "You're not leaving this bed."

"Hm, somebody has to get out of the bed and get her. Do you want to do it?"

He rolled off me immediately. "Who am I to stand in your way?"

I laughed. "I'm bringing her to you then I'm getting in the shower."

His arm shot out and he wrapped his hand around my wrist. "Bring her here and get back in."

I went to shake my head, but he shook my arm lightly. "She's cuddly in the morning. You'll love it. Come on," he urged.

I thought about the brief space of time I held her between her room and Lucky's, the sweetness of her tiny body curled around mine. It would be nice to cuddle in the bed. Lucky would be there. It would be safe.

I smiled down at him, noting the change in his face at my acquiescence.

"Good," he grunted as he lay back down. "Hurry up. I miss you already."

He sang a different tune when I got back in with Brayleigh, and she ditched him in favor of cuddling with me. So warm, so sweet, her little head fragrant still from her lavender bath the night before.

"Huh," he grunted. "The least you could do for stealing all the snuggles is take over diaper duty."

Touch her.

I smiled serenely.

"Not a chance."

He touched a finger to my cheek then folded his arm behind his head, his chest spread out like a gift. If Brayleigh wasn't there, I'd give in to the urge to lick the dark nipple that beaded so close to my face.

"What does that smile mean?"

"What smile?" I ran my hand over Brayleigh's back as her breath puffed in and out of her slackened mouth as she lay relaxed against my chest. I buried my nose in the blond tornado that appeared on her head every morning and breathed her in. So pure. So sweet. So beautiful.

"You have a different sort of smile, one that is only meant for you, like you're smiling at something internal. What is it that makes you smile?"

Meeting his eyes, I easily read the confusion in his as he voiced his thoughts. "It doesn't seem like a happy smile. I can't read it."

I shrugged though my heartbeat skittered in my chest like a butterfly trapped in a glass. "It's my OCD." I paused to work out my thoughts before speaking. "I get intrusive thoughts. They are not pleasant." I grimaced at the understatement. "With OCD, if you fight it or resist it, if you argue with it, you're sunk. You can't win an argument with OCD. So, I smile to accept that I've had an OCD thought and let it go."

"I thought you said it was like white noise?" he questioned.

I smiled wryly. "That *is* the white noise."

He studied my face, his eyes serious, then touched a finger to my cheek. "You're strong as fuck, you know that?"

I gave him a genuine smile, and his entire countenance warmed. "Yes. I do know that."

Moving closer, he lay his arm over my waist beneath Brayleigh's bum, stared into my eyes and whispered, "Proud of you, baby."

I looked away for a moment to collect myself and adjust my eyes to his light, before meeting his sober, stormy gaze. "Means the world to me, darling."

I cupped my hand around the back of Brayleigh's little head.

Lucky's lips twisted and he reached behind him for his phone.

"You going to take a picture of my bedhead?" I teased.

"It's just for me, baby. No one else."

I closed my eyes, and he captured the shot.

Brayleigh pushed herself up and reached for Lucky's phone. "Me do it!"

"No!" He laughed. "The last time I gave you my phone there were three hundred pictures of your forehead."

"Peas, Da!" she demanded, shifting to sit on Lucky's chest.

I watched them for a moment, wanting a picture of my own.

I held out my hand for his phone and he passed it over. I took the shot and sent it to myself, then slipped out of bed to begin my morning routine.

A couple of hours later, Brayleigh squealed as Lucky sent the swing soaring into the air.

"It's too high, darling," I warned.

Brayleigh leaning over the bar, toppling forward, neck bent at an odd angle, stillness on the ground, stillness all around as the world stops spinning, leaving us locked forever in that horrible moment.

He looked at me in surprise. "You think so?"

I nodded firmly even as I moved closer, hovering nearby in case she fell.

His lips quirked. "You're a mother hen," he accused.

"I beg your pardon?" I demanded, but he only laughed.

"Cluck, cluck, cluck," he teased, and I couldn't help but laugh.

"I am not a mother hen. I am prudent."

"You mean how you prudently latched her into the car seat three times before you were happy with the fit?"

"Yes. I haven't used a car seat in almost a decade. It was prudent to practice."

"Well, you've definitely got it now," he teased.

"Down, Da!" Brayleigh demanded as she attempted to pull her leg up through the hole and stand up.

"Lucky!" I yelled as he easily caught the entire swing in his arms.

I walked away, wrapping my palm around my throat to calm myself.

Lucky aligned himself behind me and placed his hand atop mine. "Calm, baby. I'm not going to let anything happen to her. Or you."

I lay my head back against his chest and slipped my hand out from under his, wanting his skin on mine.

His finger found my pulse and stroked it. "It's all good, baby."

I nodded and took a deep breath before turning to face him with a practiced smile on my face.

"Okay." Brayleigh wasn't with him. Panic flooded my system. "Where is she?" I demanded.

He pointed over my shoulder. "She's right there. She hasn't been out of my sight for a second."

"Wow." I shook my head. "Parenting isn't for pussies."

He laughed and grabbed my hand, intertwining his fingers with mine as he leaned in to brush his lips gently over mine.

"It's definitely not," he agreed.

Brayleigh seemed bent on exploring every inch of the park, getting dangerously close to the tree line.

Hands snatching, Brayleigh screaming, Lucky crashing through the trees too late.

One two buckle my shoe. Three four shut that door.

Lucky loped over and scooped her up into his arms, then put her down and chased her back to the play area.

I heaved in a breath. It would not serve to give in to the compulsion.

Hands snatching, Brayleigh screaming, crashing through the trees too late.

I squirmed against the mental distress.

Again.

One two....

I swallowed.

Smiled.

Let it go.

I didn't take my eyes off her until we headed for home. It was a relief to buckle her into the car seat where I knew she was safe.

I checked the straps, sliding my fingers between the straps and her chest to check for fit. Pulled on the latch to ensure it was secure. Then circled round the car and slid into the passenger seat. After one last visual check of the car seat, I directed my mind to planning my outfit for Drivetrain Saturday night, smiling in anticipation of Lucky's reaction.

Chapter 34 – Intrigued

<u>Lucky</u>

Sunday morning arrived too early. As soon as I felt Minty shift to move from the bed, I snagged her around the waist and pulled her back against my chest. "Stay here," I demanded.

"Next Sunday, I promise, you can keep me in bed as long as you want. Today's the last craft fair." She nestled her butt back into my groin. "I'm only doing a half day."

"Yeah? You're coming with me to the barbecue?" Barrett and Willa invited the band over to their place around four o'clock. Because of the craft fair, Minty had planned to meet me there.

"Yes, Captain. After I drop the girls off at the house. You happy now?" she teased.

I hugged her closer. "I am."

By three-thirty, we were packing my potato salad, Minty's cookies, and my acoustic into the car.

"You'll play tonight?"

I raised my eyebrows, surprised she'd ask, then realized she'd never been to one of these with us before. "Sure. Barrett will have his. Lenny and Bax might bring something. At some point, somebody will be playing something."

A smile broke over her face like the rising of the sun. "That's lovely!"

I took in her beautiful face. Before she came into my life, I believed I was happy. I wasn't unhappy, but looking back, all the days ran into each other, a monotonous routine.

"You're more beautiful than the breaking of the dawn," I murmured, touching my finger to the softness of her cheek. "You make every day new."

Always the flash of surprise, then she would duck her head for a moment before smiling, wonder and disbelief reflected in her gaze. I prayed for the day that flash meant happiness, the wonder and disbelief relegated to a thing of the past.

The properties in Bridgewater were generally larger than those in Milltown. Barrett and Willa's home was no exception. Gardens, an outdoor fireplace, scattered nooks with comfortable outdoor seating, and a patio table filled out the space along with covered areas to shield from the sun.

I could not help but compare it to my own yard furnished with fold-up loungers and wondered what changes Minty might make when she moved in. Then I wondered when that might be. Something told me not to push. I'd never been an impatient man but wanting this the way I did made it difficult to wait.

Much like the first barbecue, I watched Minty from afar with her girls. It struck me anew how well she fit in though she held herself slightly apart. More so than she did with Amber and Ruby, although there appeared to be no lack of love between Minty, Junie, and Willa.

Complicated. An enigma. Layers upon layers.

I pictured a spectrum depicting Minty's openness with the various people in her life and I wondered where I fit on the scale.

From the moment I met her, I'd longed to slip behind the veil and that had not changed. I wanted to know her mind, feel her body, hold her heart. More than anything, I wanted her to know that her heart was safe with mine.

She sat with her ankles crossed, her face soft, Rena cuddled against her breast. Between us lay the length of the backyard. I pulled my phone out and took a picture of Minty's veggie sausages on Lenny's hibachi, being sure to capture Minty's blurry image in the background.

Hours later, our stomachs full, we gathered around the outdoor fireplace while Rena slept inside. A high-tech baby monitor the likes of which I'd never seen sat on the small table between Barrett and Willa, visible to both of them.

Even Bax stayed. I hadn't expected that. Quieter even than Barrett, he was slow to integrate with the rest of the band, though he showed up for rehearsals religiously and there were no complaints about his performance. We were lucky to find him after the Sarah debacle the summer before.

Barrett refreshed drinks then sat down with his guitar. Willa lay her head back against the back of her seat and closed her eyes, a small smile on her face. I wonder if she knew how often Barrett's gaze turned to rest on her face.

Bax joined in with a harmonica and tears sprung to Minty's eyes.

I squeezed her thigh. "You okay?"

She smiled through her tears. "My dad used to play."

I intertwined my fingers with hers and sat back in my seat, oddly satisfied that she had that sweet memory. I thought of my own parents, the photo albums stuffed with happy memories lining the bookshelves in the family room and knew I wanted to make those with Minty.

"You want to take over for a bit, Lucky?" Barrett tucked his guitar around behind him.

"Sure," I cleared my throat.

Nerves. On the days Minty stayed at her place, I'd been busy. There were things I needed to say to her, but I had no words. In this way, I could borrow them.

"I've got two new ones. Three if you count the one Minty and I learned together."

Unlike Willa, Minty sat forward in her seat, eyes open, her beautiful mind spinning.

Unlike Barrett, other than the briefest of glances while I sang The Spill Canvas' *Lullaby*, I kept my eyes on my strings, unsure how she would receive these very public declarations.

When I finished, you could hear a pin drop.

Minty sat with her lips parted, gaze soft on my face.

I raised my chin and offered her a smile. "Can you handle another one?"

Her light laugh rang out and she nodded her head. "Absolutely."

With slightly more confidence, I sang *To Make You Feel My Love.*

Junie was the first to break the silence. "Somebody is so getting laid tonight."

Willa laughed out loud and swiped her finger beneath her eyes. "I think it's safe to say everybody's getting laid tonight."

Baxter spoke drily. "Better sing another one. I need all the help I can get."

Barrett's big boom of a laugh split the night. "Minty? You going to sing with Lucky?"

I swung my head around to catch her reaction.

She tilted her head to the side and smiled at me. "You want to?"

"Absolutely."

By the time we finished Penny and Sparrow's Duet, it was Willa and Junie who were left gaping.

Junie leaned over and elbowed Willa. "Remember when we did karaoke the week before you got married and Minty showed us she had pipes? Minty's got pipes!" She exclaimed excitedly.

"She used to be in a band," I informed them, flashing my dimples at Minty when she swung around to look at me.

"What kind of band? Country?" Lenny tilted his head as he studied Minty, trying to figure her out.

I laughed. Good luck, bud. "She wore thigh-high boots, leather pants, and a bustier."

"Evanescence was my jam," she confessed as she fought a smile.

"Oh my gosh," Junie interrupted. "You have to get on stage with the guys!"

Minty waved her hands. "Oh no. Absolutely not. It's been a very long time since I've performed in public."

Barrett studied her silently for a moment. "Maybe it would be good for you. Consider yourself officially invited. We'll make you an honorary member, not this Saturday, but next. That crowd will love it."

Minty began to protest, but Lenny interrupted. "Tell you what. Send us a few songs that you would sing if you decided to do it, and we'll tell you if we can cover them."

Junie clasped her hands together under her chin and widened her eyes. "Please, Minty," she begged. "Do it for the greater global girlhood."

Minty looked at her and pursed her lips. "Your big eyes don't work on me, beautiful."

Junie batted her eyelashes, and Minty laughed. "I'll think about it."

"Yes!" Junie hissed, then turned to Lenny. "Set it up!"

"It's not a done deal," Minty protested.

"Oh, please," Willa laughed. "If it was a 'no' you would have shut her down so fast her head would spin."

Minty laughed again. "Okay. You're right. I'm intrigued." Turning to look at Barrett, she continued. "I'll send you a few ideas to see if it's even feasible. If it's good for you, I'll need a couple of days to think about it."

"Done!" Willa slapped her hand down on the arm of her chair and stood up. "Mama needs to go to bed." She winked at Barrett. "And I'm bringing the big guy with me."

Minty

Warm hands splayed across my back as I lay sprawled across Lucky's chest, heaving from the morning's sextivities.

"You remember that art exhibit we went to see?" His low, husky voice slid over me like a wet dream.

A small laugh escaped my lips. "How could I forget?"

He grunted and dropped his hand to my ass to give me a squeeze. "You," he replied roughly. "You're the goddess at play." He stroked the naked skin of my back. "You're everything a woman should be."

I closed my eyes against the light.

Even still, I basked in his glow.

It made it difficult to go home, but I had plans with my boys, Junie needed me at the office, and I was determined to shop for princess dresses before Thursday.

Other than the hours spent fruitlessly searching for answers to OCD, it was a productive week, and when Thursday rolled around, I was more than ready to head back to Lucky and Brayleigh, newly purchased sparkles in hand.

Chapter 35 – I Will

Lucky

Brayleigh toddled along while Minty followed closely on her heels.

I wasn't sure it was necessary to follow her that closely. As soon as we arrived at the zoo, Minty bought a giant helium balloon and tied it to the back of Brayleigh's dress. The dress alone, so covered in 'sparklies', made her visible from outer space.

Trailing them by ten feet, it struck me how very beautiful they were together. Minty wore another new outfit. She was getting more comfortable showing her shape as well as a little skin.

I couldn't say I didn't miss the sexy librarian thing she had going on, but I wasn't complaining either.

Brayleigh possessed no such inhibition, happily wearing one of the new princess dresses Minty brought for her yesterday. It had a fucking crinoline and came with a diamond tiara. I had to pull the car over and wrestle it from her. The damn thing kept catching the light and reflecting off the rearview mirror. Near blinded me. I huffed out a laugh and whispered a plea that she would not lose that delight with herself.

I loved the joy Minty found in giving presents. She bought for Brayleigh. She brought gifts to 'her boys' when we went there. Every time she went to the craft fair she seemed to come home with gifts for her friends and the kids. Currently, Rena and Brayleigh were cleaning up.

I slid my hand over the new leather wallet in my back pocket, the word 'Captain' embossed on the inside. She bought for me, too. I couldn't remember the last time someone bought me a gift for no reason. She was a giver.

Minty dropped her bum down to her heels to listen to Brayleigh, her hand gently cupping her back to draw her close. The sun lit the gold in their hair, the barest hints of red in Minty's. I smiled. That red hinted at the passion she so carefully hid.

I rubbed the heel of my palm over my chest as I watched them together. I hadn't broached the subject of her moving in again, but it lived on the back of my tongue. I wanted this so bad I could taste it.

A similar scene with Hope and Brayleigh had unfolded countless numbers of times, so why did it feel so different with Minty and Brayleigh?

Mine.

Yes. They were mine. My girls. My loves. My life.

And I belonged, heart and soul, to them. I held my fingers up to make a frame around them. That right there was what I was going to live for. I pulled out my cell phone and snapped a pic.

Wanted to remember this feeling.

Minty

Going to the zoo with Lucky and Brayleigh was a dream. Brayleigh's pleasure flashed like a beacon from her little face and filled my heart with light.

She had Lucky's smile. I could pick out his features now, as well as Hope's, on her tiny face. Two beautiful people, inside and out, created an angel.

Her hair tie had long since come undone, and a wispy, blond hurricane danced on top of her little head as she toddled along in front of me. I constantly scanned the environment. Where there were too many people, I scooped her up in my arms.

Some of those enclosures left much to be desired.

Honestly, should a person be able to throw a baby over the fence the way I pictured throwing Brayleigh over?

Okay, there was a second enclosure, but that would do nothing if she poked her tiny arm through the fence to pet the 'pretty kitty', a scenario that played out in my head in technicolor more than once as we circled the park.

By the time we made our way to the car, Brayleigh was beyond exhausted. No matter what she did, no matter what happened, Lucky's mood never faltered. Steady as the sun and just as bright.

The same could not be said for Dolly.

She screamed and dug her heels into the seat, bucking her little hips up as I tried to secure the straps.

"Sit down, sweetheart. We're going to go home and play in the tubby. Is that a good idea?"

Too far gone, she couldn't hear me and wouldn't be able to calm down even if she did.

I remembered how Alex freaked out about the car seat when he was overtired or overwrought. Strongarming Brayleigh into the seat did not feel right, but she had to be buckled in so we could leave.

I lifted her up into my arms again to try to soothe her, but she arched back, wanting down to run. Too many hours in the sun. Over-stimulated. Hot, hungry, tired, and wired.

Lucky had already packed all of our stuff back into the car and was on his way back from paying at the parking kiosk.

I had foolishly offered to buckle Brayleigh into the seat.

"Okay, Dolly," I murmured. "We've got to get you in."

I tickled her tummy until she buckled then flipped the straps over her shoulders and strapped her in.

For half a second, she laughed, then noting her confinement, she screamed out her fury, beating her little fists on the sides of the seat.

"Okay, darling," I soothed. "How about a bottle of juice? I think we can make an exception for a day bottle. What do you think?"

I fumbled with the diaper bag, pulling the bottle of juice I'd frozen the night before for just this moment.

Her attention stumbled onto the bottle, and she reached for it, her breath hiccoughing.

Lucky draped his arm over my shoulders with a smile. "Ah, the cost of an exciting day." Patting my ass, he moved to open the driver's side door. "Come on, baby. Let's go home."

My heart galloped in my chest. "Don't you want to check the car seat?" I asked.

He shot me a questioning look before glancing at the straps briefly then tried to shut Brayleigh's door. "You got it. You know what you're doing. I don't need to check it. The sooner we get her home, the better."

I searched his face. Other than a bit tired, he looked relaxed and happy. I wished I could siphon some of it off of him for myself. Just a bit. Not enough that he'd even notice the difference, but I might.

I pushed open her door, checked the latch, and ran my fingers underneath the straps to check for snugness. My throat tightened. I tried to clear it. "Does this look good to you?"

"Yeah, baby. It looks good."

I turned to him, but his eyes were on his cell, checking the traffic report for our route home.

Brayleigh's tiny body, thrown through the windshield, bruised, broken, and bleeding on the ground, so small, so still.

The gory details bled through my brain, the picture so clear in my mind I almost expected to see her tiny form on the pavement in front of the car.

"Lucky," I said tightly. "I need you to check the car seat."

"Hm?" His eyes scanned his screen. "Okay. We're going to take the 407. Come on, baby."

"Lucky!" I yelled and his stormy eyes shot to my face.

He jerked back in surprise, a brief flash of annoyance on his face. "What?"

"Check. The fucking. Car seat," I bit out each word.

His face cleared. "Aw. Okay. You're struggling. Is this an OCD thing?"

254

His understanding eased the tension in my chest, and I pulled in a deep breath. "Yes."

"Minty," he began. "It's fine. I don't need to check. I trust you fully."

Trapped. Suffocating. I needed space.

I stalked away from the car. My dress swished around my lower thighs reminding me of Lucky's calloused fingers brushing over my quivering flesh the night before, reminding me of his eyes on me before we left, warming with appreciation and promise.

I focused on that instead of Brayleigh's broken body.

"Minty?"

"I need you to check the car seat," I whispered. I wasn't even sure he could hear me.

Gentle hands landed on my shoulders. "I don't think I'm supposed to check..." he petered off, unsure, trying to do the right thing.

Decisions.

Compromises.

Bloody, broken, and bruised.

Pavement painted red.

I pivoted on my heel, his husky voice in my ears, my heart in my throat. When I reached Brayleigh's door, I opened it fully, reached in, unlatched her car seat and gently pulled the straps down her arms.

Calm and sleepy, she reached for me.

I picked her up and cuddled her close, holding her too tightly, as I wished the image away. When Lucky reached me, I gently transferred her into his arms, walked around to my side of the car, got in and closed the door.

He quickly strapped her in, swung into the car and reached for my hand.

"Minty," he began.

"Please, Lucky," I beseeched him. "I'm exhausted. Please let's just go home."

"Okay, baby. No problem."

I leaned my forehead against the window, watching the world pass by.

What I wouldn't give to be out on his bike instead of trapped in my brain, locked in this car.

1-2-3-4-5-1-2-3-4-5

1-2-3-4-5-1-2-3-4-5

Again and again and again until I lost count and needed a reset. I flexed my fingers. Open. Closed.

They're not even.

I pressed them into the tender skin of my thighs.

1-2-3-4-5-1-2-3-4-5

Again.

Again.

I shook them out and resisted the urge to resume counting.

A transport truck cut in front of us, the sun flashing off the corner of the trailer. Lucky braked easily. An excellent driver.

Bruised and broken.

Blood painting the pavement.

I looked back and checked the straps. She slept. Her face at peace.

My fingers itched. I linked them together in my lap.

Bruised, broken, bleeding. Curled up on the pavement. Pale and still. Painted red.

Lucky reached for me across the seat, tugging my elbow, wanting my hand. I unlinked my fingers, spread my thighs, and placed his hand on my knee before linking my fingers in my lap, mentally knitting myself back together.

I leaned my forehead against the window and closed my eyes. Buildings and trees cast long shadows in front of the sun, the color behind my lids fluctuated with the flickering of shadow and light.

Once home, I carried in the diaper bag while Lucky transferred Brayleigh to her crib.

Locking the bathroom door, I splashed water on the insides of my wrists. No longer ensnared by compulsions, my failure burned. I opened the door and walked right into Lucky who immediately drew me into his embrace.

"I'm sorry. I thought I wasn't supposed to check for you," he murmured against my hair.

My voice shook with fury, fear, and adrenalin though I leaned into him heavily. "I control what I'm working on. You don't get to decide what I check and what I don't."

His chin rubbed against the top of my head as he nodded. "You're right. 100%. I was trying to do the right thing by showing my confidence in you. I'm sorry it came across the way it did. Be patient with me. Teach me how to deal with this properly."

The truth rose with a vengeance. I pulled away and crossed my arms over my chest. "You shouldn't have to."

He spread his hands wide with his palms turned toward me, exasperated. "Why not?"

"Because you're you and you could have so much better! You could have a wife and family and more kids and not have to deal with all this." I waved my hand down my front indicating all of myself.

He scowled. "Oh, for fuck's sake, not this again. Minty, I don't want anything other than what I've got right now. I'd deal with a fuck of a lot more than this to be with you. But you know what I don't want to deal with? What I shouldn't have to deal with? This bullshit of you pulling away every time you get the daft idea that I can't cope. Give me some fucking credit!"

"You just don't get it," I protested, hope whispering sweet nothings to my soul.

"You're right. But I will, baby." He pulled me against his chest and bowed his back to cover me. "I will."

Chapter 36 – Donkey Kong

Minty

When I woke up Saturday morning, I remembered that Hope planned to come early to pick up Brayleigh. Relief barreled in like a giant wave, depositing guilty debris in its wake.

Hope had a business trip the following week so Lucky and I would have Brayleigh full time. Hope decided to keep her the whole week before she left which meant I'd get a much-needed break. Hopefully a chance to get my head straight. All my hours spent researching on the computer had amounted to little more than a hill of beans. I had to sit down with Ezinne soon and get it sorted.

Junie and Lenny had booked a few days away at the same time, so I planned to stay with Lucky for the entire week. It would be like playing house, giving me a chance to think about moving in.

He brought it up again last night but agreed to adhere to my timetable. We did, however, exchange house keys. I'd never done that before.

When Hope pulled into the driveway, something loosened inside me.

Up until now, I managed my time with children so as not to trigger myself too badly. Spending as much time as I did with Brayleigh, the trigger was bound to get flipped. Worry over her wellness and safety plagued me, and the OCD thoughts that battered me at the most inopportune moments, well, those were of the soul-destroying variety.

Hope balanced a tray of coffees and a box of donuts in one hand, a gift bag in the other. I hurried to open the door for her.

"Thanks!" She smiled and gave me a once-over as she passed me the bag. "Do you ever not look perfect?" She leaned over and smacked a kiss onto my cheek as she blew into the kitchen.

It wasn't hard to see where Brayleigh got her energy. "You're hardly one to talk," I retorted with a laugh. "What did you bring me?"

I found myself weirdly relaxed around Hope. Even Lucky noticed, commenting that I was not as controlled or formal around her. It made sense. Straightforward and bursting with joyful energy like Junie, but emotional and affectionate like Ruby, with seemingly no hang-ups, she was easy to read and even easier to be with.

"Look in the bag," she answered as she opened the donut box and assessed its contents to make her selection before dropping into a chair.

I peeked in and pulled out a beautiful silk scarf. Swirls of gilt-edged color reminiscent of a summer sunset ran through my hands.

"It's beautiful." I couldn't look at her and I wasn't sure what to say. When I asked her what she brought me, I was referring to the donuts. I hadn't expected a gift. When she spoke, I lifted my chin.

"It's for your hair," Hope mumbled around a mouthful of donut before swallowing and touching an elegant finger to her lips. "Sorry. When I'm at Lucky's, I forget I'm a lady."

"It's really beautiful," I said again. "Thank you, but you shouldn't have." My voice sounded stilted and formal. I didn't like it.

She waved my words away. "I didn't. Not really. I'm a fashion buyer. I get freebies all the time. When I saw this, I thought of you." She looked me over again. "What size are you?" She stood up and circled me, muttering, "You're kind of pear-shaped. Plush booty. Hard to see your thighs in this outfit but probably relative to your butt. Yeah, for sure. Shapely calves. Hm. Tiny ribcage. Big boobs. Narrow shoulders." She finally made it back to my face to find me staring at her, mouth gaping. She stepped back, a look of horror on her face.

"I'm sorry!" Her eyes jerked back and forth as she retreated into her head, then closed them and groaned. "I'm sorry," she said again, looking at me. "That sounded horrible. I'm used to looking at models and assessing them for fit, and you're so damn gorgeous and you'd be such a pleasure to dress, and I was thinking about what I had in stock that might suit you and thinking out loud which obviously I should stop doing-"

I cut her off with a laugh. "It's okay." I sat down at the table, my shoulders shaking. The more I thought about it, the more I laughed.

Hope grinned at me as she sat back down and took another bite.

Lucky walked in with Brayleigh in his arms, a bemused expression on his face which only made me laugh harder.

He looked at Hope. "Did you put your foot in it again?"

Hope nodded with a smirk. "Both."

I snorted, and Lucky's mouth fell open.

"That didn't sound like no bell," Hope commented, her voice muffled by more donut.

Lucky laughed and punched her lightly on the shoulder. "Stop talking!"

"She circled me," I snorted again, then covered my face. "Like a prize cow."

Hope guffawed, and Lucky chuckled harder, though I doubted he could understand what I said.

Brayleigh wiggled out of his arms, and he lowered her to the floor.

"Said I was pear-shaped and had big boobs! Wondered about my thighs!" I bent nearly in half. "Guessed they were relative to my..." I laughed harder. "My 'plush booty'!"

"Hope!" Lucky yelled, his laughter breaking through.

Hope spread her arms wide. "What? Did I lie?" She shrugged, owning her lunacy. "I want to dress her. She's gorgeous." She pointed at me with the half donut she had left and raised her eyebrows as she nodded. "You could swing me the other way."

Done.

I crossed my arms on the table and buried my face, listening to Lucky laughingly reprimand Hope while she offered him a donut.

Brayleigh attempted to crawl up into my lap. I wiped the tears from beneath my eyes and lifted her. She straddled my lap and turned her cornflower blue eyes up to my face as she touched her chubby finger to my necklace.

"Mine sparky?"

"Daddy's!" Lucky yelled, exasperated and laughing.

"I has a donut?"

"Yes, darling." I passed her the box. "That you can have."

I cuddled her in my arms as we ate our donuts, conflicted between my need for a break and my desire to keep her close.

I watched from the window as Hope buckled her into the car and I took a deep breath.

Safe travels.

Lucky's arms encircled my waist from behind as he nuzzled my ear. "Do you and your plush booty want to come upstairs?"

I turned my face toward him, pressing my temple to his mouth. "We could be convinced."

It didn't take much.

Lucky

The weekend flashed by at the speed of sound. We managed to get a rehearsal in with Minty on Saturday. Stayed out far too late with Junie and Lenny, then spent Sunday lounging in the backyard, reading, drawing, playing guitar, and doing yardwork.

Darcy passed by with Abby and Ben to examine my flowerbeds and approved of my efforts. They didn't stay long. Darcy confided that dear-old-dad cancelled on the kids last minute so she was scrambling for something to do that would take their minds off it.

Minty suggested go-carting and offered to keep them company, but the kids refused to be deterred from their disappointment.

"Thank you, Minty," Darcy sighed. "I appreciate the offer and will gladly take you up on it another time?" She stood abruptly and sniffed.

I looked up, alarmed. My sister did not cry. She looked defeated, shoulders slumped, face drawn. I moved to stand, but she waved me off.

"Just tired, Lucky. Tired of his shit." She called out to her kids and transformed back into supermom in front of my eyes. "Guys! We're going to have a 'yes' day."

For the first time since they got here, their faces betrayed a spark of interest.

"What's a 'yes' day?" Minty inquired.

Darcy looked at her, a wry smile on her face. "It means whatever reasonable thing they ask for, I commit to saying 'yes'."

Intrigued, I asked, "So, if they ask for a puppy?"

She laughed. "That's unreasonable. But if they asked to go to the zoo, have ice cream for dinner, stay up late watching movies, play a marathon of board games, go mini-putt, all those things would be reasonable. And!" She held up one finger. "They have to agree on it and can only ask for one thing at a time."

"You're a good mom," Minty murmured softly. "I admire you." She looked over at Abby and Ben who were busy plotting, wide smiles on their faces. "Look at them."

"Yeah." Her face softened. "They're good kids. I'm lucky. Right!" She waved them over. "Say bye to Uncle Lucky and his beautiful lady and then you can tell me how you're going to torture me today."

They left but their disappointment lingered. "He sucks," I said.

"Hm. He certainly does," Minty agreed.

I scrubbed my hand over my hair. "I hate that he does that to them."

Minty looked at me. "You care. You're a good uncle and a good brother, too."

"I should do more."

"Do I need to distract you? Should we also have a 'yes' day?"

My head swung around. "What are the parameters?"

"Well, I don't know..." she mused, her voice low. "We never did discuss fucking limits..."

I stood abruptly. "Well, it's too late for that." I held out my hand for her. "Come distract me."

She raised an eyebrow and laughter flashed in her eyes as she stood. With one hand on my chest, she walked her fingers down to the waistband of my pants. "So many things we could get up to..."

"Inside, Minty," I turned her shoulders and gave her a gentle shove towards the back door.

She stopped at the doorframe and looked at me over her shoulder. "So many things we haven't tried yet..."

I crowded her inside then closed and locked the door.

She walked backwards toward the stairs, unbuttoning her shorts as she walked, then let them fall to the floor before stepping out of them and turning to take the stairs.

At the first step, I was on her, filling my hands with her ass, prodding her to move faster. "Oh, you don't know what I'm going to do to you," I promised.

She took a step, and I ran my hand up between her thighs. "I suppose I should take this off, too," she said, dropping her t-shirt.

"Keep going," I demanded. "You're not going to need any of this." I tugged the back of her bra strap, flicking it open.

She let it fall down her arms to the stairs, then turned and continued up the stairs backwards.

One stair down from her put me at exactly her height. I pushed her up one stair and leaned in to catch her nipple in my mouth. She threaded her fingers through my hair and held me close until I pushed off, impatient to get her horizontal.

With her hand under my chin, she tipped my face back to meet her deeply amused eyes. Why was she so amused? She wouldn't be laughing in a minute. She bent forward and kissed me while taking another step back.

Then she smiled and it was not a sweet smile that boded good things for me, but the type of smile that boded a spanking for her.

"You seem to have forgotten something," she stated softly, releasing my chin and retreating another step.

I stopped, wracking my brain. "Nope. Nothing important."

She grinned as she turned and ran, giving me a show I would not soon forget. "We're going to Yiayia's for dinner now."

Watching her plush tush bounce up the stairs, it took a moment for her words to seep into my brain. My eyebrows crashed together, as I barked, "What?"

Her laughter rang out as she breached the doorway to our room.

I took the stairs two at a time to find her playing it cool, pretending to organize her outfit. "Oh no," I reprimanded her. "You don't tease."

I grabbed her shoulders and spun her around to face me then marched her back against the wall.

"Oh, but I do, see," she cooed, dragging her palm over my erection. "Because here you are, all ready to go, and you're not going anywhere."

I smiled at her, reached down to the sides of her panties, and tugged. Hard.

She looked down in surprise. "Did you actually just rip off my panties?"

"Yup." I stared down at her as I ripped open my button and fly, then shoved my shorts to my knees. I bent to lift one of her knees and drew it up around my hip. "Open up, Buttercup."

"Lucky..." She laughed. "We don't have time."

I dipped my knees, grasped her other leg, and wrapped them both around my waist. "Are you wet enough to take me?"

"I'm wet enough to take two of you," she murmured.

I slid inside her heat, watched as her head tipped back against the wall, and rocked against her.

"Lucky," she breathed. "We really don't have time."

"You're right," I answered, licking and kissing my way up her neck. "*We* don't. But do you know what happens to bad girls that tease?"

"What?" she whispered, holding my face to her neck.

I pistoned my hips, driving into her, holding nothing back for love or money.

She gasped, "Lucky."

I squeezed her ass and let myself go, emptying inside her.

I dropped my thumb to her clit and gave it a slow roll. "They don't get theirs."

Looking at me beneath hooded eyes, I caught the exact moment she understood.

Fire lit her gaze. "Lucky," she breathed, unbelieving. "That's terrible."

I made a show of looking at my imaginary watch. "Looks like we're running late." I eased her to her feet.

She stared back at me, mutinous, then smiled and sauntered into the bathroom. "I'll finish myself off."

I slapped my palm against the door before she closed it. "You do that and it'll be the first thing I ask for on my 'yes' day."

Her eyebrows knit and her lips pursed.

"In any case," I grinned, "we don't have time. Take a look at yourself in the mirror. You look flustered and freshly fucked." I cocked my head to the side. "A tiny bit frustrated."

"Oh," she laughed. "It is on like Donkey Kong."

"Donkey Kong?" I guffawed.

She closed the door on my smug mug and seconds later I heard the shower start. We really were going to be late.

Chapter 37 – Cackling

<u>Minty</u>

"I feel great. Do you feel great?"

Lucky tapped out a rough beat on the steering wheel.

I glanced at him. So smug, dimples flashing as he grinned back at me. Remembering that slow, sweet roll sent a pulsing ache to my clit.

"I am plotting my revenge," I advised him.

He chuckled. "Sure, you do that."

When we got to Amber's, her yiayia, who lived with them, answered the door and held out her arms. "Koukla! You are koukla!"

Koukla meant doll in Greek. As loving as she was bossy, Yiayia made everyone feel at home.

"Hello, Yiayia." I leaned over to offer her my cheek and give her a hug. She seemed to get tinier every time I saw her.

"Beautiful girl, you are," she exclaimed, her eyes soft on my face as she gently cupped my cheek. "Bravo. You brought your boy."

I twisted to find Lucky looking down at Yiayia with delight. He held out his hand. "It's a pleasure to see you again, Yiayia."

She patted his cheek. "Nice manners, so handsome! Come in, come in." She welcomed us and stepped back from the door. "Lucky, what you do? You work?"

"Hi, Mr. Triggs." George slung an arm around Yiayia's shoulders. "He's my teacher. Remember Yiayia?"

"Ach. I am old lady now. I'm forgetting!"

"Don't let her fool you, she's as sharp as a tack. Knows exactly what's going on and keeps everybody in line." Gus stepped forward to shake Lucky's hand. "Good to see you again, Lucky."

Gathered around the typically raucous Vasilakis dinner table, I noticed Lucky sat perfectly at ease. Amber and Ruby's family cooked up the same flavor of noise and chaos as his own.

In my house, calm reigned supreme. For the first time, I wondered if my parents had always been like that or if they became like that for me. Because I so desperately needed peace, routine, and stability.

My attention wandered to George and the accommodations I knew Ruby and Vander had made to ease him through his transition to living with them.

Vander made accommodations for Ruby.

Gus made accommodations for Amber.

That willingness to adjust and adapt, support and stand by, was what made a family. Not blood. Not birth. But the belonging that comes from commitment and claiming.

Throughout the meal, I witnessed it firsthand. When Yiayia placed a plate down in front of me with the meat already on it, Lucky deftly scraped it onto his own. And each time Yiayia pushed me to eat more food, Lucky intervened. "That looks good, Yiayia. Put it on my plate and we'll share."

In truth, he played her like a fiddle. She had a weakness for her boys, and she'd just adopted Lucky.

With dessert, I had no issue eating my share, and managed to finalize a date for Yiayia to come to the house to bake with Ezzy, me, and the girls.

Amber and Gus insisted on cleaning up while Yiayia excused herself to lie down for a while.

Then Gus grabbed a few beers and went out to the porch with Vander and Lucky. Amber, Ruby, and I sat on the couch.

"I saw the way he took care of you at dinner," Ruby commented happily. "He's very sweet."

"Does he take care of you in other ways?" Amber's eyes crinkled.

I laughed. "He does." Then I remembered this afternoon. "You know what he did?" I explained and watched as Amber laughed knowingly while a look of horror passed over Ruby's face.

"Gus has done that before when I've been 'bad'." She smiled widely. "The key is to make sure you're bad enough to warrant a better punishment. One that is mutually beneficial in the end."

Ruby stared at us both, her mouth gaping indignantly. "That's...that's...that's clitoral abuse!"

Amber leaned forward and spit her wine across the coffee table, choking on her laughter.

Ruby patted her on the back, then grabbed a napkin to wipe up Amber's mess, her shoulders beginning to shake.

"Clitoral abuse," I repeated, my mind delighting in the new phrase and my eagerness to accuse Lucky of it later.

"You should buy one of those cock cages," Ruby nodded, agreeing with herself.

Amber fell sideways on the couch, and I snorted with laughter as I slapped my hand down on my thigh, remembering his horror at the art installation of *The Goddess at Play*.

Lucky

Cackling. Not the light, tinkling laugh I'd grown accustomed to hearing from Minty, but outright cackling complete with thigh-slapping and snorting.

The three of them sat in a huddle in the living room while we sat outside on the porch having a beer. Yiayia had long since gone to bed though how she could sleep through that noise was beyond me.

I jerked my chin up in their direction. "What the hell could possibly be that funny?"

Vander snorted. "You don't want to know."

"Why not?" I asked, surprised.

Gus grinned. "It's about us. Or sex." He shrugged. "Or a combination of the two."

I groaned. I had sisters. I should have known this. "I did not know women talked about their sex lives with other women."

Gus leaned over and placed a commiserating hand on my shoulder. "Nothing, and I mean nothing, is sacred."

It took a moment for that information to sink in before I realized something. "She's plotting against me."

Vander burst out laughing while Gus took a pull of his beer, nodding affably. "Probably."

Vander cast me a sideways look, his lips tipped up on one side, amused eyes assessing. "Do you know about aphroditesharem?"

"Aphrodite's who?" Somewhere along the line I'd lost track of the conversation.

He clarified. "Do you know about her Bookstagram nights?"

I shrugged. "Yeah. She has a little book club with Amber and Ruby, right?"

Gus's eyes crinkled. "Look it up on Instagram. You might find it interesting."

Vander chuckled deeply. "You might develop a sudden interest in reading."

I pulled out my phone, and Gus winced. "Don't do it here. Minty's like my sister." He laughed. "But don't forget to do it."

"And let us know if you want any book recommendations," Vander added with a smirk.

I pulled out my cell and snapped a quick pic of Minty and her girls through the window. It would be blurry, but that didn't matter.

Minty's face never lost its smile the whole way home. Spending time with her girls left her happy and relaxed. Although I missed Brayleigh already, I was happy to have the time with Minty.

Monday morning, we went out for breakfast and then took a walk down by the pier. Monday night I gave her double the orgasms to make up for what I did to her Sunday. Tuesday to Thursday, Minty followed her regular routine, going to work with Junie and having her boys over Tuesday night. Wednesday night, she called me, and we had a long conversation on the phone, ending with me finally catching on that she'd been busy with her vibrator.

I demanded she stop.

She breathlessly declined and invited me to hang up if it was too much for me. I listened as she panted through what sounded like a spectacular orgasm, ending with me pissed and turned on in equal parts and her laughing.

Thursday night, I pulled out the tie from Barrett's wedding, tied her to our bed, and fucked her into the mattress.

Friday, I got my 'yes' day.

Chapter 38 — Walk of Shame

<u>Lucky</u>

She shone as bright as the sun; her face lit up from within.

As she belted out the lyrics, the crowd took to their feet, hooting and hollering, not the least of which came from the back corner where all her girls cheered her on.

Her voice, always so coolly moderated, did not prepare me for the power she unleashed as she sang. Even in the two rehearsals we had she hadn't sung like this. I set my guitar down when she finished and walked over to her.

"I'm so damn proud of you." Pride that almost hurt filled my chest as I smiled down at her. "And more than a little turned on," I admitted with a laugh.

She huffed out a laugh, her smile spreading wide as she leaned into me.

"Come on," I cupped her elbow. "I'll help you down the stairs."

Barrett's dark chuckle sounded over the mic. "Do we have a doctor in the house?" He jerked his head in my direction. "Cause this boy's going to need artificial resuscitation when his woman is done with him." Barrett's wide smile flashed in his beard as he turned to me and chuckled. "Try to keep up."

I shook my head and laughed in surprise as Minty smiled up at me softly. This second song was not part of the plan, and I wondered when and how she arranged to pull this off. She fascinated me. Always had. I suspected she always would.

Releasing her elbow, I wagged my eyebrows at her and moved back to my spot, slinging my guitar into place and waiting for the song to start so I could join in.

I was a lost cause from the beginning.

Minty moved to stand in front of the microphone stand, her legs pressed together tightly. She wrapped both hands around the mic and, at her nod, Barrett strummed the sexy opening notes of Meg Myers HTIS. Energy rolled off her in waves. Her back expanded with her inhale, and she leaned into the mic. My blood sang as her husky voice confessed her sexy secret to the crowd, and they leaned in as one to hear it.

She dropped her head back then rolled it around as she began to move her shoulders and hips in a sensually mesmerizing dance before freezing, stepping wide, and telling them exactly what she'd been hiding.

Junie and the girls hooted and hollered at the back and wolf whistles pierced the air.

Minty bounced her knee through the chorus and sent me a saucy wink over her shoulder.

I couldn't even pretend to play and rested my guitar on its stand. There was no fighting my enjoyment as Minty worked the stage.

Through the second verse, she continued her confessions, her arms rising above her head, keeping time with those round hips my hands itched to pull against mine.

Then she lifted the mic from its stand and slithered toward me. Stopping half in front of me, she dropped her hand to the front of my thigh and dragged it up over my hip and my chest before trailing it lightly over my shoulders as she circled around behind me.

I watched her as far as I could then snapped my head around to the other side in time for her to step in front of me, one boot clad foot between my legs as she faced the crowd and sang the chorus.

With a sly smile she undulated against me, dropping her juicy ass to her heels before bending forward and pushing herself up in a move reminiscent of the strippers I remembered from my university days.

As if I could take any more, she leaned against my side and drew her leg up my thigh as she screamed out her confession once more before ripping her thigh from my eager grasp and returning her mic to the stand for the closing round of choruses.

As the bar erupted, she ducked her chin, nodded her thanks, then turned and threw herself at me with a triumphant laugh.

I laughed out loud as I swung her up in my arms and carried her off the back of the stage.

Minty

Adrenalin throbbed, and I shook with the need to expend it.

With my arms looped around his neck, Lucky dipped and turned sideways to bring us backstage.

"Did you like that?" I asked, though I knew the answer.

"Oh, you know I liked it," he answered roughly as he stared intently at my mouth, then dropped my legs and ushered me quickly into the bathroom reserved for performers and quickly shut the door.

It didn't even occur to me to protest.

I moved to drop to my knees, wanting him in my mouth, but he hauled me up and pressed me back against the door with his palm on my chest.

His eyes holding mine, he worked the button and zipper of my pants and slid his fingers into my panties, sliding his other hand to rest lightly around my throat. He groaned as those calloused tips encountered my slick slit.

My head fell back against the door as he found and rolled the spot God granted women strictly for their pleasure.

"Lucky," I breathed.

"Come on, baby," he urged, his body tense, face tight. "Come on my fingers."

Halfway there before he even had my pants open, it didn't take more than a minute for those divine shudders to wrack my frame, leaving me limp and languid against the door, watching him through half-closed lids.

He braced his feet on either side of my legs and held my eyes as he set my pants to rights then yanked my head back and covered my mouth in a brief, bruising kiss.

I reached for his pants, but he shook his head. "I'll get mine, don't you worry," he promised darkly. "Now you've gotta take the walk of shame back across the stage and go sit with your girls while I finish the set."

I gasped, fully alert now. "I am not walking across that stage!"

"Sure, you are," he countered. "Everyone out there is going to know you're mine, and I will never laugh at or downplay your jealousy again."

He opened the door and swatted my ass, his dimples reappearing. "Get moving. The longer it takes, the worse it looks."

I stopped dead. "Are you serious?"

"Yup," he declared, linking his fingers through mine and leading me up the steps before yanking out his cell phone and taking a picture of our joined hands.

"Aren't you going to wash your hand?"

"Nope," the word popped from his mouth.

Barrett's amused voice rang out over the crowd. "Not sure what happened to my guitarist..." He looked back, caught sight of us, and his laughter boomed. "It's okay," he intoned. "Minty is dragging his ass back."

Whistles and cheers accompanied us across the stage while fire dusted my cheeks. Lucky handed me down the stairs and pressed a sweet kiss to my forehead before patting my ass gently and bounding back onto the stage.

"We'll just wait a second until Lucky's lady finds her way back to her girls," Barrett muttered into the mic and lazily plucked the strings.

Amber and Ruby met me halfway, throwing their arms around me and bookending me back to our table and the smiling faces of the rest of my girls. Drawing me into their circle, they twittered over my performance and declared their sudden need for thigh-high boots and leather pants.

Drivetrain ripped into their next song, and Junie, Willa, and Ruby jumped to their feet. Amber, Mara, and Bex settled around the table with me across from Vander and Gus who crossed their arms and shook their heads in smiling disbelief.

I laughed out loud.

Gus grinned back at me, his devil's mark winking, eyes shining with pride and admiration.

Vander passed me my drink and lifted his own in a silent toast.

I felt free.

Free of white noise.

Free of the padded walls I'd surrounded myself with for my own protection.

Free to be myself without judgement, without the weight of others' expectations.

Without shame.

Chapter 39 – Reflection

<u>Minty</u>

Sunday morning seemed to arrive earlier than usual after the festivities from the night before. I still couldn't believe I got back up onstage. Couldn't get over the flood of joy and freedom.

Not that I wanted to join a band or anything, but that sense of stepping back into myself, and not feeling driven to examine every thought as I did so was phenomenal. I acknowledged to myself that it would be healthy if I could somehow make that the norm.

Alone in Lucky's bed, I stretched my sore limbs. A slow, satisfied smile spread across my face. The things that man did to me when we got home. Took him two hours and a couple of orgasms just to get my clothes off.

After the last song, Lucky jumped off the stage with nary a nod to the women gathered at the foot and headed to our table. People gradually peeled away until it was only Amber, Gus, Ruby, Vander, Junie, Lenny, Lucky and me. I drank too much, laughed too loud, and loved every minute.

As soon as we got into the car, Lucky yanked me across the seat and proceeded to reintroduce his lips to mine in such a way as to imprint his own onto mine for eternity.

Once home, I feigned fatigue. It wasn't a stretch. A few steps up the stairs, I looked over my shoulder to find Lucky's gaze glued to my ass.

"I'm so tired, darling. Are you tired?"

His head snapped back to meet my eyes. He easily read the tease in them and shook his head with a grin. His hands claimed my hips and propelled me up the stairs. "Did you learn nothing last week about what happens to teases?"

In his bedroom, he stood back and studied my outfit, looking befuddled.

"What's wrong?" I chuckled.

He quirked his eyebrow. "I'm trying to figure out how to ditch the pants but keep the boots."

"Ah, I see," I answered. "If you give me ten minutes in the bathroom, I can solve that conundrum for you."

"Go." He pointed to the door.

I spun on my spiked heel and swung my hips to the bathroom.

A moment later, he aligned himself at my back, one hand crossing my chest to wrap around my throat, tipping my head back against his pec. The other flicked open the button of my pants and delved inside. With his lips busy at my neck, and his fingers barely brushing my clit, my orgasm rose fast and furious, my hips bucking against his hand as he groaned in my ear.

He held me through the tremors, planted one last kiss against my temple, then pushed me toward the bathroom.

I barely recognized the woman staring back at me from the mirror. Her hair lay tousled around her head, laying evidence to the fact a man's hands had been in it. Her eyes shone with light and desire. Her mouth, puffy from his sweet kisses, had settled into a soft curve, that hint of a smile indicative of her happiness.

She carried herself with confidence. Exuded sensuality. Radiated peace.

I'd never seen her before.

I raised my hand to the mirror, touched my forefinger to hers and promised, "I will know you better."

I pulled off my boots, peeled off my pants, and freshened up before putting the boots back on.

The mirror showed me exactly what Lucky would see. Black and purple bustier, purple lace panties, thigh-high boots.

I swung the door open and stalked across the room just as I stalked across the stage: owning it. Prepared to make him beg.

He dropped to his knees, tossed me on the bed, and buried his face in my pussy, not releasing my thighs until I shattered around him. I'd come twice and he still hadn't broken.

What followed was a battle for dominance, the end of which found me on my knees in only my boots, face pressed to the mattress, wrists encased in Lucky's calloused hand as he bottomed out inside me and stilled.

Leaning over my back, he braced one hand beside my head and pressed his lips to the nape of my neck before leaning down to my ear, his voice low. "This body? It's mine. I'll dole out your pleasure as I see fit. You want to top? It's by my pleasure you do that. You feel me, baby?"

"Yes," I whispered, my body shaking with the need for release.

"Good," he grunted.

"I never imagined you'd be like this," I admitted as he pressed gentle kisses to the side of my face.

"You and me both, but you bring something out of me. You make me a different man." He trailed kisses over my shoulders and licked a line over my spine as he righted himself. "You make me want to be a better man. A stronger man. Your man."

He slowly eased out then ground back in, rocking against me. Deep inside, swelling to fill me, he took me to a place where I could not see or hear, the rush of waves in my ears rendering me incoherent with pleasure, my entire being centered around his body joined to mine.

So close, but I needed his touch at my clit.

He spoke. I didn't understand but tried to answer.

I heard his deep, satisfied chuckle, then his finger found my need and circled gently, gathering wet from our joining. He rocked harder against me, pulling noises from the woman in the mirror that I'd never heard before.

The fire roared through me, and my eyes flew open. My back curved like a bow as I sobbed out my release, Lucky's deep voice murmuring love and encouragement before setting my hands on the bed, grasping my hips, and taking his.

Lying back, he arranged me over his chest and lightly stroked my back. His chest rumbled with laughter.

I smiled and mumbled, "What are you laughing at?"

He snorted, "Retirement age." Then pressed his lips against my hair, and I knew no more.

It was an excellent night. Listening now with the morning sun peeking through the blinds, I could just make out Brayleigh's big voice coming from the backyard. I had bubbles for her. I had something for Lucky, too. I swung my legs over the side of the bed to hit the shower and head outside.

Lucky lay on his back on the grass, sunglasses shielding his eyes as he served his body up as a human trampoline.

I eased myself into a lawn chair to watch them for a moment. I think, the first thing I'd buy when I moved in, would be new lawn furniture. And a playhouse for Brayleigh. One of those plastic ones with the rounded edges.

I hoped Lucky wouldn't go all caveman on me for wanting to buy things. My eyebrows knit together. If it was going to be my home, too, I should be allowed to add my touch.

Truthfully, all it needed was bookshelves. Maybe a new kitchen table.

I looked around the backyard. Lucky's neighborhood was quieter, yet I felt the proximity of his neighbors. At my place, once the businesses downstairs closed, I was really quite isolated.

"You having a good conversation over there?"

Lucky sat on the grass, leaning back on his hands, a soft smile on his face. "I'm redecorating."

"Sparky!" Brayleigh began to make her way over to me, but my eyes were locked on Lucky's wide, hopeful ones.

He looked away for a moment, staring up at the sky, then looked back, his eyebrows raised. His voice was husky when he spoke. "You decided?"

I held his gaze. "I want to. It has to be on my timeline."

He jumped to his feet, and I continued in a rush. "I can't be hurried. And I'm not sure of all the details…"

He pulled me to my feet and pressed his forehead to mine. "Progress is progress. As fast or as slow as you want. I couldn't be happier."

I released my held breath. "Okay." I nodded. "Okay."

His smile warmed my heart and I mentally high-fived the woman in the mirror.

"Love you, my baby," he murmured.

"Love you, Captain."

"Love me?"

Lucky's dimples flashed as he scooped up his little woman and sandwiched her between us.

"Love you, too," I murmured.

Lucky's eyes misted and he swallowed hard.

"Only you, Minty. My first and only love."

Chapter 40 - Checking

<u>Minty</u>

Her chubby finger pointed to the door. "Go, Da!"

Lucky slapped his palm to his chest in mock injury. "A shot to the heart! She ditched me for Sparky."

"It'll be short-lived. A daddy's girl is always a daddy's girl," I assured him. "I'm a novelty."

"No," he sighed dramatically. "It's the beginning of the end. First, I lose her to you. Then to some undeserving man."

"How do you know he'll be undeserving?" I teased.

"Because the truth is we're all undeserving." He grinned. "It's society's best kept secret."

I smirked. "It's not that well-kept."

He grabbed his chest again. "And the hits just keep on coming!"

"Da!" Brayleigh frowned and pointed to the door. "Go!"

"Can I have a kiss, first?"

She held up her hands, and Lucky lifted her up into his arms. Her little fingers pressed into the back of his neck, their tips turning white from the pressure.

Releasing him abruptly, she lunged into my arms, treating my neck to her baby finger acupuncture. "Mine Sparky," she whispered.

I lay my hand over her back. "Yes, darling. And you're my Dolly."

Is she safe with you?

I smiled the thought away. If I was going to move in, I needed to get my head straight.

You're breaking a rule.

I focused on the feel of her baby body curled against me, soft, warm, and sleepy.

Her fingernail scratched lightly at my necklace, moving slower and slower, until her arm slipped down my chest, and she lay against me, deadweight.

Supporting her head and back, I bent to slip her down onto her mattress, then pulled her blanket up to her chest. I didn't think it should go higher than that in case it covered her nose. Too many stuffed toys in her crib. Those had to go. I'd read somewhere that stuffed toys in a baby's bed were a hazard. Was she past that stage? I left her penguin and her bear but decided to remove the rest. That looked better. Were two-year-olds allowed pillows? Lucky wouldn't have it in there if it was dangerous. I needed to do some research for keeping toddlers safe.

Brayleigh's legs kicking, her body shuddering, my hands pressing the pillow over her face. Her body shuddering as she struggles to breathe.

"Oh!" I stepped back. That was a bad one. Holding my throat, I edged over to check to make sure the pillow was in place and not covering her face.

I could feel her body twitching beneath my palms.

I linked my fingers loosely in front of me, smiled the thought away.

It's just a thought. I am not my thoughts. My thoughts are like passing birds, and I am the sky.

I reached out my hand and caressed her cheek, the nagging feeling that I'd missed some crucial step or check weighing on me.

"Goodnight, Dolly," I whispered.

I closed her door over and stepped away quietly.

Did you make sure the blanket isn't over her face? Did you put the pillow over her face?

No.

Maybe you did but changed your mind.

I could feel the sensation under my palms, as if I'd done it.

Maybe you didn't put it back properly.

I looked back at her door. Perhaps putting her to bed on the first night was rushing things. Maybe if Lucky stayed with me while I put her to bed at first, or waited in the hallway, or even checked on her afterwards, until I desensitized myself. Baby steps brought giant gains, I reminded myself.

I'd have to tell him about the thoughts.

It occurred to me that I needed to tell him anyway. He should know how I am so he can make an informed decision.

I followed the noise of clattering dishes to the kitchen and found Lucky making me tea and setting out several boxes of cookies.

When he heard me come in, he waved his arms to present the boxes.

"What are you doing?" I could hear the smile in my voice.

"I noticed you drink chamomile tea, and sometimes peppermint, so I bought both." He turned to the cookie boxes. "There are several types of chocolate cookies here, but I threw in a shortbread and a jam-filled just in case you like a little variety."

My smile grew. "Lucky, that's so sweet of you."

Holding out his hand for mine, he drew me in. Serious grey eyes looked into mine. "I want you to be comfortable here." He smirked. "It's just cookies, but-"

I shook my head. "It's not just cookies. It's care and attention and effort. Sometimes cookies mean everything."

"You're not that difficult to please, are you?" he mused.

I thought about it. "I would say I'm difficult, but not difficult to please. Does that make sense?"

He pressed his lips together. "No. I would say you're complicated, but not difficult. At all."

Perhaps this was the wrong time to talk about OCD. It was literally our first night on our own with Brayleigh. Maybe I should have laid it out for him before. The obvious truth of that struck me all at once. Here I am agreeing to move in, and he doesn't even know what he's signing up for.

"Hey." He jostled me lightly. "What are you talking about in there?"

I tilted my chin up to meet his eyes. Did I make him serious? "Were you always serious like this? Or did I do this to you?"

"I have my serious moments. And my quiet moments." He shrugged. "I guess I behave differently under different circumstances. When I'm playing, I'm filled with energy. When I'm teaching, it's another type of performance, one where I'm constantly gauging my audience. That requires a focused type of energy. With my sisters, with Hope and Brayleigh, I'm always a little cautious. Watchful."

"And what are you with me?"

"A combination. Combined with the intensity I take on when I'm learning something new."

That made sense. "There are things I need to tell you about my OCD."

"Sure. I haven't done any research other than after you initially told me about it. I wanted to wait and let you tell me how it is for you as you're ready. Would you like me to learn on my own?"

"Maybe in a couple of days we can look up some things together and I can use that to explain to you how my OCD affects me. And maybe tonight we can drink tea and eat cookies."

"Yeah," he grinned. "We'll practice for when we're old people."

"I'm going to be old before you," I groused.

"Men don't live as long as women. It was very," he paused and then smiled smugly as he used my word against me, "prudent of you to pick up a younger man." He squeezed me close, muffling my laughter against his chest. "Cougar."

"Lucky! No!" I slapped him and pointed my finger to make my point clear.

"Mm, I'm having librarian fantasies." He ran his hands firmly up my back. "You can sit at a desk with a book. I'll be loud. You can smack me with your ruler..."

"You're mixing your fantasy roles. I think that's librarian mixed with old fashioned schoolteacher...or a nun."

"You killed it." He laughed. "You killed my fantasy with your talk of nuns."

Now that I had at least broached the subject, waiting to discuss OCD seemed like a much better idea.

"Going with the smacking theme, I could be a dominatrix?"

His eyes lit with interest. The idea had merit.

"Ruby suggested I buy you a cock cage," I murmured.

His eyes bugged out of his head. "What? No! Why would she say something like that?"

I shrugged. "Could be because I told her what you did to me."

His brows scrunched in confusion. "What did I do?"

"Before we went to Amber's? You left me ... unfulfilled?"

He looked delighted, then sickened. "You really told, hm?"

"I did." I pursed my lips primly. "Ruby accused you of clitoral abuse."

He barked out a laugh and hugged me close. "I hope you at least told her I made it up to you."

"I haven't." I smirked, then grinned. "But I probably will."

He shook his head in mock dismay.

I looked down. "I have something for you."

His eyebrows arched, and he grinned. "Another present?"

"Sort of. I drew something for you."

He palmed his chest. "You made it? Let's see it. I can't wait."

I smoothed my palms down over my thighs and went out to my car to get his gift. It occurred to me, far too late, that giving someone art for their house was incredibly presumptuous. It's not like he could hide it in a closet. Where else could he put it if not in the house. Does he have a mancave?

"Darling, do you have a mancave?" I walked into the house with the wrapped canvases under my arm.

"My mancave exists only in the dream realm." He followed me into the family room.

I sat down on the couch with the canvases on my lap. "Okay, it's not necessary for you to hang these up. Wall art is incredibly personal, and I won't be at all offended if it doesn't suit you. Maybe it'll be good for when your mancave crosses dimensions."

"Baby, just give it to me."

I set the three canvases down on his lap and twisted my hands together on my lap.

"Does it matter which one I open first?"

"No. As soon as you see one, you'll know what it is." It was in fact a triptych. Three narrow canvases which when hung together forming one large square.

The first piece he unwrapped showed Barrett, resting on his back foot and looking down at his guitar. The second piece showed Lenny and Bax. Bax standing sideways to the crowd, Lenny facing forward with one stick spinning. The third featured Lucky, legs braced, the ropey muscles of his forearms straining, dimples on full display.

It was good. Objectively, it was technically excellent, but it also contained movement and you could almost hear it. That didn't mean he wanted his band hanging in his living room.

He cleared his throat, then covered his mouth with his fist.

I watched his face. "You like it."

He cleared his throat. "I love it. I've never received a better gift. The fact that it came from your precious hands..." He petered off, then lay the canvases out on the coffee table, side-by-side and stared at them. "You are so talented. Thank you, baby."

He stood up, tucked his fingers into his back pockets, and continued to study them. Finally, he turned his head and took me in, his eyes sweeping down to my hands before returning to my face.

With one finger, he separated my twisting fingers. "You're everything I never knew I wanted and far more than I deserve." Turning, he folded both my hands in his. "I'm going to make you so damn happy."

For the first time, his light didn't hurt my eyes and I didn't feel the need to look away.

"You do, darling. You truly do."

Lucky

I woke up shortly after three to find Minty swinging her legs off our bed. "Baby, where are you going?"

She froze and turned to face me. "I'm going to check on the baby. I'll be right back."

I sat up and pushed myself back against the headboard. "What are you checking for exactly?"

"I just need to make sure I didn't cover her face with the blanket. I'm just going to make sure she's okay."

I held her eyes. "I'll buy a video monitor tomorrow. Set it up on the dresser. You need to sleep."

She hesitated.

"Would you like me to check on her?"

Her shoulders slumped in relief.

I yanked back the covers. "In you go." I tucked them around her, then went to check on my daughter.

And I wondered if I should wait for her to share, or if it would be better to start reading.

Chapter 41 — Easy

Minty

The next couple of days passed smoothly. Lucky waited downstairs while I put Brayleigh to bed, then he ran up and checked to reassure me. I wrote down the steps I needed to take to reach the ultimate goal of putting Brayleigh to bed without giving into the compulsion to check. Step one was putting her to bed by myself. It didn't matter that Lucky followed up, my job was to stay in the room with her, lay her down, and walk away. Once that became easy, it would be time to take the next step.

In the mornings, the three of us spent time cuddling and playing in our bed. Lucky's presence made it safe and allowed me to enjoy that sweet time. My job was to stay with them, in my pajamas, without the armor of my daytime clothing.

When we took her out in the car, I put her in her car-seat each time and Lucky would check. Except for one time, a time I chose when Lucky would not check.

I began to dream of excursions where I took Brayleigh to the park by myself or brought her with me to visit one of my girls. I wanted to introduce her to Yiayia.

Wednesday morning when I woke, Brayleigh lay nestled between us fast asleep. Torment's icy fingers touched my chest.

Did you touch that baby?

I closed my eyes, misplaced anger aimed at Lucky coursing through my veins. Taking a deep breath, I worked to settle my nerves. He didn't know. Of course, he didn't know. What normal person would think this was a problem?

Brayleigh flailed in her sleep, her foot coming to rest on my lower abdomen. My body jerked in shock.

You like that.

I shrank away from her and gently picked up her ankle to move it onto the bed beside me. Turning my back so she wouldn't inadvertently touch me, afraid to get out of the bed in case she rolled off, I lay stiffly and battled my demons.

Battle. To battle OCD, successfully, is to lay down your arms, drop your defenses, tie yourself to a chair, and smile as it beats you. You fight by refusing to fight.

Did you touch that baby?

Maybe you did something while you slept.

You liked it when her foot touched you.

Erase it. Erase it.

One, two, buckle my....

Resist the compulsion.

Take up your arms by laying them down.

Smile.

Breathe.

Did you touch that baby?

No.

Are you sure?

I needed to talk to Lucky.

"Morning, baby," Lucky said softly.

"Hi! I didn't think you were awake." Surprised, I turned to meet his serious grey eyes. Shame bit into my soul. I did that. I dimmed the light in those laughing eyes. Was this what life would be for him now?

Confusion and worry? Instead of siphoning off a little of his calm, I'd infected him with my chaos.

He smiled wryly, unknowingly confirming my thoughts. "You're thinking too loud." He held out his arms. "Come over here."

I dipped my head toward Brayleigh, a spark of anger in my voice. "Did you forget we've got a little body here?"

His eyebrows knit. "She won't fall out. Walk around."

The space between us, the canyon separating his calm and my chaos kept me rooted in place, as if physically going to him required us to be on the same side emotionally.

"Come. Here."

My eyes flew to his. He wasn't joking but he wasn't angry, either. Determined and hopeful, perhaps a little anxious.

I moved slowly, my internal voice urging me to retreat, my heart leaning hard in his direction.

He shifted toward Brayleigh and lifted the covers. Long and lean, golden inside and out, and I was a defilement. He waved me down.

My knee hit the bed and he knifed up to gently gather me down on top of him, tangling his hand in my hair.

Quietly, he ran his hand over my back.

Gradually, I melted against him.

"That's better."

I stiffened and he snorted out a laugh. His grip in my hair tightened.

"Baby, I've got you. I see you, and I've got you. You're running scared, I get that. I am patiently waiting for you to explain, but I'm not completely clueless. I do know some of it." He cupped the back of my head and pressed his palm to my back. "You won't shock me. You won't turn me off. You don't scare me."

This could be the beginning or the end. But I needed to lay it out.

"I'll explain. When Brayleigh goes down for her nap this afternoon, I'll give it to you," I promised quietly.

His chest expanded beneath me with his rough inhale. "Good."

Lucky

Relief. Finally. With everything out in the open, we could make a plan and begin the process of weaving the threads of our life together.

Holding her against my chest, I felt the moment she fell back asleep, her hand curled against my chest.

Loving a child, I understood. That made sense to me.

This business of handing your heart and soul over to someone who could at any moment walk away with it? This was a risk. Loving someone ripped open a vulnerability in a person's soul, a space that could only be filled by them.

But I'd never seen the point in making life more complicated than it needed to be. I believed that priorities elevated a man from existing to living. For me, that meant family and friends took center stage. Fatherhood was worthy. Teaching meant something. Music fed me. And my faith rested unassuming beneath it all.

And I knew also, with a simplicity of faith that did not bear questioning, that Minty was everything. Which made the way forward simple enough, complicated as it might be.

I considered what I knew about OCD. Over the years, I'd taught two students with severe OCD. Both of those kids had mothers who advocated for them fiercely. Probably the only reason I knew how much they suffered.

One boy suffered with religiosity. Constantly questioning his worth and existence. He found his way, embracing his overactive brain and going into to ethics studies. The first in his family to go to university.

The girl, though, I remember as clearly as if it was yesterday her mother sitting down across from me, an unlit cigarette hanging out of her mouth, her entire countenance a mix of challenge and defiance. Uneducated. She struggled to keep ahead of the curve of a mental illness she didn't understand.

But she understood devotion. And she was devoted to her daughter.

We met separately from her daughter because she feared the embarrassment it would cause her. I agreed. It wasn't up to the child to educate me. Mom explained the fears that plagued her. The disturbing images and urges.

That girl still came in to visit occasionally. She lived a quiet life working with animals. She held herself in much the same way Minty did. I wondered if she, too, had white noise.

Once Brayleigh fell asleep, Minty and I sat at the kitchen table in front of my opened laptop.

Her fingers flew deftly over the keyboard, and she brought up a site that explained OCD and its various subtypes.

"I have all of these to some degree or another. Most of it is nothing but a fleeting thought. Some of it is white noise." She pointed to the paragraph on sexual OCD and admitted quietly. "This is my nemesis."

"So, inappropriate or unwanted sexual thoughts. What's different about this kind of OCD that it makes it difficult for you to smile it away like the rest?"

"Basically, I just haven't challenged it enough. I haven't been able to. It feels too risky." She lifted her hands in frustration. "You read this and it's all very clinical. It doesn't present itself as clinical."

"How does it present itself?"

"Lucky, I'm nowhere near the point where I can speak aloud the depravity that exists in my brain. I can talk about harm OCD. That one I have a handle on. That one is white noise."

I nodded for her to continue. She watched me as she spoke.

"I'll give you some examples. Willa walked into the office, very pregnant, and a movie played in my head of me stabbing her with a hunting knife. It's not a cartoon type video, it's gory. When I went to see Willa at the hospital, Barrett handed me Rena and I saw myself grabbing her by her feet and swinging her head into the corner of the wall. You were carrying Brayleigh downstairs, and I got the thought urging me to push you down the stairs."

My mouth gaped open in horror at her suffering. "And this," I sputtered. "This is white noise? How is this white noise?"

"Because it doesn't stop me from doing what I want to do. It stops being white noise when it interferes."

"Isn't it interfering? When it's causing you distress?" I wanted to take her in my arms. I wanted to take it all away. I wished I could take it from her.

"Not for me. For me, it's only interfering when it stops me from doing. I conquered harm OCD years ago. The clips have never decreased or disappeared. Sometimes they shock me, and it takes me a moment to get past it like in the case with Rena at the hospital. But I held her, and I enjoyed that. Another example is a visual I see of Brayleigh thrown from the car-seat. That is interfering. That is more than white noise because it's interfering with me taking her out. In short," she leaned over and placed her palm to my cheek, to comfort me, "if I can smile it away and carry on, it's white noise."

"It's horrible. You must be exhausted."

She nodded, looking more relaxed than I expected based on what we'd been talking about. "Sometimes. I do need my down time. And I do need to see my therapist to get help with this. I've improved, for sure. But I've never lived with a child. The circumstances have changed. The rules have to go."

"What rules?"

Minty went on to explain the rules that protected her against the distress of pedophilia thoughts as well as her current struggles. "Safety issues are the worst, food issues are difficult but manageable, issues surrounding children seem to be insurmountable because they circle back to safety." She looked down for the first time. "And there's this underlying doubt that I might actually be a monster."

I snorted. "You're not a monster."

"I'm not. I would never, ever hurt Brayleigh or my boys or any child."

Her breathing picked up as she spoke, no longer looking relaxed.

"Baby, I'm not the one you need to convince."

She stopped and looked at me.

"You're the only person who thinks that. And like you said," I shrugged, "it's not you. It's those damn birds."

She laughed, the sound like music to my ears.

293

We spent the next hour making a list of all the things she wanted to do, the steps she wanted to work on, and my role in all of it. And I realized my mistake in bringing Brayleigh into the bed without giving her a heads up.

The intricacies of dealing with the disorder were complicated.

The learning curve would be steep.

But the decision was easy.

Chapter 42 – Knees

Minty

Other than Tuesday night, Brayleigh slept through the night, and thankfully, the night terrors had ceased. Putting Brayleigh to bed was becoming marginally easier. The controlled nature of the exposure helped, and Friday night Lucky and I refrained from checking until we went to bed, something Lucky habitually did every night anyway.

My level of anxiety had not changed, but the level of uncertainty I could tolerate increased. In other words, my anxiety remained high only because I kept pushing the limits of my exposure.

Thursday morning, we tired Brayleigh out at the park. While she slept in the afternoon, Lucky played guitar and I worked on my commissions. We made dinner together, bumping hips and elbows in the kitchen, talking about nothing and everything.

Lucky chopped vegetables liked nobody's business, and had taken to marinating and grilling portobello mushrooms, sliced eggplant, and peppers alongside his burgers. I doubted his barbecue had ever met an eggplant or portobello mushroom before I came into his life. The change in my daily routine and the shifting of my future plans was a wonder.

Friday, we visited a petting zoo an hour outside of Milltown where Lucky took more pictures than I could count. Worn out from sun and excitement, Brayleigh spent the afternoon in bed and so did we.

In the evening, we headed over to Willa and Barrett's. Balancing my cookie platter in one hand, and Brayleigh in the other, threw me off balance in more ways than one. Walking up to Willa's, side-by-side with Lucky who carted all the toddler paraphernalia, was a far cry from how I usually arrived at these things. The shift had me all kinds of warm and slightly off-kilter.

Overtired and overwrought, she fought going to bed Friday night and Lucky calmly took over. Watching him, I realized that the calm I emitted to the outside world was manufactured and contrived, while Lucky's was bred into his bones. He took her tantrums in stride, her night terrors in stride, my issues in stride. Perhaps he really could handle it. Accept it. Accept me.

I commiserated with Brayleigh, I, too, was overtired.

Unused to spending this much time with other people, never mind a small person who triggered my worst fears, had me falling asleep in Lucky's big bed before Brayleigh. I woke up hours later, my butt tucked into Lucky's groin, his arm looped around my waist, and his nose tucked against the back of my neck.

He stirred in his sleep and pulled me closer. "You good?" he murmured.

"Couldn't be better," I admitted.

"Good." He kissed the nape of my neck and within moments his breath evened and slowed. I followed him to sleep shortly after.

Lucky's sister, Ava, picked Brayleigh up early Saturday afternoon, taking her to Tracy's for the day to play with her cousins, then to her place to sleep because Lucky had a commitment with Drivetrain.

As soon as she left, we took the bike out. I treasured these times. The soft blur of the fields as we whipped past. The wind beating against me. With my body synced to his, I soaked up his peace. And I sorely needed it.

Again, the relief I experienced with Brayleigh out of the house waved like a bright, red flag. I told myself it would get better. After so many years, I knew how to deal with these things. It would take time, but it would get easier until it, too, became white noise.

Hope would be back on Monday. Our routine would revert back to the usual where I wouldn't have to constantly deal with the triggers.

I smoothed my dress over my hips as I checked out my reflection in the mirror, wondering which woman would be staring back at me. I caught glimpses of the inside me, the unfettered me, the me I wanted to be, but she was not yet ready to move in permanently.

Still, I could see her, and she approved of my little dress.

Lucky rolled in behind me and his eyes slid over my form approvingly before meeting mine in the mirror.

I watched as his hands slid around my waist and he bent to rest his chin on my shoulder. "You... are beautiful. I love everything about you," he murmured, palming my ribs.

"Don't get any ideas," I replied dryly.

He grinned. "Lots of ideas but they're only in the planning stages." His thumbs brushed the undersides of my breasts. "Execution of said plans is scheduled for approximately four hours from now."

I raised my arms over my head and threaded my fingers through his hair, watching his gaze zero in on my breasts.

He groaned and cupped them in his hands.

"Four hours, darling," I reminded him.

He grunted and squeezed my nipples. "You know what I love about tonight?"

"What?"

"We don't have to be quiet."

Almost exactly four hours later, eyes wild, Lucky slammed the front door and pointed to the floor. "Knees," he gritted.

I'd spent the twenty-minute drive home telling him all the things I'd thought about doing while he was onstage.

He ripped open his pants.

I leaned toward him, tipping my head back to meet his eyes. "Say please, darling."

He gripped my hair in his fist and leaned down so that his nose almost touched mine, and growled, "Please."

I patted the hand that held my hair. "Leave this right here."

I palmed the sides of my dress and pulled it up over my hips as he watched, then slowly dropped to my knees. I tipped my head back and opened my mouth.

"Woman, you are going to kill me," he groaned as he breached my lips. His hips jerked. He hit the back of my throat and pulled back. "Sorry, baby."

I released him and looked up. "Do you want to fuck my mouth or don't you?"

He stared down at me, fingers tightening, eyes searching mine. "I want to."

"Then stop pussy-footing around and feed me that cock."

"Minty, for fuck's sake," he hissed, pushing back inside my mouth.

His head fell back with a groan as he pulled me closer and flexed his hips.

I leaned in and swallowed around him, loving the tension that rolled through his frame, the quivering that wracked his abdomen, the strain in his arms as he held my hair taut to stop me from swallowing him down.

"Where are your hands?" he demanded suddenly.

I laughed around his cock, letting him know exactly where they were.

"No way. Uh uh. That's mine," he growled. "Put your hands on my thighs."

I readily complied.

He yanked me off his dick and met my eyes. "Now you're going to know the torture you put me through in the car. Do not touch your pussy."

"Aye, aye, Captain."

He grunted out a laugh. "You make me crazy in all the best ways."

"Yes, darling, and I'd like you to return the favor sooner rather than later so let's get back to it, shall we?"

He tugged my head back, drove into the back of my throat and paused, his thumb caressing my jaw. "I love it when you get all uppity." His thumb brushed across my bottom lip stretched around him. "Now, be a good girl and suck me off."

My palms resting on his thighs, with tongue and lips and the grazing of my teeth, I drove him higher, his little grunts and moans of encouragement flooding my panties.

When his movements began to stutter, my fingers wandered behind his balls and pressed against his prostate.

His muttered curse reached my ears half a second before he bowed over me, spilling inside my willing mouth.

Easing out with a hiss, he slid down the door to the floor and pulled me into his arms. "I love you. So fucking much. You literally knocked me on my ass."

I laughed, pressing my face into his neck, reveling in the security of his arms wrapped tightly around me.

"Happy to do so, Darling."

"You might need to help me upstairs," he teased. "I'm weak."

"This does not bode well for me," I murmured.

"I'm weak, not dead. Still. You'll have to do all the work."

"I'm already doing all the work!"

"I'll remind you of your preference for a gentleman of retirement age. Far be it for me to deny you your fantasy." Grasping my hips, he helped me to my feet then knifed up, yanking his pants up. "Tell you what, whoever's first upstairs gets to call the shots."

I spun on my heel and headed for the stairs, trying to kick off the heels that were hampering my speed.

Lucky laughed and tossed me over his shoulder as he took to the stairs.

"Might I advise you, in this position, my bottom will cross the threshold before yours which means I'll be first."

"Can't have that." Turning his back to his room, he set me down on the floor on my bum, putting me at a distinct disadvantage.

I latched onto his neck and yanked him down with me, laughing, then turned and launched my body toward the door.

Lucky's laughter rang out behind me. "I had no idea you were so competitive!"

I slapped my hand down onto his bedroom floor. "I'm in. I win."

He stepped over my prone form and helped me up. "You win. On a technicality, but I'll let you have it."

I lifted my dress over my head and stood before him in lace bra and panties.

The mirror above his dresser reflected my image back to me. Hair a mess, cheeks flushed, eyes bright.

There you are.

Lucky

She was glorious.

Eyes laughing, hair a wild tangle from my hands, mouth soft and swollen.

I tucked my fingers into my back pockets and leaned back on my heels to take her in. I could not help but smile. "What do you want, baby? I'm at your command."

A saucy smile tipped her lips as she pointed to the floor and mimicked me from earlier. "Knees."

Gladly, I thought.

And I'll fucking stay there.

Chapter 43 – Smithereens

Lucky

Ava brought Brayleigh, and coffee, shortly after breakfast but didn't stay long. It had nothing to do with Minty or holding out hope for Hope and me. Ava just wasn't much of a talker. I think being the youngest, everyone simply spoke for her. In the past few years, I'd made a conscious effort to not fill the silent space between us, waiting to hear her thoughts.

She didn't share often, but when she did it was a gift.

When she left, Minty and I sat outside on the back patio. Brayleigh sat on Minty's lap examining her jewelry. The way Minty dressed and accessorized gave Brayleigh new baubles to discover every day.

Which was a good thing because Brayleigh was uncharacteristically fussy.

"I think she misses her mommy," Minty murmured. Brayleigh cuddled against her chest, her fist in her mouth. "Maybe it's teeth?"

I raised my eyebrows. "Could be. I know she's got the bottom molars but not the top yet." I smiled wryly. "We could be in for a rough night."

Minty smoothed her palm over Brayleigh's tiny back and murmured, "Doesn't seem like such a rough deal at the moment. Do you have baby Tylenol we can give her?" She pressed her lips to Brayleigh's forehead. "She's the tiniest bit warm."

I looked at her and I heard music.

She fed my soul the same way the music did. Witnessing her care and concern for Brayleigh compelled me to share my child, give my child, in a way I could never have fathomed six weeks ago.

Making a square with my fingers, I framed them.

She smiled.

"This, right here, is everything."

She ducked her head as I pulled out my cell phone.

Was she camera-shy?

Was she uncomfortable hearing how I felt about her?

I took the shot, then zeroed in on the photo I really wanted, knowing whatever else she was, she was music.

Minty

Brayleigh fussed and mewled throughout the day. As soon as the Tylenol began to wear off, she shifted back and forth between us, unable to settle for very long until it kicked back in.

Eventually, she only wanted daddy.

Finally, I got his fascination with pictures. Lucky lay back on the couch, one knee cocked up, his tiny daughter sprawled across his chest, her fist curled into his shirt. He watched tv, one arm thrown back supporting his head, his other hand curled around her bottom, bracing her so she didn't fall.

Her fussing didn't faze him in the least, he simply rolled with her moods and her needs.

I took the picture.

His gaze swung away from the tv and noting my cell phone in my hand, he smiled. Only a hint of his dimples showing.

"You love me?" he murmured.

"I do."

"I take pictures to remember how I felt at that moment. Why did you take this picture?"

"Because you're beautiful. Because you don't fight reality, you just roll with it. You don't let things upset your balance. You simply adjust. I admire that."

"There's no point in fighting reality. Why waste your energy?"

"That's kind of how I deal with OCD when it intrudes. Fighting it, moaning and complaining about it doesn't change anything." I considered something. "Does it require energy to resist fighting reality?"

"Sometimes." He grinned. "Like when you stormed out of here thinking Hope and I were hiding something, I might have bitched and complained to Hope that you didn't believe me."

I laughed. "Sorry about that."

"No sorry." He shook his head. "My point is that my instinct was to fight and rail and argue with you that you were wrong, that Junie and Willa set me up to fail. But it was far more important to simply accept where you were at, accept the fact that Hope and I needed to make changes, and simply follow through. Hoping you would see me."

For once, he was the one who looked away.

"I see you, Captain. I see you so well I struggle to believe my own eyes." I cocked my head, suddenly realizing something. "You remind me a bit of Gus. Gus is good, to his bones, he's just good. And Amber is everything to him." Oh, boy. Was I making his feelings out to be more than I should? Had I misread?

"Go on."

Looking up, I found his gaze resting on me steadily, waiting.

"You make me feel like I'm everything," I blurted out quickly. "And the reality is, you are everything I always dreamed of in a man. Kind, loyal, devoted, confident, calm, funny, and so damn good, Darling. You're just good."

His lips tipped up on one side. "Well, you're everything I never knew I wanted."

I laughed softly, not wanting to wake Brayleigh.

"It's true," he murmured. "It's as if there was a closed door in my life, but I'd been walking past it for so long I forgot it was there. Then one day, you showed up and blew it right off its hinges. Now I can't imagine my life without you."

"There's no closing that door, hm?"

"What door?" He grinned. "You blasted it to smithereens."

"Smithereens? Who says that?"

"It's a legitimate word," he argued, pulling out his cell. "Fragments. Pieces. Bits. Smithereens."

Carefully, he rolled Brayleigh onto the couch, tucking a pillow in front of her, and held out his hand. "Let's get some food going. I'm starving."

I linked my fingers through his and followed him into the kitchen. How much warmer it seemed to me now that it was filled with memories.

"Stir fry?"

"Mm, yes, please."

Lucky pulled out the cutting board and his sharpest knife.

A thick line of red, from wrist to elbow, following the path of the blade up my arm.

"Do you want peppers and onions?"

The point of the knife against his throat, my face horrified as I lose control of my hand.

"Yup. Do we have mushrooms? I'll need carrots and celery first."

I relaxed my shoulders and acknowledged the crazy thoughts with a smile while I passed Lucky the vegetables.

"Shit, fuck!"

I spun around in time to see a wide splatter of Lucky's bright red blood land across the counter.

"Lucky! What the hell did you do?" I grabbed a tea towel and rushed to press it over the cut.

"Cut myself. It's not as bad as it looks."

"Really?" I indicated the blood splattered over the counter.

The pan sizzled on the stove.

Lucky pressed down hard on the tea towel.

I turned off the heat. "Let me see," I demanded.

Lucky lifted the towel. It was a deep cut, but it wasn't the geyser I imagined it would be. "You need stitches."

"I'll call Barrett."

"Uh, Barrett is a vet."

Lucky laughed. "Same thing. It'll be like working on a goldfish."

"Goldfish do not get surgeries."

"Sure they do."

"Bear? Can you come over? I seem to have cut myself. Might need a small stitch."

I snorted.

"I know you're a vet." He laughed. "Just bring your first aid kit and get over here. Brayleigh is teething and I don't want to leave her." Pause. "Okay. See you soon."

I cleaned up the kitchen as he sat at the table and applied pressure to his hand.

"You've lost your expert knife-wielding status," I teased, though the sight of the blood still disturbed me. *Just roll with it.*

"So long as I don't lose my sword-wielding status," he retorted with a laugh.

"Not possible," I assured him.

Bantering back and forth between checking his wound, I realized long before he did that he needed to go to the hospital.

"I'm going to get Brayleigh ready to take you to the hospital," I stated.

"Just wait," he said. "And can you make me a sandwich? I'm starving. In any case, if Barrett can't do it, I'll get him to drive me."

Alarms blared. Not safe. Not safe.

I turned to the counter and began pulling out the fixings for a sandwich.

"You're bleeding to death and all you can think about is your stomach," I joked.

Is she safe with you?

"Not true," he assured me. "If Brayleigh was in bed for the night, I'd be on my back expecting some serious nursing."

You can do this.

I laughed. "Haven't you already lost enough blood? You're going to send the rest of it to your dick just so I can bounce on it?"

He groaned. "Don't give me those visuals right now. Fuck." He looked up at me, eyes hopeful. "What would you be wearing?"

With my back to him, I described it. "The white set. I'd be looking all virginal, the straps falling down my shoulders, the barest hint of a nipple showing..."

"I can picture it but I don't remember a white set."

I turned from the counter, the first few buttons of my blouse released, and offered him a peek. "This one."

His mouth fell open for a moment before he snapped it shut and glared at me. "Mean!"

I stood in front of him, cupped my breast, and offered it to his mouth. "You did ask."

He sucked it in, bra and all, humming like it was the most delicious thing he ever tasted, until I popped it out of his mouth.

"You are so going to pay for that."

The doorbell drowned out the sound of my laughter. Barrett walked in and I scooted out the back way to get myself in order.

"You okay, man? You're really flushed," Barrett said.

I clapped my hand over my mouth as Lucky snorted. "Women are the devil."

Barrett laughed. "Let's see." There was a pause in which I imagined Lucky lifting the tea towel. "That needs stitches."

"I know," Lucky huffed. "That's why you're here."

"I'm a vet."

"I'm an animal," Lucky retorted, and Barrett's big boom of a laugh shook the house.

"Mama?"

I rushed to the couch. "Hi, Dolly."

She turned her face away. "Mama."

"Mama will be here soon. One more sleep, darling."

I took off my bangles and hung them on my finger as I reached for her.

She hesitated, then came to me, tucking her face into my neck. "Mama."

My heart broke. There was no way to explain to her that she would see Hope tomorrow morning.

More laughter came from the kitchen as I made my way there with Brayleigh. It was almost time for her next dose of Tylenol.

"If it was one of two, I'd do it for you, man. But this needs to be done right. It can affect your guitar-playing if it's not done correctly because of where it cuts across."

Barrett headed over to me, a big finger held out to shake hands with Brayleigh. "Hello, little angel," he said as she grasped his finger. "You not feeling too good?"

Lucky sighed, and then looked at me. "I'll call Ava, okay, baby?"

Barrett's head snapped up in surprise, his all-too-intuitive gaze swinging back and forth between us before he turned to pack up his stuff and give us a hint of privacy.

I shook my head as the shame rolled over me. "Just leave me her number. If I need her, I'll call."

"You sure?" He looked doubtful. "She's not exactly at her best."

"I've got it, Captain."

Barrett let out a snort.

Lucky turned to him and jeered. "You're just jealous, Bear, that my woman is so enamored of my member that she has named me for him."

I laughed. "Who spilled? Willa?"

Barrett scoffed. "Who do you think?"

"Junie." I declared.

"Yup."

"Come on, Captain. I'll take you to the hospital." Barrett's mouth twisted to the side. "Somehow this feels different than when I call Rhys 'handsome'. Nope. Can't do it." He shook his head. "I'll wait for you in the car."

Lucky turned to me immediately and touched a finger to my cheek. "I'm sorry I said that in front of Barrett. I wasn't thinking about him, I was only concerned for you."

"It's okay," I assured him.

He looked at me intently. "I'm not sure what to do," he murmured. "I don't want to tell you what to do as if I know better, but I'm worried this will be too much for you."

"You won't be gone for that long. I'll probably just keep her downstairs on the couch with me until you get home."

"I'll text you Ava's number. You want me to call her?"

"No. I'll call if I have to."

I didn't want the questions. Already, I saw them in Barrett's eyes, though he was never one to judge. I didn't want to expose my shameful underbelly to the one person in Lucky's family who was the most reserved toward me.

I gave Brayleigh her medicine while Lucky grabbed his wallet and keys.

He knocked briskly on the door frame, drawing my attention. "I'll be back as soon as I can."

"Okay, darling."

He walked out the door.

And Brayleigh began to cry.

Chapter 44 – Sticky

Minty

Brayleigh cried inconsolably for both Lucky and Hope. I tried popsicles, I tried taking her out in the backyard, I tried putting music on, her favorite tv shows, I even pulled out my stash of costume jewelry. Nothing could ease her.

You're not cut out for this.

After two hours, Lucky texted to check in. I was honest, said she was upset and told him what I'd done to try to soothe her.

"Give her a bottle," he suggested. "She's probably hungry and there's no chance she'll eat right now."

You should have thought of that.

Truthfully, she hadn't eaten well all day. I grabbed her a bottle of milk, put on her favorite tv show and she finally curled up on my lap and settled.

I breathed a deep sigh of relief. We would get through this. Chances were good she'd go to sleep on the couch, and I could just sit beside her and read until Lucky got home.

The bottle drained, she continued to suck away at the teat as she drifted off to sleep. Her rosebud mouth lax, the bottle slipped away. I gently rolled her over onto the couch, uncovering the wet spot she left on my dress. Her diaper was soaked. It needed to be changed.

You want to touch her.

I swallowed hard. There was no point in waking her to change her diaper.

She's going to get a rash. You can't even meet her basic needs.

She needed sleep more than anything right now.

I covered her with a blanket while my mind continued to spin.

My cell buzzed and I picked it up. "Hello, darling. How is it going?"

"Hi, baby. They're bringing in a specialist to have a quick look before they close it up."

"That's good, darling. Better to be safe than sorry." My life's motto.

"You doing okay?"

"Yes, I'm fine." He didn't need to worry about me right now.

"What's Brayleigh doing?"

"Sleeping on the couch beside me." Tell him about the diaper. Tell him. "I didn't change her diaper," I blurted out.

"That's okay, baby. If you need to, and you want me to stay on the phone with you while you do it, I can. But I think it's better that we let her sleep."

Even he doesn't trust you to change her diaper.

"Okay. I'll leave her be."

"I'll keep checking in, okay? Do you want me to call Ava?"

"No, of course not. She's passed out. It'll be fine."

"I'll check in again. I love you. Thank you for being there for her. And me. There's no one other than Hope that I'd trust more with her."

That was high praise. And probably misplaced.

I am not a monster. I am trustworthy. I have never lost control. The idea that I might is a lie.

Things I already knew. I also knew I shouldn't defend myself. The voice of doubt wasn't even the biggest problem. It was the visuals. They sent me reeling.

I wasn't a threat.

Are you sure?

I lay back, my head resting on the back of the couch, and pulled a blanket over my legs. It was already nine o'clock. Chances were good Lucky would be home in a couple of hours and he could transfer her up to bed.

And change her diaper. Poor baby.

Lucky checked in again at eleven with an update. There'd been a workplace accident that took precedence, and Lucky was placed back in the queue. It would be another couple of hours. I assured him I believed she was out for the night and told him I'd text if I needed anything.

I tucked my hands under my thighs and closed my eyes.

Brayleigh's whimpers penetrated my sleep. I woke up with my hands, thankfully, still tucked under my thighs. Only half awake, she curled her little body into a ball. I lay my hand over her back.

"You're okay, dolly," I soothed, rubbing slow circles.

Cornflower blue eyes blinked awake. She stared at me for only a second before her face turned red and pulled into a pained grimace.

The sound that came from her diaper would have made a trucker proud.

"Ahh," she sighed. "I poop."

"Yes, you did," I agreed, laughing. Her forehead felt cool to the touch, while mine beaded with sweat at the thought of what I had to do.

"Change bum," she demanded, holding her arms up.

I gathered her up, realizing my mistake half a second too late when I sat her on my arm and the contents of her diaper squished up her back and out both legs.

She attempted to peel her little thigh off my bare arm. "Yucky."

My bladder chose that moment to let me know of its own need for release. I'd have to get her back to bed first.

"Indeed, dolly. I think we need to take you outside and hose you off like a dog."

She perked up. "Outside?"

"Tubby. We're going to have a rub-a-dub-dub. What do you think?"

311

She bounced in my arms, and I bit back a groan. Thank, God, I didn't have contamination issues, and Brayleigh was in much better form, back to her usual sunny self.

You're the contaminant.

Upstairs, I stood her up in the tub and stripped off her dirty clothes. Rolling her diaper into a ball, I stuffed it in the bathroom garbage pail. That would be ripe tomorrow.

It's okay. Compromises must be made.

Grabbing the roll of toilet paper, I began to wipe her down but mainly succeeded in painting her. "Oh, Dolly. We need wet wipes."

Wet wipes were in her bedroom. Could I leave her in the empty tub for the fifteen seconds it took to grab the wipes?

"Okay, dolly. You stay right here and wait for Minnie, okay?"

I backed away toward the door and held out my palms. "Don't move."

She looked at me curiously, then plunged her hand between her thighs. "Yucky..." Her face stricken, she held the offensive limb out for my observation then her face crumpled in dismay. "Yucky!"

I went back to her and kneeled beside the tub. "Okay, okay. No problem," I assured her, or maybe myself. "We've got everything we need right here. Lots of water."

Unfortunately, the addition of water with no washcloth simply changed her poop to the consistency of acrylic paint.

I began to laugh at the sheer lunacy of my situation. If I ever suspected God of having a sick sense of humor, tonight confirmed it.

Brayleigh, however, did not find it humorous at all, and burst into tears.

"Okay, dolly. Okay. We're going to do this." I turned the tap back on, checking the temperature several times before tugging her hands into the flow. Baby body wash rescued us both. Once her hand was clean, I spun her around, aimed her bottom under the water, and encountered the same problem as before. Acrylic paint in no color anyone would ever want.

I squirted the baby wash over her bum and tried again to no avail.

"I clean, Sparky?"

Swallowing hard, I formed my hand into a paddle, pressing my fingers tightly together, and began to wash her tiny bum.

Did you molest that baby?

Bile rose in my throat.

My need to pee grew exponentially with my panic.

"Almost, dolly," I choked out the answer to her question.

When she was clean enough, I turned off the water, and she howled. "Tubby! I want tubby!"

"You're right, you're right. I promised you a tubby." I looked at my phone. One a.m. I needed to pee.

"One minute," I bargained, holding up my finger. "Just one minute!"

She stuck her finger into the back of her mouth. "Owie."

Oh, God! Can you die of E. coli exposure from your own feces? Of course, you can. I shook my head while I turned the tap back on, poured baby wash over her hands, and rolled her little hands inside mine before rinsing them off and repeating the process again.

As soon as I released her hands, they went back to her mouth. She needed Tylenol and a popsicle. While her bum cheeks were clean, there were many folds that were not.

I pointed at her. "Don't move!"

As I ran the ten steps into her bedroom, scenarios flashed through my mind.

Locked out of the bathroom, water running, the crash of her fall. The terror of Brayleigh unattended in the bath. Her skin blue, eyes staring unseeing through the water.

My heart thudded in my chest.

Who's going to close the door? There's nobody else here.

I came back to find her standing in the same place. "Okay, darling. Minnie has wet wipes. Lie down to wipe your bum."

She lay down in the tub and pulled her legs up, hanging onto her feet.

I closed my eyes against the visuals in my brain and quickly cleaned her up, using far too many wipes, anything to keep a barrier between us.

Her entire groin and cheeks were pitch red with rash and I knew I'd have to brave the cream as well.

No matter. I settled back onto my heels, accepting what needed to be done. I'd do what I had to do and suffer the consequences tomorrow.

With the water running, I gathered her up in a towel. "Let's go get you a popsicle to have in the bath, hm?"

She pressed her tiny fingers into the nape of my neck as I took her down the stairs.

I spread my arms wide, her tiny body bounces off the sharp edges of the stairs.

It was getting harder to shake off the bad thoughts as I skirted the outer edge of my limits.

In the kitchen, I grabbed her a popsicle and caught sight of Lucky's oven mitts. "Yes!" I hissed, grabbing them up. These would do nicely.

My bladder ached to be emptied. Perhaps I could close the curtain once she was in the bath and go pee. No.

The very idea was beyond imagination. Exposing my naked body in the vicinity of a child was so outrageous a suggestion I had no rules for it.

I filled the tub, gave her the popsicle, and with the oven mitts on, I scrubbed her clean.

Once the popsicle was gone, I drained the water, wrapped a towel around her little body, and picked her up, wringing out one of the oven mitts and bringing one with me. I needed it to put on the diaper cream.

My mind reeled.

The assault on my soul, unrelenting.

Zipping up her sleeper, I set her in the crib and walked out of her room to the sound of her screams. She needed Tylenol. She needed to sleep. She needed somebody who knew what the fuck they were doing.

I ran to the bathroom and relieved myself then whipped around and threw up.

Lucky

I breathed a sigh of relief to finally be home. On the couch, where I expected to find my girls, there was only Brayleigh's blankie covered in what looked suspiciously like shit. I lifted it to my nose and recoiled. Yup. No doubt about it.

Oh no. That meant Minty had to deal with her diaper. Recalling how upset she was after the last incident, I began to worry about the state she might be in. Not so curiously, I didn't worry about Brayleigh. I knew Minty would make sure she got what she needed.

I took the stairs two at a time, the smell from the bathroom seeping out into the hall. I tied off the garbage bag and took note of the soaked oven mitt.

My heart hurt for her.

There was no sound from Brayleigh's room and the door was closed.

I eased it open and stepped inside. The overhead light was on, but both Minty and Brayleigh slept. Brayleigh in a nest of pillows and blankets from my bed, Minty on the floor beside her, curled into a ball.

How she held herself apart even in sleep.

After carefully transferring Brayleigh to her crib, I carried the pillows and blankets to our room, then went back for Minty. Her skin was cool to the touch. I swallowed the lump in my throat.

"Baby," I stroked her arm. "I'm home, baby. Come to bed."

Her eyes flickered open and took me in, the relief doing nothing to brighten the dull dishwater shade of her eyes.

"Come to bed, baby."

"Brayleigh?"

"She's in her crib."

She struggled to her feet, drowsy and incoherent. "Where are the pillows?"

"I put them back. Come to bed."

I could sense her fatigue seeping through her pores and running down her body until she was sticky with it, providing adhesive for the thoughts that would plague her.

Tucking her under the blankets, I pulled her into my arms and waited for her skin to warm.

And then I slept.

Chapter 45 – Incongruity

Lucky

Hope and I sat at the kitchen table, quietly drinking coffee while Brayleigh snuggled in her lap.

I'd left Minty in bed, lining pillows behind her back where I'd lain, hoping she'd think I was still there and sleep in.

"How was she?" Hope looked at me over the rim of her Tim's cup.

"She had a rough night. From what I could gather, Brayleigh's butt exploded requiring a bath in the middle of the night. When I got home, I found them sleeping on the floor in Brayleigh's room."

Hope smirked. "By 'she' I meant Brayleigh, but I do like where your head is at."

I huffed out a laugh and admitted, "I've got it bad."

"Is she good to you?"

"She is." I cleared my throat. "She sees me."

Hope turned her head and stared out the kitchen window. "There's the dream, Lucky." Looking back at me, she smiled. "You deserve it."

"So do you." I leaned back in my seat, stretched out my legs, and sucked back my bean juice. "Any good prospects?"

"Ugh, no." Hope curled around Brayleigh and kissed the top of her head. "This may be it for me, Lucky." She shrugged. "It's not so bad."

"It's not bad at all." I struggled to find the right words. "But if you want more, you should have it."

She sighed. "I do want more. I want what you and Minty have. Dani and Carlos. Tracy and Sean. I want all of that." She smoothed her palm over Brayleigh's tousled hair. "I might even want another child seeing as this one turned out so well."

"That's because of my DNA. You'll have to set your sights a little lower."

She guffawed then leaned forward and grabbed a donut. "How much sugar do you suppose is in my blood?"

The shower came on overhead, and I looked up at the ceiling.

"You look worried. Do you want me to go?"

"What? No! Hang around if you can, say hi and let her say bye to Brayleigh."

Twenty minutes later, Minty wandered into the kitchen looking like a lost soul, though it was hardly noticeable to the undiscerning eye.

"You look like you've been pulled through a hedge backwards," Hope greeted her.

I laughed and held out my arm, pulling Minty onto my lap. Apparently, Hope's eye was discerning. "She looks perfect," I protested, pressing my lips to her hair.

"Objectively, she does," Hope continued, waving her donut. "But look at her eyes. Was the diaper really that bad?"

Minty jerked in my arms. "What?"

Hope's smile faltered. "Lucky said Brayleigh exploded last night."

Minty looked at me, her eyebrows knitting together. "How did you know?"

"The smell hit me about halfway up the stairs."

"Ah, yes." She nodded and smiled at Hope. "It was nuclear. How was your business trip?"

"Good. There was this one asshole..."

I tuned out the conversation, my attention focused on the woman sitting stiffly in my arms. She made no move to get away from me, neither did she melt against me. I wondered if she even knew how keyed up she was.

"Hi, sparky."

"Hello, dolly," Minty murmured. "You happy Mama is home?"

"Mine mama," Brayleigh intoned.

"Yes, darling. Your mama."

"Mine Dada," she continued, her eyes darting between Minty and me.

"Yes, darling dolly. Your dada."

She pointed her chubby finger at Minty's bottom in my lap. "Your dada?"

Hope barked out a laugh. "Welp! On that note, I'll be going."

Minty laughed and approached Hope, reaching out a hand to gently cup the back of Brayleigh's head.

"Bye, dolly."

"Luck, can you put her in the car seat for me? I can't fight her this morning," Hope asked, turning away from Minty.

"Sure, I can do that." I squeezed Minty's waist and pulled Brayleigh from Hope's arms. "Say bye to Minty."

"Bye Minnie." Brayleigh lunged toward Minty, pressing a wet kiss to Minty's pale cheek. I headed for the door. The sooner I got Brayleigh into the car, the sooner I could get back to Minty.

Minty

Hope studied me.

"Are you going to hurt him?"

"Hm?"

I mentally reviewed the events of the night before, picking apart each interaction for evidence that I hurt that baby. I'd been doing it since I first woke up but had come no closer to any kind of conclusion.

"Are you going to hurt him?"

The tone of Hope's voice caught my attention, and I answered without thinking. "God, I hope not." I wrapped my arm around my stomach at the idea and shook my head to clear it of the thought.

"Do you love him?"

"Yes. Yes, I do."

"Then don't hurt him."

Hope gathered up her things and smiled wryly at me. "Have a donut. You look like you could use the boost." At the door, she turned. "Minty, remember I told you I'd be your biggest ally?"

"Yes," I answered woodenly.

"That still stands. You have my number. Use it if you need to talk."

She left before I could answer, but it didn't matter. I had nothing to say. Staring at the table, I began again at the point where Lucky left with Barrett. I didn't notice at first when he sat down across from me at the table.

"I know you had a hard time last night. I'm sorry." He enclosed my hand in both of his, the bulky bandage filling my palm as he rubbed his thumb gently over the base of mine. Those calloused fingers that brought such pleasure, played so beautifully, cared for everyone they touched.

"How is your hand?"

"No lasting damage. Stitches should come out on their own in roughly ten days."

"Will you be able to play on Saturday?"

"Not sure. It's doubtful." He stood up. "Come on. Lie down on the couch while I make you breakfast."

The couch.

My hands were tucked beneath my thighs.

Are you sure?

"I need to ..." Think? If I said think, he'd think I was breaking up with him. "Process."

"No problem. We don't need to talk about anything right now. Do you want to eat something and go for a ride?"

320

We hadn't been out on his bike in over a week. There was freedom on the bike. But no amount of wind could blow away these thoughts.

"No. I think I need to go home and regroup."

He jerked back in his seat. "We have the whole day together. We don't have to go out," he offered. "Want to watch movies and cuddle? Maybe you can ravish me? Do all the work? Seeing as I'm injured?"

I made her a nest. I didn't touch her.

Are you sure?

I closed my eyes. Began my mental review once again.

"Minty..." he whispered.

"I need to go home."

"Okay." Standing, he drew me into his arms. "I'll drive you. You don't seem like you're in a good place to drive."

No.

"I can drive." Driving demanded all my attention and offered a brief reprieve. "Driving helps."

He followed me home in his car, turning off only once I pulled into my lot. Throughout the day, he texted. My responses were brief, to the point, and extracted energy I did not have.

Early Monday evening, the boys showed up at my door as usual, and my stomach heaved. I called downstairs to make sure Ruby was still there and sent them back down. Explained that I felt under the weather.

George looked concerned.

Falling asleep beside him in my bed. Waking with his blanket tucked around me. Did I touch him in my sleep?

"I'm okay, Georgie. I just need sleep and maybe a couple of Tylenol."

Ten minutes later, Ruby knocked on the door. I sent her away as well. I couldn't look at her. Not when I didn't know what happened with George while I slept.

Then Amber called.

I sighed. "I'm so tired, Amber. I just need a few days to rest."

Sitting down with a cup of peppermint tea, I reviewed the events of the night before. If I could just get through them once without interruption, without losing my train of thought, I could put it behind me.

Baby wash.

Wet wipes.

Diaper cream.

Oven mitts.

Blanket nest.

Don't hurt him.

My review ended, as it had each and every time since I'd gotten home, with the incongruity of my chaos in the midst of Hope's easy cheer, Lucky's charm, and Brayleigh's uninhibited joy.

What could I offer? A part-time relationship? One where he had to choose between me and his child on the daily?

And what would I get in return? A one-way ticket to my own personal hell?

This is why we have rules.

My eyes overflowed. In my current state, I couldn't even have my boys, never mind that precious baby.

I recalled the list Lucky and I had made of things I wanted to do with Brayleigh.

Did you molest that baby?

Baby wash.

Wet wipes.

Diaper cream.

Oven mitts.

Blanket nest.

The thought of going back to Lucky's in only a few days froze the blood in my veins.

I sat down at the piano and played, pounding the keys, the fullness of the music filling my head and momentarily squeezing out the bitter obsessions. With the stores closed below and no neighbors, there was nobody to complain about the noise. There was nobody, period.

Tired now, my emotions ringing in my ears, I dialed Junie's number and left a message begging off work for the week. Then I sat down at the kitchen table and opened my laptop.

Chapter 46 – Words in My Head

Lucky

I texted periodically. Asinine things that meant nothing but reassured me that she was okay while I went about my day, trying and failing to focus on any task at all to keep my mind from what she might be thinking.

Finally, I gave up and eased my bike out of the garage. Snapping down my face shield, I pulled out onto the road. Once I hit the backroads leading to Bridgewater, the restlessness began to dissipate.

I thought back to the cool blond with the secrets in her eyes that first nabbed my attention. I compared her to the dream she'd become, my dream who was currently locked in her own nightmare. One I'd willingly take from her.

When she set the parameters for our relationship, it unleashed a well of insecurity I didn't know I had. Believing from the outset that I wasn't good enough, her limits suggested that she agreed.

Talking to Hope about my sex life uncovered the root of that fear: that perhaps I couldn't connect emotionally with a woman. Perhaps I did not have the makings of a life partner. Minty blew that theory out of the water.

I couldn't believe I thought she'd be uptight and shy in bed.

I huffed out a laugh. She fucking made me blush.

So much passion and fire on lockdown.

I remembered our date, the one Hope and Brayleigh inadvertently crashed, and how much I wanted to hide Minty from them. Perhaps hide them from Minty. Like a kid at Christmas, my inner child screamed ownership and I did not want to share.

Being honest, I didn't want to scare her off, either. If having a child didn't do it, I feared once she got an eyeful of Hope, I'd be finished. So much guilt for wanting Brayleigh out of the house, for wanting to hide Hope.

I'd watched my sisters with their husbands, as well as Barrett and Lenny with their women, and figured it out. The right woman holds a man's heart in a way that binds him to her and forges her likeness onto the membrane of his soul. That bond, so fragile in its beginnings, demanded protection. Holding my breath, waiting for her reaction to meeting Brayleigh and Hope. The weakness of relief that threatened my limbs when she decided to stay. That feeling of trepidation, not knowing what would happen next.

I pulled my bike back into the garage and took off my helmet. I ran my hands through my hair and climbed the steps to my front porch. Easing back into my chair, I watched the sun sink behind the roofs of the houses across the street.

Dealing with Minty's nightmare was not unlike Brayleigh's night terrors. My job was to wait them out, keep her safe until she worked through them on her own, and stay close enough to offer comfort and support.

There was no feeling of trepidation now.

Only determination to move forward.

And the drive to be there when she woke from her nightmare.

I slept fitfully, and when she called the next morning and asked me to come, I ran.

Minty

I hadn't slept since Lucky's the night before.

Instead, I wrestled with the internet. Searching for someone who was braver than I could ever be and willing to expose their OCD so I could compare it to mine.

On the days I spent at home, I searched for hours and found nothing of substance to quiet the voice of doubt inside me. I tried again. And again. Searching. Pleading. Praying.

What does your OCD sound like?

Who is the voice of your OCD?

What does OCD tell you to do?

How does it tell you to do things?

Pedophilia OCD.

Sexual OCD.

Harm OCD.

Are people with OCD dangerous?

How do I know for sure it's OCD?

I filtered through the results then went back and opened the sites I skipped in case I missed something.

My search continued through the night.

Google, YouTube, Instagram, Pinterest.

The definitions and descriptions came up again and again, but no one said what I needed to hear. 'My OCD says, 'You want to fuck _____'. Fill in the fucking blank: your child, your dog, the cashier at the grocery store, your husband's best friend, your best friend.

I understood why I couldn't find it. Who wanted to admit to these thoughts? What if everybody's OCD voice was different? What if only mine sounded like this? What if that meant it wasn't OCD?

It was OCD. 'You know this!' I thought as I pounded my fist into my thigh.

But what if it wasn't?

What did that make me?

Dangerous.

No matter how I turned it over, one truth remained: I could not deal with the mental torture and psychological agony of the fallout. I knew how to fix it, but was unwilling to participate in exposure therapy, because the exposure was to minors and that was not anyone's risk to take.

I had to be responsible.

Lucky's knock sounded at the door. Steeling myself for what was to come, I dragged my heavy limbs to the door and pulled it open.

Lucky leaned against the railing, tall and golden in the sun, stinging my eyes. His expression was more serious than I'd ever seen it. Pushing off, he cupped his hand around my hip and dropped a kiss to my temple before stepping around me and walking inside.

Behind him, the stairs beckoned, and I saw myself at the bottom.

Let yourself fall. Concrete and metal. Torn flesh and broken bone. Blood painting the pavement. Do it.

I swallowed.

"How are you doing, baby?" Lucky asked from behind me. "You don't look like you've slept."

I turned to face him. I should witness the devastation I wrought.

A line formed between his brows as his stormy eyes searched mine.

I took a breath. "I can't see you anymore."

He gaped and his eyebrows arched as he struggled to form words. "What the fuck? How did you come to that conclusion?" He stepped closer, his mouth pulling into a frown as he studied me. Compassion softened his face. "Last night was a lot. I put too much on you. That's on me."

He stilled as he waited for my response, feet braced, fingers tucked into his back pockets. Only his eyes moved as he studied me.

"No," I shook my head definitively and spoke firmly. The last thing I wanted was for this uniquely beautiful man to think he was the problem. "You are perfect. Dolly is perfect." My voice shook. "But I can't be a stepmom, Lucky."

His face fell and he opened his bandaged palm to me. "Minty, it was an emergency. I promise, it wouldn't be an everyday thing. I don't even have her with me every day. Can you not share me for the few days a week I get to be with her?"

Lover. Daughter. Family. Friends. Community.

Belonging.

Everything I'd ever dreamed of, he offered. For a moment my resolve weakened, and I wondered if I could have it.

What if you lose control?

I closed my eyes and spoke from my heart. "I am truly, to the depths of my soul, sorry, but you deserve more than I can give you, well, less than what I give you."

"Explain," he whispered harshly.

My skin stung along the path of yet another tear. "Darling." No more would I call him that. One day, probably soon, I would see him with another, his dimples flashing, his daughter laughing. "You couldn't possibly understand. You're light and I'm dark." My voice broke but I pressed on. "It plagues me," I confessed. "I feel so dirty sometimes. And when I'm with you, and especially Dolly, I'm contaminating you both."

Shame burned me from the inside out. I covered my face. I didn't want him to remember me like this.

I wanted him to remember sparkly dresses and dancing with Dolly, parks and blanket forts and giant balloons at the zoo.

I wanted him to picture me singing on stage with Drivetrain, working on my commissions while he played guitar, curled up beside him reading in his backyard, singing with him at the cookout, teasing him about musical instruments, naked Shakespeare, the goddess at play...

He touched me and I reared away from him.

"It's not that I don't want to share you." Another tear escaped. "I love Dolly. How can I not? She's yours." I needed to make sure there was no misinterpretation. "I want to take her to the park and the zoo and put her in the bath and tuck her into bed and kiss her booboos and change her diapers and buy her ice cream and do her hair and cover her with sparkles, but I can't!"

"Why can't you? Lay it out for me in a way I can understand."

"Because the OCD fallout makes me crazy. I cannot live like this. I cannot survive like this. I don't want to survive like this!"

"It's early days, baby. We can work on these things. We haven't even had a chance..."

"Captain," I whispered. "I know my limits."

"Minty...baby..." he entreated. "Don't do this." He stopped suddenly and narrowed his eyes on my face. "There's really only one thing I need to know right now. Is it too much because you don't love me enough? If that's what it is, you gotta say the words."

Lying is a sin.

Not lying is selfish.

The truth will set you free.

You need to set him free.

My shoulders hunched inward. "I can't give you those words. But I can't be with you. I'm suffering. I can't handle it. Please, Lucky," I pleaded, wanting him to go? Stay? Understand?

His face cleared and he seemed almost relieved which left a different kind of wound. "Please what, baby?" He pushed.

"Please leave." I reached for him then snatched my hand back. "I cannot." My voice broke and I began again. "It's too much, Captain. I cannot cope."

The words dropped from my lips like lead weights, and I curled into myself, turning my face away from him.

He stepped close but didn't touch me.

His voice was low and controlled when he spoke, almost calm. "You told me there was one you loved who walked away because he couldn't handle your OCD. I'm not him. I can, and will, handle you."

He touched the calloused tip of his finger to my cheek. "Beautiful. My heart."

A sob caught in my throat.

Focused on the floor in front of me, I watched his shoes as he turned and walked away.

The door snicked shut. He turned the lock from the outside with his key and knocked briskly on the doorframe. I heard his words in my head.

I'll be back.

Despite what he said, I knew it was over. I'd make it so.

Still, I leaned against the door and strained to hear the last of his footsteps as he thumped down the stairs, leaving me to the angry buzz of silence. My hands shook as I grabbed a blanket off the back of the couch and tucked myself into a ball underneath it. If I thought I'd been suffering before, it was nothing compared to the sharp spear of loss running me through now.

Even so, with the pain there mingled a sick sense of relief.

It was to that, I clung.

Chapter 47 – Compass

Lucky

I dragged my hands through my hair as I pounded down the back stairs. So that was a kick in the pants, but one I obviously needed to understand just how difficult it was for her at times. It changed nothing from my end. I still planned to be there when she woke up from her current nightmare, and I planned to be there for the next one as well. But it was most definitely a wake-up call.

I circled around to the front of the building and opened the door to Spuds.

Vander sat at a table with his laptop open in front of him. He looked up when I walked in and stood up. "Hey, man. How're you doing? You picking up something for Minty? Junie said she's sick?"

Now that I was here, I was unsure how to broach the subject.

Vander's eyes sharpened. "You want to have a seat and I'll grab us a couple of Cokes?"

"Sure," I nodded. That might give me a bit of time to come up with a plan.

Ruby swung through from the back, a big smile on her face. "Hey! Are you picking up something for Minty? Don't worry," she continued, not waiting for my answer. "I'm going to bring her lunch and dinner. My

Yiayia is home making her soup right now. Amber and Gus are going to bring it to her tonight."

"Ruby-mine," Vander murmured. "Give the man a chance to speak. There's something else going on, here."

Ruby pressed her lips together. "Right." Then, thinking she knew what was happening and that I was the culprit, she narrowed her eyes at me. "What's going on?"

Dear, God. Don't let this be a serious breach of privacy. "She's not doing too well right now. She would prefer I not be around."

"She's not doing too well..." Ruby echoed softly, then her eyes flew up to meet mine. "Is it her OCD?"

I looked between her and Vander. "You know about it?"

She shrugged. "She told us. Said it wasn't a secret. She's never even had a flare-up that I can remember."

"Well, she's having one now. She needs her girls."

Vander's brows lowered. "And you?"

"That's where you come in." I took a deep breath. "She's triggered. Told me she can't be with me because of her OCD." I scrubbed my hand over my hair. "I'm not going anywhere, but I don't want to make things worse either. I need you to monitor and keep me posted over the next couple of days. After that, I'm getting in her face either way, but I'll come sooner if I need to."

"Done. I'll talk to Gus, tell him to call you after they see her tonight. Minty trusts him, and I think Ruby is already texting Amber. We've got your back."

Now that I had eyes on her, the fact that none of them were mine hit me hard and I slumped in my chair.

"Don't give up, man. The good ones are a pain in the ass."

I snorted out a laugh. "That's the damn truth."

Ripping myself away from her building went against every one of my instincts, but I'd spent years surrounded by broken people. I taught them every single day, and I recognized the signs of a cornered soul and knew when to give space. Trapped, she'd be willing to gnaw off her arm to escape. I didn't want it to go that far.

There was one more stop I wanted to make to ensure Minty was surrounded at all points by her family compass. I pulled out my cell as I rounded the building and headed for my car. "Barrett? Can you meet me for a drink?"

Willa was at her sister's, so I headed to their place. Holding Rena was a treat. Some days I could hardly believe Brayleigh was ever that small. The unfairness of it struck me, the fact that Minty's brain sought to deny her these small pleasures.

"What do you know about Minty?"

"How do you mean?"

I shook my head. "Give me whatever you've got."

Barrett studied me in that still, quiet way he had. "She's controlled. Careful with her words, keeps her hands to herself, gets lost in her head. I don't doubt she has some kind of anxiety disorder. Maybe social anxiety. Maybe OCD." I tried to maintain my poker face, but Barrett was uncommonly intuitive. "Ah. Okay. That's a bitch of an illness."

"She's struggling. Today she ended it with me."

"I'm sorry," he said gruffly.

"Don't be." I shook my head. "It's not over. She's going to pull it together, and I'm not going anywhere."

"What do you need from me?"

Exhaling roughly, I admitted, "I'm not sure. All I know is she doesn't want to be around me, and I don't want her to be alone."

"Willa had an issue for a while that prevented her committing to me," he began carefully. "Without betraying Willa's privacy, Minty let me know something was wrong and put me in the right place at the right time to be there for Willa."

"I need to make sure I'm in the right place at the right time, but more importantly than that, I need to make sure her girls are in the right place at the right time."

"I'll make sure her girls check in." His lips tipped up. "And I'm reasonably certain both Willa and Junie owe you one."

I laughed. "They were just looking out for her, which is exactly what I need them to do right now."

Back at home, I grabbed a beer and headed to the couch with my laptop. The house was too quiet. Exactly as it used to be before Minty came into my life. For a brief flicker in time, I imagined losing Minty and having my life return to this empty stillness. I recoiled at the thought.

It simply wasn't an option.

Flipping open my laptop, I settled back and pulled up my search engine. I could kick myself for not doing it sooner.

OCD. Subtypes.

After an hour, I'd had enough. I wondered at the strength she possessed to keep eating, keep drinking, keep hugging people, letting them in, touching lives, touching souls, and showing up day after fucking day with that monkey on her back.

"Okay." I exhaled hard and rubbed a hand roughly over my hair. "Right now, she can't cope. She'll learn. I'll learn too. I'll be the best damn support person the world has ever known."

Minty

Ruby called first thing the next morning. "Yiayia made you soup. I'm coming up. You want to open up or do you want me to use my key?"

"Uh..."

"Alright. I'll use my key." She hung up.

I looked around my messy home. It had gotten progressively worse the more time I'd spent at Lucky's. Maybe she wouldn't notice. With little energy left to care, I opened the door when she knocked.

Her eyes widened when she saw me. "Whoa!" She gave her head a gentle shake. "I brought you soup and cookies."

"What kind of soup? I'm sorry but I can't handle anything with meat right now."

"Avgolemono. No chicken. Veggie broth. Amber watched and made sure." Her mouth twisted to the side. "On the downside, now Yiayia knows you don't like meat and she's worried for your 'hormonies'."

"Hormonies?" I questioned.

"Yeah. Hormones with a hint of Greek drama." Prodding me toward the couch, Ruby sat down with me and passed me a cookie. "What's going on. You're not sick."

I nibbled the edges where the dough was just a little browner that the rest. My favorite part. "Remember I told you about OCD and how I control it by controlling my environment?"

"Mm-hmm."

"Lucky and Brayleigh blasted my control to dust."

"Ah, yes. Kids do that. So do men, actually. But! A wise woman once claimed she wasn't prepared to row her own hoe. Wait. Hoe her own row?" She waved a hand. "Never mind. Another wise woman said we had mountains to climb." She stopped and peered at me before carefully suggesting, "Maybe, this one, is yours."

How many times had I used a mountain analogy when faced with a symptom I needed to conquer? Each toehold represented a step, with the peak signifying the ultimate goal. I'd made such a list with Lucky. I tried.

It was one thing to climb a mountain on your own. It was quite another to strap a defenseless child on your back and force the risk on them as well.

The hopelessness of the situation flooded my eyes. "I can't. I just can't."

"You're so tired, Minty," she murmured.

I nodded, utterly wrung out.

"Did you sleep last night?"

"A little." A tear rolled down my face. "I don't like sleeping alone anymore."

"Come lie down. I'll stay with you for a little while. Just go to sleep and I'll use my key to lock up."

I allowed her to lead me to my bedroom which was in worse shape than the front room. "I see you've been redecorating."

I huffed out a dry laugh.

"No, no. It's a good plan. Get everything out of the closets to see what you've got. I've seen this method on tv."

I began to laugh then the laughter turned to tears.

"Okay," Ruby said softly, taking my hand. "Come lie down. I'll cuddle you until you fall asleep."

Ruby curled around my back.

"Don't let me have sex with you in my sleep," I blurted out.

"Don't worry. I'm all about the dick," she assured me breezily, making me laugh again. She stroked my hair back from my temple. "I got you. Sleep."

Hours later, I woke somewhat refreshed. The mental clarity I'd acquired cast a spotlight on my heart.

And it was broken.

I crawled out of my bed and made my way to the kitchen. Evening cast its long shadows through my windows, but there was enough light from the streetlights to allow me to sit in the semi-darkness and still be able to see.

I ate more of Yiayia's cookies.

I ran my tongue over my fuzzy teeth. Gross. Maybe I'd brush my teeth. Maybe. I was disgusting. What did it matter if I brushed my teeth?

I picked up my cell phone to clear the messages I knew I'd find from Ruby and Amber.

I scanned the notifications, Ruby, Amber, Willa, Junie, and several from Lucky. I answered Ruby and Amber first, then checked in with Willa and Junie. And they had worried that he would be the one to pull a dick move.

My thumb hovered over Lucky's messages. I briefly contemplated ignoring them, but what if there was something wrong with Dolly? What if he was hurt? What if something happened to someone in his family? Or Hope?

The first message was a blurry photo. I clicked to open it and figured out it was a picture of Barrett's and Willa's hands with their wedding rings.

This is one of the first memories I ever captured of you. I take pictures of memories, not people. And the thing I wanted to remember from that day was the woman who ensnared me by teasing me about her knot-tying skills. Look again and you'll find yourself in the background. You're off to the side, watching, looking utterly complete on your own but we both know you're not. I'm here. I'm waiting. I love you.

The second picture was a bunch of masculine hands holding beer bottles, clinking their amber necks together over a barbecue. I could see Willa, Junie, Bex, Mara, and me sitting in a circle. We were leaning toward one another, laughing, hands grasping onto each other.

Before I took this picture, I'd already decided I wasn't going to follow up on my attraction to you. I'd already decided you were too good for me, and I couldn't offer you my usual spiel. You remember how long that decision lasted. I like this picture better. You're surrounded by people who love you, as you always should be.

The third picture showed a nearly empty coffee cup.

This one is from the coffee shop where you lay out your parameters for our relationship. This cup signifies what I left with which was coming to be the exact opposite of what I wanted from you. I knew even then.

The fourth picture showed his extra helmet.

I took this one after our first night together to remind me of how perfectly your body moved with mine on my bike, and in my bed. To remind me that you had a jealous streak signifying an insecurity I needed to keep a mind toward protecting.

I wasn't sure I could take anymore. The pictures were odd, but the memories and words were so very sweet and rang with his truth. I had no choice but to keep going. I couldn't have stopped even if I wanted to.

The next picture was my piano.

This picture means so very much to me. It signifies the moment I identified you as the source of music in my life. The things you had done for my kids at school cemented your place in my heart. It was also the day you told me about one who left, and I promised you that once I said 'I love you', I never would.

The next message said, *In case you missed it, I love you.*

A picture taken through the window of me laughing with Ruby and Amber. *That night I learned I never truly knew what it meant to be happy before you.*

A picture of the ticket stubs for The Goddess at Play and naked Shakespeare, *we don't need to speak of this.*

My alarm panel, *to remind me that you're fragile, sensitive to rejection, and you operate by a code that I need to learn and respect.*

The thin strap of my sundress over the back of my shoulder, my hand cupped around the back of Brayleigh's head, our hands joined after I sang with his band, one that depicted Brayleigh and me at the zoo that I knew immediately I had to draw, Brayleigh's little fingers pressed white on the back of my neck.

A sob broke through, the desire to claim that baby ripping through me even as I cowered away from her.

And Lucky's words, *the very place I long to press my kiss,* called to mind the many times he'd done just that, in bed, in passing, even the day he pinned me to the door when I almost walked away from him, even that day he pressed his lips to the nape of my neck.

I moved to message him back, to apologize, tell him I love him, ask for his forgiveness.

Are you sure?

You can't jerk people around.

How do you know you won't leave again?

Are you going to discard Brayleigh the way your parents discarded you?

I carefully placed my phone down on the coffee table. The truth was, I could not be sure. I curled up on the floor while my brain spun its vicious rumors and I cried.

Chapter 48 - Heartstrings

Amber

It had been a long time since I'd seen Minty in this state. Two decades, in fact. I watched Gus take in the mess, his face a mask of shock.

I nodded to the lump on the floor that was Minty, and his face crumpled. Gently he scooped her up with one hand under her knees, the other around her lower back and held her high against his broad chest.

I whispered instructions to Gus while quickly gathering up the pillows and blankets from the floor to make up her bed. Time was of the essence. She wouldn't want help once she was fully cognizant. I pursed my lips. As if she could ever be a burden.

Gus and Minty had a special relationship. I don't know how it developed, they didn't spend time together apart from me, but their two souls recognized each other. I used to imagine he was a brother she'd never met.

"Bedroom?" he asked, looking at me, his perception of her now stripped of her carefully constructed illusion.

I nodded and placed my finger over my lips to remind him to be quiet then ran my hand down his broad back to comfort him before moving ahead to fix the bed.

My throat tightened painfully. But now was not the time.

Minty lolled in his arms for a moment then seemed to realize she was airborne and cracked her eyes open. Seeing Gus, her entire body stiffened like a bow, arching out of his arms.

"No," she moaned low, her voice guttural. "Don't touch me." She spread her fingers wide and held them in front of her eyes as if to assure herself they were there. A violent sob broke from her throat, and she begged pitifully. "Don't let me touch you."

Gus stopped moving and held her closer. He'd spent hours on the computer last night reading about OCD. Over the past couple of days, we all had. She was there for us and our boys in every way, and we should have done better by her. We would do better by her. Tears coursed a violent path down his craggy cheeks to the corners of his mouth.

"Amber," he gasped.

Already on my way back to him, I wrapped my arms around Minty from the other side. "Hang onto her, agapimeno," I murmured. "Hi, my beautiful friend. We're going to get you into bed, then we're going to stay with you awhile."

Minty balled her hands into fists and tucked them against her chest, curling into herself. "I'm so dirty, I'm so dirty. It's going to be all over you," she cried, sickened.

"You're not dirty," Gus murmured gruffly. "You're all that's good and pure and right."

My throat, thick with tears, prohibited me to speak. I pressed my forehead against hers. "Minty," I finally begged. "Minty, please."

"You don't know," she wept. "You don't know."

"I do," I assured her. "I do know. I know about the pictures, the movies, the sexy stuff, the violent stuff, the stuff with the kids. I know. And I know where it comes from."

I smoothed my hands over her ravaged face, her face that flamed with shame upon hearing my words.

She turned her face into Gus's chest to hide and her tears fell faster.

Gus bent his neck to press his temple against the top of her head, his chest expanding with his heavy inhale.

"Amber," he warned.

"Let's go," I replied, pulling them gently towards her bedroom, still talking. "I started researching OCD after you told Ruby and me last year. I know all about the different subtypes. It wasn't hard to figure out which ones you struggle with."

We reached her bedroom door, and I pushed it open, keeping one hand on my dearest, oldest friend.

"I'm sorry I didn't say anything sooner. I didn't know it was this bad."

Gus stepped through and stopped in shock.

"What the fuck?"

I took in her bedroom. It looked like a tornado had touched down.

I looked at Minty's ravaged face. "It's also clear which subtypes you are not afflicted with."

My joke earned me a huff and a weak smile but didn't unfurl her fists.

Gus lay her down on the bed and she seemed to fade into the mattress until we got in beside her.

Her lids shot open in alarm. "What are you doing?"

I nodded at Gus to lie down beside her. "Getting in beside you."

"I don't think that's a good idea," she said, a look of horror on her face, and Gus paused.

"Minty," I whispered, my palm against her cheek. "Please just let us love you. We won't come too close if you don't want us to."

She closed her eyes, and I noted the pain on her face, the same pain that sometimes flicked across her face when the boys hugged her.

"It's just a thought, Minty. It means nothing," I murmured.

She drew in a shuddering breath and pressed her palms to either side of her head. Her chest heaved.

Her breath rasped, her face twisting into a grimace. Fisting her hands in her hair, her face scrunched, and she closed her eyes tight.

"It's not what you want, Mint. You know that."

She rapped her knuckles against her skull, and Gus whispered a pained, 'Fuck'.

"You think we would give you our boys if we thought you were a danger?"

Her eyes flew wide, brimming with tears, and her trembling mouth pulled down into a deep frown. "I would never hurt your boys," she promised even as her eyes begged for reassurance.

I passed my hand gently over her head, shielding her from her knuckles. "I know that. Gus knows that. Ruby and Vander know that. Jace and Alex and George sure as fuck know that. And Lucky knows that. You need to know that, trust in that. Trust in you."

"Like we do," Gus whispered.

She looked at Gus over her shoulder and her face crumpled. "I'm so ashamed," she admitted brokenly.

"There's no shame in this," he whispered back.

Her head dropped.

Her tears flowed.

Without meeting my eyes, she raised her arms to me like a child and allowed me to wrap myself around her, while Gus hovered over us both.

One minute bled into two into five into an hour before she spoke. "I'm sorry I worried you all."

"That's okay, Minty. Do you want to share what happened?" I asked softly.

"Lucky had to go to the hospital for stitches, and I had Brayleigh all night. I had to change her diaper, give her a bath, and the pictures were relentless." She paused. "I'm feeling a little more clear-headed today. I don't believe I'd do anything bad. I know I wouldn't. But the pictures and the constant doubt kills me. And I can't stop the pictures and videos. Those I can't stand."

"You fight them."

"I...I do. And that's where I'm going wrong."

"I don't know how you cope," Gus murmured. He lay on his back behind her, careful not to encroach on her too closely. "I thought about it.

Thought about having the type of thoughts you do. At first, I figured it wasn't much different from the brief thoughts any of us might have in passing and dismiss just as easily. I looked into it more and I need to know. In your mind, are Van and I a thing? Am I top or bottom? I need you to not make us a thing."

Her laugh erupted with a surprised bark. "Well, I am now," she said dryly.

"I think," he began quietly. "I might be wrong, but humor may be an excellent antidote."

She pressed her lips together and looked at him over her shoulder. "And when it's a child? When it's A-A-Alex or Jace or George? How is that funny?"

His face grew serious. "It's not. It's horrendous, but it's also a testament."

"How?" she asked, completely exasperated.

"See," he pulled up an article on his cell phone, "it says right here that the intrusive thoughts often reflect the things that would be most abhorrent to the sufferer, especially when including those they love or care for." He shrugged. "The fact that your thoughts revolve around these scenarios with our kids only shows the depth of your love for them." He waved his hand in a circular motion. "In whatever weird, fucked-up way your brain has flipped it on you."

She stared at him for a moment, then burst into a semi-hysterical laugh. "That's how you see it?"

"No." He shook his head. "That's how I see you. And it's through that lens that I understand your OCD."

"Thank you, Angus. I needed to hear that. I can't live like this," she admitted.

"So, don't," I murmured. "You've been fighting when fighting doesn't work, but you know what does work," I murmured. "Do you want me to call Ezinne?"

"No. I'll go see her tomorrow. I'll sort it out tomorrow. Has anybody heard from Lucky?"

Gus chuckled. "We've all heard from Lucky. Repeatedly."

Her tension evaporated. "I love him, you know."

"He loves you, too," Gus assured her. "Go back to sleep. You're going to need it. Parenting a toddler is no easy feat."

Minty

I woke to the soft sounds of an acoustic guitar playing Lucky's and my song. "Lucky," I whispered.

"Right here, baby."

I couldn't turn around, couldn't look at him. "I'm so sorry."

"Nothing to be sorry about." He continued to play, the notes smoothing the ends of my frayed nerves. He didn't speak, but the callouses on his fingers communicated what I could not fail to understand, and the strings of his guitar untangled the convoluted reasoning that knotted my brain.

"Thank you for the pictures... I wanted to call you, but I was caught in a thinking trap."

"I know. It's okay. We'll work out a system."

"You're not mad?"

"No," he answered simply.

"Did I..." I unsuccessfully attempted to swallow the lump in my throat then pushed my voice past it. "Did I hurt your feelings?"

His fingers continued to dance over the strings. "Scared me a bit, but I already knew I wasn't going anywhere. It was the kick in the pants I needed to be the man you need going forward. Remember I was a love virgin before you."

I smiled. "Indeed."

"It's true. No other woman could fit the space God created in my soul for you. He made me to fall in love with you and you alone."

"You might need to give up your nickname," I teased gently.

He ignored my self-deprecating jab. "I learned a song for you."

"Will you play it for me?" I asked softly.

"I have a couple to play for you," he murmured. "I'm not good with words, but I can recognize my truth in someone else's. Consider these my own heart's strings."

He played Nathan Wagner's *Love* as though it expressed his heart's deepest desire. Because it did.

I rolled over so that I could see him, golden and beautiful, lighting up all my dark.

The second song, *Worthwhile*, also by Nathan Wagner, had me pressing my face into my pillow to stem the flow of my tears. When the music stopped, the bed dipped, he curled his long body around mine, and I could finally breathe.

Vulnerability. Exposure. The stripping away of walls and defenses. To be known and accepted. That's the path to belonging. That's the antidote to loneliness.

"Lucky?"

"Yeah, baby?"

"I might have overreacted."

He chuckled softly. "Yeah, baby."

"Can you give me a few days?"

"So long as you let me sleep beside you for the rest of them."

He waited while I had a shower, which I sorely needed, helped me change my bed, and made me something to eat. The last thing he did before he left was hand me a picture in a frame.

"Willa gave me this for you," he said softly. "It speaks volumes."

I took it from his hand and gasped. It was us at Willa and Barrett's wedding. The photographer had caught me with a soft smile on my face, my hands frozen in time as I knotted the tie around Lucky's neck. Lucky's eyes were focused on my face, lips parted, his expression a mix of wonder, worship, and not a small amount of confusion.

"I look like I'd just been hit by one of Cupid's arrows." He laughed. "You didn't stand a chance, baby. I was made to love you."

Chapter 49 – Pussy Intervention

Minty

Early the next morning, I headed to Ezinne. As usual, as if she had a sixth sense, she met me in the doorway.

"Humph," she grunted. "Have you not hit rock bottom yet or did you just neglect to call me when you got there?"

I laughed. Ezinne and I did not have a professional patient-therapist or boss-employee relationship We'd long since crossed all those lines. She treated me now as a friend would advise another friend. Much the same way Amber would have had I ever asked. I never asked. With Ezinne, I never stopped.

"I'm crawling my way back out," I admitted, and her face lit up. "Why are you so happy?"

"Tired of waiting, my beautiful friend, for you to get the life you deserve."

A few hours later, having mapped out a plan, the obsessions were already losing their grip on me. Honestly, nothing about the process was new. Other than during my childhood years, it had always been this way for me. As soon as I accepted that the thought was OCD, I could dismiss the errant thoughts relatively easily. Dismiss, not eradicate, but I could deal with the white noise.

This case was different only because of the metric ton of shame attached to it. And that shame felt an awful lot like guilt, leading me to question if there was any truth to the thoughts.

Keeping my disorder a secret worked for me on a number of levels. A private person at heart, I also valued my independence. Neither of those traits compelled me to share. Combined with the fact that early on I needed to break myself of the compulsion to constantly ask for reassurance, a type of checking behavior, it was simply easier not to tell.

Now, I could admit shame also played a part in my silence. Especially with this particularly distressing subtype. It was easier not to tell, but infinitely more harmful. Like mold, shame thrives in the dark.

I needed to deal with my shame, and I got the opportunity to do just that a little sooner than I would have preferred.

Not long after I left Ezinne, Junie called to inform me she and 'the girls' were coming over. I'm not sure who all 'the girls' entailed, but she gave me no time to ask questions.

"No questions! And from what I heard, you need to clean up your front room. Get your shit together, you sexy bitch. We'll be there at seven and we're bringing snacks."

I looked around my home and laughed. Willa and Junie would love to see it like this.

By the time seven rolled around, everything, save my bedroom, was shipshape.

"Huh," Junie grunted. "I expected to see something." She seemed almost disappointed, and Willa laughed.

I laughed. "Let me assure you, it was bad." She looked skeptical. "You can go take a look at my bedroom if you don't believe me."

My laughter followed them as they took off down the hallway and increased when hearing Junie's whoop of delight.

"Finally!" she yelled. "A discernible fault!"

I turned to lock the door, but it flew open instead. "Hey, beautiful," Ruby greeted me, Amber right behind her.

"Hello, lovelies," I said softly. These two. My God, what would I do without them?

They dropped their platters on the table and encompassed me in a group hug.

"I love you so much," Ruby choked.

"I love you, too," I whispered. "Sister-friend."

Amber laughed. "Maybe we should have planned to get high tonight. Or at least get Ruby high. That was fun."

"Fun for you, maybe," Ruby grumbled.

A knock sounded at the door, and Amber turned to let Mara and Bex inside. Mara's arms were overladen with containers and Bex carried two large bags. She held them up in explanation. "We're making boards!"

I swung my head around eyeing Junie. "Is there anyone else?"

Her face paled. "Frig. Did I miss someone?"

"No!" I laughed. Although Ezinne would have been tickled to see this.

"Okay!" Junie rubbed her hands together. "Let's get the drinks and the food going, then we'll talk."

I sat slightly apart, as usual. They were so beautiful. All so different, but oh, so beautiful in their own ways.

Not one of them could be called appropriately ladylike, though Willa and Amber probably came the closest. Mara was quietly hysterical, Junie obnoxiously so. Bex and Ruby, petite but oh so feisty, ready to take on the world at a moment's notice, and they were here to take on the world for me. All of them. Even Bex and Mara, who I'd only really gotten to know over the past six months, were here to lend their support.

"Mara, how are you finding the girls?" I asked.

She brightened. "Good! The first time I went they were very quiet." She blushed. "I did what you suggested and gave them a copy of my book. She cleared her throat. "They were much more relaxed around me the next time and we spent a great deal of time discussing certain parts."

Amber laughed. "They are a really good group. Your name came up during one of our sessions. They really love you. And I'll tell you, the journaling? They are loving it."

"That makes me so happy," Mara sighed.

"Bex?" I turned to Rebecca. "How did you find it?"

"Easy-peasy," she replied. "I went in with Merry, piggy-backed on her success."

I looked around. Seeing them here all together made me realize just how intertwined their lives had become with the shelter. One of my girls worked with Ruby. Amber ran group sessions. Willa had taught art lessons on many occasions. Now, Mara and Bex were going occasionally having jewelry-making parties and writing lessons. Even Yiayia went in and baked with them. And Junie, sweet Junie, had recently presented me with graphics and a social media plan to beef up our fundraising campaigns.

"So," Junie began. "Think of this as a girl posse convention."

"More like a pussy convention." Ruby laughed.

"A Pussy Intervention, if you will," Junie concluded.

Amber covered her face with her hands. "Here they go."

Mara shrugged. "I like it. Pussy Intervention has a certain ring to it."

"I agree," Bex replied, then slapped her hands down on her thighs as she looked at me. "We are here to help you in any way we can."

"We're sorry if what we said about Lucky in the beginning led to any of this," Willa interjected, pressing her lips together.

"You two belong together. Anyone can see that," Junie agreed.

Amber and Ruby moved to bookend me, offering silent support.

"I think we're going to be okay," I began cautiously. "Willa, thank you for that picture. I love it. It holds a place of honor between my mother's tea set and my dad's art tools."

Willa smiled, and I promised to show everyone later.

"The thing is, I have a..." My shoulders rose to hug my ears as the room closed in around me. Amber lay a gentle hand on my arm, and Ruby pressed her thigh against mine. "I have a disorder that fucks with my brain sometimes."

"Hm," Willa hummed, nodding her understanding.

"I have OCD."

"It makes life difficult for you?" Mara asked quietly, her eyes soft with compassion.

"Not always." I paused, then mentally shrugged and said, 'fuck it'. My shoulders relaxed and I launched into my recitation. "OCD has many subtypes. Some people only suffer from one or two, some people suffer from all of them, some people cycle through them. As they conquer one set of symptoms, another pops up to take its place. I'm a cycler. I go through all of them. The two that have shamed me are sexual OCD and pedophilia OCD. I couldn't handle the OCD assault that came from spending so much time around Brayleigh."

I visibly shrunk away from their stunned gazes.

Junie jumped in. "I did some reading," she began. "Correct me if I'm wrong, but sexual OCD tells you to fuck everything that moves, and pedophilia OCD makes sure that includes children."

"Essentially," I murmured. Heavy silence lay between us.

Someone cleared their throat. "I used to hallucinate when my PTSD was triggered." Grateful for her confession, my head whipped up to find Willa's thunder and lightning eyes steady on mine. "I still do sometimes."

"I can't leave the house without four different escape routes and a back-up plan," Ruby added.

"I have fibromyalgia and I get migraines. There are times I'm in bed for days, unable to care for my children or run my business," Bex offered.

"I, um, get insanely jealous and my mind makes up pictures of my husband with other women," Mara admitted, flushing deeply.

"Me, too," Amber whispered.

I swallowed hard. "My brain makes up pictures of all of you naked with your husbands. My brain gives me pictures of everyone naked and getting sexy." I wouldn't tell them anymore than that. They didn't need to know more than that.

"Me and Lenny?" Junie leaned forward. "Have you pictured me and Lenny?"

"Of course," I looked at her quizzically.

She smirked and wagged her eyebrows. "Do I look hot?"

I laughed. Hard. Amber shook beside me, and Ruby chortled and slapped her thigh.

"My, Lord, Junie!" Willa reprimanded her, chuckling, but Junie only shrugged.

"Gus wanted to know if she pictured him with Vander," Amber choked out. "He wanted to know if he was top or if Vander was top."

Ruby fell to the side. "Please can I tell Van?"

"No!" Junie interjected. "This is a pussy convention intervention. No dicks allowed. What is shared in the pussy convention stays in the pussy convention."

"Agreed." Mara smiled at me. "I know a lot about OCD. It often goes hand-in-hand with autism, and Olivia is developing signs of it. I think you're incredibly brave. I would trust you with Olivia. I would love it if she had you to lean on when she needs it."

"I trust you with Rena," Willa added.

"I trust you with my boys," Ruby declared.

"I trust you with Alex," Amber murmured.

Just like that, the shame dissipated. I did not fool myself into believing that it would never return, it's much too sticky a problem not to, but the easy acceptance and compassion offered by these women who had earned my respect, centered me. Surrounded me. Offered me intimacy. Belonging. An end to loneliness.

"Thank you," I gulped.

"You're fucking welcome," Junie deadpanned.

"Let's eat," Bex clapped her hands together. "I'm starved."

Chapter 50 – Thank You

<u>Minty</u>

I paced laps around my apartment. Needlessly hesitating. A fine residue of doubt still clinging to my poor, disabused mind.

The girls left late the night before. Surprisingly, it was Junie who stuck around the longest.

"So." She wagged her finger back and forth in the space between us. "We're okay? I didn't overstep?"

"We're good, beautiful. I love your heart and I thank you for your care. It means the world to me."

Junie sniffed and then shook her head. "Ah! No mushy stuff. I need to go home and bang Lenny's lights out and I can't do that if I'm all weepy."

She skipped down the stairs, a fairy with the heart of a lion and the mouth of a trucker.

My thoughts returned to my current dilemma. I should just call. Or message. Or maybe I should just go to his house. Would that be weird? Stalkerish? Do I need a reason to call?

I sat down at my kitchen table and firmly reprimanded myself. "You are overthinking."

A knock sounded at my door. "Open up, baby."

"Lucky!"

I ran and opened the door.

He stood with his hands braced on the doorframe above his head. He wagged his eyebrows. "Time's up."

I rolled my eyes. "Thank, God. I've worn a path into the floor with my pacing."

He quirked an eyebrow. "Why?" Dropping his hands, he rested one on my waist as he steered me back into my house.

"I wanted to call you, but I didn't know what to say. I was trying to channel my inner Junie."

He barked out a laugh. "Please don't. You're enough of a handful on your own without channeling Junie. And for further reference, say, 'Hi, darling,' in the sweet way you do, and I'll take it from there."

I smiled up into his stormy, grey eyes. "Hi, darling."

"Hi, baby." He wrapped his hand around the front of my throat and pulled me closer, leaning his forehead against mine. "You want to pack a bag and come to my place? I'm not playing tonight. Stitches aren't fully healed."

"Yes," I replied softly, my hands on his waist. "I'd like that."

"We'll go for a ride down to Bridgewater? I'll take you to Bliss Kitchen for dinner then we'll go home." He finished on a whisper. "I need to hold you."

"And I need you to hold me."

The space between us pulsed with hope for our next chapter. We were really going to do this.

Not an hour later, after helping me with my helmet, he pulled my body close to his and eased the bike down the driveway.

I loved the initial take-off. His body swaying to the left as he turned out of the driveway, my body leaning with him.

Lean in.

Don't fight.

Don't resist.

And it bore repeating, lean in.

There was a lesson here. Several, probably, that my fastidious mind would delight in picking through later. For now, the wind breaking around us as the world sped by was enough. More than enough. It was freedom and unity at once.

I clasped my hands around his tight tummy, and chuckled to myself, remembering that first ride when he warned me not to explore.

He patted my hand briefly, his own chuckle vibrating through his chest. I wondered if he knew what I was thinking.

Taking the scenic route along the backroads softened my shoulders, relaxed my jaw, and allowed my body the time it required to melt against his. Odd how much I enjoyed giving over control to him at times. The bike rendered me utterly dependent on him, my only contribution being the alignment of my will with his while the world sped by, and the wind blew my cares away. A brief but welcome reprieve. An escape from my reality.

We ate well and swung back onto his bike. Tender anticipation marked the way home. Unlike the first time, we knew what we were to each other, what we planned to be to each other always.

He led me up the stairs, his fingers linked through mine, and stripped off my clothes before laying me down on our bed. Lying on his side, propped up on his elbow, he rolled me onto my stomach, the palm of his hand following the curves of my body, brushing down the length of my spine, rounding the swell of my butt, cupping the line where it met my thighs before stroking the length of my inner thigh as far as he could reach until I melted into the mattress.

Dropping a kiss on my naked shoulder, he urged me to turn over and continued his tender ministrations over my collarbone, my breasts, my tummy, then gently cupping my mons, he sighed and brought his beautiful mouth to mine.

"Minty," he breathed. "I love you, my heart."

I smiled against his lips. "I love you, too, my darling."

Home. Belonging. Peace. It was all here where he and I came together.

I spread my fingers across his naked chest, seeking out the reassuring beat of his heart.

Shifting to cover me, he joined his body to mine, rocking against me gently while I shuddered and quaked around him before finally gifting me with his seed.

And I slept.

<u>Lucky</u>

Her hair spilled over her pillow onto mine. Any bit of her could spill onto anything and everything of mine. She could have it all.

"Good morning, darling."

Lost in thought, I hadn't even noticed her awaken. She looked pensive.

"What's on your mind?" I asked.

"How would you feel about moving in with me?"

My eyebrows knit together. "You mean on the days and nights we don't have Brayleigh?"

She held my gaze. "No. Both of you moving in." She closed her eyes. "I know your place is better in the long run for raising a family, but I need time to transition. I think being at my place will help me with that. I could move in here slowly, but I really don't want to wait any longer to be together." Her eyes popped open. "If that's still what you want! I understand completely if you'd like to slow things down." She went to move from the bed, deep in flight mode.

"Minty, baby." I could hear the smile in my voice. "I would be happy to move into your place until you're settled." I drew her back into my arms. "We need to go shopping though. Brayleigh will need a crib."

She stiffened in my arms. "Oh, God. I never dreamed I'd ever get to do that!"

I ached for her even as she rejoiced, and I thanked God that I had a child to give her. "You want to do that today?"

"I do. And I also want to pick out paint for her room. I'll get the boys over to help me paint..." She swung her legs over the side of the bed and headed for the shower, planning the whole way.

Monday morning, she called her boys and elicited their help for project baby, then took me to meet Ezinne.

"We won't stay long, and I can't show you the house today, because some of the girls are skittish around men."

"Maybe I shouldn't go?" I worried aloud.

"No, you absolutely should. Ezinne has already given them a heads up. They know you're connected to me, and they also know it's your classroom that sparked the idea for the collection of musical instruments, cameras, and such. They're loving the program and they're curious about you. Even so, I'd like to give them lots of time to get used to you." She paused. "It's not even just men. It's anybody new, really. Mara and Bex both had a time waiting to be accepted. It's a process."

Ezinne, an absolutely stunning black woman somewhat older than Minty, met us at the door.

She extended her hand. "Welcome, Lucky. It's a pleasure to meet you."

"The pleasure is mine. I've heard wonderful things about you."

"Ah, well," she said, leading us down to her office. "Only believe half of what you hear."

I laughed, charmed by her easygoing manner. Soon enough, I learned it belied a backbone of steel.

She and Minty drew out a plan for Minty's Mountain as they'd termed it, including such things as babysitting Rena, having the boys sleep over one at a time, as well as the entire list we'd made for her and Brayleigh.

Both women explained my part in Minty's recovery, and how best I might support her. When Minty told her Brayleigh and I were moving in, Ezinne dropped her professional demeanor and hugged Minty tightly, rocking her back and forth until Minty laughed and begged off.

By Wednesday, Brayleigh's room was complete, and Minty waited nervously to uncover the big reveal.

Brayleigh puttered around Minty's family room and kitchen, exploring corners and sitting on her haunches to look at the books on Minty's shelves.

"You're training her to love abs," I accused.

She patted me on mine and smiled. "A girl's gotta have standards." She pressed her lips together. "You want to see first? Or bring Brayleigh at the same time?"

"Brayleigh? Come see your new bedroom," I called.

"Mine room?"

"Yes, dolly. Your room at this house."

"Mine room this house," she echoed.

Minty opened the door, and Brayleigh gawked.

A delicate, crystal chandelier in the shape of a crown threw light and color at the soft pink walls. Faux fur trimmed the curtains at the window, and fairy lights lined the top. Her new crib sat alongside one wall while low shelving housed a few stuffed animals and toys. A wide chair, big enough to curl up in, sat in one corner, a standing lamp tucked behind it, a small table holding children's books beside it.

I spun in a circle, taking it all in. The bedding, the lighting, the prisms of color, the wall art, it was a wonder. I stopped short when my eyes fell on the last wall.

It was my memory. The one of Minty and Brayleigh at the zoo with the enormous balloon tied to the back of Brayleigh's ridiculous dress. Done in pen and ink with the barest hints of watercolor.

"That's actually for you," Minty said softly.

My heart lodged in my throat, and I couldn't swallow it down. Only in that moment did I allow myself to acknowledge what I'd nearly lost, and it was for that moment only. I turned to my future wife and said, "Thank you. Thank you for giving me you."

A high-pitched squeal drew my attention away from Minty's flushed face.

Brayleigh stood with her arms akimbo, her mouth wide open with joy, looking at the fairy lights, and screamed, "Mine sparky!"

Chapter 51 – Compensation

Minty

"In line with your right knee, at a forty-five-degree angle, there's a good toehold," Vander called up to Alex.

Vander took all three boys rock-climbing at least twice a week all summer long. Today they asked all of us to come, because each of them had conquered the highest wall in their skill level.

"That's it, buddy," Vander encouraged.

"Dad." Jace stood beside his dad, watching Alex scale the wall. "He's doing it faster today."

"He is, agori mou. He sure is." Vander smiled. "Almost there, buddy!"

Gus stood off to the side, ready to belay George, his face beaming as he watched his son. He looked back at Amber who sat beside me with a wide smile on her face.

Ruby stood between Vander and Gus, shifting from one foot to the other as she clapped and cheered for Alex.

Lucky stood farther back, watching Brayleigh as she played on the toddler equipment.

Vander and Gus held the lines. The harness kept the boys tethered. The boys gave suggestions and high fives. Everyone shouted encouragement, everyone applauded their achievements and their efforts.

"There's a toehold..."

"You're doing just fine..."

"I'm so proud of you!"

"Can you do more or are you done for the day?"

'There's a toehold.' Have the boys sleep over one at a time.

'Straight up above your head, there's a handhold. Grab it.' Babysit Rena.

'You can do it!' Put Brayleigh to bed, give her a bath, change her bum.

Step by step. Bit by bit. My people standing by, my lines secure in their hands, ready to guide me to the next toehold.

Ezinne, Amber, Ruby, Willa, Junie, Mara, Bex.

Vander, Gus, and Lucky.

Even Barrett and Rhys would help if I called them.

Maybe even Hope one day.

I sighed and swung my head around to look for Lucky. He sat leaning back against his hands, his eyes smiling on me. My heart smiled back.

Alex rang the bell at the top, pumped his fist into the air, and scaled down the wall, his freckled face split wide with laughter. As soon as his feet hit the floor, Jace and George crowded around him. In the beginning, Alex was the one who was most afraid. Now he had the best time.

Vander and Gus stood together, hands on hips, grinning at their boys while Ruby bounced around taking pictures. Our little trio of wounded hearts had healed and grown.

I glanced at Amber. "We've come a long way."

She looked surprised for a moment, then nodded thoughtfully. "Did I ever thank you for what you did for us?"

"I didn't do anything. I just loved you guys."

"Yeah." Amber laughed. "That."

"Thank you for the other night. Not just with the girls, but you and Gus coming over and," I swallowed the lump in my throat, "holding me."

"It's just us loving you." She teased then grew serious. "He loves you the same way you love him. It broke his heart to see you like that. Neither of us would have wanted to be anywhere else but by your side. Please don't let it get that far again. Just call. We'll be there."

"Thank you." We sat quietly for a moment, watching while Gus hooked himself to George and started gathering line.

Amber nudged me with her elbow. "Just between us girls. Vander and Gus... who was top?"

I laughed loud enough that Lucky looked over and winked.

"Truthfully, that's one picture that has never crossed my mind." We both looked to where Gus and Vander stood, legs braced, looking up.

"Can you imagine though?" she whispered, awestruck at the thought.

I snorted. "I try not to."

We took the boys out for dinner to West End Diner to celebrate. The owners, who were Greek, took all three boys back into the kitchen as was their usual routine. We ate and laughed and not once did the pictures trip me up. That's not to say they didn't show up, they just showed up as white noise. Even when the boys hugged me goodbye, there was no shame. No guilt.

Free. I was free.

Lucky

She shot up in bed. "Lucky!'

"What? Fuck!"

She laughed and lay a cool hand on my arm. "Sorry! I just had a tremendous idea!"

I rubbed my palm over my chest. "Well don't have any more. You're going to give me a heart attack."

She got up on her knees and straddled my waist. Things were beginning to look up.

"I've got your attention now, do I?" she teased.

"Baby, you've always got my attention." We'd been living at her place for a week. Most of Brayleigh's things were here. I moved those in one day. I had no intention of delaying once Minty gave me the go-ahead.

Everything I needed from the house was here except for about half of my clothes. Minty still needed to shift her things around to make more space. The woman had clothes. And shoes. At this point, I figured I'd take over the dresser and closet in the guest room.

"This place has four bedrooms," she began excitedly.

I grinned. "I'm way ahead of you. I'll use the closet and dresser in the guest room for the rest of my clothes. That will leave the boys' room and Brayleigh's room free for them. And you don't have to make any more space in here for me."

She ducked her head. It looked like she was fighting a smile.

"What are you laughing at?" I eyed her suspiciously.

"Well, darling," she began. "If we moved into your place, I could expand the shelter." She paused, assessing my reaction. "Isn't that wonderful?"

"You want to move into my place."

"Um, yes?"

"When?"

"Um..." She moved to get off me, but I snagged her around the waist.

"When?" I demanded, laughing.

"As soon as possible?" she squeaked.

I rolled her under me. "I'm going to kill you. I'm actually going to kill you. Do you know how much I hate moving?"

"It was hard to miss. You complained the whole time."

I barked out a laugh. "That's because I hate it! I don't hate anything the way I hate moving. My sisters have moved, in total, seventeen times. Seventeen!" I pressed my body into hers and caged her laughing face between my forearms. "And do you know who they called each and every time to help?"

"You," she guessed.

"Me!" I yelled, exasperated.

361

"Raiden didn't help? Sean didn't help? Carlos didn't help?"

"You don't seem to understand. There could have been ten men and it still would have been an astronomical feat. You have clothes. Dani has cooking supplies. Two kitchens worth and she demands two kitchens in every house they own. Not to mention the fact that she has three kids. Tracy has twins. Twins! And Sean is a collector," I spat the word out like a bitter taste. "Don't even get me started on Ava!"

"What about Darcy?"

"Darcy's smart. Like me, she flies light."

I looked down into her laughing eyes and caressed her temples with my thumbs. "You know I'd move seventeen times for you alone. Maybe even eighteen if you promised me a blow job."

She laughed like I knew she would.

We laughed a lot.

I continued. "Brayleigh's going to be heartbroken to lose her sparkly room."

Minty cringed beneath me, her nose wrinkling. "About that... we're going to redecorate her room before we move back in. We'll bring everything from here!" She squealed as I buried my face in her neck.

"Tell me about the shelter," I spoke into her neck, my voice muffled.

She ran her hands up and down my back. "We only have room for five girls at the house. Three of the girls who are there now are almost ready to transition out. They could easily be moved here. This apartment could house those women who no longer need the same level of support as they did when they first arrived. I could double the impact either by helping more women, or by extending the time they can stay."

"I have one week of summer vacation left and I have to spend it moving," I only half pretended to gripe. I rolled onto my back, bringing her with me. "Let's talk compensation."

She laughed.

Just like I knew she would.

Epilogue

<u>Six Weeks Later</u>
<u>Minty</u>

"It's this house that's the problem. She didn't have one nightmare when we lived at my place," I whispered. I curled onto my side so I could see him.

Stretched out with one arm thrown behind his head, all golden and ruffled, his beard scruffy, he looked delicious.

"We were only there one week," he retorted, his lips tipping up into a smile. "And she only slept there three nights."

"Maybe we should move back?"

He peeked at me through narrowed eyes. "You're lucky she's in here with us or I'd show you exactly how I feel about that idea."

Brayleigh had woken up crying in the night. A normal cry, not a 'ohmygodsomebodyskillingme' cry. With school back in session, Lucky was back at work and Brayleigh began attending nursery school where every second child had a cold. And judging from the way she woke up last night, she had just succumbed.

My routine had changed immensely. I still helped Junie out a couple mornings a week but spent more time at the shelter with Ezinne and the ladies, working toward expanding. We'd already given our first donation of gently used musical instruments, cameras, and microscopes to students at Lucky's school, and I bought George a used acoustic guitar so he would not stand out from the other kids.

On Wednesdays, I kept Brayleigh home with me. It was our girls' day and we got into all kinds of sparkly things. Who would have ever thought?

Not me.

"It's early, but I want coffee," Lucky whispered. "Hope won't be here for another couple of hours. You want to come out to the kitchen with me?"

I wouldn't mind a cup of coffee, but my tired body insisted on staying in bed.

You're going to molest that baby.

"You wore me out last night. I'm older than you, you know," I teased.

"Baby, I can honestly tell you, I am struggling to keep up." He swung his long legs out of the bed and pulled a pair of pajama pants on over his boxers. Mornings were getting chilly. "Retired," he snorted.

I smiled and stretched like a satisfied cat. "I'm going to stay here with Brayleigh, make sure she doesn't roll off the bed."

"Lazybones," he murmured.

Bending low over the bed, he brushed his lips across Brayleigh's smooth forehead, then pressed his lips firmly to mine. "I'm seriously missing out on our sleepy Saturday morning fuck," he murmured.

My womb contracted while my lady parts demanded a mental promise to collect on that later. "We'll have a sleepy Saturday afternoon fuck."

You're exposing a toddler to sex.

My brain launched its first visual missile.

I smiled it away.

White noise.

Lucky watched, knowing the battles I faced, and offered me a fist bump as he left our room.

Laughter. So much of it. From morning to night.

Brayleigh stirred in her sleep. It was much too early for her to get up. I rolled her toward me and nestled her in against my breast.

Her little fist sought and found the neckline of my shirt.
She held on.
And so did I.

The End

Thank you for reading Mountain Road.
I hope Minty and Lucky's love story filled your heart the same way it
did mine.
Read on for a sneak peak at Hope and Ares' story,

Sweet Everythings.

One Can Only Hope

Hope

I rolled to a stop at the red light, my attention drawn to the park across the street. I huffed out a laugh. He was 80 if he was a day. Smiling and shirtless, he tugged his beanie down over his ears, then pulled his voluminous shorts up around the ancient, sweat-stained girdle that supported his military posture. He threw his wrinkly knees high with every step across the grass.

I shook my head. Only in Milltown.

He tossed a friendly wave to a young woman pushing a rather aggressive stroller with a toddler hanging off her back.

My eyebrows rose. That was some determination to exercise.

I glanced down at the box of donuts on the seat beside me then to the soft rounding of my tummy. I shrugged. At thirty-eight, I was finally beginning to fill out. Besides, if I showed up at Lucky's in the morning without Tim Horton's, Minty might not let me in.

Accelerating through the intersection, my thoughts turned to my best friend. Lucky always stood by me, even when the others drifted away.

A tomboy, most of my friends were boys until the sudden appearance of my breasts short-circuited their adolescent brains. Those that stuck around only did so until they earned a girlfriend who quickly put a stop to time spent with me.

Lucky never looked at me differently. Other than my parents, he was the one constant in my life. Now, for the first time, I had to share him. He'd recently found 'the one'.

I didn't know if I believed in 'the one' anymore, but Lucky and Minty made a convincing argument.

Minty and I got off to a rocky start. Like the rest of the women Lucky dated over the years, Minty viewed me as competition. But I bought her off with cookies and continued to ply her with donuts. Over time, she learned I was no threat.

Despite the fact that my daughter was in fact his.

It was a drunken fluke. The first glass of cherry brandy warmed me all the way through. The second popped open the lid on my fear that I would never find 'the one'. The third dropped my inhibitions as well as my panties once I convinced Lucky to test my theory that we might have chemistry.

We did not. Which surprised me because God did not shortchange Lucky in the looks department, and you could bounce a quarter off his abs. In addition, he was kind, loyal, and funny. He taught at an inner-city school and played electric guitar in a rock band.

And he loved me. What more could I possibly want?

Was it really that great a leap to believe the one I'd been waiting for might be the one who'd been there all along?

The next morning, the edges dulled by alcohol the night before sharpened to points as we woke up equal parts horrified and hysterical with laughter. We decided never to talk about it again. Lucky spat into his palm, made me do the same, and we shook on it.

Two weeks later, I showed up on his doorstep with my heart in my throat and a positive pregnancy test in my hand.

In true Lucky fashion, he never faltered.

Custody, family dinners, Christmas, Easter, birthdays, outings, we shared it all. We made a family, and we were life partners in almost every sense of the word.

Until Minty.

I pulled into Lucky's driveway and bent to extract our daughter from her car seat. She dipped her chin and looked at me from beneath her tiny brow. "Mine mama."

"Yes, Tweetie," I agreed. "I am most definitely your mama. And you're my baby."

"Tweetie," she replied, her finger to her chest. "I, Tweetie."

"Yes," I agreed again. "You're Tweetie, and I'm Mama."

"Mine mama," she reiterated, pulling my face to hers. Locking our gazes, she pressed her nose to mine and whispered, "Mine mama."

I swallowed the lump in my throat. I'd often wondered if the routine Lucky and I took for granted was difficult for her. Though she'd never known anything different, it had to be tiring to go back and forth between two homes, to be constantly separated from either mom or dad, rarely having them together at the same time.

Was I projecting? I cried a river when my parents separated in my teens. I shook off the unhelpful thoughts. It was better to focus on problems I could solve.

With Brayleigh on my hip, her diaper bag over my shoulder, and the box of donuts in the crook of my elbow, I headed up to the door.

Lucky opened the door wide, and Brayleigh threw her chubby arms into the air.

"Da!"

He caught her up in his arms with an easy grin, and she pressed her face into his, the tips of her fingers turning white where she pressed them against the back of his neck. My little girl loved hard.

Walking around them, I dumped the diaper bag on a kitchen chair and pushed the donuts across the table. "For Minty," I informed him. "Don't scarf them all down before she gets one."

He laughed. "You take your chances like anyone else who brings treats." Belying his words, he set them aside and quickly assessed me. "You good?"

"Yup." I popped the 'P' and flopped into a chair.

He sat Brayleigh in the highchair between us and gave her a donut before offering the box to me with a grin.

I took my favorite and shoved half of it in my mouth.

Which is when Minty walked into the kitchen.

"Why?" I protested through the donut stuffed in my cheeks. "Why do you always enter when I'm acting like a teenage boy?"

At the sound of Minty's laughter, Brayleigh waved her donut in the air and squealed, "Sparky!" A nickname that suited her well. Minty was indeed sparkly.

"Hello, dolly," she murmured softly and ran her palm over Brayleigh's soft curls. She then turned her cool brown eyes to me. "As for you, it's not often you don't have something in your mouth. I've gained ten pounds in the weeks I've known you." She pivoted to peek into the box. "What did you bring me?"

"All your favorites," I bragged.

She laughed. "You did." She reached an elegant hand out and snagged the one I knew she'd choose. She brought it up to her nose to inhale the sweetness before taking a delicate bite and closing her eyes around her moan.

My eyes flitted to Lucky. He stared at Minty with his mouth hanging half open.

I snorted. For damn sure he'd never looked at me like that.

Minty settled into the chair beside Lucky and turned to me. "What do you have planned for today, beautiful?"

Lucky looped his arm around her waist and tugged her closer.

The details of their sweet interactions stood out in stark relief, imprinting a template on my brain for how things could be.

They gave me hope.

Because if Minty could get past my role in Lucky's life, perhaps I could find someone who would accept Lucky's presence in mine. If not, it was a hit I'd have to take. We were a family, and I had no intention of letting anybody break us.

"Mine Sparky," Brayleigh frowned at her dad's arm around Minty.

Lucky bugged his eyes out at our daughter and started their game of arguing over who owned 'Sparky'.

Minty's cool gaze rested on me while she awaited my response.

I took a moment to chew.

And think.

Swallowing, I grabbed a napkin, buying myself another second. "I'm going to do a little shopping. Maybe stop by the bookstore if I have time, and I have plans to see a movie tonight."

Minty's brows rose. "Hm, anyone interesting?"

I waggled my eyebrows at her. "One can only hope."

Technically, I didn't lie.

After kissing Brayleigh goodbye, I headed straight to the grocery store and bought myself a bag of sweet chili heat Doritos and pink lemonade. At Indigo, I treated myself to a Double Chocolate Frappuccino before picking up one of Juliette Banks sexy vampires.

I spent the afternoon reading in my favorite armchair. In lieu of dinner, I washed the entire bag of Doritos down with pink lemonade while watching *The Will* on Passionflix. It starred one of my all-time favorite book boyfriends which more than qualified him as 'interesting'.

And if I went to my bed feeling the gaping space within me that marked Brayleigh's absence and Lucky's changing focus, no one needed to know about it but me.

In any case, there was no one I could tell.

Special Acknowledgements

They say writing is a solitary endeavour, but oh, my Lord, there are some folks who turn it into a team sport!

I need to thank (expose) some of my brilliant team members who helped me come up with the alternatives to 'boyfriend' for one very special scene.

Darley: boy-toy.

Amanda: mighty man meat and life-size vibrator.

Sionna: Purveyor of Pleasure.

Jenn Lynn: Commander of Orgasms.

April: Daddy. (Oh, how we laughed!)

Cali: Mr. Incredible.

And, although Minty got the final say and went with Captain Cock, your contributions made that scene. Thank you!

Street Team: I appreciate you all so very much. Some of you have been with me from the beginning and you've been so incredibly consistent with your support!

- @the_retro_reader
- @bibliophilewritrix
- @blessedmommy_booklover
- @keza.campbell
- @mto32
- @bibliophilwritrix
- @susieq_reviews
- @darley.collinsauthor
- @spilltheteawithmichelle
- @books_fiction_desire
- @jen_ner_reads
- @bookaddictblog
- @alternateuniverse_bookclub

- @crystals_book_blab
- @allyoureadislove
- @nolamariereads
- @krippy.reads.books
- @anitathebookaddict
- @readingwithlola
- @mommalikestoread
- @books_n_brownie
- @ispankmyshelf
- @tina_alicea
- @marla_0519
- @city_of_roses_romance_reads
- @emmas_reading_corner
- @the.open.bookish.mom
- @whenitrainsitpoes

I've been blessed to have met up with some members of my team in person! They've become friends and are wonderfully supportive. Amanda, Jen, and Andrea, I love our girls' nights.

ARC Team: You guys, I can't thank enough. Your feedback makes me a better writer and compels me to keep going. You add the fuel to my fire.

My SuperBetas! Nola, Sionna, Rachel, Crystal, Amanda, and Amara. Thank you from the bottom of my heart. Without your screening, I would not be half as brave about putting my stories out into the world. Rachel, Crystal, Amanda and Amara, you've been with me from the first book. Thank you.

Crystal Kaiser. My fearless PA. Your kindness, generosity, willingness to learn, and general feistiness have been such a gift. It's been a year! A year that we've been friends! You're a blessing and a treat.

I've encountered excellent people in the Bookstagram community, women I admire, not just for their talent which is astounding, but for their kindness and generosity of spirit.

@swati.mh
@amararaeauthor
@lily_baines_author
@barbarakellynauthor
@ciaramwren

@debbie_cromack_author
@dariawrites20

There are two other women who I admire tremendously. They are talented writers and possibly better friends. One is slightly evil and won't mind me saying so. She's aware and revels in it.

Nola, thank you for your analysis of my writing, your assistance with my graphics, your friendship, and your generosity.

Sionna, thank you for your support, for offering your excellent proofreading skills, for being an excellent sounding board, and for your kind encouragement, always.

I thank both of you for allowing me the privilege of giving back a bit to you as well and I cannot wait (well, honestly, I can. February seems to be coming much faster than usual and I could totally skip the whole airplane part...) to meet in person in Kansas City!

Panda Squad: Nola, Sionna, Crystal, Daria, Anita ---- You're dazzling! Anita, I miss you!

@obsessivelyeverafter – thank you for being brave enough to fearlessly expose the depravity of the OCD bully. You gave me the ounce of reassurance I needed to write this book, a book I'm tremendously proud of.

To my readers. When you message me to tell me what the book meant to you, it makes every word worthwhile. When you thank me for writing it? That's the stuff my dreams are made of. Thank you.

Handsome. I love you. Always and always. Thanks for being a superfan and the world's best research assistant. Your pride in me... I cannot express what it does for my heart.

My kids. I love you all so much. I hope you're half as proud of me as I am of you.

God. Thank you for all my blessings. They are too numerous to count.

About the Author

Known for writing real, raw, and deeply emotional stories, Devin prefers mature characters who know what they want and go after it.

Devin's big-hearted heroes melt hearts, disintegrate panties, and know exactly how to love a woman.

Devin's relatable heroines could be your neighbor, your sister, or your best friend, and after reading their stories, you'll wish they were. You might even recognize yourself.

Devin doesn't shy away from tackling tough topics in her Bridgewater and Milltown Series, including those not often seen in contemporary romance. As one who struggles with mental illness herself, Devin believes seeing fictional representations of ourselves persevering and finding healing is strong stuff and she delivers. As in the real world, there are no easy answers, but her HEAs make a heart happy.

At home, Devin is outnumbered by one husband, four kids, a dog, a cat, and plumbing issues that never quit. You can most often find her curled up on her front porch, earbuds in, music cranked, nose stuck in a book...hiding from her favourite people in the world who require far too many meals, and her husband, who is without a doubt the hero in her very own love story.

Also by Devin Sloane

Find me here: devinsloane.ca

The Bridgewater Novels

Live Again

Breathe Again

Feel Again

The Milltown Novels

Broken Road

Chosen Road

Mountain Road

The Sage Ridge Novels

A Lifetime of Afters

The Mulberry Place Novels

Sweet Everythings

Milton Keynes UK
Ingram Content Group UK Ltd.
UKHW021839240823
427419UK00016B/471